PUSHKIN
VERTIGO

PRAISE FOR THE
HARITH ATHREYA SERIES

'Like stepping back into the Golden Age of the classic mystery'

Rhys Bowen, author of *The Tuscan Child*

'Perfect for fans of Agatha Christie, Arthur Conan
Doyle and readers who – like me – just can't
get enough of atmospheric mysteries'

Harini Nagendra, author of *The Bangalore Detectives Club*

'A slice of sheer pleasure… blends the feel of classic crime with
the modern world, while presenting a proper thorny puzzle'

Observer

'I love RV Raman's Harith Athreya with his
cool, curious resourcefulness'

Ovidia Yu, author of *The Mimosa Tree Mystery*

Following a corporate career spanning three decades and four continents, RV RAMAN now lectures on management, mentors young entrepreneurs, serves as an independent director on company boards, and writes. He has written three previous books in the Harith Athreya series, *A Will to Kill*, *Grave Intentions*, and *Praying Mantis*, all of which are available from Pushkin Press. RV Raman lives in Chennai.

www.rvraman.com

RV RAMAN

THE LAST RESORT

PUSHKIN VERTIGO

Pushkin Vertigo
An imprint of Pushkin Press
Somerset House, Strand
London WC2R 1LA

Copyright © RV Raman 2023

The Last Resort was first published by Polis Books in 2023

First published by Pushkin Press in 2023

1 3 5 7 9 8 6 4 2

ISBN 13: 978-1-78227-940-2

Designed and typeset by Tetragon, London

Printed and bound in the United Kingdom
by Clays Ltd, Elcograf S.p.A.

www.pushkinpress.com

THE LAST RESORT

DRAMATIS PERSONAE

Harith Athreya	An imaginative investigator recuperating in Kumarakom after a serious illness
Veni Athreya	Athreya's wife; a bubbly, garrulous go-getter with an encyclopaedic knowledge of Bollywood
Kurup	Veni's cousin and host; lives in a lake-front villa in Kumarakom
Akuti	Kurup's daughter-in-law; a yoga instructor who handles her motorboat adroitly
Mahesh Gauria	A doyen of Bollywood; the wealthy filmmaker hires Athreya to script a murder mystery film at their resort
Manjari Gauria	Mahesh's pious and silent wife
Hiran Gauria	Mahesh's elder son; a moderately successful filmmaker
Pari Gauria	Hiran's wife and the creative head of Gauria Studios; a film director of some repute
Danuj Gauria	Mahesh's younger son; a filmmaker who is on a 'luckless streak'
Ruhi Gauria	Danuj's wife; a beautiful Bollywood star
Kanika Mehra	Mahesh's money-minded daughter
Jeet Mehra	Kanika's subservient husband
Sahil Sachdeva	A young, successful filmmaker; Danuj's childhood friend and Ruhi's ex-suitor
Kishan	A Bollywood fixer and a knife for hire; has threatened to 'track down and cut up' Ruhi
Bhagya	A struggling actress who has a sorry story to tell

7

Inspector Anto	A comic police inspector who is sharper than he seems; speaks with a thick Malayali accent
Sub-Inspector Joseph	Anto's deputy
Dr Saju	A starchy police doctor
Inspector Holkar	A police inspector in Mumbai who has been keeping tabs on Kishan and Bollywood
Marisa	A policewoman with a flair for technology

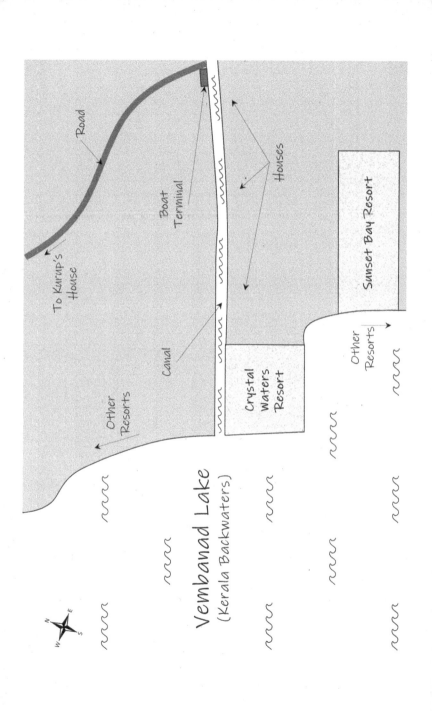

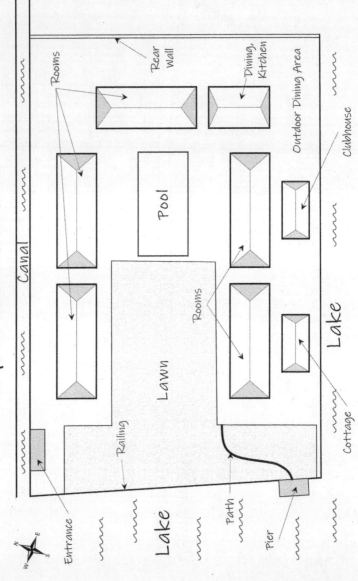

Crystal Waters Resort

THE GAURIA FAMILY

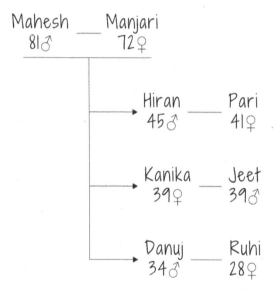

Mahesh
81 ♂
___
Manjari
72 ♀

Hiran
45 ♂
___
Pari
41 ♀

Kanika
39 ♀
___
Jeet
39 ♂

Danuj
34 ♂
___
Ruhi
28 ♀

1

Dawn was breaking over picturesque Kumarakom when the small motorboat sped over the waters of Vembanad Lake, churning its way southwards. Around it, the vast, undulating expanse of Kerala's backwaters was empty save an occasional houseboat or fishing vessel. Here and there, green patches of water hyacinth marred the otherwise clear blue water. The western horizon beyond the lake was marked by a long stand of tall coconut trees. On the opposite side—the east—was the famous Kumarakom shore, lined with upscale resorts that drew tourists from all over the world. It was to one such resort—Crystal Waters—that the motorboat was heading.

Crowded into the small boat were three people.

Crouched in the front, recuperating after a nasty bout of dengue fever, was Harith Athreya, an investigator of some renown. His last case, which had taken him to a mosquito-infested town for a few weeks, had laid him low with the debilitating illness.

Though he had recovered from the initial fever symptoms, he was far from his usual self. Fatigue and weakness were constant, if unwelcome, companions. His fine-haired mane was shot through with more grey strands than had been the case a few months ago. The silvery patch in the front gleamed more prominently now, as did the matching silver tuft on his chin. Having stayed away from barbers during his illness, his long hair made him look more like a bearded collie than ever before.

Huddled behind him, with her knees digging into his back, was his affable and sparkly wife, Krishnaveni. A striking woman who had graciously accepted going grey in her mid-forties, Veni, as she was called, was the Yin to her husband's Yang.

It was her genial but persistent badgering that had brought Athreya to Kumarakom, where they were staying at her cousin's lake-front villa. Once this gregarious go-getter made up her mind to do something, it usually got done. After contemplating the medical advice the doctor had suggested for Athreya, she had decided that her husband needed a break in a salubrious environment, where he could recuperate at his own pace.

She wanted to take him away from polluted cities to a place where the air was fresh and clean. Kumarakom was her automatic choice. Her cousin, Kurup, had been delighted at the suggestion and had at once offered to host them at his vast ancestral home on the banks of the Vembanad Lake.

Behind Veni, piloting the small motorboat, was Akuti, Kurup's daughter-in-law and a yoga instructor who was much in demand at Kumarakom's resorts. The twenty-seven-year-old, who could converse in multiple languages with tourists, held yoga sessions at three resorts, the first of which began at 6 a.m. at Crystal Waters. As all three also were on the lake, her preferred mode of travel from and to her lakeside house was this motorboat, which was small enough for her to handle on her own.

As usual, the garrulous and affable Veni was talking. How she found something or other to say in any situation was a perpetual mystery to Athreya. This was the one mystery the famed investigator had not cracked, even after decades of marriage to this lady on whom he depended for almost everything except solving cases.

Veni suddenly broke off in mid-sentence and shot an arm over Athreya's shoulder, pointing over the boat's bow.

'See that?' she asked. 'That man is watching the resort through binoculars. That, too, so early in the morning. Is it just idle curiosity, do you think? Or is he watching someone?'

Looking where she pointed, Athreya saw a stationary motor-boat occupied by a middle-aged man and a young woman. Their attire and appearance—he in a turtleneck pullover and she in a well-cut sleeveless jacket—suggested that they were not locals, but tourists. The man was peering intently through his binoculars as the woman sat silently beside him, looking bored. That the boat was not moving suggested that they were not on a merry cruise.

In any case, few tourists would be up and about at daybreak, and even fewer would be piloting a boat into these backwaters. Being on the west coast of India, it was the sunsets that were popular on this lake, not sunrises. Only fishermen and other locals who used the lake as a part of their daily routine were out so early. Athreya's curiosity was piqued.

Even as he studied them, the young woman in the boat noticed Akuti's motorboat approaching and warned the man. He lowered his binoculars at once and tucked them away between his knees. He then stonily watched their motorboat come closer as the young woman feigned nonchalance.

They were strangers to Athreya. The man, who seemed to be in his late forties, had a rough, impassive face that reminded Athreya of some unpleasant characters he had encountered in his career. Their faces too had worn this studied inscrutability. Hard eyes stared back from a leathery face that sported a thick black moustache. The woman was pretty and much younger, perhaps in her mid-twenties. She looked everywhere but at Akuti's approaching boat.

Athreya's right index finger began tracing invisible words on his knee—a sign that his mind was churning. He began imagining what the man might have seen through the binoculars. The open layout of the resort meant that he could watch the doors of most, if not all, the guest rooms.

Akuti slowed her motorboat and veered towards the small pier attached to the resort that the man had been observing.

They were arriving at Crystal Waters, which occupied a rectangular protrusion of land into the lake. On two sides were the lake waters, while a canal marked the third. An unbroken fifteen-foot-high wall formed the rear boundary of the resort. Crystal Waters had no land access. The only way in or out was by boat.

Realizing that Akuti was stopping at Crystal Waters, the man in the other motorboat started his engine and moved away.

'What were they doing?' Akuti asked, as she glided her boat to the pier with practised ease. 'What's there to snoop on so early in the morning?'

'Did you recognize the girl, Aku?' Veni asked, waiting for Athreya to alight first.

'No, Aunty. Who is she?'

'I don't know if it's her real name, but her screen name is Bhagya. She is a bit of a failed actress. Does item numbers now.'

Item numbers were catchy, provocative dances that were popular in Indian cinema. Often, they had little to do with the film's story and were inserted as nuggets of raunchy entertainment.

'That's an example of your aunt's encyclopaedic knowledge of Bollywood,' Athreya chuckled, as he prepared to disembark. 'The other encyclopaedias she carries in her head deal with cooking, cricket and politics.'

'The four most popular topics in the country!' Akuti laughed.

'And all your uncle knows about,' Veni retorted good-naturedly, 'is crime—murder, robbery and an assortment of the most disagreeable things.'

A man dressed in a colourful lungi and a white banian was waiting for them at the pier. He greeted them in Malayalam with a wide, toothy grin. As the boat bumped gently against the wooden platform, he took the mooring rope and secured it. Athreya was the first to get off the boat.

'I wonder what an item girl is doing at dawn on the backwaters,' Veni mused aloud as she rose, took the lungi-clad man's hand and followed Athreya onto the pier. Akuti skipped lightly from the boat to the wooden platform.

Any further discussion on that topic was cut off by a voice that boomed from the large lawn that bordered the lake.

'Good morning, Aku,' it said. 'I'm hoping to catch you come a minute late one of these days. I've been trying for a week, but you seem to have a Swiss watch embedded in your head.'

Mahesh Gauria, a jovial octogenarian filmmaker who was accustomed to getting his way, was sitting in his usual chair with his metal walking-stick by his side. A wide smile split his pouchy and spotted face as he looked affectionately at Akuti with watery eyes. His idea of participating in her yoga classes was to sit in his chair and egg on the people who were actually doing the asanas. Every now and again, he would good-naturedly needle someone or crack a silly joke. If his intent was to make the yoga class enjoyable, he was succeeding very well.

'Good morning, Uncle,' Akuti replied with a smile and a wave as she strode to the lawn where the class was to be held. 'Good morning, everyone!'

A chorus of greetings flew both ways as all in the class wished the three newcomers well, who, in turn, greeted them back. On reaching the lawn, Athreya and Veni spread out their yoga mats side by side. Danuj and Ruhi Gauria, Mahesh's younger son and daughter-in-law, came and spread out their mats as well. Danuj was a film producer while Ruhi was a successful actress.

'Good morning, Danuj, Ruhi,' Veni greeted them. 'Nice yoga pants, Danuj! New?'

'Yes, Aunty,' Danuj replied, cracking an infectious grin. 'We picked it up at Kottayam yesterday. Bright, isn't it? Ruhi bought one in a different colour combination. Good morning, Uncle.'

17

'Good morning, Danuj,' Athreya replied. 'Hello, Ruhi. A penny for your thoughts? You seem distracted today.'

'Oh, it's nothing, Uncle,' Ruhi replied, putting on a smile. 'Good morning, Aunty, Uncle.'

'Are you better today, sir?' Danuj asked. 'You were feeling weak yesterday. I hope the illness has stopped dogging you.'

'Oh, I'm okay. It comes and goes, you know. I think Kumarakom is doing me a lot of good.'

'Aunty, I hope your knee is not hurting today?' Ruhi asked, glancing at Veni.

'It's fine, Ruhi,' Veni replied. 'Thanks. Yoga helps.'

Akuti began the class by instructing everyone to start with *pranayama*.

As he began his first breathing asana, Athreya glanced at the backwaters lapping at the resort edge a few feet away. A couple of houseboats were anchored a short distance away and a crude barge was making its way past the resort with its sole occupant pushing at the lake bottom with a long bamboo pole to propel it.

The motorboat carrying the item girl and the man was nowhere in sight.

Forty-five minutes later, when the yoga session came to an end, Danuj and Ruhi rolled up Veni's and Athreya's yoga mats as they usually did. They then went to a nearby table where tender young coconuts were stacked and brought one each for Mahesh, Veni and Athreya.

'These are absolutely perfect after a yoga session,' Danuj remarked, sipping the coconut water through a straw.

'I couldn't agree more!' Veni concurred.

'I just can't have enough of these Kumarakom coconuts,' Danuj went on. 'We don't get such good ones in Mumbai. So sweet and refreshing!'

'These backwater coconuts are a speciality of Kerala,' Veni added. 'Not just the coconut water, but the pulp inside is very sweet too.'

'Yeah! It's a pity we can't take some back with us to Mumbai. They are just too bulky! No, Ruhi?'

Ruhi nodded silently as she drank from her coconut. Athreya's gaze lingered on her for a moment. She seemed to be preoccupied and reticent today. He didn't know if it was his imagination, but he thought he detected traces of fear on her face this morning.

A slurping sound came from Danuj's coconut as he finished the water in it and drew air.

'Sorry!' he grinned. 'I didn't want to leave even a single drop.'

He dropped his coconut into a nearby bin and picked up his and Ruhi's yoga mats.

'We'll shower and change before breakfast,' he said. 'Coming, Ruhi?'

'Just a sec,' Ruhi replied.

She finished her drink, got rid of the coconut and hurried after her husband. Veni watched them go with a smile on her face.

'They make a delightful couple, don't they?' she asked. 'He is so boyish despite his age, and she is *so* pretty! A film producer and a star make a great pair.'

Athreya grunted noncommittally as he remained focused on his tender coconut.

'But despite that, they are so friendly,' Veni went on. 'No airs or conceit. Danuj is not arrogant like his sister or aloof as his brother. And Ruhi comes from a middle-class family and is naturally affable. Her success in Bollywood hasn't turned her head. I'm absolutely delighted at her success.'

Athreya didn't say anything.

'You know,' Veni continued, 'when Danuj and Ruhi got married last year, the press touted them as the perfect Bollywood couple. I couldn't agree more.'

Drawing no response from her husband, she turned to him with a glare.

'Hari! Are you even listening?' she demanded. 'I'm talking to you.'

Athreya hurriedly finished his drink and nodded.

'I am, my dear,' he replied. 'You said that they make a great couple. Come, let's also go shower and head for breakfast. We are due at Mahesh's suite shortly.'

2

After a traditional Kerala breakfast of *appam, idiyappam* and *puttu,*
Veni and Athreya adjourned to Mahesh's 'Presidential Suite',
where steaming tumblers of filter coffee awaited them along
with Mahesh and Danuj. With them was Pari, Mahesh's elder
daughter-in-law and the Creative Director of Gauria Studios.
She was twirling a pen and balancing a notebook on her knee.
The forty-one-year-old was already a film director of considerable acclaim.

The five of them were working together on a project into
which Mahesh Gauria had drafted Athreya a couple of days ago.

When he had first learned of Athreya's identity, Mahesh had
grown excited. The filmmaker had then buttonholed Athreya
and enlisted the investigator's services for a film project he had
in mind.

'This is an ideal place for a closed circle murder mystery,'
Mahesh had said. 'Look at this resort, Mr Athreya... it has the
lake on two sides and a canal on the third. The landward side
has a high wall without gates. The only way to enter or leave this
resort is by boat—be it through the canal or the lake.

'And when you use a boat, you *will* be seen, especially
since this is the very last resort when you come by the canal.
At least a dozen people will see you on the canal before you
get here. It would be very difficult for an outsider to enter or
leave the resort undetected. The murderer *must* be one of the
residents.'

'Did you know that the locals sometimes call this "the last
resort"?' Athreya had asked. 'Because it is at the very end of the
canal?'

21

'Do they? An interesting play on words! Maybe, we'll name the film "The Last Resort".'

'This film... do you have anything specific in mind?'

'All I know at this point is that I want to make a film set in this very resort—a murder mystery where residents get killed one by one. I need to conceptualize it and work out the details. For that, I need your help.'

'*My* help!' Athreya asked in surprise. 'I know nothing about films. Zero!'

'That doesn't matter. Between Pari and myself, we know all there is to know about them. However, we have no practical insight into real-world mysteries and criminal minds. I fear that what we come up with might not ring true. That's where you can help.'

'What exactly would you want me to do?'

'Just be our consultant. Brainstorm with us and answer the million questions we will throw at you. We'll put our heads together to develop options that we can toss around. We will then narrow it down to one, and sketch out the story. You'll have fun, I assure you. And it'll be an entirely new experience for you. What do you say?'

Athreya had asked for some time to think about it.

Later that day, when Athreya told Veni of Mahesh's proposal, she had jumped at it and insisted that she too would join the project. The idea of developing a film's story from scratch appealed to her creative side. As far as Athreya was concerned, she said, it would give him something to do. It would keep him from moping, which he invariably fell into when he had no work on hand.

As usual, once she had made up her mind, it was only a matter of time before it became a reality. On hearing of her interest, Mahesh had welcomed her participation and had sought her help in convincing her husband. If Athreya were to have

22

disagreed with Veni, he knew he would have lost the battle. Soon, he had signed up for an astonishingly generous fee.

Today was their second meeting. They were about to brainstorm multiple ways to commit murder at Crystal Waters.

'Right,' Pari began, pushing back her lustrous brown hair that matched her eyes. 'Let's get started. We agreed yesterday that the story would have up to three murders. Two for sure and possibly a third. For today's discussion, let's assume that we'll have three.'

'We had talked about one aspect of the murders,' Danuj added with contagious enthusiasm. 'Should they be similar to each other or completely different? Both have their advantages—similar murders reinforce certain aspects of the mystery and drive home the fear strongly. However, in the interest of variety and unpredictability, we can make the three murders completely different too. One victim would be poisoned, and another would be killed with a dagger. We need to come up with the third murder. Any thoughts?'

'Let's discard the gun as the murder weapon,' Veni replied. 'First, people don't carry around guns in this part of the world. Second, gunshots wouldn't go with the tone of the story.'

'That's right,' Danuj nodded, his clear brown eyes shining. 'We want something stealthy and devious, preferably something that strikes fear.'

Athreya cleared his throat softly. The ill-effects of dengue were still dogging him. The others there turned to him enquiringly.

'Did you hear of a particularly horrifying murder that took place a hundred kilometres south of here?' he asked a shade weakly. 'It's a real story.'

'I don't think so,' Mahesh rumbled in his gravelly voice. 'What happened?'

'A man killed his wife by getting a snake to bite her when she was asleep.'

'Snake! Ew!' Pari cried, wriggling uneasily in her chair. 'That gives me the creeps!'

'It is a creepy story, all right, but a true one,' Athreya went on in a voice rendered soft by dengue-induced fatigue. 'A man called Sooraj bought a Russell's viper from a snake catcher. One night, he drugged his wife before they went to bed. Once the sedative took effect and she was fast asleep, he retrieved the viper and forced it to bite her.

'The viper, as you know, is highly venomous. The poor lady suffered for many weeks, undergoing procedure after procedure, including plastic surgery. But she managed to cling on to life and survived a fifty-two-day ordeal.

'After she recovered and returned home, Sooraj got hold of a more venomous snake—a cobra this time. Once again, he sedated her and made the cobra bite her. Apparently, he had starved the snake for days to induce it to bite. This time, the lady died.'

'Astonishing,' Danuj exclaimed with a horrified expression on his face. 'This really happened, Uncle?'

'Yes, in 2020. In this very state. Not far from here.'

'Gosh!' Danuj exclaimed, his boyish face now alight with curiosity. 'How did the police work out that it was a murder?'

'When the victim's father suspected foul play, the police did a brilliant job. They enlisted the services of herpetologists and proved that the snake bite that had killed the lady was not a natural one. Rather, it was an *induced* bite.'

Danuj's eyebrows shot up. 'How did they prove that?' he asked.

'By measuring the distance between the punctures made by the two fangs. The distance was larger than would have been the case had it been a natural bite. To force the snake to bite and to make the venom flow, Sooraj had pressed its head down.

24

That made the fangs move apart. The police built up the case and obtained a conviction.'

'Amazing!' Mahesh boomed. 'Phenomenal! I had no idea our police were this good.'

A moment passed in silence as they contemplated the gruesome incident. Perched on her chair, Pari had tensed up while Athreya was narrating the incident. She had pulled up her feet to tuck them under herself as if there were snakes on the floor. Clearly, she hadn't enjoyed Athreya's little narration.

With a playful grin on his youthful face, Danuj decided to tease his sister-in-law.

'Watch out, *Bhabi!*' he cried, pointing to the floor. 'Under your chair!'

Pari let out an involuntary squeal before she realized that Danuj was pranking her.

'Danuj!' she snapped exasperatedly, throwing a stern glance in his direction. 'Grow up!'

Danuj's reaction was to broaden his grin.

Pari then closed her eyes and slowly relaxed, letting her clenched fists open and the tension ebb away from her body. Gradually, her pretty face relaxed, and she reopened her eyes.

'Eek!' she complained, the single word capturing her feelings aptly. 'I hate snakes!' She looked at Mahesh and went on, 'Papa, do we want snakes in the film?'

'Why not, Pari? You found it creepy. So would the audience. Many will pick up their feet from the floor like you did. It'll make an impact, won't it?'

'I'm not sure I want *this* kind of an impact,' she mumbled. 'Let's go back to the other two murders. I'd like to hear your thoughts on them, Mr Athreya.'

'Well,' he replied, 'we can come up with any number of ways to kill in the resort—knocking the victim from behind, throwing

25

them into the lake, drowning them in the wading pool, stabbing them when they are on their post-dinner walk along the resort perimeter, and so on. However, those would be simple and straightforward acts of killing.

'Instead, let's see if we can add some intrigue to the modus operandi of the murders themselves. Let's not make the film just a "who-dun-it" but also make the murders "how-dun-its". Let's add some mystery to how the murders are committed.'

'I like that!' Pari enthused and wrote 'how-dun-it' in her notebook. 'Please go on.'

'We can set the dagger murder in a locked room. I propose that the victim be found with their throat slit in her room. The lock in the door has been turned, and the key is on a table *inside* the room. The duplicate key to the door is in a safe in the manager's office that hasn't been opened. All the windows are barred. How then was the victim killed inside a locked room?'

'You've got my attention!' Pari replied. 'How did the murderer escape?'

'They had a *third* key.'

'Where did they get this third key when only two existed?' Danuj demanded, his keen face alight with interest.

In response, Athreya pulled out his mobile phone and showed him a photograph of two room keys.

'The key on the top is yours,' he told Danuj. 'And the other one is to the room I'm temporarily using. Remember, you were sitting near me at breakfast? When you went to pick up food from the buffet, I placed the keys side by side and photographed them. Notice that the chequered napkin under the keys has very regular chequers.

'I wager that I'll be able to make a copy of your key from this photograph. The chequers on the napkin supply an accurate scale, and my key provides the physical reference and dimensions needed. That's all a skilled locksmith needs to make a key. Of course, these are only my initial thoughts. I'll have to prove this by having a copy of your key made.'

'Nice!' Pari gushed, writing furiously in her notebook. 'Very nice indeed! I don't think I've come across this before. In older novels, a key's impression is taken on wax or a piece of soap. I see no reason why your photo shouldn't work.'

'Hari,' Veni asked her husband, regarding him with a twinkle in her black eyes. There was also a hint of pride in her voice. 'When did you think of this? I haven't heard this before either.'

'At breakfast this morning,' Athreya chuckled. 'Hey, it's no big deal—it's just a random thought. Now, let's look at the other murder—the poisoning. I suggest that this victim be poisoned at the table where others are dining as well. Yet nobody sees the poison being administered. Everyone at the table partakes of the same dishes, and nobody else is poisoned. The mystery here is about how the poison was delivered. Unseen and with precision.'

'Ooh! That's good too!' Pari said, going back to wielding her pen. 'Do you know how it was delivered?'

'I haven't fully worked it out yet, but it's got to do with the victim preferring to take the same seat at the table at every meal.' Athreya turned to Mahesh. 'I've noticed that you always sit at the head of the table. Your wife is always to your right. And Ruhi is usually at the other end of the table. It seems to be a habit for the three of you. Isn't that so?'

Mahesh nodded and grinned widely.

'Yes. That's how we sit at home—I am the oldest and Ruhi is the youngest. We sit at opposite ends. We seem to have unconsciously carried that habit here too. At home, I always use a particular chair that is my favourite. Thanks to you, I now realize that it's not a smart thing to do. Someone could get rid of me by poisoning my cutlery well before I come to the table. No need to tamper with the food at all. Coat my spoon or my glass with colourless poison, and I'm done for.'

'Precisely!' Athreya said. 'That's what I had in mind.'

'That's not amusing, Papa,' Pari cut in. Athreya saw that she was more than a little upset. 'Why would anyone want to kill you? You are the kindest and the most generous man I know.'

Ruhi, who had been passing through the room, paused for a moment and glanced their way. Athreya remained silent. But Mahesh couldn't be held back.

'One of the downsides of being wealthy, my dear,' he teased, refusing to take Pari seriously. 'Someone is always waiting for you to kick the bucket.'

'Papa!' Pari objected fiercely. 'That's *not* funny. Please don't say that again.'

'Okay, okay! Don't get upset,' Mahesh said, raising his hands. He had, at last, realized that she was serious. 'It was only a joke, Pari.'

'We can do without such jokes, Papa. Please.'

With a determined look, she changed the topic.

'How about having the third murder on a houseboat?' she asked. 'I am *not* in favour of using snakes.'

'Good idea, Pari!' Veni cheered as Mahesh nodded agreement. 'This time, the killer could either be an outsider or someone from the resort itself. *Anyone* could board the houseboat at night.'

'Remember,' Athreya added, 'every time someone boards or gets off a houseboat, it rocks. Let's use the boat's repeated rocking as clues in the film.'

Pari was writing as fast as she could.

'Yes, let's include an outsider or two,' Mahesh said. 'Even if it's a red herring. People known to the victims but not staying in this resort.'

'Let's see now,' Danuj said eagerly, 'if an outsider were to come at night, either to the resort or to the houseboat, how would they cross the water? We have water on three sides and a high wall on the fourth.'

'If I were to do it,' Veni volunteered, 'I'd use a small boat that can be poled across the water.'

'Poled?' Danuj asked, his head slightly cocked to one side in enquiry. 'How?'

'You will have seen how they propel boats on the backwaters here, Danuj. They don't use oars. Instead, they use long bamboo poles and push off the floor of the lake. That makes the boat move forward almost soundlessly. This lake is shallow enough for that. You've seen how silently they move, haven't you? Unlike oars, poles create no loud splashes and make little noise.'

Danuj rose and began pacing the room in excitement. He seemed to be taken up with Veni's suggestion.

'Personally,' she went on, 'I'd use a coracle—a basket boat made of bamboo that is small enough and light enough for a single person to carry it. But it takes some getting used to, lest it capsizes and dumps you into the water. Once you have some practice, you can move pretty well with a single paddle, even if you don't want to use a pole.'

'That's right,' Athreya added. 'You'd also maintain a low profile when you use a coracle. Unlike boats, which stand out several feet above the water, a small coracle is only about a foot high. If you crouch, you might just pass undetected.'

'Stealth!' Mahesh applauded. 'I like it! What a creative couple you two make! See, this is why I wanted your help. Are coracles easily available, Veni? Do you have a photo of one?'

'Oh, yes, they are easy to obtain,' she replied. 'At least here at the backwaters.'

'Here, Papa.' Danuj walked across and showed his phone to

Mahesh. As Veni had been talking, he had pulled up a picture of a coracle.

'Ah! I see your point,' Mahesh said, studying the picture. 'You can avoid being seen at night if you keep a low profile. Let's use this, Pari. It also gives an authentic local flavour to the story.'

They went on to talk about how unstable a coracle was and how easy or difficult it was to propel and steer it. Having used one in her younger days, including during her childhood visits to Kumarakom, Veni happily expounded on the subject. Once you had acquired the skill, she said, it was a breeze. Mahesh was delighted. He was entirely taken up with the notion of a shadowy outsider coming in a silent coracle in the dead of night. And the fact that it was unstable added extra intrigue.

As they discussed animatedly, the other Gauria family members walked in and out of Mahesh's suite. Curious glances came their way as the five talked excitedly about murders at Crystal Waters.

Mahesh and Athreya strolled out onto the lawn after the discussion in Mahesh's suite. Veni was still inside, chatting with the two Gauria daughters-in-law and Danuj. The two men walked slowly as Mahesh leaned heavily on his metal walking-stick after every other step.

'I heard about one of your recent cases, Mr Athreya,' Mahesh said. 'Bhaskar Fernandez of Coonoor.'

'Yes?' Athreya asked.

'I believe Bhaskar wrote two wills—one that came into effect if he died naturally, and another that kicked in if he was killed. I was wondering why he did such a thing. Was he expecting to be killed?'

'Well, yes. There had been several attempts on his life already. He hoped that writing two such wills would discourage whoever was trying to get rid of him.'

'Did the two-will ploy work?'

'The answer is too complex for a simple yes or no. Why do you ask? Are you planning to write two wills too?'

'No, no! Just curious,' Mahesh chuckled. 'That wouldn't work for me, you know. I have assets that the taxman knows nothing of. Many of them are overseas. I can't very well include them in a will, can I? Some of them are not even in my name. So, my will is a very simple one. I was just curious if Bhaskar's plan worked. There is too much greed in some families, Mr Athreya. Not every scion is a saint.'

He broke off as Veni emerged from the suite along with Ruhi.

'Before I forget,' he went on loudly, changing track smoothly as the two women came within earshot, 'I'd like you and Veni to join us on a cruise of the backwaters tomorrow—Friday. I've chartered a large boat that can accommodate all of us comfort-ably. The entire family will be there. We'd love it if you and Veni could come too. I asked Aku, but she isn't free tomorrow.'

'Sure, Mr Gauria,' Athreya replied, catching Veni's quick nod to him. 'Thank you very much. Veni and I would love to join you.'

'Wonderful! We'll leave after breakfast. Lunch will be served on the cruise, and there are enough bedrooms on the boat for a siesta if you care for it. We should be back by 4 p.m. or so. See you tomorrow.'

The patriarch of the powerful Bollywood family turned and hobbled away, leaving his actress–daughter-in-law with Veni and Athreya.

'Ruhi is coming with us,' Veni said, as she led the way to the landing spot from which a boat would take them to the mainland.

With Akuti having left the resort at the end of the yoga ses-sion, Veni and Athreya had to take the resort's own canal boat to the boat terminal, from where they would walk to Kurup's house. The boat was a sturdy, practical wooden vessel with four plastic chairs and enough space in between for luggage. Its sole purpose was to ferry the resort guests and their suitcases between the resort and the boat terminal. The three sat in silence as the boatman poled the boat along the canal that was a little more than a dozen feet wide. Two boats could just about squeeze past each other if they were to meet in the canal.

On the left side of the canal was a walled property, and on the right were the backyards of several small houses. Poultry and goats roamed there beside the greenish water of the canal. Some houses had small boats pulled up to their backyards and tied to trees. This channel was a part of a network of canals that the local people used to move about.

They reached the boat terminal in a few minutes, where they got off and began walking towards Kurup's house. Athreya was curious about Ruhi accompanying them but kept his counsel. The beautiful actress had not said a word since she had joined him. Clad simply in a *salwar* set, she had padded beside Veni, who was also uncharacteristically silent.

As if on cue, Ruhi came close to Athreya and began speaking. He saw that her pretty face was puckered in worry, and there was a paleness on it, which could have been caused by fear.

'I'm sorry to barge in uninvited, Mr Athreya,' she said softly, as they reached the main road from the boat terminal. 'But I need your advice. Veni Aunty thought you wouldn't mind. Do you, Uncle?'

'Not at all, Ruhi,' Athreya replied. 'How can I help?'

'I wanted to ask about wills. I'm sure you know all about them.'

'Wills?' That took Athreya by surprise. Mahesh too had just talked about wills. Coincidence? 'Aren't you rather young to bother with wills?'

32

Ruhi was all of twenty-eight.

'Perhaps. But I want to play safe. Will you advise me, please?'

'Of course, Ruhi. What do you want to know?'

'Does a will need to be printed on stamp paper and registered for it to be valid? Or can a simple handwritten will on plain paper suffice?'

'The law is very clear on this matter,' Athreya began in a measured manner. 'A handwritten will on plain paper is legally binding if it is properly signed by the testator—the person who writes the will   and is witnessed by two other persons. However, practically speaking, a will that is printed on stamp paper and registered would be preferable if there is any chance of it being contested.'

'Okay… does a handwritten will on plain paper need to be in any particular format?'

'No. As long as it's legible and unambiguous, it is fine. Why these questions, Ruhi?'

'I've written a simple will, Uncle.' She briefly held up the envelope she was carrying. 'I wrote it last night. I want to have it witnessed.'

'I'd be happy to do it. The second witness can be Kurup, Aku's father-in-law.'

'That's what Veni Aunty said too.' She threw a grateful glance at Veni. 'She said Mr Kurup would be happy to help.' She let out a sigh of relief. 'Thank you so very much, Uncle. I just want to make sure that everything I have goes to my mother if… if… something happens to me.'

Athreya looked at the worried young woman with concern. What was making her take such a step now? And so suddenly in the middle of a family holiday? Had something happened last night? He recalled her distracted look during the morning yoga class.

'Why so suddenly, Ruhi?' he asked. 'Why now?'

'Please, Uncle, I don't want to go into that. I've had a decent acting career so far. My films have done well, and I enjoy a good standing with the audience. I don't know how long it will last.

'I've saved quite a bit, by the grace of God. If I die without a will, my mother and sister will get nothing. I don't want that to happen—they aren't particularly well off, you know. I come from a middle-class family.'

'Who else knows about this will?'

She frowned and bit her lip.

'I am not sure... I've told no one. But Danuj might know. Papa probably suspects it. He is very sharp, you know, and he is like a second father to me. He knows all of us inside out. But don't worry, I'll make a proper will and register it as soon as I return to Mumbai. Everyone will know then.'

Athreya let it pass. He had no business probing her reasons for hurriedly writing a will now. She had only asked him to witness it, and he had no reason not to.

'What do you plan to do with this will after Kurup and I witness it?' he asked instead.

'I... I don't know,' she said uncertainly.

'I told Ruhi to leave it with someone she trusted,' Veni cut in. 'She wouldn't want it to go missing after taking the precaution to write, sign and get it witnessed.'

Athreya threw his wife a quick glance. Precaution? Against what? The only event that triggered a will was death. Were there any threats to Ruhi's life?

'I don't want to leave it with anyone in the family,' Ruhi said, breaking into his thoughts. She looked pensive with a furrowed brow. 'That could complicate their lives unnecessarily. But whom else can I leave it with?' An idea struck her. She turned to Veni. 'Will you keep it for me, Aunty? I know I have met you just recently…'

'Of course, my dear.' Veni wrapped an arm around Ruhi's slim shoulders. 'I'll keep it till it's time for you to return to Mumbai. I'll lock it up in my suitcase after it's been witnessed.'

3

The cruise boat turned out to be much larger than Veni had expected. Unlike most boats in Kumarakom that were long and narrow, this one was broad and almost rectangular in shape—much like a luxury barge. Although they were only ten passengers on the cruise, the boat Mahesh had chartered could have accommodated thrice that number.

Much of the forward half of the boat was given to an extensive sitting-cum-dining area filled with sofas, cane chairs and low tables. Bamboo spines and thatched mats formed an elegant, arched roof to shield them from the sun and rain. Aft was a smaller sitting area appropriate for private chats. Between the two were four small cabins where one could catch forty winks if desired. On either side of these cabins were passages that connected the two sitting areas.

Looking at the cruise boat, Veni was sure that Mahesh would have struck a bargain at this off-season time. He might be careful with money, but he had not compromised on luxury and space. All in all, it was a very comfortable-looking boat.

Given their proclivity for punctuality, Veni and Athreya had reached the pier promptly at 9 a.m., the time Mahesh had indicated. As none of the Gauria family members had yet turned up, they waited there for their hosts to appear. A few minutes later, Mahesh and his wife, Manjari, arrived. An attendant came behind them, carrying their duffel bag.

Bespectacled and limping slowly, Manjari smiled at them and joined her palms in a silent gesture of greeting. Veni and Athreya returned the *namaste*, along with courteous dipping of heads to the older woman. Manjari's left hand held her metal walking-stick with three spokes splayed at the bottom. In her right hand, the devout septuagenarian carried her *rudra mala*, her prayer-bead necklace, which was her constant companion. She spoke very little and spent much of her waking time silently chanting prayers in her mind. When she wasn't, she was listening to devotional songs or reading a spiritual text.

Veni and Athreya followed their hosts onto the boat and took their seats in the larger sitting area. Athreya and Mahesh sat together and began chatting, while Veni occupied a sofa near Manjari that gave a clear view of the resort. Veni was pretty sure that the rest of the Gauria family would take a while to arrive singly and in pairs. That would give her the opportunity to study them in the light of the previous day's will-related discussions with Mahesh and Ruhi.

To Veni's slight surprise, Ruhi, the youngest of them all, arrived first. She came alone, walking quickly towards the boat. Her eyes flicked left and right as if she was watching out for something, and they were wider than usual. Her face was pale. Her eyes softened as she saw Veni and Manjari. She came up the boarding plank, touched her parents-in-law's feet in respect and took a seat beside Manjari, who reached out and held her hand. An unspoken message passed between the two.

To Veni, whose imagination sometimes rivalled her husband's, the young woman seemed to be seeking comfort from her mother-in-law, which the older woman gladly gave. Mahesh's worried eyes rested on the young actress for a moment before moving away. Realizing that not a word had been said, Veni greeted Ruhi. Ruhi promptly returned the greeting and did a *namaste* to Athreya.

Next to arrive were Kanika Mehra and Jeet Mehra, Mahesh's daughter and her husband. As usual, they walked close together, with Kanika leading the way by half a step. She was talking animatedly as her husband listened and watched her face. She wore expensive, well-chosen clothes that accentuated her attractive figure. However, her beauty was marred by the hard, unforgiving cast of her face. Jeet was in his usual blue jeans and a T-shirt, with the habitual half-smile pasted on his face. A pair of binoculars hung from his shoulder.

It occurred to Veni that Kanika and Pari were very similar in height and build and looked alike from a distance. But close up, their faces were the opposites of each other. While Pari's was open, beautiful and friendly, Kanika's calculating visage could have been made of marble, with black agates for eyes.

From the time Veni had met Kanika and Jeet, she had taken an instinctive dislike to them. Within ten minutes of chatting with them, Veni had leapt to the conclusion that Kanika was self-centred and Jeet was too slick to be trusted. Their incessant references to money, combined with how they treated those less wealthy than themselves, led her to believe that the couple measured people by their monetary worth. She also got the distinct sense that the slimy Jeet was well and truly under his domineering wife's thumb, but also like others in the family, he was wary of her. Veni's opinion of Kanika was simple and black and white—she was 'a wolf in wolf's clothing'.

It, therefore, came as no surprise to Veni when, as soon as Kanika boarded the boat, she gestured peremptorily to a two-seater sofa that was away from the others. The couple went there and sat side by side, murmuring to each other. They didn't spare the others even a perfunctory glance, nor did they respond to Ruhi's polite smile. They continued talking, oblivious to the others. Having been ignored on an earlier occasion by the couple, Veni did not offer a greeting. Athreya, of course, was stoic as he exchanged a few words with Mahesh from time to time.

Veni turned to see Pari and her husband, Hiran, walking down the pathway towards the boat. Pari stopped abruptly, said something to her husband, thrust her handbag into the thin man's hands and rushed back the way she had come. She seemed to have forgotten something.

Waiting for his wife to return, Hiran began whistling a song and kicking the grass. He was neatly turned out in his usual half-sleeve shirt and trousers. The few times Veni had met him had left her with an impression that while he looked almost emaciated, he was a brainy man of the scholarly kind. His pinched face had an intelligent look that his round glasses accentuated.

Pari returned in a few minutes, and the couple hurried to the boat. Hiran seemed nervous as he stepped on the boarding plank. He kept a wary eye on the gap between the boat and the pier as if he was afraid of falling into the water there. Once they boarded, they began apologizing profusely for being late.

'We are on a vacation, *Beta*,' Mahesh answered. 'We have all the time in the world. In any case, Danuj hasn't yet come.'

'He'll be here anytime, Papa,' Ruhi added in her husband's defence. 'He got a phone call just as we were locking the door. He told me to go on ahead.'

'That's fine, then,' Hiran said in his usual courteous way. 'Pari feared that we were the last. She hates that.'

Hiran and Pari touched Mahesh's and Manjari's feet and greeted Athreya and Veni. Pari then went and sat beside Ruhi and began chatting. Ruhi's face lit up. Not for the first time, Veni felt that the two Gauria daughters-in-law seemed to be on excellent terms.

Veni turned as running footsteps sounded and Danuj came sprinting down the path towards the cruise boat. As was often the case, this handsome man turned heads wherever he went. In many ways, he was the classic image of a dashing film hero, especially when his luxurious mane bounced as he ran.

'Sorry! Sorry! Sorry!' he gushed, as he ran up the plank and stood there panting. 'I got *three* calls one after another. I hope I've not delayed everyone too much. Apologies for making you wait, Aunty, Uncle. Sorry, Papa, Ma.'

He went to his parents and touched their feet. Like his siblings, Danuj too was well turned out in high-quality clothes. Seeing that his wife was sitting with Pari, he turned to Athreya.

'Can I sit with you, Uncle?' he asked breathlessly.

'Of course,' Athreya answered. 'It would be my pleasure.'

'Thank you, sir.'

Danuj sat down beside Athreya, placed his phone on the low table next to him and tried to recover his breath. In his left hand was an ornate dagger in an equally decorative wooden scabbard. He took a few deep breaths and turned to Athreya.

'Nice piece, isn't it, Uncle?' he asked, holding it up. 'Papa picked it up at a souvenir shop in Kochi. One each for the three daughters of the family.'

The weapon had a brown-and-gold hilt of lacquered wood. The scabbard was of similar material, but with designs inlaid in bronze. Veni had seen such daggers in handicraft shops in tourist spots, including in Kochi, the nearest major airport.

'Whose is it?' Athreya asked. 'Ruhi's?'

Danuj clicked it open and held up the blade for Athreya to see. A name was engraved along the spine: *Ruhi*.

A blade with Ruhi's name written on it? A dark interpretation of the phrase occurred to Athreya's fertile mind. He glanced at the young actress and saw that she was watching Danuj. There seemed something unfriendly about the way she stared at her husband. Perhaps, there was an undercurrent that

40

Athreya was not aware of. The look on Ruhi's face vanished the moment her eyes met Athreya's. She gave him a quick smile and turned away.

Mahesh watched Danuj and Athreya talk as Manjari continued to count her *rudra* beads and chant a soundless prayer. Ruhi and Pari had continued the muted conversation of their own. Kanika and Jeet had paused their whispering at the sight of the blade. Jeet came up and put out his hand.

'Can I have a look at it, Danuj?' he asked. 'I think the three daggers Papa bought are slightly different from each other. I'm interested in seeing the differences.'

'Sure!' Danuj handed it to Jeet. 'You know more about knives than I do.'

'Kind of a hobby,' Jeet explained to Athreya as he returned to his seat with it. 'I used to throw knives as a student.'

He clicked the lock on the dagger and pulled it out of the scabbard. The slightly curved five-inch blade shone dully. Kanika contemplated the weapon in her husband's hand with a slight frown. It seemed to have triggered a thought.

'So, have you come up with new ways to kill us all at the resort?' she asked Athreya loudly enough for everyone to hear. 'I heard bits of your discussion in Papa's suite yesterday.'

'We came up with a few, all right,' Athreya replied, 'but I'm not sure if any of them are really new. There has been so much evil since the dawn of civilization that there is very little left to discover, as far as killing is concerned.'

'And yet a man had the ingenuity to kill his wife by making a snake bite her. Is that for real?'

How much of the discussion in Mahesh's suite had Kanika heard? Athreya wondered.

'Unfortunately, yes,' he said. 'Far too real.'

'He was foolish enough to get caught.'

41

'In my experience, Kanika, very few murderers are smart enough to get away undetected. There are some, of course, who don't make a single slip up. But they are the exceptions.'

'Figuring out the killer is one thing,' Kanika said shrewdly. 'Proving in court is quite another, isn't it?'

'Absolutely right.'

Meanwhile, the boat operators had pulled up the boarding plank and pushed off from the pier. Danuj took up the conversation.

'Instead of the usual whodunit film where the murderer gets caught,' he asked earnestly, 'can we make a film in which the murderer is the centrepiece? An anti-hero, if you like. In a twist at the end, he outsmarts the detectives and goes scot-free. That would be a dark kind of film—very different from the usual ones we make. I can think of a couple of such Hollywood films that did well.'

'That's an interesting thought, Danuj,' Athreya said. 'It would be a first for me, even as the audience. But I have no idea if such a movie would do well commercially in India.'

'Waste of money!' Kanika barked at Athreya from afar. 'Complete *bakwas*!' Complete nonsense.

'Pari *Bhabi*?' Danuj turned to his sister-in-law. 'Would it work? It would be very different from the usual fare, wouldn't it?'

'It would certainly be an interesting creative exercise, Danuj,' Pari replied. 'But I am not sure our Bollywood audience would care for such a theme. They want good to prevail at the end and the baddies to get punished.'

'Come on, *Bhabi*! If *you* don't break the mould, who will?' Danuj turned to Mahesh. 'Papa, what do you think? I'm sure Mr Athreya will help us come up with a top-notch plot. We already have parts of it.'

Mahesh shook his head firmly.

'This is not the first time someone has thought of it, *Beta*,' he explained. 'It's financially risky.'

'Exactly!' Kanika cut in again. 'Why waste money? It doesn't grow on trees, you know, Danuj. In any case, it would be Papa's money, not yours. Don't waste another fifty crores on a whim. You have blown up enough.'

'Let's do a low-budget project—20 crores,' Danuj persisted. 'I'll be the central character, the murderer. Ruhi can be the victim. Neither of us will charge a fee.'

'You can't act for nuts, Danuj,' Kanika chuckled. Danuj looked hurt. A slow flush crept up on his face. 'Not even to save your life. As for Ruhi,' she went on mockingly, 'she is a *star*! Why would she do free films?'

Glancing at Ruhi, Veni saw the young actress lower her gaze and stare silently at her hands, which were folded on her lap. Veni had seen Ruhi refrain from responding to Kanika's taunts in the past. What was making Kanika publicly goad her? Veni wondered. Was it jealousy? Or something else?

'I was serious, Papa,' Danuj said with a wounded expression on his face. 'I know I've made some bad decisions as a film producer. But not all my ideas are bad, are they, Papa?'

'The idea itself is fine, Danuj,' Mahesh rumbled. 'It may work overseas but Bollywood is different. Pari is right—it may not go down well with the audience.'

'Well, it was just an idea!' Danuj barked and rose.

He turned his attention to an empty chair and kicked it fiercely a couple of times, taking Veni by surprise with his sudden display of anger.

'Just look at the backwaters around us,' Pari said, sitting up and turning on an aura of good cheer to change the mood. They had left the pier behind and were into the open waters of the lake. 'It's so beautiful! No wonder they call it "God's Own

Country". It will be a delight to shoot a film here. I'll make sure that we have enough scenes on the water. A cruise boat like this one would make a wonderful set.'

Jeet returned the dagger to Danuj and pulled out his binoculars to train them on the far shore.

'As it is a backwater,' Hiran asked in an attempt to move the conversation away from Danuj's proposal, 'it's a saltwater lake, right?'

'Not entirely,' Veni replied. 'Much of it is actually freshwater, and the part near the sea has saltwater. That's so because Vembanad Lake is fed by river water as well as the sea. It's a pretty large lake, you know—almost a hundred kilometres long, north to south.'

Danuj pocketed the dagger and drifted away moodily as the conversation moved from murders to the Kerala backwaters. Veni happily held forth on the topic she knew much about and had recently gathered local knowledge from her cousin, Kurup. Besides, by virtue of having been a quizzer in her younger days, she had an endless supply of random facts to throw into any conversation. Ruhi listened without contributing, while Hiran, Pari and Mahesh asked never-ending questions. Athreya remained content watching, apart from offering an occasional remark.

A couple of hours passed as the boat took them to different parts of the backwaters and to villages on the lake. Kanika and Jeet remained wrapped up with each other, with her doing the bulk of the talking and Jeet offering an automatic smile whenever anyone looked their way. They took turns to peer through their binoculars from time to time.

Danuj sat by his wife, sipping beer and trying to make desultory conversation with her. But he met with little success as Ruhi quietly watched the scenery go by and remained abstracted. Was she ignoring him? Veni noticed Athreya glance at Ruhi a few times with a contemplative look on his face. She wondered if he was thinking about Ruhi abruptly deciding to write a will.

What had prompted a twenty-eight-year-old in the prime of life to suddenly do that? Veni wondered. That too, in the middle of a family holiday? What was so pressing that she had to do it immediately? Was there some specific threat that she was worried about?

As lunchtime approached, Danuj and Hiran picked up beers and wandered aft to the smaller sitting area. Veni was standing amidships, leaning on the port-side railing and watching a fishing village pass by. She didn't notice the two brothers move aft to the starboard side and became aware of them only when the breeze brought their voices to her.

'Where were you all of yesterday?' Hiran's voice asked.

'Kochi,' Danuj replied. 'Why?'

'I wanted to talk to you alone. I didn't want Papa or Ruhi to overhear.'

'Kya ho gaya, Bhaiya?' What's happened, *Bhaiya*? 'Something urgent?'

'I wanted to warn you,' Hiran said quietly. 'Kishan is here.'

'Here?' There was an edge of fear in Danuj's voice as it rose. 'In Kumarakom?'

'Shh! Keep your voice down. We don't want others to hear.'

Veni's curiosity was roused. She glanced towards the larger sitting area. The other family members were busy in their own chats. She slid a few feet aft along the railing so that she could hear the brothers' conversation better.

'Are you sure, *Bhaiya*?' Danuj asked softly. 'Kishan is here in Kumarakom?'

'He is staying at the adjacent resort—Sunset Bay. I saw him yesterday and tried to find you to warn you, but you were away. I tried calling you, but you didn't answer.'

'Where did you see Kishan?'

'He's been prowling on the lake in a boat, watching our resort through binoculars. Bhagya is with him.'

An image of the stationary boat at dawn flashed through Veni's mind. In it were the thug and Bhagya. So, the thug's name was Kishan. And the two were staying next to Crystal Waters.

'Oh, God!' Danuj exclaimed. 'I should have known. Is she spying on me? Why is Kishan here?'

'To carry out his threat, why else?' Hiran replied. 'He threatened to harm Ruhi, didn't he? "Cut her up" or some such thing he said.'

'Worse! He said that he'd track us down and kill her.'

'Why kill *her* if his problem is with *you*?' Hiran asked.

'If he kills me, he won't get his money back. That's why he is threatening the family. He won't dare touch Papa. So, who's left? You or Ruhi. "*Khoon baha doonga!*" he said.' I'll make blood flow!

'Shit, man!' There was a trace of fear in Hiran's voice. 'You better do something about it. Kishan is ruthless. From what I hear, he has killed before.'

'I know, I know. But where do I go for so much money?'

'Don't you have even half the amount? Pay him that and say that you'll pay the rest in a few months. That'll keep him off Ruhi's and my backs.'

'I'm broke! As you know, our last three films didn't do well. How much can you lend me? I promise I'll pay it back. Come on, *Bhaiya*, you must help me.'

'I'm in the same boat as you, my friend. We are in it together, thanks to our partnership.'

'But you have dough stashed outside the country, don't you?'

'Emergency funds! I can't touch that. Even then, how much loss can I absorb? Our firm is almost bankrupt! Sorry, Danuj, you'll have to get it from elsewhere.'

'Where?' Panic made Danuj's voice squeak. 'Papa won't bail me out this time. If you won't help either, my only hope is Sahil.'

Who was Sahil? Veni wondered. She knew of a successful Bollywood producer by that name, and film gossip said that he and Danuj were childhood friends. She moved a step closer to the talking brothers.

'Sahil?' Hiran asked, puzzled. 'Why would he help you? After all that has transpired.'

'Hmm... let me work it out,' Danuj replied pensively. 'I'll find a way to convince him.'

'Shh! Someone's coming.'

Veni heard soft footsteps on the starboard side. She moved along the railing away from the brothers, but not so much that she couldn't hear them. A couple of seconds later, she heard a female voice, speaking softly.

'Both of you are here,' Kanika said. 'Good! I wanted to have a frank chat. This is as good a time as any. I have a suggestion to make.'

'What about?' Danuj asked warily.

'The family wealth,' she replied. 'It's best that the three of us have an open chat without our spouses and come to an agreement. I think that would be best for all of us.'

'Go on,' Hiran said. 'We're listening.'

'Okay, as we have discussed several times, the family wealth is being eroded by the continuous losses you guys are incurring. Your last three films have lost money—'

'Come on, Kani,' Danuj protested. 'It's just that I'm on a luckless streak. Soon—'

'Your streak has been going on forever!' she retorted. 'It's not just these last three films that failed.'

'I'll make a blockbuster one of these days and we'll all be fine.'

'We've been through that, Danuj. Let's not go down that path again. I don't want to interfere in your and Hiran's filmmaking, or in the projects you guys undertake. At the same time, I don't want your failures or successes to impact my inheritance. So, just hear my proposal.'

'Okay.'

'My proposal is simple. Let us—all three of us—go to Papa after we return to Mumbai and tell him to trifurcate his wealth and hand over our inheritances to us. Once that is done, the two of you can fund your projects and films from your shares of the inheritance.

'I do hope that you do well and that you actually end up making blockbusters. You two can then share the profits between yourselves. I won't ask for a penny. I and you would be financially insulated from each other.'

Abruptly, Veni's attention was drawn to a movement in the larger sitting area. Deciding that it would be awkward to be caught overhearing the conversation among the Gauria scions, Veni turned and went to the forward sitting area.

Lunch turned out to be a quiet affair, partly because Veni, the most voluble of the lot, did not trust herself to speak. Anger, fear and sorrow churned her mind. Anger at Kishan simmered in her on Ruhi's behalf, accompanying the sorrow for Mahesh and Manjari. Kishan's threats had made her blood run cold—the thug was targeting the gentlest of them.

After she had overheard the conversations and returned to the forward sitting area, she had thrown furtive glances at Ruhi, wondering if she was aware of Kishan's presence in Kumarakom. There was no doubt that she was visibly worried. Her contributions to the chatting with Pari throughout the cruise had been desultory and patchy.

The second conversation Veni had overheard—the one among the three Gauria scions—hadn't moved her, even though it was intriguing. How they divvied up their wealth was their business, not hers. She had no interest in it.

On their return to the forward sitting area, both Danuj and Hiran had been preoccupied. Pari cast worried glances at her husband but said nothing. Ruhi too looked at the two brothers from time to time, as did the inscrutable Mahesh. Veni wondered how much the old man had guessed. His wife, meanwhile, devoted herself to her silent prayers.

At a private moment when they were not being observed, Athreya raised a discreet eyebrow at the sudden dip in Veni's loquacity and drew the slightest of head shakes from his wife. Mahesh's wise eyes continued to flit from person to person.

When the lunch buffet began, Ruhi brought food for her mother-in-law with much alacrity, and looked after her needs. Only when Manjari had almost finished her meagre meal did Ruhi pick up a plate for herself. Veni felt sure that this was out of affection rather than any hierarchy-related expectations within the joint family. Meanwhile, Pari looked after Mahesh. It appeared that the two daughters-in-law had a tacit understanding between themselves.

On the other hand, Kanika was focused on herself, with her husband hovering around her in attendance. The two Gauria scions sat separately at opposite sides of the boat, speaking to no one.

When the cheerless lunch came to an end, the boat made a U-turn and began its long journey back to Crystal Waters. Desultory conversation resumed, and Manjari retired to one of the cabins for her afternoon nap. Mahesh and Athreya sat together in companionable silence.

When they reached Crystal Waters a little after 4 p.m., the sky had become overcast. Grey, woolly clouds had moved in from the Arabian Sea. The evening, one of the cruise boat staff had predicted earlier, was going to be wet.

As they reached the pier and the boat operators lowered the gangplank, the travellers prepared to disembark. Kanika got off as soon as the plank was in place, without bothering to help her aged parents or saying goodbye to the two guests. Jeet followed dutifully after a nod to Athreya.

Danuj came to Athreya and Veni. He still seemed distracted.

'Not the merriest of cruises, but it was very scenic,' Danuj said with a rueful smile as he shook Athreya's hand. 'I'll see you both at the yoga class tomorrow. Goodbye, Aunty. Bye, Uncle.'

Meanwhile Ruhi was helping her mother-in-law get up as Pari helped Mahesh. When Danuj had disembarked and strode away, Veni noticed that the dagger he had been playing with was nowhere in sight. In fact, she hadn't seen it after Danuj had gone to the aft sitting area to talk to his brother.

Veni waited for the others to get off before alighting with Ruhi, who now seemed to be in a better mood. Veni didn't know whether it was a put-on to hide her distress or if Ruhi's spirits had indeed lifted.

As they walked up the path, Veni saw Danuj at the top of the path, near the resort rooms. He was talking to a man of the same build as himself. The stranger, whose back was to Veni, seemed neatly turned out like Danuj. But, unlike Danuj, who was smiling and at ease, the stranger's bearing was markedly tense. His hands were clenched, shoulders hunched, and the head was thrust forward.

Veni also noticed a young woman on the lawn. She was sitting on a lawn chair and watching the two men. Veni recognized her at once: Bhagya, the failed actress who did item numbers now. What was *she* doing here? Surely, she was not staying at this resort!

But that didn't mean that she couldn't come here—the boatmen would ferry anyone who looked like a guest. For all Veni knew, the boatmen might even recognize this screen personality, as many Hindi movies were screened in Kerala with Malayalam subtitles or dubbing. But the key question was: whom had she come to meet at Crystal Waters? Danuj or the man he was talking to? Or someone else? Or was she just snooping?

Veni's focus shifted again as Danuj gave a cheery farewell to the stranger and ambled away. The man stood rooted to the spot, looking after Danuj. Hearing footsteps behind him, he turned and glanced down the path. Veni saw that he was the same age as Danuj and nearly as handsome. The next moment the stranger's gaze fell on Ruhi. He froze. So did Ruhi. In mid-stride. Slowly, an angry flush crept up the man's face as his smouldering eyes glowered unblinkingly at her.

'Oh, God!' Ruhi whispered and clutched Veni's arm.

Veni glanced at the younger woman's pretty face and saw that it was blanched. Instinctively, she put an arm around her and pulled her close. Ruhi and the stranger stared at each other as if spellbound.

Then, the man took a step down the path. That broke the spell.

'Come, Aunty,' Ruhi pleaded and dragged Veni away from the path. 'Let's get out of here.'

She hastened across the lawn in a near-run just as the skies opened up and large drops of rain began falling. Bhagya had risen from the lawn chair and was staring at Ruhi now. With Veni following her, Ruhi veered at the centre of the lawn and made for Mahesh's suite. Struggling to catch up with the fitter woman, Veni didn't have a chance to glance back at Bhagya, the stranger or the other Gaurias. Only when they reached Mahesh's suite did she look back. The rain was falling heavily now, and both Bhagya and the man had vanished.

'Who is he?' she asked Ruhi, who, by now, was shaking. Her good cheer had evaporated, and her eyes looked haunted.

'Sahil.' Ruhi's voice was a trembly whisper. 'We were once very close... before I married Danuj. Oh, God! Why is *he* here?'

4

They were again at a yoga session on the Crystal Waters lawn the following morning. The Saturday had dawned bright and sunny with a gentle sea breeze that dimpled the lake's surface with small waves. The rain clouds of the previous evening were nowhere in evidence. Birds had set up a merry chatter at dawn, as if to welcome the new day that was perfect for an outdoor yoga session.

Mahesh was in his chair, joking and egging on the group as Akuti led them through the daily routine. Danuj and Ruhi had not joined them that morning, but Manjari was there beside her husband. She gazed over the blue waters of the lake, past the one-bedroom houseboat anchored a couple of hundred feet from the resort's edge. Another houseboat—a luxury one—floated lazily a short distance away. An odd fishing or transport vessel plied the waters beyond. It was precisely the kind of day Veni had hoped for when she had brought Athreya here for recuperation.

Athreya tried emptying his mind of everything other than the yoga asanas he was doing. As always, the deep breathing of *pranayama* had brought him a contented balance of mind. The group had finished doing four of the mandatory five *surya namaskars* and were in the midst of the fifth. Some of the less fit members were struggling to complete the last one.

'Way to go, Mrs Kumar!' Mahesh called in encouragement to one of the stouter members of the group. 'An additional coconut water for you if you complete five! Come on!'

The said lady tried to respond but found herself too short of breath to speak. Contenting herself with an answering nod, she threw herself into the last *surya namaskar*. They all knew that Mahesh would treat them to young coconuts after the yoga session. In fact, a nearby table was already laden with fresh coconuts, with a sickle-wielding, lungi-clad man in attendance.

'Rohit!' Mahesh targeted a lethargic performer. 'Raise your head higher, young man! Surely, the borrowed yoga mat can't smell so sweet for you to bury your nose in it. That's right, arch your back! That's the spirit!'

Thanks partly to Mahesh and partly to the glorious morning, the group's mood was upbeat, and their minds relaxed. Several smiles were in evidence. Athreya too was enjoying himself— doing yoga with others was so much more fun! Especially when Mahesh played yoga master.

Athreya felt at peace with himself as he completed his last *surya namaskar*. He closed his eyes, breathed deeply and focused inwards.

Suddenly, the tranquillity of the idyllic morning was shattered by a piercing scream. Athreya snapped his eyes open and tried to place its source. He quickly glanced around the lawn and found nothing amiss. A second scream—much like a wail—gave him the direction, and his head turned towards the lake.

Everything seemed normal on the backwaters, but there was one change from when he had looked that way a couple of minutes ago: in the one-bedroom houseboat stood a young woman in her nightie. Her hands cupped her face, partly covering her eyes and ears. She had a horrified look about her as she stood rooted to the spot.

A third cry came from her—not a scream this time, but a distressed call for help. As she swooned and held on to the boat railing for support, Athreya recognized her.

Ruhi.

'Aku!' he called, his voice laced with urgency as his dengue-induced fatigue retreated in the face of the shot of adrenalin that surged through him. 'Your boat! Quick!'

He rushed to the pier where Akuti's motorboat was moored, but she beat him to it. At Athreya's call, the quick-witted woman had spun and sprinted to her boat. By the time he reached it, she had cast off the mooring rope and started the engine. Athreya had hardly placed both feet on the boat's bottom when it sped away from the pier. He clutched the side and sat down hurriedly as the boat swung in a tight semicircle and raced towards the houseboat.

On reaching it, Akuti yanked the rudder so that the little motorboat came side by side with the larger boat and bumped against it. Clutching the mooring rope in one hand, she leapt up and clambered over the railing of the houseboat near Ruhi. She quickly tied the rope and unlatched the small boarding gate built into the port-side railing. She then held out a hand for Athreya to climb up.

Feeling surprisingly energetic, Athreya took her hand and launched himself upwards to clutch the railing with his free hand. A couple of moments later, he passed through the open gate to stand on the deck of the houseboat a couple of feet from Ruhi.

'Uncle!' Ruhi moaned as she reached out and clutched his arm with one hand.

With the other trembling arm, she pointed forward from where they stood. Before them was the sitting area of the houseboat with one sofa, a couple of cane chairs and two low tables.

Someone lay on the sofa. But the person's upper half was hidden by its back. One leg jutted straight out under the armrest, and the other dangled to the floor. Both feet were bare but said little about their owner.

As Athreya leaned forward to peer, Ruhi now clutched him with both hands as if she was afraid to be left alone.

'Aku,' Athreya called softy.

Akuti came up and put an arm around Ruhi and drew the distraught young woman to herself. Ruhi responded by letting out an anguished gasp and hugging Akuti.

Once free of Ruhi's grasp, Athreya stood still for a moment. Wanting to record the scene before treading any further, he pulled out his mobile phone and shot a series of photographs and a video. He surveyed the deck before him to ensure that he would not be stepping on any potential evidence. Satisfied that he wouldn't, he went to the sofa and looked down on the person lying there.

Danuj.

He had been stabbed repeatedly in the chest, and his pale blue T-shirt was soaked in blood. The brown-and-gold hilt of a dagger protruded from one of the wounds. It looked very much like Ruhi's dagger, which Danuj had been playing with on the cruise the previous day.

One wound in the left side of his chest had bled profusely, making the blood run onto the sofa and the coir mats covering the wooden deck. Judging by its position, Athreya decided that the blade had punctured the heart. Blood must have gushed out from that wound. Considering how much it had congealed, Athreya concluded that Danuj had been dead for a few hours. His eyes were closed as if he were sleeping, and his mouth was slightly open.

Even without touching him, Athreya knew that the young film producer was beyond all help. Nevertheless, he stepped carefully past the blood to touch Danuj's neck and forehead for a pulse. It was indeed too late.

The immediate things for Athreya to do were to preserve the crime scene and summon the police. He debated whether to keep Ruhi on the boat till they arrived or to send her away. Given the small size of the houseboat, two people on it might disturb the crime scene. That meant that he would send Ruhi back with Akuti to the resort and ask the latter to get the resort manager to call the police. He would stand guard on the houseboat until they arrived.

He turned and went to the two women to issue instructions, but was taken aback. Ruhi, who had been very distressed a minute ago, had recovered and was utterly dry-eyed. Not a solitary tear was in evidence.

'But how?' she whispered. 'Kishan had threatened to kill *me!*'

Meanwhile, back on the resort lawn, Veni was beside herself with worry and curiosity. She had been in her ninth posture of the *surya namaskar* when the first scream had jolted her. Not having been particularly well-balanced to begin with, she had tried to crane her neck to see who had screamed. The result was that the rotund lady toppled sideways and rolled off her mat. By the time she regained her breath, rolled over to her side and stood up, the third cry had sounded, and Athreya was running towards the motorboat.

With a single look, Veni had recognized Ruhi in the clear morning air. As before, the motherly instinct surged in her, and she hurried to the railing that separated the lawn from the lake. But with two hundred feet of open water between her and the houseboat, she couldn't see what was happening there very clearly. She saw Akuti board the houseboat, followed by Athreya. Thereafter, the three of them were too close together for Veni to get a good sense of what was going on.

Nevertheless, she knew that something was really wrong. The way her husband had summoned Akuti and hastened to the houseboat was indication enough. Having absolute faith in

Athreya and knowing how exactly to read him, his uncharacteristic haste telegraphed the situation's urgency to her.

Several times in the past, she and Athreya had discussed the value of observing people in the immediate aftermath of a crisis or a tragedy. Realizing that she was now in a unique position, Veni turned her attention to the lawn, where everyone was standing up and watching the houseboat.

Except for Manjari, who remained in her chair with her eyes tightly shut. She was no longer chanting her prayer or counting the beads of her prayer necklace. The agonized expression on her face suggested that the elderly lady knew that something terrible had happened, something from which she was trying to shut herself off.

Mahesh looked broken and a hundred years old. The dismayed look on his face said that his sharp mind had already summed up the situation and arrived at a dreadful conclusion. The consternation briefly gave way to tenderness as his eyes shone with unshed tears. But not for long. His habitual self-control eased his face out to inscrutability, and his eyes blinked rapidly to dry the tears. Within a minute, his face had set in severe lines.

At the sound of a boat engine, Veni turned back towards the water to see Akuti bringing Ruhi to the resort. Beyond them, Athreya was moving slowly around the houseboat. Veni hurried to the pier and offered Ruhi a hand as soon as the motorboat arrived.

Ruhi seemed oblivious to the fact that she was still in night clothes—a kaftan-type, full-length cotton nightie and rubber slippers. Her hair was all tousled up, just as it would have been when she rose from bed. As a rule, film stars were acutely conscious of how they appeared in public. That certainly wasn't so with Ruhi now. She seemed utterly unmindful of her appearance.

Her face was blank as if she was numbed with shock, but her eyes were open wide and dry. She had taken Veni's hand and climbed onto the pier in a trance. She said nothing. Her eyes were riveted on Mahesh and Manjari in the distance as she made straight for them. Veni still held her hand and went along silently, as Akuti ran to the resort office. Veni and Ruhi walked past the others on the lawn as they looked on mutely, and reached the couple.

'Danuj is dead,' Ruhi said, staring at Mahesh with deadened eyes. 'Killed… with one of the daggers we bought at Kochi.'

Mahesh froze. He might have been carved from stone. For a long moment, he and Ruhi locked eyes unblinkingly and in silence. Veni wondered if some unspoken message had passed between them. Then, Mahesh's face crumbled, and he let himself down into his chair.

Ruhi's eyes remained dry and her face impassive. It was as if she had reported a mundane household matter. Only when she turned to Manjari did emotion begin to break through. Manjari had now opened her eyes and removed her glasses. She looked tearfully at her daughter-in-law for confirmation, but in total silence.

Ruhi knelt beside Manjari, took her hands in hers and spoke gently in Hindi, 'Mummy… *Danuj ab nahin rahe.*' Danuj is no more.

Manjari's glasses fell unheeded to the grass. The dam broke, and tears cascaded down her lined face as only a mother's tears could. Ruhi watched wretchedly and gently squeezed her hands. That was when Ruhi's own eyes moistened for the first time. Her husband's murder had not brought tears, but her mother-in-law's grief did. Veni wondered why.

Manjari lifted Ruhi's hands and buried her wet face in the back of her daughter-in-law's hands. Her bony shoulders shook as silent sobs racked her fragile frame. Ruhi continued holding

Manjari and let her sob into her hands. A long moment passed as Veni marvelled at how quickly the old couple had absorbed the news of their son's death. There was no disbelief or question. Just acceptance. Meanwhile, the others on the lawn drifted away to give the distraught Gaurias space and privacy.

'Manju,' Mahesh whispered tenderly to his wife and stroked her grey head. His voice barely reached Veni. 'Manju… *jiska dar tha, wo ab ho gaya. Yehi Bhagwan ki ichha hai.*' What was feared has now happened. This is God's will.

Standing only a couple of feet away, Veni's mind reeled, and her blood ran cold. Mahesh's words suggested that Danuj's death was not just expected, but they had actively feared it. Why? What misfortune had transpired in the Gauria household that had made them anticipate their son's murder? She was left with the distinct impression that unspoken messages had passed between the three Gaurias before her.

Her thoughts were interrupted by the sound of running feet. She turned to see Akuti and the resort manager hurrying towards them. Behind them, Veni noted with relief, was the resort's doctor-on-call. He would take care of Manjari and Mahesh. Veni stepped back to give them space. While the manager and the doctor went to the couple, Akuti came to Veni.

'The police have been called,' she gasped breathlessly.

'Hari asked you to?' Veni asked in a whisper.

Akuti nodded.

Veni turned around and looked towards the houseboat. Her husband's thin, dengue-ravaged figure could be seen moving slowly along the boat, pausing often to inspect something. What had he discovered? Veni wondered.

Athreya had got down to work as soon as Akuti and Ruhi had left. It was a small one-bedroom houseboat, not one of those luxury ones that were heavily advertised. Why had Danuj, who came from a family that enjoyed luxury, hired a simple houseboat and not a fancier one? Athreya wasn't sure how stable the higher-end houseboats were, but this basic one kept moving disconcertingly under his feet as the lake's waves passed under it. A part of him wondered if he could put up with the movement for a whole night.

Much of the length of the deck—the entire rear half and a few more feet—was taken up by the bedroom and its attached bathroom. Forward from there was the sitting space where Danuj lay lifeless.

Athreya pulled out his phone, turned on video capture and went around the boat twice, ensuring that every detail was recorded. He shot the spaces behind and under furniture too, to make sure that nothing was missed. He then captured the surroundings, including the water and the nearby luxury houseboat, wondering why Ruhi's screams had not woken its occupants. After all, they were no more than a couple of hundred feet away—the same distance Ruhi's boat was from the resort lawn.

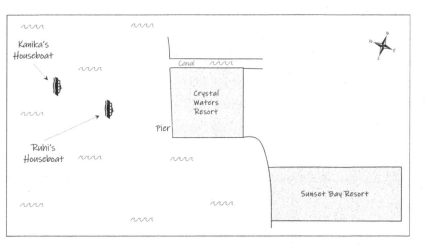

The first thing Athreya established was that there was nobody else on Ruhi's houseboat. She and Danuj had been alone that morning, and probably through the night as well. He wondered why neither a pilot nor an attendant was aboard.

He recalled that the small boarding gate built into the railing had been latched when he and Akuti had reached the houseboat in response to Ruhi's call. He remembered clearly that Akuti had climbed over the railing and unlatched the gate for him to enter.

On his first round of the boat, he had seen wet two patches on the deck—one at the boarding gate, which was on the port side, and another at the corresponding spot on the starboard side, which too was low and close to the water. These were places where the deck was most accessible from the water, making them the preferred boarding points.

The wood of the deck at both these spots felt decidedly damp to his fingers, which came away with a film of water. However, he was unable to judge how old the patches were. On the one hand, the moisture-laden air over the lake would retard evaporation, especially in the absence of sunlight. On the other, there was the steady breeze, as was the case every morning, which would help dry them.

A foot forward from the boarding gate, a short piece of rope hung outward from the railing. It was tied firmly to a post and hung down three or four feet outside the hull. The curious thing about it was that it had been cut very recently with a sharp blade. The freshness of the cut was obvious from the colour and lustre of the cleanly severed end. A small maroon-brown spot tarnished that end. Athreya pulled up the rope and examined the stain. It looked like blood. A thin, shiny film of coagulated blood had formed. Very near the spot where the rope was tied, at the very edge of the deck, was a dark spot the size of his thumb.

Athreya crouched there for a moment, contemplating the implications of the stains. Out of habit, he folded his arms to his chest so that he did not touch anything accidentally, including the railing. Except for the rope, which wouldn't retain fingerprints anyway. His, Akuti's and Ruhi's prints would be found on the railing as they had been made recently. But would the police find any others? The dew would probably have erased or smudged older prints. But they just might get lucky with the vertical surfaces where the dew hadn't settled. Hoping for the best, he let the rope drop in precisely the place it had hung and stood up.

Next, he went to examine the dagger lodged in Danuj's torso. It was buried to the hilt. He wished he could pull it out and take a closer look at the blade, but he couldn't do so until the police had done their work. Yes, it looked very much like Ruhi's dagger which Danuj had been fiddling with the previous day on the cruise boat.

He turned his attention to a low table on which lay two mobile phones. He bent over and studied them—both seemed high-end iPhones. But he couldn't be sure unless he flipped them over, something he couldn't do without touching them. He would wait for the police to examine them. Tiny drops of dew had misted over the backs. Surely, that would have erased any fingerprints on the phones.

He stood up and surveyed the coir mat on the deck. A large part of it had soaked up blood that had flowed from the stab wounds. One of Danuj's slippers was in the midst of the coagulated pool, probably stuck to the mat because of the dried blood.

But the other slipper lay on its side, with blood on its sole. The upper side and the strap also had some blotches of blood. Athreya stared at it, trying to imagine how that could have happened. If this is how it had lain when Danuj had been killed, only the part of it that rested on the coir mat would have had blood. How did blood reach the sole, the upper side and the strap? He took two more photos of the slipper and went to inspect an

63

irregular stain of blood a couple of feet towards the starboard from the large patch of blood.

Unlike the main patch, where blood had stagnated, soaked and congealed, this blood was not thick. It was too far from the body for blood to have dripped here from any of Danuj's wounds. Then, what had created it? He studied it for a minute, but was none the wiser. He contented himself with taking a few close-up photographs.

He straightened up and went to the bedroom where he had seen potentially significant evidence while recording the video of the boat. The sliding door was already open—that's how he had found it when he had boarded the houseboat. Ruhi had not closed it after she had come out of the bedroom and seen Danuj dead. Athreya studied the bedroom from the doorway, noting that the bed had been slept in, and Ruhi's day clothes were neatly folded on the dressing table.

Danuj's clothes were nowhere to be seen. He hadn't changed into his nightclothes—he was wearing a pair of three-quarters shorts and a T-shirt when he had died.

On the dressing table was a strip of alprazolam pills. One pill was missing from the otherwise fresh strip. Alprazolam, Athreya knew, was used more extensively in India than it should be. Many found it useful in managing anxiety and insomnia. Some misused it, too—it was easy to obtain small quantities of this drug without a prescription, even though the law required one. The question now was: who had consumed the missing pill from the strip? Ruhi or Danuj?

The tiny bathroom provided no clues. A toilet bag with floral prints was open, with a toothbrush and a tube of toothpaste lying next to it. Probably Ruhi's, Athreya guessed from the flowery pattern. Come to think of it, neither the bedroom nor the toilet showed any evidence of Danuj having been there. Athreya wondered when and how precisely Danuj had died, and what events had led to it.

Athreya came out and held his handkerchief up in the air to test the wind. A light breeze was blowing from the north-east— from the shore towards the houseboat and onwards to the open lake beyond. He went to the bow of the houseboat and gazed south-west. Small waves were moving in that direction, but he could see nothing on the open water. He silently berated himself for not having checked this earlier. Had his delay allowed something to float way from the boat?

Turning, he studied the position of the houseboat relative to the resorts on the shore and the luxury houseboat. He realized that he needed a way to record their positions. Perhaps, he could ask the police to use a drone to capture footage and take photographs from above. He would also request them to ensure that the boats were not moved for a few days.

He then went to the starboard side where he had seen something blue clinging to the outer surface of the hull. He leaned over the railing without touching it and studied the rectangular patch of blue a few feet below him and a few inches above the waterline. It was a widely used 'spring file', and was completely soaked with water.

It was the kind of folder that securely held papers that were punched with a pair of holes. Two thin springs in the file would pass through the holes and be bent back to keep the papers safe. However, the sodden cover, which was made of thick paper, was open and empty, and was stuck to the dripping hull as wet paper often clings to surfaces.

A couple of minutes of examination over the railing yielded no additional information. He made a mental note to point out the file to the police as soon as they came, lest the file dropped off once the sunlight warmed up the morning air.

He went back to Danuj and looked at his bloodied chest. The brown-and-gold hilt of the dagger glistened in the morning sunlight. A frown appeared on his face as he stared at it. A question arose in his mind: why had the murderer left the dagger in the wound?

After contemplating the implications, Athreya turned away to complete his inspection of the houseboat. Just as he turned, a thought that had been gnawing at the back of his mind surged forward. He froze in mid-turn and his eyes snapped wide open. Why had it not struck him earlier? Had the emotional intensity of the situation prevented it?

Danuj's murder was disturbingly like the third murder they had envisaged for Mahesh's upcoming film! There, the murderer was to board the houseboat in the dead of night and kill his victim who was staying on it. Just as it had happened in reality last night!

All the members of the Gauria family had been within earshot when Pari had proposed a murder on a houseboat and when they had discussed details. Several Gaurias had walked in and out of the suite when the murders were being discussed. What did that mean, if anything? Was one of the Gaurias the killer?

If so, was he, Athreya, responsible—at least partly—for this murder? Had he supplied the blueprint for it? It was a chilling thought, which brought with it more than a trace of guilt. Never in his career had he provided the inspiration for murder.

Before he could think about it any more, the sound of an engine reached his ears. He turned to see a motorboat approaching. Four khaki-clad men were looking expectantly towards him as the fifth man piloted it.

The police.

5

Veni and Ruhi were with Manjari and Mahesh in their suite when Athreya returned from the houseboat. Silence reigned as each person sat engrossed in their own thoughts. Ruhi stared blankly at the opposite wall as Mahesh's gaze flitted from her to his wife. Manjari seemed stoic as she gazed unseeingly at the carpet at her feet. Her *rudra* beads lay orphaned on a nearby table—the first time Athreya had not seen them in her hand. She was the only one who didn't look up when he entered.

'The police have come,' Athreya said, getting down to business right away. 'They are on the houseboat now and will be here soon. Let's put the few minutes we have before they arrive to good use. Ruhi, can you tell me what happened?'

The young widow gave a quick nod and began speaking rapidly.

'Before I tell you what happened last night,' she said, 'you need to know one thing… that my marriage was on the rocks.'

'Meaning?' Athreya asked.

'Danuj and I were heading for a divorce, but we kept that from showing in public. Everyone in the family, of course, knew it but it was not common knowledge outside.'

Athreya didn't reply right away as something clicked into place in his mind. So, that's why Ruhi had been preoccupied and had often fallen silent in public. He recalled the unfriendly look on her face when she was watching Danuj on the cruise boat. Athreya had sensed an undercurrent, but he had not suspected the extent of the problem. There had been nothing to suggest that her marriage was in peril. In retrospect, the only real indication was that she had not talked much to her husband.

On his part, Danuj too had given no indication of it. Nor had the rest of the family. Athreya marvelled at how well they had prevented it from showing in public. This family of storytellers had maintained a harmonious public image. Acting, it seemed, was in their blood.

'I see,' he said. 'I'm indeed sorry to hear that. I was not aware.' He glanced at Veni, who shook her head. 'Nor was Veni. How far gone was it?'

'I have drawn up the papers,' Ruhi replied. 'I was going to file for divorce as soon as we returned to Mumbai.'

'I presume Danuj was aware of that?' he asked.

'Of course. The marriage began falling apart in the third month.'

'The reason?'

'Infidelity. Papa and Mummy will tell you that I offered to let the past be past if Danuj would turn over a new leaf. I tried everything to preserve the marriage. As did Papa, Mummy and Hiran *Bhaiya*.'

'We tried to counsel Danuj many times,' Mahesh concurred. 'But...'

'But nothing worked.' Ruhi completed the sentence for him. 'Danuj refused to change despite everyone imploring him. He felt that marriage should not fetter him in any way, including in enjoying extramarital relationships. This led to irreconcilable differences between us. At the end of it, there was only so much I could take. I spoke to Papa and concluded that divorce was the only way forward.'

Athreya contemplated her silently. The fact that she was saying all this in front of Danuj's parents lent considerable credibility to her words. Athreya and Veni had spent a few days with the Gauria family, but neither of them had developed the slightest suspicion of infidelity on Danuj's part. This was indeed a surprise.

As Athreya considered the situation, he felt that the clarity and sureness with which Ruhi spoke suggested that her answer was not unrehearsed. The words had been carefully chosen. But then, she was already on the verge of divorce. Her lawyer would have coached her on what to say—a phrase like 'irreconcilable differences'. He further felt that Ruhi would have stood up to Danuj and that would have resulted in clashes between husband and wife.

'In retaliation to my decision to file for divorce,' Ruhi went on, 'Danuj became increasingly violent and abusive. And he began accusing me of infidelity as well, suggesting that I was having an affair with an old and mutual friend by the name of Sahil.'

'A top film producer,' Veni chipped in for Athreya's benefit. 'Sahil Sachdeva was the one who produced several of Ruhi's hits, including her first film.'

'That's right,' Ruhi continued. 'A more pertinent fact is that he has been a close friend from before my marriage. Sahil and Danuj were friends too, but that relationship had lately become strained.'

'Because of Danuj's accusations?' Athreya asked.

'Yes. More so because all of us know that there is no truth in the accusations. Danuj threw them in just to complicate the divorce process. Besides, Sahil was also angry at how Danuj was treating me.'

Athreya wondered how Sahil had known about the private relationship between husband and wife. Had Ruhi confided in him?

'Sahil is the person whom Danuj met as soon as we returned from the cruise yesterday,' Veni added. 'Remember, we all saw Danuj speaking to him when we disembarked.'

'Yes, I remember,' Athreya nodded, keeping his eyes on the newly widowed actress. He recalled the anger on Sahil's face on seeing Ruhi. 'If I remember correctly, you became upset.'

'What else would you expect, Uncle?' Ruhi countered. 'Here I was, being accused of an extramarital relationship with Sahil. And he turns up at my resort when I am on holiday. My first thought was that it would bolster Danuj's fictitious claim. I feared it would complicate the divorce even more.'

'Why did Sahil come here? I presume you didn't call him?'

'Of course not! I have not been in touch with him for months now—not taking his calls or answering his messages. Why would I call him to come here? I didn't even tell him that I was coming to Kumarakom.'

'Had your lawyer told you not to be in touch with him?'

Ruhi nodded.

'Tell me,' Athreya asked, 'Danuj's accusations... did he believe that they were true?'

Ruhi fell silent for a long moment, thinking about the question. Slowly, she nodded.

'Hmm... yes... yes, it's possible that he did come to believe his own claims. I had, of course, thought that he had flung them to put spokes in the wheel as far as the divorce was concerned. He perhaps did it on his lawyer's advice. But you know how it is—if you repeat something often enough, you end up believing it yourself.' She glanced at Mahesh. 'What do you think, Papa?'

Mahesh, who had been listening silently, nodded thoughtfully. 'It's possible, *Beti*. The more he talked about it, the more he believed it. It was his nature.'

'Okay,' Athreya said after a brief pause. 'What bearing does all this have on the events on the houseboat?'

'It's this... Danuj threw a fit after we returned from the cruise yesterday. He accused me again of having an affair with Sahil. If Hiran *Bhaiya* hadn't stepped in, I'm afraid that he might have tried to hit me. Danuj could be an absolute monster when he lost his temper.

'On the spur of the moment, he snatched away my mobile phone and demanded that I stay in our room until he returned and locked me in. He came back fifteen minutes later and told me to pack for the night—we were going to spend it on a houseboat. He said that he didn't want Sahil and me under the same roof at night. Kanika had earlier booked a houseboat for herself and Jeet for the night. Danuj booked another for us.'

'Let me understand this.' Athreya raised a hand to stop Ruhi. 'The decision to spend the night on a houseboat was not pre-planned?'

'No. It was a sudden one.'

'Prompted by Sahil turning up at this resort?'

'Yes.'

'Who knew about it?'

'I guess everyone in the family,' she replied with a frown.

'Outsiders? Sahil? Kishan?'

She shook her head. 'I don't know. I told nobody. I don't think anyone in the family would have either. Papa?'

'I agree,' Mahesh replied. 'But some of the resort staff would have known. They were the ones who gave Danuj the phone numbers of houseboat owners. They could easily have told someone.'

'Okay.' Athreya dropped his hand. 'Go on, Ruhi. What happened next?'

'He kept me inside our room until we went for dinner. Oh, God! How tense that dinner was! But we maintained a façade of normalcy. Anyway, after dinner, he led me to the pier where we boarded the houseboat. It was quite dark by then. When the houseboat was a couple of hundred feet from the shore, he told the pilot to anchor it. Danuj then told the pilot and the attendant to go away for the night and return at 9 a.m. this morning.'

'They went away? Were they surprised?'

'Well, they said that they sometimes stayed on the boat to serve the guests, but people often preferred to be alone, especially on one-bedroom boats such as ours. In such cases, they would go away for the night. Honeymooning couples too preferred to be left alone, they said.'

'How did they go?'

'A small boat picked them up.'

'Time?'

'About half past eight, I think. I am not sure.'

'The spot where the houseboat was anchored… was it chosen by Danuj?'

'Yes. I think he wanted to be close enough to the land to get a mobile phone signal.'

'And where was your phone?'

'Probably left behind in our room at the resort. I haven't seen it since Danuj snatched it from me yesterday. I came straight here to Papa's suite from the houseboat.'

'Then, you were without a phone last night?'

'Yes.'

Athreya recalled seeing two high-end phones in the sitting area of the boat. Perhaps one was Ruhi's.

'What happened after the pilot and the attendant went away?' he asked.

'We had a fight almost at once. A real shouting match… I was fed up with be being controlled like a puppy on a leash. I told him what I thought of it, and he reacted in his usual way—abuses, profanities and physical threats.'

She stretched out her arms to show bruises on her forearms. Athreya's face darkened at the sight as he felt anger rise in him. Glancing at Mahesh, Athreya saw anger and sorrow cross the old man's face too. He heard Veni hiss through her teeth.

'We quarrelled so loudly,' Ruhi went on quickly, 'that we must have been heard at the resort and on *Didi*'s houseboat.'

Mahesh nodded. 'We did hear you. So did others at the resort. Until you went into the bedroom and the shouting stopped.'

'Anyway,' she pressed on, 'I went into the bedroom. Danuj told me to stay there and not come out. I replied that I didn't want to see his face anyway and shut the door.'

She stopped abruptly and seemed to go into a trance. Athreya waited patiently even though he knew that the police could arrive at any moment. A full minute passed in silence. Four pairs of eyes were riveted on Ruhi.

'That,' Ruhi continued hoarsely, 'was the last time I saw him… alive.'

Another long pause.

'I can't believe that he is gone,' she whispered haltingly. 'I suppose I ought to feel sad… but I'm not sure if I do… I am *truly* sorry for all that has happened… but grief at his passing? I don't know. You probably noticed, Uncle, that I didn't cry after I discovered that Danuj was dead. I can't understand my own feelings now.' Her gaze moved to Manjari. 'I'm sorry, Mummy, but that's the truth.' She looked at Mahesh. 'Papa?' she appealed.

'It hasn't yet hit you, *Beti*,' he replied gently. 'You are in shock. Go on, tell Mr Athreya what happened next. We don't have much time.'

'Next?' She blinked rapidly a few times. 'Nothing. Danuj didn't enter the bedroom all night, and I didn't go out. I had a terrible night… nightmares and the wobbling boat. I slept fitfully… on and off. Later, I might have dropped off into deeper sleep. When I woke up in the morning and came out, I… I… saw him with the dagger in his chest. I think I screamed. The next thing I remember is you and Akuti beside me.'

'Did the bedroom door remain locked all night? Till you opened it this morning?'

Ruhi nodded.

'Did you hear anything during the night?' Athreya asked kindly.

'Yes... at least, I think so. I don't know what I imagined and what I really heard. I was in a daze... I am so muddled now... those dreams! It was a terrible night and the boat wobbled continuously.'

'What did you hear?'

'I'm sure I heard Danuj talking on the phone... at least two or three times. I also heard him moving about and heard his cigarette lighter. I think I heard some other noises too—thumps and creaks and scratching noises. But I think all boats creak at night. I also heard water splashing, but that is to be expected, I suppose. We were floating on a lake.'

'Did you hear any other voices?'

'Other than Danuj's? I am not sure... I was drifting in and out of sleep. If I did hear any, I can't remember them now.'

'Did you *feel* anything, Ruhi?'

'Feel? Apart from the constant wobble of the boat?'

Athreya nodded. 'Small boats wobble. Did you feel anything apart from that?'

'Yes... the boat rocked several times. It was far more pronounced than the continuous wobble. But isn't that normal? When another boat passes yours, the waves rock your boat, don't they?'

Athreya remained silent. That was not the only reason why a boat rocked. Besides, very few large boats plied the backwaters after dark, and those that did were poled over the water. Poled boats made small waves that didn't travel far. Unlike those made by motorboats.

The more probable cause of rocking was something else—someone getting on or off the houseboat. Just as they had planned for Mahesh's proposed film. That was consistent with the two wet patches on both sides of the boat. And the thumps could have been another boat bumping into the houseboat.

He recalled what he had said when they were discussing possible ways of committing murder at Crystal Waters:... *every time someone boards or gets off a houseboat, it rocks. Let's use the boat's repeated rocking as clues in the film...*

And now, the rocking of Ruhi's boat was going to become real evidence for a real murder. He decided not to delve into it at this time.

'Anyway,' he heard her say, 'I was half asleep when the boat rocked. I am not sure what I felt or heard in that state.'

'But you're sure it rocked several times?'

'I think so.'

'You had a terrible day yesterday,' he said softly. 'A heart-wrenching one, I'd think. Didn't that keep you awake?'

'It would have, I suppose... but for Mummy's remedy.' She glanced at her mother-in-law.

'Remedy?' Athreya asked.

'Restyl... alprazolam. I took a pill after I went into the bedroom.'

'There was a strip of it on the dressing table. Did you open a fresh strip?'

'Yes. I borrowed it from Mummy... she gave it to me at dinner that night.'

'Do you take it often, Ruhi?'

'No. Actually, this was only the second time in my life. It had been a terrible day, as you say, and I was anxious and very restless. I needed something to relax and sleep. Mummy takes it daily to help her sleep. It worked for me… I felt myself relax and I drifted off into sleep.'

'Do you know anything about a blue file?' Athreya asked. 'A file made of thick paper, in which documents are filed?'

Ruhi blinked at him for a moment, seeming to not comprehend.

'Did you or Danuj take a blue file to the houseboat?' he clarified.

'Oh, yes!' A penny seemed to drop in her mind. 'The infamous blue file! Yes, Danuj had it with him on the houseboat.'

'Infamous? Why?'

'It is a file that Danuj was very touchy about,' Mahesh clarified. 'He said that it had some of his most important personal papers. He would not let anyone see it. Always kept it under lock and key. Hiran used to joke about it, saying that it held Danuj's dirty secrets.'

'Didn't you ever see it, Ruhi?' Athreya asked.

'I've seen it very often, Uncle,' she replied, 'but only from the outside. I have never seen the papers that were in it. He didn't want me to see them, and I respected that.'

'Tell me… could it have held something that he could have been killed for?'

'You mean to say that someone might have killed him to take the file?'

'Is that a possibility?'

'Honestly, I don't know.' She glanced at Mahesh. 'Papa?'

Mahesh shook his head. 'I don't know either. None of us saw the papers in it—'

A knock on the door interrupted them. As Veni went to open it, fear seized Ruhi. She seemed to know what the knock implied.

A neatly attired police inspector walked in.

. . .

'Hello!' the newcomer greeted them with the cheery wave of a hand as he came in. His moustache, eyebrows and hair were jet black, and he was immaculately dressed in a police uniform. 'Good morning, all! A beautiful morning, isn't it? I am Inspector Anto, and this is my assistant, Sub-Inspector Joseph.' He jerked his thumb backward towards the short, khaki-clad man who had followed him into the room. 'We are in charge of this case.'

He beamed at everyone in the room, taking in the five people seated in it.

'No! No!' he protested, waving both hands as Mahesh made as if to rise. 'Please don't get up, sir. I am so much younger than you! Please sit! Please sit!' He turned to Ruhi, who sat with a puzzled expression on her face. The comical inspector's demeanour and words were so out of place that she had forgotten her apprehension for a second. 'And you, madam—' He bowed ceremoniously '—must be Ruhi Gauria. I have watched at least three of your films.'

His expression changed to a doleful one as he continued mournfully, 'My condolences, madam. Sincere condolences. What a tragedy! What a tragedy!' He turned to Mahesh and Manjari. 'And to you both too... my deepest sympathies. What a thing to happen in your sunset years!'

Anto then turned to Veni and cocked his head enquiringly as a polite half-smile played on his lips.

'My wife, Krishnaveni,' Athreya introduced her. 'We call her Veni.'

'Of course, of course!' the inspector gushed and turned to Athreya. 'And are you *the* Arridh Aadhreiah?'

The thick accent distorted his name so much that Athreya himself failed to recognize it. But Veni, having spent many years in Kerala, was up to the task.

'Yes, he is *the* Harith Athreya,' she confirmed. 'He was down with a severe case of dengue. He has come here to recuperate and improve his health.'

'What a pleasure! What a pleasure! I'm sure.' Anto lunged forward and took Athreya's right hand in both of his and shook it warmly. 'It's a privilege to meet you, sir. Welcome to God's Own Country. May you regain your health quickly. My apologies for not recognizing you when we met on the houseboat. You seem to have lost a lot of weight.'

'Dengue,' Veni explained drily.

'Perfectly understandable, Inspector,' Athreya replied. 'A crime scene is tough on everyone, including on seasoned officers like yourself. Especially when the victim is a young person. This was a gruesome sight.'

'How true, how true! Thank you, Mr Aadhreiah.' He glanced at Mahesh and went on, 'With your permission, sir, can we begin the formalities?'

The inspector's eccentric behaviour and ridiculously inappropriate and quaint words had lightened the atmosphere to such an extent that a hint of a smile tugged at Ruhi's mouth.

'Please do, Inspector,' Mahesh replied. 'I would like you to start as soon as you can. We are at your disposal. I am very eager to find out who killed my son.'

The atmosphere changed abruptly, and fear returned to Ruhi's face.

'Thank you, sir. We will do our best. For starters, we seem to have the murder weapon. Joseph!'

He held out his hand, and the sub-inspector placed a transparent plastic bag in it. In it was the brown-and-gold dagger from the crime scene. Anto silently held it up for all to see, making sure that all five saw it clearly.

Again, the question arose in Athreya's mind: why had the murderer left the dagger in the wound?

'Can any of you identify it, please?' he asked mildly, as if he was requesting someone to pass the salt at a dinner table.

'It looks like one of the daggers Papa bought at Kochi on our way here,' Ruhi said slowly. 'But I can't be sure.'

'Why not?'

'Because there were dozens of such daggers in the souvenir shop where we bought it.'

'Ah! Of course!' The inspector pulled out his mobile phone and brought up a photograph, which he showed to them. 'Did all of them have your name engraved on the blade?'

It was a photograph of the unsheathed dagger, showing its naked blade with splotches of blood. Engraved along the spine of the blade was a name: *Ruhi*. The name started near the hilt and went down towards the tip. Seeing it, Ruhi gasped. Blood drained from her face. A moan escaped Mahesh while Manjari suffered silently.

A frown furrowed Athreya's brow. This made no sense! Why would Ruhi leave her dagger in the wound if she had killed Danuj? Surely, the inspector could see that!

'Is that a photo of the dagger in the bag, Inspector?' Veni asked, interrupting Athreya's thoughts.

'Of course, madam. I assure you it is.' He turned to Ruhi. 'Now, is this your dagger, madam?'

'It could be,' Ruhi croaked. 'I'm not sure.'

'Not sure?' Anto's eyebrows rose theatrically. 'Why not?'

'Because I've seen my dagger only once.'

'Only once?' he repeated.

'Yes. When Papa bought it in Kochi. I haven't seen it since.'

'You are sure, no?'

'I… I think so.'

'You'll have to do better than that, madam,' the inspector urged. 'This is not good enough. When did you see your dagger last?'

'I… am not sure.'

'No? Why not?'

'I think I can explain, Inspector,' Veni cut in. 'May I?'

'By all means, madam. By all means.' He was all courtesy.

'We went on a cruise yesterday, Inspector,' Veni began, deliberately putting on a light Malayali accent. 'The entire Gauria family and the two of us. During that cruise, Danuj had a very similar dagger. He was playing with it. We don't know if that dagger was Ruhi's, or one of the other two that Mr Gauria bought. That's why none of us can be sure.'

'Are *you* sure of what you just said, madam?' Anto asked Veni.

'Yes.' Veni nodded vigorously. 'Very sure.'

'I can corroborate that, Inspector,' Athreya added softly. 'It was a similar-looking dagger. Jeet too inspected it. You should ask him too. However, I do recall that the dagger we saw on the cruise had Ruhi's name engraved on it. Danuj showed it to me privately. I don't think Ruhi saw it.'

'All the three daggers I bought were similar,' Mahesh rumbled. 'There were some minor differences, but I couldn't tell one from the other. That's why I had the three names engraved on them.'

'Ah! Of course! Why did you buy them, sir?'

'As gifts to the three younger ladies of the family—Kanika, Pari and Ruhi. As mementos of our visit to Kerala. Something to keep in their showcases.'

'Of course, of course! If the other daggers carried the names of Kanika and Pari, this one, which has Ruhi's name, must be Ruhi's. No?'

'I guess so,' Mahesh conceded. 'Unless someone bought a *fourth dagger* and had Ruhi's name engraved on it.'

'Who would do that? Why?'

'I don't know, Inspector. I'm just voicing it as a possibility.'

'But is it possible?'

'I should think so. There were dozens of daggers in that shop.'

The inspector turned to Ruhi. 'When did you last see your dagger?' he asked. 'If you disregard the one you saw on the cruise.'

'In the shop in Kochi. I put it into our duffel bag when we left the souvenir shop.'

'You didn't see it after that?'

Ruhi shook her head. Anto returned the dagger to Joseph and took a large, transparent plastic pouch from him. In it was a blue paper file, sodden and dripping with water. He held it up to Ruhi.

'Have you seen this before, madam?' he asked.

Ruhi took the pouch and studied both sides of the file. Apart from the brand of the file and the words 'Office File' nothing was written on it. Ruhi nodded and returned it to the inspector.

'Yes, this seems to be Danuj's file. He had it on the houseboat last night.'

'When did you see it last?'

'Just before I went into the bedroom of the houseboat. It was on the table next to the sofa.'

'Ah, of course! Was it dry?'

'Yes.'

'Was it empty then, or did it have papers in it?'

'It had papers.'

'Why is it empty now, madam? Where are the papers?'

'I have no idea.'

The inspector's face seemed to harden.

'What kind of papers did your husband keep in the file?'

'I have no idea. He never showed them to me.'

'I see!' Anto handed the file back to Joseph. 'And you also have no idea who took the papers from it?' he asked.

Ruhi shook her head mutely.

'Will you take us to your room, madam?' he asked, suddenly grave. 'We would like to search your room and ask you some more questions.' His voice hardened. 'Alone, please.'

6

A heavy silence hung over the group after Ruhi left with Inspector Anto. Feeling sorry for the young woman, Veni had escorted her to the door, given her an encouraging pat and whispered reassuring words in her ear. When she turned from the door, she saw that Athreya's eyes were on Mahesh and Manjari, studying their grief-stricken faces as their agonized gazes followed their daughter-in-law. Silent tears cascaded afresh down Manjari's face. Feeling another pang, Veni went and sat beside her, holding her hand and offering silent support.

'Peculiar man, that inspector,' she heard Mahesh say gruffly, breaking the awkward silence. Veni agreed wholeheartedly with him. 'He says the most inappropriate things and behaves a bit like a buffoon. What did you think of him, Mr Athreya?' he asked.

'Peculiar, yes,' Athreya replied. 'Interesting too. I noticed that his funny behaviour distracted us. As a result, we let our guards down. I wouldn't underrate him.'

Trust Hari to notice that! Veni herself had been taken up with the incongruity of Anto's words.

'Hmm.' Mahesh nodded at Athreya. 'I see your point. Do you think he is up to the task?'

'Of finding the killer?' Athreya asked. 'That remains to be seen. But Anto is no fool. I'm told that he is known as "Bulldog Anto" in the local police circles. Very tenacious.'

'You do realize, don't you, that Danuj's murder is very similar to what we had discussed for the film?'

Athreya nodded. 'I do, but I am not sure what that means. Many people heard our discussion that day.'

'Do you think that Ruhi is Anto's prime suspect?' Mahesh asked.

'Yes. At this point, many things point to her: she was the only one on the houseboat last night, she and Danuj had a bitter fight, and he was stabbed with her dagger. Not to mention the insurance and the inheritance that would come to her after Danuj's death.

'She also had ample opportunity to commit the crime, a very strong motive to do so and a weapon to carry it out. Anto would be remiss in not considering her his prime suspect.'

Mahesh nodded slowly. 'Unfortunately, that's true. Poor Ruhi... just when we thought that things couldn't get worse for her, they do.'

'But in my mind,' Athreya mused aloud, 'there is one thing that speaks in her defence.'

'What is that?' Mahesh asked, his face brightening.

'The fact that Ruhi's dagger was left in the wound. Why would Ruhi do that if she was the one who killed Danuj? Why would she implicate herself?'

'Indeed! You know, Mr Athreya, I don't think she killed him.'

'Why not?'

'Because it's not in her nature. I have seen many, many people in my lifetime, Mr Athreya, and I consider myself a good judge of character. Ruhi is not the kind to kill for any of the motives you mentioned. I think she is utterly incapable of driving a dagger into anything, let alone another human.'

'People do uncharacteristic things in the heat of the moment, Maheshji. Anger sometimes makes them do things they would otherwise not do.'

'I agree. But that was not the case here. You see, Manjari and I were watching the houseboat during and after their quarrel for quite a while after the last shouts had faded. Ruhi didn't come out of the bedroom and Danuj didn't enter it. An hour is quite ample for Ruhi's anger to subside. She usually regains her composure far sooner. There was no "heat of the moment" here.'

Veni watched Athreya as he listened silently and didn't react to Mahesh's explanation. Neither did he offer an opinion. Seeing the contemplative look on his face, Veni knew that multiple possible scenarios would be flashing through his mind, some involving Ruhi and some without her. Ruhi, Veni knew, might not be the only one with a motive to wish Danuj dead. Athreya would therefore be keeping an open mind.

As if Athreya had read his wife's thoughts, he popped the question to Mahesh.

'Are there other people who might have wanted Danuj dead?' he asked.

'I was just going to talk about that,' Mahesh replied, glancing at his silent wife as he shifted on his sofa. 'I am going to say things now that we've kept within the family. You and Veni will be the first outsiders to hear them. If you are to help us, Mr Athreya, you need to know the truth about our family. At the same time, I'll rely on your discretion.'

Athreya nodded. 'Of course.'

Veni glanced at Manjari. She had not said a word, which was not unusual for her. It was only last night that Athreya had said that he hadn't heard her voice at all. Her interactions with him so far had been limited to gestures, *namastes* and smiles. He hadn't even overheard her speaking to someone else. This silent lady had taken the murder of her son stoically. Some inner strength was aiding her.

'Danuj was my son, and I loved him like any father would,' Mahesh began. Veni turned her gaze to him. 'But I was not blind to his faults. Quite the contrary! You will hear me use words that parents seldom take while talking about their children. What I will now say is the unfortunate truth. Some of it may shock you because the Danuj you saw and the Danuj we know within the family were two very different people. Everyone in the film industry will tell you that I call a spade a spade. That's what I'll do now.'

'I appreciate that,' Athreya replied softly. 'It makes the job easier.'

'Early in Danuj's adolescence, our family's wealth, the fact that we are big names in Bollywood and his own good looks went to Danuj's head. Nothing Manjari or I did could remedy that. We tried many different approaches; we tried scolding, cajoling, threatening, but all was in vain. We had been more successful with Hiran, but we failed utterly with Danuj.

'Since adolescence, Danuj has had a streak of promiscuity. As you can imagine, the temptations in Bollywood are endless, especially for a good-looking scion of a prominent family. We are a film-crazy nation, Mr Athreya, and there was no dearth of girls willing to please someone like Danuj in the hope of getting a break into films. Danuj exploited this to the hilt. He was far too fond of women. Unfortunately, he left many broken women in his wake.

'I had hoped that he would change after marriage, but my hopes were dashed very quickly. My heart went out to Ruhi, but there was nothing I could do to prevail upon Danuj. Divorce, I soon realized, was inevitable... it was only a matter of time. But I seriously erred in asking her to stay in the marriage. My only defence is that I didn't realize the extent of Danuj's abuse and violence until lately. Had I known it, I wouldn't have asked her to stay.

'I am deeply grateful to Ruhi that she stayed in the failed marriage for so long at my request. I now view her as a daughter. I know that she was not the cause of the divorce. Danuj was… one hundred per cent. For all that I've made her endure, I want to give her a share of the family wealth. Of course, it doesn't lessen the trauma she has suffered, but it is a gesture on Manju's and my part. It's small compensation for what Danuj did to her.'

'Does she know?' Athreya asked.

Mahesh shook his head. 'I haven't told her. She would refuse to accept it. But I did tell my children—they needed to know.'

'How did it go down with them?'

'Not well, as you can imagine. Different people reacted with different levels of intensity. But I was very clear in my mind that this is a decision for Manjari and me to make. Our children had no say in it. My wife agreed fully.'

'Were there quarrels over it?'

'Of course! Many quarrels. There still are. Some are very acrimonious. But Manju and I didn't yield. As a result, if I were to drop dead this moment, Ruhi will inherit a minor fortune. She doesn't know it yet.'

Athreya nodded in appreciation. 'Thank you for being candid,' he said. 'Please go on.'

Mahesh let out a long breath and continued.

'Going back to Danuj's growing up… before long, Danuj joined the family film production business. He had tried his hand at acting but found that he didn't have a flair for it. Nor was directing his cup of tea. He took up film production and began losing money hand over fist.'

Veni was unsure what to make of that. Despite not having a 'flair' for acting, Danuj had projected an image in public that was very different from who he really was! Which suggested that he could act when he really wanted to.

'Now, you need to appreciate that things are not always legal and above board in our business,' she heard Mahesh say. 'That's the nature of the beast. However, trust is all important, especially when you can't put everything down in writing. Soon, I began hearing that Danuj was not keeping his word. He made reckless promises, only to break them at other people's cost.

'To cut a long story short, many people who lent money to Danuj felt cheated and the family name was getting tarnished. That affected me as well as Hiran, who has shown promise as a film producer. I stepped in to make good Danuj's promises and ensured that people who engaged with the Gauria family were not short changed.'

Listening to Mahesh, Veni felt a pang of pity for the octo-genarian filmmaker. Film stars and ordinary folk alike bowed to his will, but his own son utterly disregarded this powerful man's wishes. Manjari remained still, saying nothing.

'However,' Mahesh went on, 'I could do little for the young women Danuj left broken in his wake. Offers of monetary com-pensation in such situations, I soon realized, were seen as insults rather than olive branches. They were perceived as a rich man's callous response to his profligate son's philandering. So, there was nothing I could really do, except to apologize on Danuj's behalf. On her part, Manjari prayed to God for His help and redoubled her prayers.

'Coming back to his business dealings, Danuj was soon deep in debt. Initially, I would step in to pay his debts, but soon real-ized that it only made Danuj more reckless. If I was there to bail him out every time, there was no incentive for him to reform or to exercise caution in his business dealings.'

'I can imagine.' Athreya nodded. 'That would encourage shady people to cut flawed deals with Danuj and take your money in the end. They have nothing to lose.'

'Exactly,' Mahesh concurred. 'It encouraged bad faith deal-ings. That's exactly what happened with a rogue called Kishan.

He had lent Danuj 25 crores at usurious interest rates for yet another failed project. Unsurprisingly, Danuj couldn't repay the loan when it fell due, and the interest charges added another 10 crores to it.

'Enough was enough, and I refused to step in. I decided to let Danuj face the music himself. It was high time he learnt his lesson the hard way.' He paused for a long, contemplative moment. When he resumed, his tone was regretful. 'But unfortunately, I had picked the wrong deal to teach Danuj a lesson.'

'How so?' Athreya asked.

'I was not aware that the lender was Kishan—a thug who has links with the mafia, and a man who is said to have killed in the past. When Danuj defaulted on the loan, Kishan threatened to kill not Danuj, but Ruhi or Hiran. Sadly, this man's threats are to be taken seriously.'

'I believe he is in Kumarakom right now,' Athreya said. 'Staying close by. Is that right?'

'Yes… but how you know that, beats me. Yes, Kishan is staying at Sunset Bay with Bhagya, a young actress with whom Danuj had an affair a couple of years back. In fact, I met Kishan a couple of days ago. I attempted to negotiate a settlement by offering to pay him off and close this matter.'

'What happened? Was he agreeable to your paying it off?'

'We are still negotiating. I've offered to repay the principal amount of 25 crores. But I have refused to pay the interest of 10 crores as the rates were unreasonable. People will tell you that I am a hard negotiator. I was so in this instance too. If Kishan turns down my offer, he won't get his 25 crores either. He knows that. Word has reached me that he needs his capital back rather urgently, because the money is actually not his. I was fairly sure that he would cut a deal.'

'Was?' Athreya asked. 'What do you mean?'

'Danuj's death changes everything,' Mahesh replied. 'Surely you see that?'

'I do. Especially as Kishan is now a potential suspect.'

'Exactly. With his reputation, he will feel the heat. I'm sure he will now want to take my offer of 25 crores, cut his losses and vanish.'

'Will you agree to that, Mr Gauria?'

'We'll see. My negotiating position is stronger now.'

'Could Kishan benefit by stealing the contents of Danuj's blue file?'

'I don't know… Honestly, I have no idea what was in the file.'

'I see.'

'Now, coming back to Danuj,' Mahesh went on, 'Kishan is not the only one Danuj owes money. There are others too. There is talk that they have come together and have been meeting Kishan in an attempt to punish Danuj, who, I believe, was *really* scared. Danuj was desperately seeking money to pay off his debts. He pleaded with me a couple of times. Finally, I agreed, but only after extracting written promises from him.'

'What promises?'

'That's no longer relevant… now that Danuj is no more. They were promises to reform. Coming back to Kishan, one of my conditions for paying him 25 crores was that he backed off from Danuj *completely* and *never* had any more dealings with him. Another condition was that Kishan would not accept any contract to harm anyone of this family. He is quite capable of taking money from Danuj's creditors to kill him. Hence this condition.'

'Maheshji,' Veni asked in a low voice, 'how difficult would it be for a creditor to hire someone to kill Danuj? One hears of such people having links with the mafia.'

'Unfortunately, it's not at all difficult if one has the contacts, Veni. I could do it if I wished. It could be done anonymously too. Where there is glamour, there is crime. Where there is both glamour and money, crime is unavoidable.'

'Then,' Athreya mused, 'there are multiple people who wished Danuj ill. Any one of them could have hired Kishan.'

Mahesh nodded. 'Or someone else. There are enough knives for hire.'

'Indeed,' Athreya agreed. 'Anto must be told of this.'

'I leave that to you,' Mahesh said. 'Meanwhile, there is something else I want to say to you.'

'Please.'

'You see, Mr Athreya, I am an old man whose days are numbered. But I don't want to die without knowing who killed my son. I don't think it was Ruhi, but my judgement might be coloured by my affection for her. She is like a daughter to me and not a daughter-in-law.'

For the first time in the discussion, Manjari stirred. Veni let go of her hand and gave her an additional cushion.

'Danuj was far from perfect,' Mahesh went on, 'but he was my son. I am not surprised that this happened. In some ways, my worst fears have come true. But this is nasty business, Mr Athreya. Bad for the family, bad for Ruhi, bad for Danuj's memory.' His eyes glistened with moisture as he went on. 'It breaks my heart to see Manju go through this agony. She has taken it very well, but no mother should ever have to go through this.'

Veni stayed silent, not trusting herself to speak. Watching the elderly couple in grief had brought a lump to her throat.

'I don't want any of what I've said to come out in court, Mr Athreya,' Mahesh went on. 'I don't want our dirty linen washed in public. God knows there are enough vultures out there who have been waiting for something like this to happen. Only you can help us, Mr Athreya. Please accept my commission and take on this case. You will not find a more generous client.'

Mahesh blinked his eyes to dry the accumulating moisture. He stretched out his arm and covered Manjari's hand with his. A couple of tears fell from her eyes as she squeezed them shut. Unbidden, a tear rolled down Veni's cheek too.

Manjari, who had been silent through all this, who had accepted her son's murder stoically, joined her palms beseechingly to Athreya and dipped her head in silent supplication. Words were not necessary. Her plea was evident.

'Do this unfortunate old couple a huge favour, Mr Athreya,' Mahesh whispered hoarsely. 'Solve this case before it goes to court. Spare us and Ruhi the media trial by cracking it quickly. Find Danuj's killer before we return to Mumbai. You are our only hope. We will forever be in your debt.'

The door burst open and Pari ran in, wild-eyed and panting. A few steps behind her came the skinny Hiran, looking as distressed as his wife.

'Papa!' Pari cried. 'Is it true? We just heard about Danuj! The resort manager said that Danuj is… is…'

She broke off staring wildly at the four seated people. The palpable pall of sorrow that hung over them, and the teary, helpless expressions of agony on their faces must have supplied the answer to her question.

'Oh, God!' she gasped, trembling all over. 'Papa, did you see him… see Danuj?'

'No, *Beti*… I've been here and Danuj is on the houseboat. Only Mr Athreya has seen him.'

'Uncle!' She turned beseechingly to Athreya. 'Tell me it's not true. Tell me it's all a bad dream. Please!'

Athreya rose quickly and went to her. He took her hands and guided her to a chair. He sat her down silently, still holding her hands.

'I wish I could, Pari,' he said gently. 'But I can't. Unfortunately, the news is true. Danuj is no more.'

An agonized wail burst through her lips, and she turned to her husband in desperation. Hiran came quickly and crouched beside her. She turned her watery gaze back to Athreya.

'They say he was killed?' she asked. 'Is that true?'

'Yes, Pari. During the night.'

'But he was on a houseboat! Alone with Ruhi.'

Athreya nodded silently.

'Then… how? Why? It's just like what we discussed the other day! Somebody came at night and—.' A fresh bout of panic hit her. 'Is Ruhi okay?' she demanded. 'Is she hurt? Where is she?'

'Kishan!' A furious hiss sounded, making Athreya's head jerk up.

It was Hiran. His face suffused with anger as he turned to his father. His spare frame was trembling with emotion. Pari looked at him uncomprehendingly.

'Kishan!' he said again more loudly. 'It was him! He is here at Kumarakom. He killed Danuj just as he threatened to. We must tell the police at once.' He looked around the room perplexedly. 'Where is Ruhi? Is she safe? Kishan threatened to harm her too. We must find her.'

Hiran made for the door.

'She is safe,' Athreya cut in quickly, raising his voice to make Hiran stop mid-stride and turn back. 'Don't worry, she is safe from Kishan right now. She is with the police.'

'Police?' Hiran echoed. 'They are already here? Why have they taken Ruhi?'

'To search her and Danuj's room. Now sit down, please. I'll order some tea.'

'I'll do it, Hari!' Veni jumped up and went to the telephone to do the needful.

'Hiran,' Athreya asked, looking squarely at the dead man's brother, 'did Kishan specifically threaten to kill Danuj?'

In his mind was the conversation between the two brothers that Veni had overheard on the cruise boat. Danuj had said that Kishan had threatened to kill Ruhi or Hiran. Danuj had believed that his own life wasn't in danger because Kishan wouldn't get his money back if he killed Danuj.

'Yes,' Hiran answered, giving a different version. 'He threatened to kill Danuj.'

'How do you know that?'

'Danuj told me.'

'When?'

'Yesterday, during the cruise. He and I were talking shortly before lunch.'

'Ah, yes!' Athreya nodded. 'You and he went to the sitting area in the rear of the cruise boat.'

'That's right. He told me of Kishan's threats to kill him. Danuj was terrified when I told him that Kishan had followed him to Kumarakom.'

Athreya looked away, seeming to close the subject. Why was Hiran misstating what Danuj had said? Was it deliberate? Or was he misremembering? Athreya had complete confidence in Veni's memory, especially when it came to overheard conversations. He was certain that she had reported to him exactly as she had heard it. Almost verbatim.

His thoughts were interrupted by Hiran.

'You must tell the police about Kishan at once, Mr Athreya,' he insisted. 'Now that his job is done, he will leave Kumarakom at the earliest opportunity. He might have even gone away already.'

'I agree,' Athreya said briskly. 'I'll speak to Inspector Anto right away. I'm told Kishan is staying at Sunset Bay. Is that right?'

'I believe so. He hired a boat and was snooping on us through binoculars. A young woman named Bhagya was with him.'

'What can you tell me about Bhagya?' Athreya asked, looking from Hiran to Mahesh.

'I'll tell you,' Hiran answered and took a seat. 'Papa, if you don't mind, I'll be candid with Mr Athreya. After all, he is helping us.'

'Of course, *Beta*,' Mahesh agreed. 'Please tell it as it is.'

'Bhagya was a good upcoming actress,' Hiran began. 'Not a brilliant one or a star, but not bad either. I had done a couple of films with her and found her to be good in support roles. She learnt quickly and improved due to her hard work.

'Besides being a quick learner, she is good looking and spunky—the kind of girl that attracted Danuj. Soon, Danuj started seeing her, and one thing led to another. Over the next few months, he made promises to her that he couldn't keep—he assured her roles and even vowed to marry her. But, in reality, he had no roles to offer and had no intention of marrying her. All he was interested in was to have a fling with her. Soon, he tired of her and moved on to other women.

'Unsurprisingly, the spirited Bhagya hit the roof. Before you knew it, the matter became public and very messy. Accusations flew both ways and neither of them wanted to back down. The spat peaked when Danuj put out word that anyone giving her roles would incur the Gaurias' wrath.

'This had the expected effect and Bhagya stopped getting roles. Her career nosedived and she was left to take up item numbers that came her way. That's the story of Bhagya… She became yet another broken woman Danuj left in his wake.'

Athreya glanced at Veni—she would be able to tell him more, he was sure. He would ask her later. For now, what Hiran had said was enough to establish Bhagya's motive. He felt sorry for the unfortunate actress. The irony was that her name translated to 'lucky' in English, but she seemed to be anything but that.

Athreya pulled out his mobile phone and rose. It was time to call Anto. He walked away from the group as he dialled the number the inspector had given him on the houseboat.

'Did you just come from your room?' Veni asked Pari as Athreya drifted away.

Pari nodded absently.

'I was wondering if you too spent the night on a houseboat,' Veni went on gently, 'like Ruhi and Kanika.'

'No,' Pari shook her head. 'We are booked for tonight. Kanika said that we shouldn't all be away on the same night. It might be better if Hiran and I stayed on the resort last night, just in case Mummy or Papa needed us. Kanika and Jeet might not be able to come quickly enough if they were on a houseboat.'

'Oh, I see. That makes sense. I wondered because you were not at the yoga session today. You had intended to attend.'

'We didn't sleep well, Aunty. Couldn't wake up in time for the yoga. After witnessing the fight last night, we were so upset. We sat here, talking with Mummy and Papa for a long time. Then, Hiran and I talked late into the night—we just couldn't sleep. We took a walk on the lawn too… just to get ourselves to unwind a bit.'

'Did you see or hear anything when you were on the lawn? Especially anything from Danuj's houseboat?'

'No.'

'The police were asking if any boat approached their house-boat,' Veni lied. 'The killer would have come by boat.'

'No, Aunty.' Her voice was firm. 'Nothing.'

'Pity.' Veni fell silent.

'But we heard a cry early in the morning,' Pari said. 'It woke me up briefly. I know now that it was Ruhi. But back then, I had no idea. The sound broke my sleep, but I thought it must be some child wailing. I turned over and went back to sleep. Oh, God! Poor Ruhi. I must go to her.'

'I'm sure she'll be back soon,' Veni assured her. 'Ah, Hari!' She looked up at Athreya as he returned to the group after speaking to Anto. 'Did you get through to the inspector?'

'Yes,' Athreya nodded. 'He was grateful for the information, Hiran. He asked me to thank you.'

'Where is Kanika?' Pari asked suddenly and looked around.

Seeing Veni shake her head, Pari jumped up from her chair. 'Does she know?' she asked.

'Probably not,' Hiran answered, rising quickly and gesturing to his wife to sit down. 'They are on the houseboat. In any case, she and Jeet sleep late. I better call them. Kani will be devastated... her little brother is... my God!'

7

When Kanika finally arrived, it was with a scowl on her face that signalled her mood. It was as if she was blaming the world and everyone other than herself for the tiresome disruption to her life. Her 'little brother' seemed nowhere near the top of her mind. Clearly, Hiran was mistaken about Kanika's feelings for her younger brother. Or perhaps, he was being hopeful.

From the long delay between him sending a boat to fetch her from her houseboat and her turning up at Mahesh's suite, it was apparent that Kanika had taken her time to ensure that she was eminently presentable when she stepped out of her room. As always, her attire was expensive and stylish. She had even given thought to the colour, it seemed—she was wearing black with matching black pearls. She seemed to have stopped for a long while at her room and taken the time to change her clothes and apply make-up.

Having taken a mild dislike to her, Veni found that annoying. Wasn't this the time to show sympathy to your broken parents who had lost their youngest child? Shouldn't the young widow's well-being be high on your mind now? How could the most important thing be your dressing up for the occasion? Black pearls indeed!

Even as these thoughts passed through Veni's mind, a part of her felt that she was being too harsh on Kanika. Time to forgive, she told herself.

'What happened?' were Kanika's first words as soon as she blew into the suite with Jeet in tow. 'Hiran said that Danuj is dead.'

She sat down opposite her parents and smoothed out her flaring black dress before looking up at Mahesh enquiringly. Apart from a quick glance, she didn't pay her mother any attention.

Manjari was anyway lost in her thoughts, with a tear or two dropping on her lap from time to time.

When Mahesh, deeply preoccupied, didn't respond for a second or two, Kanika turned to Hiran.

'Tell me,' she instructed her elder brother.

Hiran summarized the events of the morning as Kanika listened silently with a frown. Jeet stood behind her chair with his hands resting on the back.

'Anything stolen?' she asked when Hiran finished.

In response, Hiran turned to Athreya. Kanika and Jeet did likewise.

'We don't know for sure yet,' Athreya replied. He had decided not to speak of the papers in the blue file. 'The police and Ruhi are searching Danuj's room right now.'

'How about the houseboat?' Kanika asked. 'Ruhi would know if anything was stolen from there. Did you ask her?'

'No. I didn't think it was important enough to ask that question at this stage.'

'Robbery is the most frequent motive for murder. Surely you know that? I'm told you were associated with the police earlier?'

'Is that the most frequent motive for murder?' Athreya asked innocuously. 'I'm afraid I wasn't aware of that.'

'Come on,' she barked irritably. 'Someone climbs into the boat in the middle of the night and kills Danuj. Why would a random stranger do that if he had no intention to steal? Danuj must have surprised him, and he killed Danuj.'

'Kishan is here,' Hiran cut in. 'In Kumarakom.'

'Aha!' Kanika snapped her fingers. 'You too saw him, Hiran?' she asked. 'In a stationary boat, snooping on us through binoculars.' She turned to Athreya. 'So, there is your first suspect.' She blinked twice rapidly. 'Unless...' Her eyes bored into Athreya's. 'Unless... you think Ruhi killed him.'

A sharp intake of breath sounded from Pari, and her face took on a deeply disapproving look. Manjari's eyes focused on her daughter and her look of sorrow deepened. Hiran and Mahesh just stared. Jeet shuffled his feet and seemed to make a half-hearted protest.

'Kani,' he whispered to her, 'this is not—'

She stilled him with a gesture of her hand.

'We are all adults here, Jeet,' she went on. 'I'm sure Athreya has seen it all before. Spouses often have the strongest motive.'

Veni saw Athreya's face harden. She knew how particular he was about not making accusations without just cause. Besides, even Mahesh used the title when he addressed the seasoned investigator. But Kanika didn't think it necessary, even though Athreya was two decades older than her. Veni felt her dislike for Kanika rise again.

'More than thieves?' Athreya asked innocently.

'Well!' Her eyes flashed. 'I'm sure you know what I'm talking about. By the way, what are you doing here? Are you—'

'I've commissioned him,' Mahesh cut in fiercely, 'to find Danuj's killer.'

Kanika flushed in anger.

'How much—' she began to ask, but a look from her father stopped her mid-sentence.

Veni knew what Kanika's question was going to be: it was about the fees Mahesh was to pay to Athreya. Money was always Kanika's prime consideration.

'Were you on the other houseboat?' Athreya asked evenly, as if the sparring had never happened. 'There is a high-end houseboat nearby which I am told you had hired for the night.'

'Yes,' Kanika answered. 'We had booked it a couple of days back. Only for one night. We went at about 7 p.m. and even had a romantic candlelight dinner on the deck.' Her voice crackled in anger. 'And the killer had to pick this night to do his work!'

'Did you hear anything when you were on the boat?' Veni asked.

'Yes... yes.' Kanika threw an unfathomable glance at her husband.

'No point hiding it, Kani,' Jeet volunteered. He turned to Athreya. 'Danuj and Ruhi had a terrible fight on the boat last night. Their voices carried to us.'

'Yes, they were heard here at the resort too,' Athreya agreed. 'But that's not what I meant to ask. I was wondering about later in the night... when Danuj was... you know...'

'No, I didn't hear anything,' Kanika said.

'I would take your suggestion seriously—the possibility of a stranger boarding the houseboat at night,' Athreya persisted. 'If you or your husband heard anything at night, you must tell me.'

'No, I didn't hear anything,' Kanika replied. 'Nor did Jeet.'

'I had hoped that you had. Sounds carry well over the water.'

Kanika shook her head firmly. 'Sorry. We didn't hear or see anything... except Ruhi fighting with Danuj earlier in the evening. How they shouted! No decency.'

Athreya lifted his gaze and looked enquiringly at Jeet, who also shook his head and gave an apologetic half-smile.

'There is another angle you should look into,' Kanika said, as she rose from her chair. 'Sahil is here. He is staying at this very resort... he was here last night too.'

'Sahil?' Athreya asked, although he already knew who he was.

'Ah!' Kanika purred. 'Don't you know? You must ask Ruhi. You will soon have more motives than you can handle, Mr Investigator. Come, Jeet!'

She spun around and made for the door with nary a glance at her gutted parents. Jeet followed obediently. At the door, she turned and looked at Athreya.

'If Ruhi doesn't tell you,' she said, 'come to me!'

Hardly had Kanika been gone for more than a couple of minutes than a knock sounded at the door. Expecting that the tea she had ordered had arrived, Veni went to the door and opened it. Instead, she found a handsome man. He was the same age as Danuj and as well-dressed. He also seemed vaguely familiar, but Veni couldn't place him right away.

'I'm sorry to bother you at such a time,' he said apologetically in a gentle sort of way. 'But I was wondering if I could see Maheshji?' His voice was courteous and well-modulated.

Unsure how to respond, Veni asked, 'Your name, please?'

'Sahil Sachdeva. I came from Mumbai yesterday. The Gauria family know me well.'

Even as a penny dropped in Veni's mind, Mahesh's voice sounded from inside the room.

'Come, Sahil,' he said. 'Come in, *Beta.*'

Veni stepped aside to let Sahil enter.

'Thank you,' the visitor whispered to her and entered the room with his hands folded in a *namaste.* First, he went to Manjari and touched her feet in respect before stooping beside her.

'*Yeh bahut bura hua, Aunty Ji,*' he said, covering her hands with his. '*Bhagwan aapko aisa din nahin dikana chahiye tha.*' An awful thing has happened, Aunty Ji. God shouldn't have shown you such a day.

Manjari nodded silently and touched the top of his head with her right hand as if blessing him. Sahil accepted it with a bowed head, stayed thus for a moment before straightening up and going to Mahesh.

He touched the old man's feet and did a *namaste* to him. He then merely shook his head a couple of times as if he were at a loss for words. It was apparent that the two men shared the moment of grief.

'*Bhagwan ki marzi*,' Mahesh said presently. '*Kya karen?*' God's will. What can we do?

Sahil remained silent with a commiserating expression on his face as Veni looked on with interest. The last minute or so had been revealing as far as Sahil's relationship with the Gauria family was concerned. Here was the man whom Danuj had been accusing of having an affair with his wife; of being the cause of the split between him and Ruhi. Yet, neither Manjari nor Mahesh showed the slightest animosity towards Sahil. Rather, they had welcomed him into their midst at this difficult and intensely personal time and had shown affection. Mahesh had even called him '*Beta*'—son. Clearly, that suggested that they didn't believe Danuj's allegations.

Veni threw a glance at Hiran and Pari. Their eyes were trained on Sahil and there was no animosity in them either. Nor was their body language hostile. Rather, their facial expressions suggested that a good family friend had just joined them.

'We have known Sahil since he was three years old,' Mahesh supplied, as if reading Veni's thoughts. 'He, Danuj and Kanika have been friends since childhood. Hiran is like a big brother to him.'

'*Bhabi*,' Sahil addressed Pari with a *namaste* before going to Hiran and silently grasping his arms.

He then looked enquiringly at the two people he didn't know in the room.

'This is Mr Athreya,' Mahesh introduced him. 'The renowned investigator. He is here in Kumarakom to regain his strength after an illness. And this is Veni, his wife. They have been very kind to us in this hour of need.'

Sahil greeted both with silent *namastes*.

Often quick to judge, Veni felt herself warming to this courteous and genteel man. Perhaps, the contrast of seeing his sensitiveness immediately after Kanika's callousness, had made her overreact. She could tell that Mahesh and Manjari were pleased to see him.

'Mr Athreya has kindly consented to look into this matter,' she heard Mahesh say. 'The police, of course, are investigating, but there is no better person than Mr Athreya to help us at this juncture. As you will appreciate, Sahil, this is a terrible mess. We need Mr Athreya to find Danuj's killer and lead us out of this tangle.'

Sahil nodded earnestly. He seemed to understand the situation perfectly.

Mahesh went on, 'Please give him full cooperation, *Beta*. Given the sensitivities and the cross-currents, I think it's best that each of us speaks to him alone. Hiran, Pari, I would ask the same of you too. Let's help him help us.'

'Of course, Papa,' Pari replied at once.

'Of course, Uncle,' Sahil echoed, pulling out a visiting card from his wallet and giving it to Athreya. 'I'm at your disposal, sir. Whenever you want. My mobile number is on this card.'

'Thanks,' Athreya replied. 'Let's talk a little later in the day. I'm waiting for Ruhi and the police inspector to return.'

'Then I better leave,' Sahil replied. 'I'm not sure she'll want to see me at this time.' He turned back to Mahesh. 'Uncle, do you know whom I ran into last evening? Kishan! He is staying at the next resort—Sunset Bay.'

Once again that infamous thug! Veni glanced at her husband. His expression was contemplative, and his right index finger was tracing quick words and patterns on his knee—a sure sign that his mind was in high gear.

'Yes, *Beta*.' Mahesh let out a long sigh. 'We know. That's part of the complications. Bhagya is here too. But I am curious about something else... what brought you here to Kumarakom? Surely, Ruhi wouldn't have called you? Or did she?'

Sahil shook his head. He then grew fidgety and threw a quick glance at Hiran, as if seeking his support.

'I came because... er... someone else called me here... for a discussion. He asked me to come here for a couple of days.'

'Of course!' Athreya exclaimed as if something had clicked into place in his mind. 'And he asked you to stay here at Crystal Waters, I suppose?'

'Yes.' Sahil's face snapped towards Athreya. 'How did *you* know?'

Athreya gave the faintest of smiles. 'I didn't,' he said. 'But it to seemed fit in. When did this happen?'

'He called me two or three days back.'

'Who?' Hiran cut in sharply. 'Who asked you to come here and stay at this resort, Sahil?'

The puzzled look on Sahil's face deepened as he looked at Hiran.

'Danuj,' he said. 'I thought you were in the loop, *Bhaiya*. Danuj said that you and he had discussed it and decided that it was time to resolve matters without bothering Maheshji. That's why I came.'

Frowns and raised brows were aplenty as the people in the room looked at each other in surprise. None of them, it appeared, was aware that Danuj had called Sahil to Crystal Waters. What had Danuj been up to? First, he secretly invites his supposed enemy to Crystal Waters. Then, he uses Sahil's presence at the resort as the reason—or pretext—to take Ruhi away in a houseboat. It was meant to appear as a spur-of-the-moment decision.

Why had Danuj orchestrated this subterfuge? Veni glanced at her husband to see how he had received all this and was surprised to see him completely at ease and displaying no sign of puzzlement. Even his right index finger was still. He was watching the faces in the room.

All of a sudden, a random thought flashed through her mind. She recalled Athreya telling her about actors and actresses featuring in crime novels of yesteryear. 'When there is a stage or screen personality in a crime story,' he had told her, 'keep in mind that he or she is a good actor who can convincingly portray false emotions, or impersonate someone, or both.'

She quickly looked around with this new perspective. But nobody here was actually an actor. They were producers or directors. Only Ruhi—who was not in the room—was an actor, and an accomplished one at that. Having watched her films, Veni knew that to be a fact.

Suddenly, the door opened and Ruhi walked in, followed by Inspector Anto. Behind them came Kanika, Jeet and a hotel steward pushing a trolley with tea, coffee and an assortment of cakes and cookies. Ruhi took a couple of steps into the room and froze mid-stride. She had just seen Sahil.

Sahil too stared at her, immobilized. His face was a picture of pity and pain, and a slow flush rose in it. He stood rooted to the spot. Nobody other than Ruhi might have existed in the room for him. After a couple of seconds, he took half an involuntary step forward before stopping himself. Ruhi continued to stare at him, speechless. Veni couldn't decipher the expression on her face.

Kanika and Jeet had quietly taken seats and were watching, with unholy curiosity, the meeting playing out.

'I'm so sorry that this has happened, Ruhi,' Sahil said with great tenderness. 'God has not been kind to you.'

That broke the spell. Ruhi blinked and exhaled. As if in a trance, she let Veni guide her to a sofa.

'Perhaps,' she replied, in a voice dripping with anguish, 'He is testing me.' Her eyes moved to Mahesh. 'I'm probably the prime suspect, Papa. It looks like I had the motive, means and the opportunity. Apparently, my dagger, which was used to stab Danuj, is the clincher.'

'No!' Sahil hissed fiercely. 'No way! You did *not* kill him!'

'No?' Anto asked in his thick Malayali accent. 'Pray, why not, sir? May I introduce myself, please. Inspector Anto at your service.' He went on with words that seemed to have been picked out of a nineteenth-century novel. 'You would have a very strong reason, I'm sure.'

'Because Ruhi is utterly incapable of killing!' Sahil retorted, his angry eyes snapping to Anto. 'She is not that kind of a person.'

'You know her well, yes?'

'Of course, I do, you—!' He stopped himself in time. His voice mellowed and became genteel again. 'I produced and directed three of her best films, Inspector. I *know* her.'

'Of course, of course!… And you are…?' Anto cocked a theatrical eyebrow.

'Sahil Sachdeva. A family friend of the Gaurias. A film producer.'

'Ah! I'm sorry. I should have known, but I mostly watch Malayalam movies. My apologies.' He looked at Ruhi enquiringly. 'Have you acted in any South Indian movies?' he asked irrelevantly.

Veni chewed her lip thoughtfully as Ruhi shook her head in response. Sahil was the second person that morning—after Mahesh—to insist that Ruhi was not capable of murder. Yet she was Anto's main suspect. Where was all this heading? Veni was utterly confused and hoped her husband was not. She glanced at him and saw that he was sitting back in his chair and listening to the conversation with great interest.

'A family friend, is it?' Anto mused aloud. 'Of course, of course. You are a producer too. By the way, how did you get here so quickly from Mumbai?'

'I'm staying here, Inspector. I came yesterday.'

'Did you now? Did you now? By chance, or…?' Anto left the question hanging.

'Danuj asked me to come.'

'Why, may I ask?' Anto was all politeness.

'I am not sure,' Sahil replied. 'I didn't get to speak to him much.'

'I see, I see! You didn't speak to him *much*. May I request you to stay within the resort until further notice? We—'

'Certainly,' Sahil interrupted. 'I'll stay here for as long as needed. Anything to find the murderer.' Sahil's tone lost some of its suavity as he asked, 'Have you seen Kishan? He is in the resort next door.'

'No, but I will,' Anto replied. 'I will.' He turned to Athreya. 'I'm going to see Kishan now. Would you like to join me, Mr Aadhreiah?'

'Yes, I would.' Athreya rose quickly. 'Thank you for asking.'

'How could I not, sir?' Anto beamed, his brilliant white teeth flashing from under his black moustache. 'When we have the famous Arridh Aadhreiah with us? Please come, please come.' He ushered Athreya towards the door as if he were inviting him to view the roses in his garden.

'Would you like to have tea before you go?' Veni interrupted, putting on her own Malayali accent. 'Inspector Anto? Hari?'

'Very kind of you, madam!' Anto bowed to Veni and went on in his affected way as he backed away towards the door.

'But duty beckons, you know. No time to lose. Perhaps another time.'

Anto and Athreya took the police boat from Crystal Waters to the boat terminal, from which they walked to Sunset Bay Resort. There was no other way, although the two resorts were side by side. They found Kishan in the swimming pool. Anto had been quick in contacting the Mumbai Police and getting hold of some basic information on the gangster. A young inspector there by the name of Holkar, who was keeping tabs on Kishan, had been very helpful. It was news to him that Kishan was in Kumarakom and he was keen to know what he was doing in Kerala.

Anto and Athreya watched Kishan for a short while as he swam a couple of lengths of the pool with powerful strokes. Clearly, he was a strong man and a very good swimmer. Beside him was a young woman who kept pace with him. With her swimming cap and goggles covering much of her head and face, Athreya was unable to identify her. But he surmised that she was likely Bhagya, the unfortunate actress whom he had seen with Kishan in a boat.

When the thug stopped for breath at the near end of the pool, Anto went up to him and said that he wanted to speak to him. Kishan looked up at Anto, largely disregarding Athreya, who was still in his yoga clothes. Kishan nodded perfunctorily and came out of the pool, no questions asked.

Meanwhile, the woman with Kishan had stopped swimming and was staring at Anto from the side of the pool. When she removed her swimming goggles, Athreya confirmed that it was Bhagya. She seemed curious as her eyes darted between Anto and Kishan. She stayed in the water as Kishan came out.

Athreya saw that Kishan was taller than he had supposed, having seem him only once, seated in a boat. Now, as he stood erect and towelled himself vigorously, Athreya saw that he was an inch or two over six feet, well-muscled and sinewy.

Kishan said something to Bhagya in Malayalam that Athreya didn't catch. The young woman nodded and put on her swimming glasses. The next moment she was streaking through the water towards the far end of the pool.

A few minutes later, the three men were seated in the sitting room of Kishan's lake-facing cottage. The lapping water of the lake was just a few yards from them. On hearing Anto's request to talk to him, Kishan had been neither hostile nor polite. Nor had he asked why Anto wanted to speak to him. He had accepted the request and led the way to his cottage.

There, he had gone into his bedroom and changed his clothes. He hadn't offered them chairs as they entered the sitting room, leaving them to find their own seats. Glancing about the room, Athreya counted three bottles of Johnny Walker whisky and two bottles of local dark rum. A carton of cigarettes lay beside the liquor. A woman's *dupatta* hung on the back of a chair.

Kishan returned from the bedroom and sat opposite Anto, with nary a glance at Athreya. He lit a cigarette as his eyes quietly assessed the inspector. To Athreya, the look on Kishan's face was that of practised inscrutability. His leathery face remained immobile while he sat back and stroked his chin with a large hand. He hadn't spoken a word yet. He was waiting for Anto to make the first move.

Here was a seasoned offender, Athreya thought to himself, a tough nut to crack. Being interviewed by the police was not new to Kishan. He had run up against them several times before. He displayed no signs of apprehension—something most ordinary people would feel when confronted by the police. Athreya had no idea if he was aware of the reason that had brought Anto to him. Irrespective of that, Athreya anticipated Kishan to be frugal with words during this interview.

'Do you know why I am here?' Anto demanded at the outset.

He had chosen an aggressive approach to a suspected crook. Athreya was surprised to note that there was no trace of his Malayali accent. Nor was there any hint of the buffoonery he had displayed in Mahesh's suite. Anto, it seemed, was a deeper man than he appeared.

In response to Anto's question, Kishan merely shook his head.

'You are from Mumbai, yes?' Anto went on.

Kishan nodded.

'When did you come here?'

'Wednesday.' Kishan's voice was gruff as he spoke slowly.

'Sure?'

Kishan nodded. 'I can show you my ticket and boarding pass.'

'What brings you here?'

Kishan shrugged. 'Why do people come to Kumarakom?' he countered.

'Did you come for tourism or to meet someone?'

'Both.'

'Are you aware of the death that occurred in the adjacent resort last night?'

Nod.

'Did you know the deceased?'

'Don't know who died.' Kishan had smoothly sidestepped a potential trap.

'What have you been doing during the past three days?'

'Walking around. Hired a boat. Relaxing.'

'Why the boat?'

'Birdwatching.'

'With binoculars?'

Nod.

'Have you been watching the Crystal Waters Resort too? And its residents?'

Shrug. 'Maybe. Birds fly everywhere.'

'The deceased is a thirty-four-year-old man. Know him?'

'Name?'

'Danuj Gauria.'

Nod. 'I know him.'

'How do you know him?'

'He's a Bollywood producer. I work in the film industry too.'

'What work do you do?'

'I arrange things for clients.'

A fixer, Athreya thought. That was Kishan's nominal day job.

'What kind of things?' the inspector asked testily.

'Money, people, equipment, vehicles… anything they need. Filmmaking takes a lot of different resources.'

'Have you dealt with Danuj?'

Nod.

'Many times?' Anto demanded, growing annoyed.

Head shake. Negative.

'Did you lend him money?'

'That's confidential. Sorry.'

'This is a murder inquiry!' Anto thundered in response.

Kishan was unimpressed. He didn't blink an eye at the mention of murder. Nor did he react to Anto raising his voice. He stayed silent, lazily smoking his cigarette.

'Did you meet Danuj here at Kumarakom?' Anto asked.

Head shake.

'Did you meet anyone else from the Gauria family?'

Nod.

'Who?'

Kishan knocked the cigarette ash into an ashtray. 'Confidential.'

'If you don't cooperate,' Anto threatened, 'I'll have to take you to the station.'

'On what charge?' Kishan asked mildly. 'I'm answering all your questions except where client confidentiality prevents me.'

Anto glowered at the man who was six inches taller than him and at least twenty kilos heavier. He knew there was little he could do. Kishan was on firm ground.

Athreya cleared his throat softly. Anto turned to him and nodded. Kishan too looked at the man he had dismissed as unimportant so far.

'Mr Kishan,' Athreya began, 'Mahesh Gauria has asked me to look into his son's death. I am here on his personal behalf. Anything you can tell me would be useful.'

Kishan studied Athreya unhurriedly and with new interest. At length, he nodded.

'Maheshji is a great man,' he said. 'And a fair one. I will help if I can. Are you a policeman?'

'No,' Athreya answered. 'I am helping Mr Gauria in a private capacity.'

Kishan nodded again. 'What do you wish to know?'

'Your cottage stands on the lake shore and gives you a clear view of the backwaters. Even now, you can see the two houseboats clearly through the French windows. Danuj was in the nearer houseboat when he was killed last night. If you saw or heard anything that could help me, I would appreciate your telling me.'

Kishan's face remained immobile for a couple of seconds, with his eyes on Athreya. Then, he spoke in a measured manner, using words he had obviously thought through.

'I wasn't here,' he replied. 'I returned only after 2 a.m.'

'Where were you, if I might ask?'

'Kottayam.'

Kishan reached out and picked up a piece of paper. Proactively, he wrote a name and a phone number on it and handed the paper to Anto.

'Before you ask, this is the person I was with.'

Anto accepted the paper with an angry frown. Athreya knew why. A seasoned killer worth his salt would have an alibi that would stand up in court. Most likely, the alibi would be provided by a professional witness.

'You can check with the resort security guards too,' Kishan added. 'I left at 8 p.m. and returned at 2 a.m.'

Athreya had no doubt that Kishan's claim would be borne out. The distance between the resort and Kottayam was about fifteen kilometres. That wouldn't take more than half an hour to cover by car.

Besides, as Vembanad Lake's shoreline wasn't monitored, nothing prevented Kishan from taking a boat at a lonely point and rowing to Danuj's houseboat. Of course, all this was conjecture.

'Did you see or hear anything after you returned?' Athreya asked. He glanced at the bedroom door. 'I suppose your window opens towards the lake?'

'It does, but I keep it closed. Prefer air conditioning to this humidity. No, I didn't hear anything. I was in my bedroom.'

'Any corroboration?' Anto asked. 'Witness?'

Stony eyes moved to regard Anto. 'I sleep alone, Inspector. There can be no witnesses.'

'What about Bha—'

'Are your suggesting that she spent the night with me?' Kishan's drawl remained even. 'Think twice before insinuating that, Inspector. She may not like it.'

'Anything you can tell me, Mr Kishan?' Athreya interposed, changing the topic. 'Anything at all?'

'I don't know who killed Danuj,' Kishan said calmly. 'All I can say is that it wasn't me. Some would say that he got what he deserved. Many had reason to see him dead... not just the people he cheated... deceived. Sahil too has a reason... and Danuj's own family.'

'His own family?' Athreya echoed, watching Kishan for reaction. 'They are all grief-stricken. It's been a huge shock to them.'

'You do realize, don't you? They are a family of actors.' Kishan stubbed out his cigarette and contemplated the cigarette packet as if he was considering lighting another. 'Producers and directors also know acting well. How else can they make good films?'

Kishan paused as he pulled out another cigarette and lit it.

'Besides,' he murmured, as he let out the smoke, 'things are not all hunky-dory in some wealthy families—too much money involved. Too much greed.'

8

As they stepped out of the cottage, Athreya heard the sound of a door opening. He darted to the corner of the cottage and peeped around it. Bhagya was just coming out onto the veranda through a French door. It was, Athreya surmised, the bedroom door to the veranda. So, Bhagya had been listening from the bedroom. He waited for her to walk away from the cottage before following her. At a gesture from Athreya, Anto began making his way back to Crystal Waters. Athreya caught up with Bhagya at the main block.

'Good morning,' he said pleasantly. 'Bhagya, I presume?'

She turned to him with a dazzling smile as her eyes studied him. Seeing her face to face, Athreya found her vaguely familiar. No doubt, he had seen her on-screen in some movie.

'Good morning,' she greeted him and waited for him to speak.

That was a good sign—she was willing to talk. She seemed curious too. It was probably a good thing that the police officer was not with Athreya.

'Can I get you a cup of coffee?' he asked. 'At the restaurant?'

'Sure. I'd like that.' The smile widened. 'You are?'

They began walking towards the restaurant. Athreya couldn't help but notice the studied grace with which she moved. Like her attire, everything about her was designed to attract attention.

'Harith Athreya,' he replied. 'I am trying to help Mahesh Gauria.'

'A good person, Maheshji.'

'You know what's happened, don't you?' Athreya asked.

'Yes. Danuj died last night. The news came some time back.'

'Was his name mentioned?'

116

She nodded.

'You knew him, didn't you?'

She threw back her head and let out a musical laugh.

'Know him?' she asked. Her tone turned hard. 'Of course! Which pretty girl in Bollywood doesn't know him?'

'What was your reaction to the news?'

'Well… he had it coming. Sooner or later. No, sir, I am far from sad.' She threw a sidelong glance at him through half-closed eyelids. Her lips curved upwards sensually. 'Before you ask, let me tell you that the news that he had been killed on the houseboat travelled fast.'

Athreya nodded absently. This woman was forthright and plucky. Was it her nature or a put-on? After all, she too was an actress.

'Why should you be sad?' he asked, studying her profile.

'You will learn soon enough. If you don't, I can enlighten you. I was once in love with him. He considered himself a Casanova for whom girls fell like ninepins. But the truth was that he was a rich producer with dubious abilities. He ran a casting couch that gave some very unremarkable girls a break. He didn't pick his actresses based on their acting abilities. No wonder his projects flopped.'

Athreya wondered what was making Bhagya so outspoken with him. Was it her hatred for Danuj? Or was it something else? Didn't she realize that she would be an automatic suspect? If not as the murderer, at least as an accessory? Especially when she had come here to Kumarakom with Kishan, a man with a formidable reputation?

His silence must have been expressive. She picked up the implication at once.

'Talking too much, am I?' she asked, as they entered the near-empty restaurant and went to a table in a corner. 'That's how I am. But what is there to hide? You will discover soon enough that there was bad blood between Danuj and me. If you have not already done so, that is.' The pitch of her voice rose abruptly. 'He cheated me! Promised me many things and betrayed me!'

Realizing that her voice was carrying, she stopped with a gently heaving breast.

'Sorry, I got carried away,' she continued in a lower, husky voice. 'Happens sometimes.'

She raised an elegant arm and summoned a waiter. While Athreya ordered South Indian filter coffee, Bhagya gave the waiter elaborate instructions about how her coffee was to be prepared.

'Do you know anything about Kishan's movements last night?' Athreya asked when the waiter left.

'Kishan?' She expressed surprise. 'Why ask me? I'm neither his nanny nor his keep.'

'But you are friends, I presume?'

'Ah, yes. But don't get ideas, please. All I know is what he told me: that he was going to Kottayam for dinner to meet a friend.'

'Did he go?'

'No idea.'

'Any idea when he returned?'

'Nope.'

Athreya changed track.

'Any thoughts on who could have killed Danuj?' he asked.

'Someone with the guts to confront him and the strength to stick a knife into him,' she answered. 'God knows that enough people wanted him dead.'

'People here in Kumarakom?' he asked.

'Yes... at least three men and one woman... and that vixen of his wife.'

Again, her voice grew shrill. She realized it at once and stopped.

'Tell me more about the murder,' she said a moment later. 'What exactly happened?'

'I'm sorry, Bhagya, I can't. We've just started the investigation.'

'Then, you came to pump me for information?'

A frown creased her brow and she seemed to abruptly lose her good humour. She was ready to get up and go. Bhagya was turning out to be a volatile woman.

'As I said,' Athreya replied softly, 'I'm doing this for Maheshji.'

He had deliberately spoken the name in an effort to get her to talk some more. It worked. She sat back in her chair.

'What do you want to know?' she asked.

'Did you hear or see anything in the night? The houseboat might have been visible from your room.'

'Nothing. I had better things to do than to watch Danuj's houseboat.'

'Till when were you up?'

She shrugged her shapely shoulders. 'I seldom go to sleep before two o'clock.'

'Were you in your room, or were you outside?'

A slow flush crept up her face. All of a sudden, she grew angry.

'You think I killed him?' she hissed, leaning forward. 'That's what you came here to ask?'

'Bhagya.' Athreya tried to pacify her. 'I am trying to find out who was up and what they saw. I'm asking everyone the same questions.'

'You know what?' she raged as if she hadn't heard him. 'Everyone around him had a motive to kill him. Everyone! Some good soul beat the others to it, and everyone will now be happier for it. Including his family! Especially his siblings! Nobody other than his mother will grieve for Danuj. Snoop around, policeman! You don't have to look far to find his killer. But I hope you don't find him! Danuj deserved what he got!'

119

She got up and strode away in anger, ignoring her coffee the waiter was bringing. Athreya stared at her retreating figure, her last few words resonating in his head: *'Nobody other than his mother will grieve for Danuj. You don't have to look far to find his killer.'*

For some reason, her words, though heated, rang true. What did she know that she hadn't spoken about?

Sahil was waiting for Athreya when the latter got off the canal boat on his return from Kishan's resort. Sahil had a serious look about him as he paced the lawn with his head bent in thought. On seeing Athreya, he came up and enquired if they could talk right away. Having missed breakfast, Athreya was hungry. On learning that Sahil too hadn't eaten, Athreya asked for some *uthappam, vada* and coffee to be served on the lawn.

'I wanted to tell you my piece as soon as possible, Mr Athreya,' Sahil began quietly, as they sat at an isolated table. 'There are some things you need to know; things that I cannot say in front of Maheshji. I'll give you an unvarnished dump, and you can decide what is important and what isn't.'

Athreya nodded encouragingly, pouring out chilled water into two glasses. The time was approaching noon and it was warm even in the shade. There were no other guests about.

'I know that matters look bleak for me,' Sahil went on. 'It's best that I be open and honest with you.'

'Why do they look bleak for you?' Athreya asked.

'Come on, sir. I was not born yesterday. It's crystal clear that I had a motive and the opportunity. And I have no alibi. It's only a matter of time before Anto realizes it and comes after me. In fact, I should have been his prime suspect, not Ruhi. Shall I begin?'

'Please do.'

'I'd known Danuj virtually all my life. I'm told that we've been friends since we were three years old, although my memories

120

don't go that far back. Of the thirty years I've known him, we've been great friends for twenty-nine and a half. It's only in the past few months that we've moved apart.'

'From when he began accusing you of having an affair with his wife?' Athreya asked.

Sahil nodded. 'So, you know. That makes it easier for me. For the record, there is no affair between me and Ruhi. Yes, I love her, and have loved her for a while now. Unfortunately for me, she married Danuj before I could express my feelings for her. You may find it interesting that the only people who knew that I loved her were Danuj and Kanika—two of my childhood friends.'

'Just a moment... Danuj *knew* that when he married Ruhi?' Athreya asked.

'Yes... but I don't blame him. He was quicker than me. I remained tongue-tied.'

'How did he justify his action to you?'

'There was no need to justify. Ruhi is a lovely woman, and he was as attracted to her as I was. Of course, I was heartbroken, but I accepted it philosophically. Then Danuj began cheating on Ruhi and treating her very badly... abusing her verbally and physically.'

'How did you know that he was ill-treating her?'

'Aunty and Uncle asked me—at least thrice—to talk to Danuj and make him change his ways. They felt that I could make a difference as a long-time friend. Of course, they knew nothing of my feelings for Ruhi.'

'What did Danuj say when you spoke to him?'

'He brushed it off and said that it was none of my business. But I persisted. Soon, he began insinuating that I was interfering in his marriage because I was infatuated with Ruhi. He said that I was using Aunty and Uncle's request as a pretext to meddle in affairs that were none of my business.'

'Was that when he began accusing you of having an affair with Ruhi?'

Sahil nodded. 'Shortly afterwards. He began throwing tantrums at home, and the genesis of the accusation lay in one of those outbursts in which he invented this alleged affair. Everyone in the family came to know of my feelings for Ruhi. Kanika took some delight in talking about it. She even suggested that a film be made of this love triangle story.'

'All this must have been embarrassing for you,' Athreya observed. From a distance, a liveried waiter was coming towards them with a large tray.

'Acutely embarrassing,' Sahil agreed. 'I stopped visiting the Gauria household. Ruhi too decided not to take my calls or respond to my messages. Why add fuel to the fire? That was about three months ago. I haven't spoken to her since... until today.'

'Does Ruhi have feelings towards you?'

Sahil shook his head firmly. 'I don't think so, even if Danuj liked to believe so. As I said, I never really expressed my feelings towards her. She only ever saw me as a close friend.'

They fell silent as their late breakfast arrived. The sight of onion-tomato *uthappam* reminded Athreya of his hunger. They waited for the steward to serve them before resuming their discussion.

'Was Danuj in touch with you?' he asked Sahil as he dug into his *uthappam*.

'No.' Sahil began his breakfast with a *vada* and chutney. 'At least, not until about a week back, when he called me out of the blue and said that he had a proposal for me. I met him to hear it out—the proposal was about Ruhi.'

'What was his offer?' Athreya asked.

Sombre lines creased Sahil's face as he picked at his food.

'Danuj said that he was willing to divorce Ruhi if I met four conditions.' He counted them on his fingers. 'One, I had to give him 35 crores to repay Kishan. Two, Ruhi should waive alimony entirely. Three, she must forgo all claims to Gauria wealth. And finally, nobody other than he and I should know of the deal.'

'What was your reaction?'

'I was shocked... utterly shocked. And offended too... more on Ruhi's behalf than on mine. Danuj was selling his wife!'

'Did he say why he was doing it?'

'There was no real need to... Everyone knew that he was deep in debt. But he did justify it to me by saying that he was getting death threats, and unless he paid up, Ruhi was in serious danger. That last part made me consider his proposal—I still care deeply for Ruhi. I told Danuj that I would think about it.'

'Did he say who was threatening them?'

Sahil nodded. 'Kishan.'

'You knew Kishan from before?'

'"Knew" is not the right word. "Knew of" is more appropriate. He has a reputation in Bollywood.'

'Okay. That wasn't the last time you spoke to Danuj, I suppose?'

'It wasn't. He called me on Wednesday—three days back—and asked me to come to Kumarakom. He said that he had discussed the proposal with Hiran and that he wanted to finalize the deal here, away from Mumbai's eyes and ears. He also added that Maheshji knew nothing about it, and that he and Hiran had decided to put it through without troubling their father. He wrapped up by insisting that they were doing it only because of the death threats.'

'You agreed to come, obviously,' Athreya remarked, finishing his *uthappam* and starting on his *vadas*. Sahil had eaten very little.

'Yes, but I made no commitment other than to hear him out. I didn't promise to pay him 35 crores or any such money. I would hear what he had to say and respond accordingly. By this time, of course, I knew that he couldn't be trusted. I guess he brought in Hiran's name to lend some credibility to the proposal. In any case, this was too dire a matter for me to disregard his claims. What if there was a sliver of truth in what he said? Especially about the death threats? I couldn't risk Ruhi getting hurt… or killed.'

'From what we heard today, Hiran wasn't aware of his invitation to you to come to Kumarakom.'

'So it seems. I was dumbstruck. But then, Danuj was a practised liar. I should have suspected it.'

'Did Ruhi know about the proposal?'

Sahil shook his head and pushed away his plate. 'I don't think so. I spoke to nobody about it.'

'What happened next?' Athreya asked, pouring out their coffee.

'I took a flight to Kochi and landed here yesterday, but Danuj had gone on a cruise. I waited for him to return and met him as soon as he disembarked. He made some disparaging comments about Ruhi and me. I got angry but didn't respond. He taunted me again and walked off, asking me to await a message from him. Tentatively, we were to meet at 11 p.m.'

'That was the brief meeting at the top of the walking path, wasn't it?'

Sahil nodded. 'You must have seen me, I suppose.'

'We all did. Then, on seeing Ruhi, you grew angrier. Why?'

'She is such a lovely woman, Mr Athreya. Not just good looking but a genuinely nice person. I was seeing her after three months. The fact that Danuj was abusing her was already making me see red. In his place, I would have worshiped her. The thought of fate's cruelty made me angry.'

'I can imagine,' Athreya concurred.

'I didn't see Danuj or Ruhi again. I waited and waited for his final message, but it didn't come. He didn't answer my calls either. I remained in my room all night, not sleeping a wink. In the morning, I heard about Danuj's death and came to see Maheshji.'

'One moment! Did you say, "*final* message"?' Athreya asked.

'Yes,' Sahil replied, fishing out his mobile phone. 'There was an earlier message, which he sent at about 8 p.m. Here it is.'

Sahil held out his phone for Athreya to see. There was a text message from Danuj at 8:03 p.m. It read:

> '*Come to my houseboat tonight. Tentatively at about 11 p.m. Wait for my next message. I will text you once the coast is clear.*'

. . .

Dr Saju, the police doctor, was a tall, spare man with thick, curly hair that had mostly turned grey. The large bifocals on his hawk nose glinted as if they had just been polished. His sparkling white, half-sleeve shirt looked freshly laundered, as did his pleated grey trousers. The unsmiling, grave-mannered doctor had a habit of blinking his eyes every so often.

'Five stab wounds,' he said solemnly, as he, Anto and Athreya sat in the vacant room that the resort manager had made available to them for discussions; it was their temporary office. 'All in the chest, all inflicted from the front.'

'Any indication of the body's position when the wounds were made?' Athreya asked.

'No definite medical evidence, but the direction of all the five stabs is more or less the same.' He blinked thoughtfully. 'One possibility is that the deceased was lying on his back when stabbed.'

'Did he not move or resist after the first stab? That doesn't seem very natural, does it?' Athreya probed.

'Perhaps not, I agree,' Saju said absently. 'But that would be an inference. I would like to go through the facts first.'

'Of course, Doctor.'

As Athreya waited for the doctor to continue, the question that had been buzzing in his head arose again: why had the murderer left the dagger in the wound?

'For obvious reasons,' Saju went on, 'the wound over the heart bled the most. With the heart punctured, blood would have gushed from it as soon as the dagger was withdrawn from the wound. That would cause a quick drop in blood pressure and in the quantity of blood in the body. That, in turn, probably caused the subsequent wounds to bleed less.'

'In your opinion,' Athreya asked, 'was the stab to the heart the first one?'

'Yes,' Saju replied earnestly. 'I'm fairly certain of that.'

'Are all the wounds deep?'

Saju blinked a couple of times. 'I haven't measured them yet.'

'Is the body still here, Doctor? Or has it been taken away?'

'Still here,' Saju replied, adjusting his glasses. 'Why do you ask?'

'I was wondering if you could make a quick examination of the five wounds again. I would like to know each one's dimensions—depth and width.'

'I can do that now if you wish. Do you want the information right away?'

'If possible, Doctor. I'd be much obliged.'

Saju looked at Anto for guidance. The inspector nodded. The doctor stood up and turned to go.

'In addition, can you inspect the wound edges and the tears in the T-shirt as well? I would like to know if the edges are cleanly cut or ragged.'

Saju nodded briskly and went away to fulfil Athreya's request.

'Why these questions, Mr Aadhreiah?' Anto's accent was back in evidence.

'I'll tell you shortly,' Athreya replied. 'But before I do, I'd like to quickly check a few things with Ruhi. Can we call her?'

'Of course, of course! By all means.'

Anto rose quickly and hurried away. As soon as he left the room, Athreya pulled out his mobile phone and called Pari.

'The dagger that Mr Gauria bought for you at Kochi,' he asked. 'Is it readily accessible?'

'Yes, it's right here,' she replied. 'Do you want it?'

'Can I come to your room and pick it up?'

'Of course.'

Athreya went over to her room and brought back Pari's dagger. A minute later, Anto returned with Ruhi in tow.

'How are you feeling?' Athreya asked once he had ushered Ruhi into a chair.

'Still in a daze, I think,' she mumbled uncertainly. 'It feels like a horrible dream... a nightmare. Being alone in that room is so frightening.'

'Can someone be with her?' Athreya asked, turning to Anto. 'Veni would be happy to help, I'm sure.'

Anto thought for a moment and nodded. 'It should be okay as long as it's not another susp—' He broke off. '—as long as it's not another family member or someone connected with the case.'

'Thank you, Inspector.' Athreya turned to Ruhi. 'Veni will be a bit of a comfort to you.'

Ruhi nodded eagerly. She seemed to have brightened up a bit. 'Yes, Aunty's presence would be a great help.'

'Good. Now, I wanted to clarify some points about last night. I need some more details about what you told me this morning. Can we talk about it?'

127

She nodded again, but unenthusiastically. 'If you think it's important.'

'It is, Ruhi. Let me start. Now, I know that it's difficult to pinpoint the times of every event, but please try and do your best. I need to understand the sequence of events a little better. Okay?'

Ruhi nodded.

'You had said,' Athreya began, 'that the pilot and the attendant went away from your houseboat at about eight-thirty in the evening. Is that right?'

'I think so, but I can't be very sure of the time.'

'I understand. But this is your best estimate.'

'Yes.'

'After they left, you and Danuj had a fight, which was overheard by several people. It went on for a while. You then went into the bedroom and stayed there all night with the door locked. What would have been the time when you went into the bedroom?'

'About 9 p.m. or so. Again, I can't be very precise.'

'That's fine, Ruhi,' Athreya assured her. 'Just do your best and don't worry. What did you do after you went into the bedroom?'

'I sat down on the bed and cried… Danuj had said some *very* harsh things… harsh even by his standards. I felt rotten about the names he had called me. I thought about how Mummy and Papa would feel about it and cried some more.'

'How long would you have cried?' he asked gently.

Ruhi shook her head. 'I don't know… I don't know. I had no sense of time. But it couldn't have been hours, I'm sure.'

'How so?'

'Well, I did glance at my watch at about ten o'clock, when I decided to take a pill of Restyl.'

'Alprazolam?' Anto asked, sitting up. 'Do you have a prescription for it?'

Ruhi shook her head again. 'No. I don't take it regularly. This is only the second time I've had it. The first time too was after a bad fight with Danuj.'

'How did you get it? It is a restricted drug that should not be sold without a prescription.'

'My mother-in-law takes it every night—one or two pills. She sleeps very badly—no more than three or four hours a night. Her doctor has advised her to take it. There are always a few strips of Restyl with her.'

'How do you know that?'

'Pari *Bhabi* or I usually administer Mummy's medicines and keep track of them. Even in Mumbai. My strip was from her stock.'

'Does she know?'

'Yes, of course. So does *Bhabi*. Mummy encouraged me to take it—said that it could help me sleep.'

'People are not supposed to use other people's medicines,' Anto fumed, sitting back defeated. 'Not good, not good!'

'Did you feel better after taking it?' Athreya asked, bringing the conversation back on track.

'Not immediately, but I did after a little while. I felt myself calming down. I lay down on the bed and closed my eyes. Sleep didn't come right away but I think I went into that half-asleep–half-awake state for a while before I finally dozed off. I had some terrible thoughts in that twilight state... don't know if they were real or nightmares. The sleep, if I can even call it that, was shallow and disturbed.'

'Is that when you felt the boat rock?' Athreya asked.

'Yes.'

'Over and above the incessant wobbling?'

'Yes, that was the first time... the boat rocked at least twice. It was quite unmistakable. I also heard various noises—thumps, some scraping sound, Danuj talking into his phone, and things like that.'

'How many times did the boat rock?'

'I really can't say… several times, I think… it's so confusing.' Ruhi rubbed her face vigorously as if to rid herself of her mental cobwebs. 'It rocked twice for sure a little while after I took Restyl. I think it rocked afterwards too. You see, Uncle, I was trying to shut the world out and get to sleep. I was not really thinking of the boat or the water or Danuj. I just wanted to sleep. Nothing more.'

'And after that?' Athreya probed gently.

'I must have drifted into a drugged half-asleep–half-awake state. I really don't know the time—everything feels so surreal.'

'Before you drifted off,' Athreya asked, 'did you hear another boat?'

'No. I don't think so.'

'Any motor or engine?'

Ruhi shook her head. 'Nothing.'

Athreya rose and escorted Ruhi out. Veni was waiting outside the room in response to Athreya's text message.

'Veni,' he whispered to her, 'see if you can get some information from the housekeeping staff. I want to know if they saw anything out of place in any of the Gauria family rooms and Sahil's. Especially wet clothes.'

Veni nodded, took the young actress under her care and guided her back to her room. As Anto had instructed, Ruhi would have to remain there until further notice.

Back in the room where Anto and Athreya sat, Dr Saju returned, taking long, rapid strides. He shut the door behind him and turned to Athreya with visible respect.

'You were right, sir,' he said. 'The wound in the heart is eight inches deep and two inches wide. The blade cut through very cleanly and entered deep into the heart. It was fatal by a long way.'

'Eight inches deep?' Athreya asked. 'Are you sure?'

'Yes, sir. I measured it three times. The other wounds—four of them—are five inches deep and an inch wide at the entry point. Exactly the blade dimensions of the dagger.'

Athreya turned to Anto. 'Do you have the dagger here?' he asked.

Dumbfounded, Anto nodded and opened his briefcase. From it he took out the transparent plastic bag in which Ruhi's unsheathed dagger lay. He laid it on a table and looked at Athreya, who was ready with a tape measure in hand.

With it, he measured the length of the naked blade in the plastic cover. It was five inches long. He then measured its width at the hilt. It was an inch wide.

He pointed to the cross guard of the dagger, which protruded about an inch from the blade on either side.

'This cross guard would have prevented the dagger from going deeper,' he said to the doctor. 'Both the cross guard and the hilt. Do you agree?'

'Yes, I do,' Saju replied. 'Only the blade could have entered the body.'

'And as the blade is five inches long, the wounds inflicted by this dagger would be, at most, five inches deep.'

'Correct,' the doctor nodded.

'So, this dagger was the cause of four of the five wounds.'

Saju nodded silently and blinked. He knew where Athreya was headed.

'The deeper wound, the one that is eight inches deep, the one that reached the heart, could not have been caused by this dagger.'

'Correct, sir,' Saju agreed. He took off his glasses and began polishing them vigorously with a microfibre cloth he took from his pocket. 'In addition, the fatal wound is also too broad for this dagger's blade, which is, at most, an inch wide. The wound is two inches wide.'

'Then this dagger,' Anto summarized with much perplexity, 'is not the murder weapon?'

'So it seems, Anto,' the doctor agreed.

9

Much to Anto's surprise, Athreya hurried out of the room without saying anything. He returned five minutes later with two pillows under his arm and a long knife. He set them down on the bed and turned to the inspector.

'Let's conduct an experiment,' he said conversationally. 'I hope to remove any lingering doubts you have about the murder weapon.'

He went to a cupboard and opened it. From inside, he drew a dagger lodged safely in its scabbard.

'I thought I put it back into my briefcase!' Anto yelped at the sight. 'Put it down, Mr Aadhreiah! Don't touch the evidence!'

'This is not Ruhi's dagger, Anto,' Athreya chuckled, pulling the blade out of the scabbard and showing it to the inspector. 'See the name engraved on it? It's Pari's.'

'It looks just like the dagger we found!'

'That's because Mahesh Gauria bought three such daggers, remember: one each for Kanika, Pari and Ruhi. I've borrowed Pari's for our little experiment.'

He laid the unsheathed dagger on the bed beside the pillows and also the kitchen knife he had brought. He then invited Anto and Saju to examine the two blades.

'What can you tell me about the dagger and the knife?' he asked.

'Well,' the doctor began, 'the dagger is the same size as the one found at the crime scene. The knife is longer and broader… heavier too.'

'Correct,' Athreya agreed. 'What else?'

'The knife is bloody sharp,' Anto added. 'The dagger isn't.'

'Well done, Anto!' Athreya enthused. 'That's exactly right. I've brought the sharpest knife in the kitchen, much to the chef's displeasure. I tested it... believe me, it's very sharp.'

'I've seen many such daggers in souvenir shops,' the doctor rumbled. 'As a rule, they are never sharp. That's deliberate, I think. The shops sell curios, not weapons.'

'Indeed!' Athreya nodded. 'They wouldn't want to supply sharp weapons to anyone who has the money to buy one. They could get into trouble. So, the daggers they sell are little more than letter openers, as far as their killing capability is concerned.'

'Unless the buyer sharpens it,' Anto said darkly.

'Correct. Look at Pari's dagger. Tell me if it's been sharpened.'

Anto picked it up and tested the edge. He then passed it to the doctor, who did likewise.

'Has it been sharpened?' Athreya asked.

The other two men shook their heads.

'You will see that Ruhi's dagger hasn't been sharpened either,' Athreya went on, as he positioned one of the pillows at the edge of the bed and picked up the sharp kitchen knife.

'Now, let's start our experiment... ready?' he asked.

When the others nodded, he raised his arm and stabbed downwards. The long blade glinted as it flashed down and entered the pillow with a faint rasping sound. When Athreya's arm stopped, the entire eight-inch blade was buried in it and the mattress underneath.

With a jerk, he pulled the knife out. It came out easily and with almost no sound.

'Please examine the tear, Doctor,' Athreya said, as he put down the knife. 'What do you see?'

Saju bent down, adjusted his glasses and studied the tear.

'A clean cut,' he said. 'Smooth edges.'

'Thanks. Now please stand back.'

Athreya picked up Pari's dagger and approached the other pillow. He raised his arm and repeated the stroke he had earlier done with the kitchen knife.

The time too, the blade entered the pillow, but with a louder rasping sound. Athreya pulled it out and invited Saju to look at the tear made by the dagger.

'Jagged edges,' the doctor pronounced. 'The cut is not as clean as the previous one.'

'Correct,' Athreya agreed. 'That's because this dagger is not sharp, while the knife is. Incidentally, it also took more effort to puncture the pillow with the blunt blade.'

He laid down the dagger and turned to Saju.

'How do these tears on the pillow compare with the wounds on Danuj?' he asked.

The doctor has already done his thinking and was ready with the answer.

'The deeper wound—the one in the deceased's heart—is a clean cut with no ragged edges. It was caused by a very sharp weapon like the knife you just used. However, the other four wounds have ragged edges just like the second tear in the pillow.'

'Inference?'

'The four five-inch-deep wounds were made by a dagger very similar to this one and not sharp. The fatal wound was caused by another, as yet unknown, blade that is very sharp and at least eight inches long and two inches wide.'

'One last question, Doctor,' Athreya said softly. 'Is it possible that the four shallow wounds were made *after* Danuj died?'

Saju blinked and paused for a long moment, his face getting graver by the minute. When he spoke, it was slowly.

'Yes, sir… I hadn't thought of that. That's indeed possible. But it could not have happened very long afterwards. They did bleed, after all.'

'But why would someone stab him repeatedly *after* he was dead?' Anto interrupted, scratching his head.

'That, Anto,' Saju said, as he picked up his bag, 'is for you to figure out.' He turned to Athreya and shook his hand warmly. 'It's been a pleasure working with you, sir. Absolute pleasure.'

'Just one more request, Doctor,' Athreya called after him. 'Can you please look for traces of alprazolam in Danuj's blood?'

Back in Ruhi's room, the young actress was frowning and deep in thought. She and Veni had sat in silence for the past few minutes. Seeing Ruhi's furrowed brow, Veni felt that she was contemplating something—probably considering telling Veni something. She waited.

After a couple more minutes of silence, Ruhi looked up at Veni and spoke haltingly.

'Aunty,' she said. 'There is something Uncle probably needs to know. It's about a conversation Danuj and I had yesterday.'

'When yesterday?' Veni asked.

'After we returned from the cruise but before we went to the houseboat. I don't know if it's relevant as it was one of those arguments between husband and wife. But considering what has happened, I thought I'd tell you. Please tell Uncle and he can decide if the police need to know about it.'

'Certainly, Ruhi, I can do that.'

'I am not sure if I can say this in front of Papa and Mummy. It would hurt them, I think.'

Veni nodded. 'Get it off your chest, Ruhi. We can then decide whom to tell and whom not to.'

Ruhi paused for a moment and began.

'After seeing that Sahil was at the resort, Danuj locked me in our room,' she said. 'I was sitting on the bed and thinking about the implications of Sahil unexpectedly turning up at the resort, and what complications that could lead to. That's when the door opened, and Danuj came in. He shut the door and came to stand in front of me with his hands on his hips. His face was like thunder.

'So,' Danuj said brusquely, 'have you decided?'

Ruhi looked up at him.

'Yes,' she said, 'I have. I'll file for divorce once we return to Mumbai. The papers are ready.'

'So, that's it, then?'

'I am not happy about it, Danuj, but you've left me no choice. Divorce was always the last resort—you know that!' Ruhi paused for a moment. When she continued, her tone was sombre. 'I have a fair idea where you were in Kochi yesterday. So do Papa and Mummy. You are breaking their hearts.'

'Breaking hearts! So speaks the one who is filing for divorce. What delicious irony!'

'You know that I've tried to avoid it. I've begged you... I've swallowed all my pride and pleaded with you to reform. Am I really such a bad wife that you should go to other women?'

'What's that got to do with anything?' He seemed surprised. 'Men will be men. Variety is the spice of life.'

'No, Danuj. Most husbands are faithful to their wives. You've gone too far... no woman can put up with this. I've tried hard to make this marriage work, prolong it. If not for you, at least for Mummy and Papa. They have been so good to me! You know that I've delayed the divorce for them.'

'So speaks the vulture! You are in great form today.'

'Vulture?' Ruhi was puzzled. 'How? I've given you everything. I've taken nothing... except abuse and betrayal.'

'Don't pretend. You know that Papa is going to change his bequests, and you know what changes he will be making. You'll get your share even if you divorce me. You've twisted the old man around your little finger, haven't you? Conned him into passing on a part of his wealth to you.'

Ruhi was taken aback. She had done nothing of that sort.

'I didn't know that Papa was going to do that,' she said, still puzzled. 'Honestly, I had no idea. I'll speak to him and ask him not to do it. The Gauria wealth belongs to the Gaurias. I'll no longer be one after our divorce.'

'No, don't stop Papa!' Danuj cut in aggressively. 'That's what I wanted to speak to you about now. So, here is my proposal... I will not object to Papa's new plan. In fact, I'll support it unreservedly. I'm sure Kanika will throw a dozen tantrums, but I'll be on your side. Once a Gauria, always a Gauria... that'll be my stand. I'll ensure that you get your share.'

'How very kind!' Sarcasm dripped from every word. 'What do you want in return? That I drop the divorce?'

'No, no. In fact, I won't contest the divorce either. It'll go through smoothly.'

Ruhi blinked. This was unexpected.

'Wow!' she said. 'I'm impressed. Such benevolence! That too, with no strings attached! Surely, I'm missing something? What's the catch?'

'All I ask is fifty per cent of what you get from Papa. An equal split between you and me. You'll be free to lead your life as you wish and marry anyone you want.'

Light dawned on her.

'I see... that's one way to get a larger share than your siblings do. Clever! And if I don't agree to your proposal? What then?'

'I'll contest every inch of the way!' Danuj's voice had hardened. It now dripped venom. 'Both the inheritance and the divorce. I'll ruin your name in the industry. You'll never get a role again. You'll be in such a bloody mess that you'll regret it.'

Ruhi's anger rose.

'Just as you did to poor Bhagya?' she cut in icily. 'But you no longer have the clout needed to do that.'

'Haven't I?' His voice was full of scorn. 'See how far Bhagya has fallen. She wanders around like a wacko.'

'You are cruel, Danuj. So unlike your parents.'

'At last, you get it! Think it over, my dear wife. I know what you want.'

Ruhi's puzzlement deepened.

'What do I—' she began to ask, but Danuj cut her off.

'Let's not pretend, okay? There is a way out of this mess for both of us. A smooth way that gives everyone what they want. We'll talk about it soon.'

A couple of hours later, Athreya was about to begin another experiment, this time on the houseboat. He had requested Anto get a couple of men and arrange for some boats and a coracle. The sun was approaching the western horizon, making the sky glow in different hues ranging from yellow to orange to red. A spectacular sunset was in the offing. But nature's beauty was lost to the two of them on Ruhi's houseboat.

The body had been removed and whatever fingerprinting was possible had been done. The overnight dew had made it a futile exercise. Little could be gleaned from the smudges that were once fingerprints. Except in the bedroom, but those prints only confirmed that Danuj had not been there, except to drop off his suitcase.

'I will take Ruhi's spot in the bedroom,' Athreya told Anto. 'I'll close the door and lie in bed. To the extent possible, I'd like to recreate the conditions of last night.'

'To what end?' Anto asked.

'I want to see what sounds I hear and how much of the

boat's rocking I feel. The rocking of the boat could be crucial evidence.'

'Okay. Where would you like me to be?'

'At Danuj's spot, lounging on the sofa in the sitting area. Nobody other than you and me will be on the boat.'

'What about the men you asked for? What do you want them to do?'

'They will do a series of things one by one. First, let us have the other houseboat and the barge pass by this houseboat one after another.'

Anto shouted a series of instructions to his men in Malayalam and settled on the sofa in the sitting area. The sofa, cushions and mats had been replaced after the murder. Athreya retired to the bedroom and lay down on the bed.

Over the next half hour, a motorboat, the other houseboat, which had a motor attached, and the barge, which was poled over water, made several passes past Athreya's houseboat, a few minutes apart. Each pass was at a different distance from the houseboat. At the end of the exercise, Athreya and Anto compared notes.

'The motor-driven houseboat was clearly audible,' Anto said, 'and it rocked our boat the most when it passed very close to us. The barge, however, neither made much sound nor sent waves to rock our boat. I barely heard it.'

'Check,' nodded Athreya. 'Exactly my experience too. Now, let's get the small rowboat to bump into our houseboat at different spots—near the bow, at the rear, at the boarding point to port as well as to the low point on the starboard. Let's see how much the boat rocks and how much sound is produced.'

Athreya lay down again on the bed with a pen and notebook. Taking as the base the amount of rocking the earlier exercise had produced, he calibrated the rocking caused by the rowboat bumping into the houseboat. He also noted the sounds produced and their loudness.

'The thumps were clearly audible,' Anto said when they compared notes again. 'The sound obviously is very different from what we heard the last round.'

'Correct,' Athreya agreed. 'The sounds we heard the last time were mostly those of the motor. There were no thumps. Did you hear creaks too this time?'

'Yes, of course. Creaks and scratching too when the boats rubbed against each other.'

'Check. And the rocking?'

'Not much... not as much as when the motorboat passed close to us.'

'Correct. And the rocking this time was for a shorter while too. It faded very quickly.'

'Yes. Shall we try the coracle now?'

'Sure.'

The coracle—a basket boat made of bamboo—was very light. Its thump against the houseboat barely registered, and if it did rock the houseboat, Athreya didn't feel it. However, he did hear a scratching noise when the coracle rubbed against the houseboat. Anto's experience was the same.

Next was the critical experiment to see how much the houseboat rocked when a person boarded it or disembarked from it.

Straight away, it became clear that the rock was very noticeable when a person boarded the houseboat at the gate, which was to port. Boarding at the corresponding spot to starboard was very similar too. However, when the boarding was done towards the bow or the rear, the rocking, while noticeable, was not as much.

Disembarking, they found, caused as much rocking as boarding did.

141

They came and sat in the sitting area of the houseboat. The sun had set by the time they completed their experiments.

'So, Anto,' Athreya asked with a smile, 'what's your conclusion?'

'Somebody boarded the houseboat, sir,' Anto replied at once with conviction. 'I'm now sure of that. The thumps and scratchings Ruhi heard were due to a small boat rubbing against this houseboat, and the rocking was caused by the boarding or disembarking of some person.'

'That's my conclusion too. The boat rocked each time someone boarded it or got off it. So, for each visitor to the houseboat, there would have been a pair of rockings. The intensity of the rocking depends on how quickly or slowly the person got off the boat or boarded it and on the person's weight. The quicker the act, the more the rocking. Agree?'

'Agree. However, we don't know how many times the boat rocked, or the thumps sounded.'

'Correct. Ruhi felt the first pair of rockings clearly. She felt the boat rock a few times after that too but is not sure how many times. Ruhi had Restyl at around 10 p.m. and fell sleep an hour or two later. What she felt and heard after that is unclear.'

'Does this really help, Mr Aadhreiah? That still leaves us in the dark about many things.'

'Yes, but we are making progress, Anto. Without these experiments, the significance of the rocking of the boat would have been speculation or conjecture. Now, it has been tested. We now know that some person or persons boarded the houseboat at night. At least once, but most probably more than that. What's more, the results of our little experiments will stand up in court.'

'Provided Ruhi is not lying,' Anto countered. 'What if the entire story she gave us is concocted?'

'Good point. We must answer that question.'

'That's not going to be easy, I'm afraid.'

'You know what I fear, Anto?'

'What, sir?'

'That this case might turn out to be one of those where we have little evidence to go by—no prints, no witnesses, no physical evidence, nothing. Lots of people have the motive and the opportunity, but there is very little by way of actual evidence. The crime scene is surrounded by water and there was nobody around except for the murderer, the victim and Ruhi.'

'Have you come across such a case before, sir?'

'Yes, I have. Like this case, the cards were stacked in the murderer's favour. There too, the killer had been smart to take advantage of the conditions.'

'Then, how did you crack it?'

'We waited for the murderer to make a mistake. He was a very intelligent man who had executed the crime very well... well enough to leave no trail. But that success made him over-confident, and he turned greedy. He overreached by perpetrating another crime. This time, he was not as careful. He made a mistake, and we got him. Had he remained content with his first crime, he would have gotten away. Here too, if the murderer remains content with killing Danuj, he or she can remain hidden.'

'Do we have a clever murderer here too?' Anto asked.

Athreya nodded slowly. 'I think so. All the people here have been successful in their professions, some more than the others. Everyone involved in this case is intelligent.'

Anto pulled out his small notebook and opened it to a page marked by a slip of paper. He glanced at it and went on.

'So, who are the potential suspects we have?' He counted the names on the page. 'Eight people we know had the opportunity and a motive to kill Danuj.'

'The Gauria family?' Athreya asked.

Anto nodded. 'Except Mahesh and Manjari. I can't see them going to Danuj's houseboat at night and running a blade through him. Do you?'

'No. I don't think they are physically capable of such an act.'

'That leaves five Gaurias—Danuj's two siblings, their spouses and his wife. All of them had the opportunity to kill him. His wife was right here on the boat. Kanika and Jeet were in another boat nearby. Hiran and Pari were a similar distance away on the shore. Hiran can't swim, but he could have taken a boat. Any of them could have taken a boat to Danuj.'

'Indeed. I take it that your men are making enquiries for anyone who might have hired a boat?'

'Of, course, Mr Aadhreiah.' Anto looked a little hurt. 'Basic procedure.'

'It is, I'm sorry.' Athreya managed to look a little abashed.

'No problem, sir,' Anto replied magnanimously. 'And their motives? Larger inheritance?'

'Correct. Now, Hiran's and Kanika's shares of the inheritance will be considerably larger. That's motive enough for the two siblings and their spouses.'

'And as far as Ruhi is concerned, this was one way to free herself from Danuj, even if we don't consider the financial angle—insurance, inheritance, et cetera.'

'Yes, but she was filing for divorce anyway. Why kill?'

'Hmm.' Anto paused for a moment. 'The other suspects are Kishan, Bhagya and Sahil. Each has their own motive.'

'Agree. That makes it eight, unless you want to add an unknown stranger who came by at night, killed Danuj and vanished.'

'That possibility always exists. We don't need to write it down.'

'Fair enough,' Athreya concurred. 'Notice that half the suspects are women. Do you think they could have done the act?'

144

'Yes, of course!' Anto was emphatic. 'All of them are young and able-bodied. Three of the four had a man with them. And as far as the fourth is concerned, Ruhi was right here on the houseboat. And none of them has an alibi.'

'Did anyone see any of the eight up and about at night?'

'Joseph is making enquiries. We'll know soon.'

'It looks like you've covered the bases. Have you also taken an expert opinion on the wet patches on the port and starboard sides?'

'Yes, I did. Sorry, I forgot to tell you. Four locals who know about such matters, including the owner of this boat and his assistant, agree that the wet patches must have been made at night. They judged it by the amount of wetness.'

'There you go, Anto!' Athreya offered the inspector a big smile. 'You are getting your ducks in line. Well done! You were put on the case a mere twelve hours ago. Quick work!'

To Athreya's surprise, Anto blushed. Athreya quickly changed the subject to help the inspector out of his embarrassment.

'What about the rope that was hanging near the gate?' he asked. 'What did you find out?'

'The rope is new, sir,' Anto answered gratefully. 'It wasn't there when the pilot and the attendant left the boat last night. It was tied to the railing sometime that night and then cut.'

'Very good! I think you can safely assume that the houseboat had nocturnal visitors. I hope someone is following up on the severed rope too. It would be helpful if you could find the other half of the rope with a cleanly cut end that matches this one.'

'I have men out searching, Mr Aadhreiah. I hope they find something.'

'And you are having the lake surface searched as well?'

'Yes, motorboats to the south and the west. As you said, the breeze last night was from the north-east. I've also requested the services of a chopper. We'll be able to cover a wide area tomorrow morning.'

'Anything on the irregular patch of blood?' Athreya asked. 'The one that was two feet towards the starboard side from the main patch?'

'Nothing, sir. We lifted the coir mat and looked underneath. As expected, the blood had not soaked through. Not much had spilled at that spot.'

'Tell me, Anto. Did the small patch look as if blood had been *smeared* there?'

The inspector though for a moment. Then, he nodded.

'Yes, sir. It does look like that.'

'Ah!' Athreya exulted and rubbed his hands. 'That could be interesting!'

When Athreya came ashore from the houseboat, he saw the gaunt figure of Hiran walking on the lawn and speaking over his mobile phone. Seeing that the Gauria scion was alone, Athreya decided to have a chat with him. As he walked towards Hiran from the pier, the younger man looked up and saw Athreya. He terminated his call and made his way towards the investigator.

'I saw several boats going up and down past Danuj's houseboat,' he said in his habitually polite manner. 'It looked as if you were conducting some experiments. Did you discover anything new?'

'Nothing conclusive,' Athreya replied noncommittally. 'We were testing certain theories. How long have you been watching?'

'Oh, on and off since you and the inspector boarded the houseboat.'

'Did any ideas strike you as you watched us?' Athreya asked.

'Not sure,' Hiran replied. 'The houseboat seemed to rock considerably when the waves from the motorboat hit it. Must be pretty uncomfortable sleeping in there.' He gave a tepid smile. 'Pari wanted to spend a night on a houseboat. I was steeling myself to go along with her.'

'Why the reluctance?'

'Well… I'm never comfortable in or on water. Gives me the willies. I *am* a little afraid of water, you know.'

'Is that why you didn't learn to swim?' Athreya asked.

Hiran shrugged.

'I'm not sure which is the cause and which the effect,' he said. 'Am I afraid of water because I can't swim? Or did I not learn swimming because of the fear? I really don't know.'

'Do you have some time for a chat, Hiran? I haven't had the chance to talk to you in private.'

'Of course!' Hiran nodded emphatically. 'Nothing is more important than discovering who killed Danuj.'

'Come then, let's stroll along as we talk.' They fell in step with each other. 'Did you hear or see anything last night? I heard what you said in front of your parents and Pari. Is there anything you'd like to add?'

Hiran frowned as he tried to recollect. A few seconds later, he shook his head.

'Can't think of anything,' he said. 'Apart from Danuj's quarrel with Ruhi, I heard nothing. I didn't see any boats either. But then, I must confess that I was pretty distracted last night, and did a lot of navel-gazing, so to speak. What with Sahil landing here all of a sudden, Danuj's impulsive decision to hire a house-boat and the altercation on the boat, I was worried that things were coming to a head.'

'A head?'

'Danuj's marriage, you know. It was already falling apart. I wondered if last night's blow-up would be the last straw. How much more could Ruhi put up with? With such thoughts buzzing in my head, I was preoccupied, and I found it difficult to sleep. Pari too was on pins and needles—she went for a swim.'

'Didn't you accompany her?' Athreya asked, although he knew what Hiran would say.

'Don't forget I can't swim.' Hiran threw a quick glance at Athreya. 'Guess I could have stayed in the wading pool, but water doesn't interest me. While it relaxes Pari, it tenses me up.'

'I understand.' Athreya nodded. 'Were you in your room, then?'

'No. I walked around quite a bit—around the pool, across the lawn and along the shore. Till late into the night. Walking seemed to offer temporary relief from my anxieties.'

'Anxieties about Danuj's marriage falling apart?'

Hiran nodded. 'That, and business matters too. Maybe, I should explain. You see, Danuj and I were equal partners in our film production company. Unfortunately, we have been incurring heavy losses the past few years.'

'Due to failed films?' Athreya cut in.

'Yes. Danuj must have made six to eight films recently that bombed at the box office. At a minimum of 20 crores a film, we are talking losses of 160 crores plus. As a result of his misadventures, we are in debt, Mr Athreya. Deep in debt.'

'You too?'

Hiran nodded. 'We are equal partners.'

'How have your films done? You said that Danuj's films lost money.'

'My films have done all right. While they may not have raked in big money, they haven't lost it either. Most of my projects are in the black and made a decent profit.'

'Okay. Wasn't your father helping you out with Danuj's losses?' Athreya asked.

'Yes, but for how long? He doesn't have an endless supply of money. He had started saying that he would not fund any more of Danuj's hare-brained projects. That's one of the reasons why Danuj ended up borrowing from the likes of Kishan. Unfortunately, as Danuj and I were partners, I ended up picking up half the losses.'

At the mention of Kishan, Athreya's mind went to the thug's companion—Bhagya.

'What about Bhagya?' Athreya asked. 'What part does she play in all this? Has she come here to Kumarakom to exact some sort of revenge on Danuj?'

'Probably, but I really don't know.' Hiran spread out his arms. 'Who knows? She is such an impulsive woman. After her psychiatric issues, she hasn't been the same. She's rather unpredictable and volatile now. But I don't see her *killing* Danuj. Harassing him? Yes. But murdering him? Definitely not.'

Athreya chose not to react to the information that Bhagya had 'psychiatric' issues. It could be important, but there was no need to emphasize it now to Hiran.

'I believe Danuj has cheated many young women,' he remarked instead. 'Bhagya was not the only one.'

'Unfortunately, that is true. Danuj used to play fast and loose with women. I've always said that it would come back to bite him.'

'Meaning?'

'Meaning, many women might have wished him ill.'

'Any thoughts on who could have killed him?'

'I can't say, but if I have to bet on anyone, I'd bet on Kishan.'

Veni had been waiting eagerly to update her husband on the task he had given her. She had had no opportunity to do so until they had eaten dinner and had retired for the night to their bedroom in Kurup's house. Acting on Athreya's request, she had chatted in Malayalam with the housekeeping staff—two young women—who were in charge of keeping the Gauria and Sahil rooms clean. During the friendly chatter, Veni had managed to elicit the information Athreya wanted.

'I have two reports for you,' Veni said, once their bedroom door was closed. 'First, I found out something from the house-keeping girls.'

'Wonderful!' Athreya replied. 'I knew you would get it out of them. What did you learn?'

'All rooms except Mahesh and Manjari's suite had wet clothes that hadn't been there the previous evening when the house-keeping women had turned down the beds and prepared them for the night.'

'Any specifics?' Athreya asked.

'Hiran and Pari's room had one wet swimming costume—that of Pari. It looks like she had used the pool late in the night. Hiran can't swim, apparently. Pari seems to have entered the pool alone.'

'Hmm... she went to the pool after dinner?'

'So it seems. While she was in the swimming pool, Hiran was seen walking around texting and talking on his phone.'

'What about Kanika and Jeet?'

'They too had wet swimming costumes in the morning.'

'They spent the night on their houseboat,' Athreya mused. 'From 7 p.m. onwards. Wet swimming clothes in their room mean that they took a dip in the lake. Unless they used the pool in the morning.'

'That's unlikely, Hari,' Veni countered. 'Remember, Hiran woke them up with news of Danuj's death. They came straight to their room, freshened up and came directly to the suite. They didn't use the pool this morning. So, they must have swum in the lake at night.'

'And Sahil? What did they find there?'

'No wet clothes, but his shoes were wet—soaking wet as if he had stepped into water. And as there were no corresponding wet clothes, he couldn't have got wet in the rain.'

'Excellent, Veni,' Athreya praised. 'What's the second report you have for me?'

'A message from Ruhi.'

Veni went on to narrate the conversation between Ruhi and Danuj that Ruhi had told her about.

When she finished, Athreya switched off the light and went to the window. There, he moved the curtain an inch and peered out. Their room was on the first floor and at the front of the house. It overlooked the street.

A moment later, he beckoned to Veni and gestured to her to remain silent. When she came, he pointed to the opening in the curtain. Veni put an eye to it and looked out.

'There's a man there,' she whispered. 'Seems to be watching the house. Who is he?'

'Don't know,' Athreya whispered back. 'Have you seen him before?'

Veni shook her head.

'Maybe he's waiting for somebody. We can't be sure that he is watching this house,' she said.

'We'll keep an eye out. If we see him again, I'll tell Kurup. I hope we are not putting him and the family in any danger.'

10

Athreya's next day—Sunday—began earlier than he had expected. With Akuti's yoga sessions at Crystal Waters temporarily suspended, he had planned on going to the resort after a leisurely breakfast with Kurup's family. But Anto's morning phone call—early even by the standards of the early risers of Kerala—put paid to that plan.

Anto had sounded impatient over the phone and was eager to share news of developments that had happened after their meeting last evening. He wanted to discuss them in person rather than over the phone. So, off Athreya went, after apologizing to the Kurups, to find Anto, Joseph and Dr Saju waiting for him in the temporary office they had met in the previous day.

Grave as usual, Saju adjusted his spectacles, blinked and began in a sombre voice.

'I performed the autopsy yesterday,' he began. 'We now have some of the answers you were seeking. First, the time of death. Before I share the details, I would like to say that the uncertainties in this case are a little more than usual because the body lay for several hours in the open air on the lake. The moisture-laden air and the overnight dew are factors that must be considered.'

'Sure, Doctor,' Athreya replied. 'We understand that. Just give us your best estimate.'

'Thank you.' Saju seemed relieved. 'Based on multiple parameters, of which I won't get into the details now, I believe that death occurred between midnight and 2 a.m. Within that time window, the highest probability lies between 12:30 a.m. and 1:00 a.m.'

'Thank you, Dr Saju. That's useful. We'll work with the 12:30 a.m. to 1:00 a.m. window, keeping in mind that it could stretch to the broader range. Any doubt about the cause of death?'

'None. The wound in the heart was clearly fatal. The consequent blood loss would have caused loss of consciousness very quickly. Death would have followed very soon after.'

'Okay. And the other wounds? The shallower ones?'

'Though grievous, none of the four, by themselves, would have been immediately fatal,' the bespectacled doctor went on laboriously. 'Collectively, they would have caused death within, say, ten minutes. However, as you had suggested, the shallower wounds were made just after death, maybe within a minute or two after the stab in the heart with the longer knife.

'Second, there is another curious thing about this death. The deceased seems to have been lying on his back when the wounds were made. That's also the position we found the body in.'

'Which means that the stabs were made downwards,' Athreya said. 'Any idea why he didn't resist the attacks?'

'Ah, yes! I think I can answer that question. The reason is alprazolam. There is a high level of that drug in his blood. As the body stops metabolizing the drug after death, our tests are quite conclusive. I am certain he was deep in a drugged sleep when he was killed.'

'Could the level of alprazolam you detected have been caused by the missing pill of Restyl we found in the bedroom?'

'No. The strip we found was of Restyl 0.25 milligram. That would not result in the high level we found. Even a 0.5 mg pill wouldn't. I suspect he ingested about 1 mg or more.'

'*Four* pills of Restyl 0.25?' Anto asked. 'Unlikely, isn't it?'

Saju shrugged.

'He could have taken two 0.5 mg pills, I suppose?' Athreya suggested. 'Or one pill of 1 mg?'

Saju nodded. 'That's probably what happened, but I can't confirm that. Please be aware that 1 mg pills are not as common as the smaller dosages are. As we don't know when exactly he ingested the drug, I am not able to tell if he took 1 mg or a little more.'

'Mrs Gauria—Danuj's mother—takes Restyl daily, but I am not sure of the dosage she takes,' said Athreya.

'Ah!' Saju took out his spectacles and began polishing them with his microfibre cloth. 'Inspector Anto has been proactive there. He can probably enlighten you.'

Anto cleared his throat and spoke a little self-importantly.

'She usually takes 0.5 mg or 1 mg,' he said. 'But on occasion, she has gone up to 1.5 mg. I'm told that she has all three dosage pills in her stock.'

'Good work, Anto,' Athreya said. 'Does she self-medicate?'

'To some extent, but within the limits prescribed by her doctor—between 0.5 mg and 1.5 mg. How much she takes depends on how she feels that night. But 1 mg is what she takes most often. If she feels good on a particular night, she drops it to 0.5 mg. If she is disturbed, she steps it up to 1.5 mg. In any case, all her medicines, including Restyl, are administered by one of her daughters-in-law.'

'I see…' Athreya's index finger began tracing imaginary figures and letters on his chair armrest—a sign that his mind was churning. 'Then, Pari would have administered it on the night of the murder.'

'Why?' Anto asked.

'Danuj had locked Ruhi in her room, you remember? Then, he took her to the dining room for dinner, after which they went straight to the houseboat. Ruhi had no opportunity to administer Mrs Gauria's medicines that night.'

'Of course!' An abashed Anto admonished himself silently.

'Alprazolam from Mrs Gauria's stock must have somehow ended up in Danuj's blood,' Athreya mused aloud. 'We need to find out how that happened and whether it was accidental or deliberate. The best way to do that is to start with the source—Mrs Gauria's stock of medicines. I will ask the Gaurias one by one.'

'Speaking of Ruhi,' Saju said when Athreya paused, 'I also had her blood samples analysed yesterday.'

'Excellent, Doctor!' Athreya smiled widely. 'What did you find?'

'Alprazolam was in her blood too. The level was much lower than Danuj's. It was consistent with her having taken 0.25 mg at 10 p.m.'

'And only one 0.25 mg pill was missing from the strip,' Anto mused a bit irritatedly. 'Then she was telling the truth. She said that she borrowed it from her mother-in-law.'

'Yes, Mrs Gauria might have given it to her during dinner.'

'Yes, yes.' Anto nodded vigorously. 'But what I have in mind is something else now: the Gauria household seems to be a veritable drugstore! They have medicines of different dosages in their possession like the rest of us have potato, tomato and onion in our kitchens. These are prescription drugs that shouldn't be floating around as if they were banana chips!'

'Well, yes.' Athreya couldn't help smiling at Anto's vexed diatribe. 'But both the elderly people in the household have all manner of health problems—diabetes, insomnia, anxiety, blood pressure, and whatnot. They do take a lot of medicines.'

'If you don't mind,' Saju interrupted. 'I need to go soon, and I have only one more piece of information for you. May I finish?'

'Of course, Doctor.' Athreya turned to him. 'Please tell us.'

'Joseph gave us a piece of rope,' Saju said, 'which he asked us to examine. One end of the rope had a bloodstain. Joseph wanted to know if it was human blood. And if it was, he wanted to know if it matched with Danuj's blood.'

'Ah!' Athreya glanced at Joseph appreciatively. 'Is that the rope we found tied to the railing, Joseph?'

'Yes, sir,' the sub-inspector answered.

'Good. That will be interesting to know.'

'The short answer,' the doctor concluded, 'is that the blood on the rope is Danuj's.'

Once he left the room, Anto turned to Athreya.

'We examined the two mobile phones we recovered from the crime scene,' he said. 'Danuj's and Ruhi's.'

'What did you find?' Athreya asked.

'Nothing. The call logs in both the phones largely bear out what we heard. It looks like Sahil and Ruhi were telling the truth for the most part.'

'Most part? Was there something in the call logs that is new?'

'Yes. There was a call from Ruhi's phone to Sahil's a few minutes after 9 p.m. on the night of the murder.'

'At 9 p.m., both Danuj and Ruhi were on their houseboat. And from what Ruhi says, her phone had been taken away from her. Then, if she didn't have access to her phone, was it Danuj who called Sahil at 9 p.m.?' Athreya speculated.

'Possibly, sir. Of course, we don't know for sure. But the call logs show no outgoing calls or messages from Ruhi's phone except the one to Sahil.'

'Incoming ones?' Athreya asked.

'Several calls. All went unanswered. They show up as missed calls on her phone.'

'Okay. Anything else?'

'We checked with the shop in Kochi from which Mahesh Gauria bought the three daggers. The shopkeeper confirmed that only three were bought, and that all of them were blunt.'

'Any breakthrough on fingerprints?'

'Unfortunately not. The dew really played havoc. This is a rare case where we don't have a single print to help us,' said Anto.

'Anything further on the irregular patch of blood?'

Anto shook his head. 'Nothing further.'

'And the blue file?'

'No, sir.'

Athreya leaned back in his chair and stared at the ceiling in silence. His right index finger began scribbling again on the chair armrest. Anto watched him curiously, with an amused expression on his face. He remained silent, as he could see that Athreya was deep in thought. But after a couple of minutes' silence, he could bear the suspense no more.

'What is it, Mr Aadhreiah?' he asked.

'Interesting, isn't it, Anto?' Athreya responded, still gazing at the ceiling.

'What is interesting, sir?'

'The file. The blue file.'

'Why? It's just a plain blue file with no markings.'

'True. But think about it for a minute... about the circumstances.'

Anto frowned and he tried to discern what Athreya was leading up to. After a long moment, he shook his head.

'I can find nothing unusual about it,' he admitted.

'Okay,' Athreya replied. 'Two things about the file strike me as being curious. First, why did the intruder kill Danuj?'

'Sir?' the inspector asked in bewilderment.

'Saju told us that Danuj would have been fast asleep after consuming a large quantity of alprazolam. If he was knocked out, why didn't the intruder just take the file and go? Why did he—or she—need to *kill* Danuj? Why commit murder?'

'Hmm… you have a point there, Mr Aadhreiah,' the inspector conceded.

'The second interesting thing about the file is this: why did the thief take the papers but not the file?'

'Why is that interesting?'

'We don't know whether the papers were stolen before Danuj was killed or after. For a moment, let's assume that Danuj was alive when the intruder stole the papers. Despite Danuj being there, the intruder spends precious time removing the papers from the file. He would have to open the cover, unhook the two springs that hold the papers, pull them out slowly without making noise, and throw the empty file overboard.'

'Yes.'

'Wouldn't it have been far easier—and much quieter *and* much quicker—to take away the whole file? Why run the risk of being caught if Danuj woke up when he—or she—was removing the papers?'

'True… true,' the inspector agreed. A look of admiration stole upon his face as he gazed at Athreya.

'On the other hand, if we assume that Danuj was already dead, and was lying there with a dagger in his chest,' Athreya went on, 'why would the intruder spend even *one second* more than is *absolutely necessary* with the corpse? Each additional second increases the risk of him being discovered with the body. Remember, Ruhi was in the bedroom just a few feet away! He would want to get away from there as quickly as he possibly could! But no! He spends the time needed to remove the papers from the file and then throws it into the water. Why?'

'Why, indeed!' Anto concurred, now thoroughly perplexed.

Joseph was a soft-spoken man in his twenties, who looked more like a sensitive artist than a tough policeman. He had been sitting in a corner when Saju was speaking. Once his turn came, he rose, came to stand in the centre of the room and threw a crisp salute. From his pocket, he pulled out a small notebook bound by an elastic band.

'We have been making enquiries in and around this resort, sir,' he began, opening the book. 'We have spoken to dozens of people about what they saw or heard on the night of the murder. With your permission, I will give you a summary.'

'Please,' Athreya nodded. 'Let's start with the summary and get into details wherever needed.'

'The primary purpose of yesterday's enquiries was to understand who was where on the night of the murder. As you probably know, the security cameras are not switched on during off season due to the low tourist traffic. So, we had to speak to a lot of people. We found that most of those related to the case were up and about until late in the night. I'll take them one by one.'

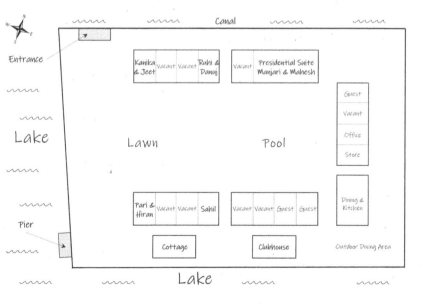

Athreya studied the young sub-inspector approvingly. He was in a neat, starched uniform, was neatly groomed and carried himself erect. From the way he spoke, he seemed organized as well.

'Starting with the head of the family, we now know that Mahesh and Manjari Gauria were up later than usual. Lights were burning in their suite till 11 p.m. or so. During this time, Pari and Hiran Gauria came and went several times. Once the lights were switched off in the suite, they returned to their room, which is closest to the pier. Sometime in between, Pari took a dip in the pool.

'The interesting thing is that Manjari Gauria was seen walking about in the corridor outside her suite even after the lights were switched off.' The corridor was a covered walkway that ran outside all the guest rooms in the resort, and they all opened onto it. 'I'm told that it has been a common thing to see her there at all times of the night over the past few days. She apparently suffers from insomnia, and any number of medicines she takes doesn't completely solve her problem. She doesn't sleep for more than three to four hours a night, maximum. She ends up walking about at night but doesn't switch on the light for fear of disturbing her husband.'

'Then, she might have been in the corridor when the murder took place,' Athreya remarked.

'Yes, sir. But I'm told that she doesn't usually wear her spectacles during her nocturnal wandering. Which means that she wouldn't have been able to see the houseboat very well.'

'Would she have been able to see other people who might have been walking within the resort?'

'Possibly, sir. We haven't interviewed her yet.'

'Okay. Please go on.'

'Sahil was seen outside his room at least a couple of times. The second time was around midnight.'

'Where specifically was he seen?'

'In the corridor outside his room and on the lawn. He could have gone elsewhere too.'

'Such as?'

'The pier or the water behind his room. The lake is just a dozen yards away, with only an unoccupied cottage in between. Nobody would have seen him walking to either place as there were no guards there.'

'Sahil is interesting,' Athreya commented. 'Found anything else about him?'

'Yes, sir. He asked the watchman and a couple of others if there was a boat he could hire. He wanted to go out on the lake during the night. The watchman gave him the phone number of a boat owner who lives in a house on the canal that borders this resort.'

'What time was this?'

'Around 9 p.m., but the watchman is not very sure of the time.'

'And did Sahil call the boat owner?'

'We don't know yet, sir. One of our constables is on his way there to find out.'

'That makes four Gaurias and Sahil,' Athreya observed. 'Five in all. Anyone else?'

'Yes, sir. Kishan and Bhagya. They are staying in the adjacent resort. Kishan's cottage faces the lake and is just a few yards from the water's edge. He could have accessed the lake without anyone seeing him.

'The French windows of Bhagya's room open out onto the swimming pool, which extends to the lake. The wall separating the pool and the lake rises only a few inches above the lake level. Anyone in the pool can slip into the lake almost unseen. Bhagya was seen walking around till at least midnight. Like Sahil and Kishan, she too could have stepped into the water without anyone seeing her.'

As they were speaking, Athreya had sat back in his chair and opened his notebook absent-mindedly. Almost without his knowing, he had picked up a pencil and begun sketching something on a clean page.

'The interesting thing is that Kishan's alibi checks out,' Joseph went on. 'He left the resort at 8 p.m. and returned at 2 a.m. He was with a friend from 8:30 p.m. till 1:30 a.m. They were seen at a restaurant from 9 p.m. to 10:30 p.m. The resort security guards confirm Kishan's claim.'

'A cast-iron alibi, eh?' Athreya commented.

'Yes, sir. That's not surprising, as you would agree. Professional criminals usually have solid-looking alibis. It's once you break their alibi that they find themselves in deep water.'

'Anything on this friend with whom he spent the evening?'

'Nothing concrete, but he is known to the police as a shady character.'

'What else did you learn about Kishan and Bhagya?' Athreya asked.

'They spend a lot of time in the swimming pool, individually or together, be it day or night. They both are excellent swimmers who are, I believe, practising for some competition.'

'A Bollywood fixer entering a swimming competition?' Athreya grinned. 'Eh, Anto?'

Anto grinned back. 'Interesting, isn't it?'

'That makes it seven at the resorts, Joseph. The others—Kanika, Jeet and Ruhi—were on boats that night.' Athreya turned to Anto. 'So, all your suspects were up and about at night. All of them had the opportunity, and none of them—except Kishan—has an alibi.'

'And as far as we know,' Anto added, 'all of them except Hiran swim well, some better than the others. Any of them could have even swum to the houseboat… it would take less than five minutes to cover the two hundred feet.'

'The only trouble is the medical evidence. Danuj was killed, in all probability, between 12:30 a.m. and 1 a.m. What Joseph has unearthed deals mostly with before midnight. Except for Kishan.'

Anto nodded. 'Being off season, there is less activity than usual now. Not many places are open beyond midnight, and few people are out late.'

'The last piece of information,' Joseph went on, 'is more a validation of what we already know. A watchman confirmed that he heard a male voice from Danuj's houseboat well after the fight he and Ruhi had. He also saw someone moving about the houseboat.'

'Time?' Athreya asked.

'At about 11 p.m. Then again after half an hour.'

'So, by all indications, Danuj was alive at 11:30 p.m. I wonder when he took the Restyl. Thank you, Joseph. You've done a fine job. See if you can get anything more. Especially people's movements after midnight.'

Silence fell over the room as Joseph saluted and left. Except for the scratching sounds Athreya's pencil was making. Curious, Anto rose and came to look at the notebook.

'What is this, Mr Aadhreiah?' he asked.

Surprised, Athreya looked down at what his fingers had drawn without his conscious knowledge. It was not a very good sketch, but it was recognizable, at least to him.

It was a round basket floating on water. A coracle.

11

A sharp rap sounded on the door of Anto's temporary office, and it opened. In came Kanika with Jeet following her a couple of steps behind. Once again, she was dressed immaculately, in an intricately embroidered orange top and fawn trousers. Red high heels and a burgundy handbag completed her attire. Her hair was carefully brushed and fell around her shoulders. Her appearance, Athreya decided, was a product of much time and effort spent at the dressing table. Veni was right—even at such a time of grief, Kanika's priority was herself.

'Good morning,' she said breezily as she walked in.

Anto jumped to his feet and ushered her into a chair.

'Good morning, good morning!' he greeted, his accent and buffoonery back on display. 'I hope you haven't taken it too badly. It must be very difficult for the family. What a tragedy! What a tragedy!'

If Anto was trying to get her off her guard with his curious behaviour, he seemed to be succeeding. Kanika favoured him with an amused and condescending glance as she took the seat he offered. When her eyes rested on Athreya briefly, there was caution and hardness in them. Athreya was sure that she wouldn't have forgotten the sparring that happened the last time they had met.

'Would you like some tea?' Anto asked, with courtesy that would have befitted a hostess.

'Yes, but you don't bother, Inspector. Jeet will attend to it.'

Without having to be told, Jeet went to the phone and ordered Thurbo Darjeeling tea, a single-estate premium tea.

'You have been very busy,' Kanika went on, her flattering gaze trained on Anto. 'I'm told you covered a lot of ground in just one day. What have you discovered?'

So, was she trying to pump the inspector for information? Athreya wondered why.

'For one,' he cut in before Anto could answer, 'we have the answer to the question you asked the last time we met.'

Annoyance flashed on her face but only for an instant. She regained control almost at once and turned on her charm.

'And what was that question?' she asked Athreya with an enchanting smile.

'Whether something was stolen or not.'

'Ah, of course! And the answer is...'

'Nothing of any intrinsic value was stolen. Neither from the room nor from the houseboat.'

'Intrinsic value?' she asked.

'Material value... like gold, diamonds, money, watches and suchlike.'

'That's good, isn't it?' She turned to Anto. 'What do you think, Inspector?'

'Robbery was probably not the motive, madam,' Anto replied with a trace of affected pomposity.

Athreya didn't miss the fact that he was merely stating the obvious. He suppressed a smile and sat back to watch the exchange.

'But I'm sure you have some other ideas too,' Anto went on. 'Would you like to share them with me? You know all the people involved very well, don't you?'

'Yes, I do,' she answered modestly. 'It's a complex set of relationships, as you can imagine, especially when so much money is involved.' She glanced at Jeet, who had just ordered tea and taken a chair. 'The Gauria family produces films, but Jeet and I keep our distance from filmmaking. It's too murky for our liking. We stick to more tangible forms of investment.'

'Like?'

'Oh, real estate, financial markets and things like that. Filmmaking is too much of a gamble.'

'Your father has done very well,' Anto offered. 'Very well indeed.'

'He has a nose for it, Inspector. Not everybody does—especially my brothers. Papa made tons of money and his sons keep losing it. Neither of my brothers has a clue about what kind of films make money and what don't. Unlike Papa, who is *really* hard-nosed about money, they get carried away by their own fancies—'

'Would you consider yourself hard-nosed, madam?'

Irritation at being interrupted showed for a moment on her face.

'I would like to think so,' she replied tersely. 'If you ask around in Mumbai, I think you will hear people say so. I don't let grass grow under my feet. But that's not the point—we were talking about my brothers. Why, Danuj even wanted to make a film of Ruhi's affair with Sahil!'

'Affair?' Anto asked, displaying the requisite amount of interest to encourage her. 'Really?'

'Don't you know?' Kanika asked innocently. She glanced at the inscrutable Athreya, who was quietly listening. 'I had mentioned it to Athreya in passing the other day.'

When the seasoned investigator didn't rise to the bait, she shifted her gaze to Anto and continued, 'There has been a lot of talk about an affair between Ruhi and Sahil. Most of her box office hits were produced by Sahil, you know. They were very close from before her marriage to Danuj.'

'And after marriage?'

'Ahem!' Kanika chose not to give an answer.

'So, this affair... is it real or just a rumour?'

'The answer depends on whom you ask.'

'If I ask you, madam?'

'I'd say "no comment". Come on, we are talking about my family here. What do you expect me to say?'

'Coming back to what we were discussing, you were saying that your brothers are not very savvy film producers. Both of them?'

'I think so. Danuj wasn't savvy for sure—he lost tons of money and was deep in debt. He was forever asking Papa and Hiran to bail him out. But he knew better than to pester me. Hiran isn't far behind his brother. He may not have been as reckless as Danuj, but few of his projects have made any significant amounts of money. Of course, he has lost heaps of it through Danuj's failed projects. They were partners, you see.'

'How was the relationship between the two brothers?'

She shrugged. 'As good as it could be when Danuj was one of the two parties. But then, Hiran is no saint either.'

'Not a saint?' Anto cocked an eyebrow.

'Doesn't matter, Inspector.'

'And the rapport between their wives?' Anto went on.

'Ruhi and Pari?' Kanika grimaced. 'For some reason, they seem to hit it off very well. Both make a pretence of caring for Papa and Mummy. I wonder how fond they would have been had Papa not been as rich as he is.'

'How is their relationship with you?'

'They keep their distance and don't mess with me.'

'And your brothers' rapport with you, madam?'

'You are a man of the world, Inspector.' Kanika smiled pleasingly at Anto. 'Who likes a person who tells the truth? Especially about poor business judgement.'

'But, but, but!' Anto protested comically. 'I'm told that you all get along very well with each other. You went on an intimate family cruise. The Gauria lunch and dinner tables are always cheery and cordial. Staff at this resort are impressed at the bonding within the family.'

'Of course, they are impressed.' Her hand waved in a dismissive gesture. 'We are a family of actors, Inspector. We know how to project an image.'

She shifted in her chair and favoured Anto with a heavy dose of charm.

'You haven't answered my question, Inspector,' she purred. 'Have you found out anything of interest? Who killed poor Danuj? Athreya seems to suggest that it wasn't an outsider.'

'It's too early to answer that question, madam,' Anto replied smoothly. 'We are still making enquiries but haven't covered everyone yet. We haven't even been able to talk to you.'

'We can talk now if you wish.'

'Thank you. I believe you and your husband were on your houseboat from 7 p.m. onwards. Is that right?'

'Yes. We had a candlelight dinner on the deck.'

'For how long, madam?'

'A couple of hours. Jeet opened a bottle of Johnny Walker and we got quite tipsy.'

Anto smiled knowingly. 'You finished the full bottle, madam?'

'There might have been some left,' she said carelessly. 'That's probably because the last half hour of our dinner was ruined by the fight Danuj and Ruhi had. What an embarrassment to the family!'

'Did you see their houseboat arrive? It must have reached that spot after you dropped anchor.'

'Yes, at about 8:30 p.m. Their pilot and attendant left the houseboat at once. Then, the shouting match began.'

'Did you send away your pilot and attendant too?'

'Of course! Who wants them around after dinner? Bloody *kabab mein haddi*!'

Kabab mein haddi referred to an unwanted irritant, like a 'haddi'—piece of bone—in a kabab—mincemeat.

'Of course, of course! I fully understand, madam. Even though it is Hindi.'

Athreya cleared his throat. The others looked at him.

'When your boat was anchored,' he asked, 'was its nose pointing southwards?'

'Er... I'm not sure which way is south,' Kanika answered.

'Was the resort to your left when you stood facing towards the boat's nose?'

'Er... I think so.' She looked uncertainly at Jeet.

'That's right,' Jeet confirmed. 'The resort and the coast were to our port side—our left.'

'Thanks. Was Danuj's houseboat also facing the same direction as your houseboat?'

'Yes.'

'Then, you would not have had a clear view of the boarding gate of Danuj's boat, right?'

'That's correct,' Jeet answered with certainty. 'I'm not sure where you are heading with these questions, but if your point is that we couldn't see who boarded their houseboat, you are right. We wouldn't have seen a nocturnal visitor to their boat unless he came to the sitting area.'

'That was exactly what I intended to ask, thank you. Their boarding gate wouldn't have been visible even through your binoculars.'

'Correct—' Jeet began but was cut off by his wife.

'Who told you that we had our binoculars?' she asked fiercely.

'Didn't you have them?' Athreya asked, without answering her question.

Jeet's face, he saw, was a picture of confusion. The way Athreya had led up to the question left it unclear whether someone had seen them with their binoculars or not. Consequently, Jeet didn't know whether the correct answer was yes or no. He shut his mouth and let his wife handle the situation.

'What if we did?' Kanika asked.

'Nothing,' Athreya answered evenly. 'I was just curious. You brought them on the cruise the other day.'

'Well, I'm not sure if we had taken them on board that night. Do you remember, Jeet?'

Obediently, her husband shook his head.

Athreya now had no doubts that they had taken their binoculars with them that night. He was also quite sure that they had watched Danuj and Ruhi through the binoculars, especially during their fight. Veni's assessment of Kanika was that she had incurable curiosity about people and couldn't help nosing about their affairs.

'Oh, that's a pity,' he said, watching Kanika's face. 'I was hoping that you might have observed something on Danuj's boat that would be useful to the investigation.'

'Well, they had a long fight for which we didn't need binoculars. Ruhi went into the bedroom after that, leaving Danuj in the sitting area.'

'Time?'

'About 9 p.m.,' Kanika replied before she could stop herself.

That matched with what Ruhi had said. If there were any doubts in Athreya's mind that Kanika had been watching her brother and sister-in-law that night, they were completely dispelled.

'Did you look towards their houseboat after that?' he asked.

'I guess we did,' she answered cagily. 'We had a full bottle to finish. In any case we seldom go to bed before midnight. Usually later.'

'Did you look towards the resort too?'

Kanika shrugged. 'We might have. Who remembers?'

'Did you see anyone up and about?'

'Sahil, for one. He too goes to bed late. Hiran and Pari too—they were going in and out of Papa and Mummy's suite.'

Athreya suppressed a smile. Given the darkness and distance between her houseboat and Mahesh's suite, she couldn't have seen that without binoculars.

'Thank you, Kanika,' he said. 'The fact that you didn't see anyone coming to Danuj's houseboat is important information.'

'But we were not watching all the time,' she countered. 'Only on and off. And we also kept going into our bedroom.'

She stopped as a knock sounded at the door. Anto went and opened it. It was Mahesh.

'Good morning, gentlemen, Kani,' he greeted them. 'Mr Athreya, I wanted to have a word with you. Would you like to join me for breakfast on the lawn?'

'Certainly,' Athreya replied, rising. 'Good morning to you too. I have something to ask you as well.'

'Oh, Athreya,' Kanika called after him as he went to the door, 'You may want to ask Sahil if he visited Danuj's boat that night.'

Fifteen minutes later, Mahesh and Athreya were alone at a table under a tree with a hot breakfast of *dosa*, *idli* and *sevai* laid out between them, along with a jug of orange juice. They talked about how the Gauria family was taking the tragedy. Ruhi had come out of shock but had grown quiet. Mahesh was concerned that she might be heading for depression.

'She is a strong girl,' he said. 'She'll weather the storm. But I'm not sure how she'll react to the accusations that are sure to fly.'

'That she killed Danuj?' Athreya asked.

'Yes. It usually takes far less than this for tongues to wag. I'm sure rumour mills are already at work. I'm glad we are not in Mumbai now.'

Presently, Mahesh finished his sparse breakfast and drew his coffee towards him.

'I have something to tell you, Mr Athreya. I didn't want to say it in front of the inspector. You decide what you need to share with him.'

'Of course.'

'I don't know why, but Manjari blames herself for what happened. She feels that she is responsible for Danuj's death.'

'Responsible?' Athreya asked in surprise. 'She's done nothing, said nothing.'

'I don't understand her reasoning. I wanted to also tell you that Manjari has taken *maun vrat*—a vow of silence. She will not speak now. Another word will not pass her lips until Danuj's killer is identified.'

'But why? She blames herself for his death, but why *maun vrat*?'

'I am an atheist, Mr Athreya. I have never understood why she chooses to do certain things. She hardly sleeps at night and wanders about the house in the wee hours. She has been doing that here at the resort too.'

'Despite taking Restyl?'

Mahesh nodded sadly.

'And during those waking hours, when the world is asleep, her mind sometimes works in peculiar ways. So would yours and mine, should we become as sleep deprived.'

'I feel sorry for her. She is such a pious and gentle lady.'

'Yes… she has lived with this problem for years now. She is very religious too and this *maun vrat* is both a penance and a prayer for her. She believes that her penance will help you find the killer and that her prayers will support Ruhi.'

'Please convey my thanks to her. Now that I think back, I haven't heard her voice even once.'

'She speaks very little nowadays. Prefers to converse with God instead.'

Both men fell silent with their own thoughts. The implication of Manjari taking *maun vrat* was that she wouldn't speak to Athreya or Anto. Was that why she had taken the vow? Did it suggest that she had seen something that night, about which she didn't want to speak? Had she seen a family member in suspicious circumstances?

Athreya recalled a case from his earlier days when an elderly relative of a murdered woman had held back telling the police a vital piece of information. By the time she had decided to speak to the police, the killer had come to suspect that she held incriminating evidence. The unfortunate woman had not survived the next night.

Athreya, therefore, had to think of some way to get her to communicate, even if it was through her husband. However, the immediate priority was to find out about the alprazolam.

'I have something to ask you,' he told Mahesh softly.

'Of course.'

'We found high levels of alprazolam in Danuj's body—high enough to put him to sleep on the sofa where he was found. He was probably fast asleep when the killer came. It made the killer's job easier.'

A soft groan escaped from Mahesh. He looked broken.

'I think the alprazolam came from your wife's stock of Restyl,' Athreya went on. 'I need to find out how it ended up in Danuj's body.'

Mahesh drained his coffee cup and set it down.

'You are probably right,' he said in a strangely strangled voice. 'Manjari's stock is the one source of alprazolam here. But I have no clue how the drug ended up in Danuj's body. I wish I knew.'

'Okay,' Athreya persisted. 'What can you tell me about the fatal night?'

Mahesh let out a long breath and stayed silent for a moment.

'The night when Danuj died was a difficult and peculiar one, Mr Athreya,' he said haltingly. 'All of us were on the edge. We guessed that something was simmering and were afraid of what might happen. The news that Kishan was around didn't help, and Sahil turning up at our resort only further deepened our anxiety. It felt as if things were inexorably converging towards something unpleasant.

'Manjari is very sensitive to these unspoken undercurrents and quickly perceives things that others miss. She expressed her fears to me privately, but she too couldn't say what specifically had made her anxious. Perhaps, it was something in Danuj's behaviour that she had noticed, which made her fear that he was on some sort of a reckless warpath.'

'I understand the feeling. It's a kind of premonition.'

'Correct. I wonder if her anxiety made her do something… unfortunate.'

'Like what?' Athreya asked softly.

'I don't know, Mr Athreya. And there's no point in speculating either. But what I can tell you is that Manjari, for some reason known only to her, is blaming herself for Danuj's death.'

'You said you don't know why.'

Mahesh nodded silently.

Athreya too fell silent, contemplating the old man's lined and sorrowful face. His instinct suggested that there was a strong reason behind Manjari's decision to take *maun vrat*. And the reason probably had little to do with religion.

12

Athreya was returning to the temporary office when he saw Sahil at a distance and hailed him. The younger man came at once and Athreya saw that he was as neatly turned out as he had been the previous day. He wore a simple pair of jeans and a T-shirt of a muted colour. The one difference today was that he was wearing flip-flops instead of the shoes he had been wearing the previous day.

'Slippers today?' Athreya asked after the pleasantries.

'My shoes are wet,' Sahil answered with a smile.

No sooner had he uttered this than his smile froze. Wariness brightened his eyes. Instinctively, Athreya knew why—there was an implication from his shoes being wet, especially when the housekeeping staff hadn't found any wet clothes in his room.

'I need to speak to you, Sahil,' Athreya said softly. 'Shall we walk to the end of the lawn so that we are not overheard?'

Sahil nodded and fell in step with him. When they reached the railing that separated the lawn from the lake, Athreya turned to him.

'You haven't told me everything, have you, Sahil?' he asked mildly.

'Haven't I?' Sahil asked. 'What have I not told you?'

'How you got your shoes wet, for instance!' Athreya chuckled. He decided to make a calculated guess. 'The crude wooden boats in these parts often have a few inches of standing water in their hulls. The unwary sometimes step into it, especially at night.'

Sahil blanched. Athreya had hit the mark.

'But, seriously,' Athreya went on, 'I think you know what I am talking about. You were trying to hire a boat the night Danuj died. The police will soon have the details—they have gone to talk to the boat owner. It's probably best that you tell me now if you visited Danuj that night.'

Sahil remained silent, staring out over the water and staying still. His hands were in his pockets and his face gave nothing away. Athreya knew that he was weighing his options. After an extended pause, Sahil let out a long breath.

'All right,' he said. 'I have not told you everything. Maybe, I should have, but I was not sure as things were moving so fast. I guess it's bound to come out once the police make enquiries.' He glanced at Athreya. 'Do you think the inspector would have found it out on his own? Without your help?'

'Believe me, he would have. Underestimate him at your own peril.'

'Right!' Sahil removed his hands from his pockets and rested them on the railing as he leaned forward. 'Let me pick up where I left off in our last conversation. I said that Danuj had messaged me to come to his boat at 11 p.m. but had told me to wait for a confirmation. I further said I did not receive another message confirming the appointment.

'Technically, that is correct—he didn't send me another text message. However, he called me from Ruhi's phone a little after 9 p.m. I thought it was Ruhi calling and eagerly answered the call. But it was Danuj, playing a cheap trick on me. After having a laugh at my expense, he asked me to come to the houseboat at 11 p.m.'

'Did he say why?'

'Briefly. He indicated Ruhi might be willing for a settlement along the lines of his proposal to me. He wanted us to finalize the terms.'

'When he said "us", did he include Ruhi?'

'That was unclear. When I asked, he said that we would discuss it in person on the houseboat. However, he did imply that Ruhi was supporting the proposal.'

'Was she?'

'I didn't believe him. I didn't think that she would ever agree to something so demeaning.'

'In that case, why did you decide to go to the houseboat? I presume you did go.'

Sahil stood erect and turned to face Athreya.

'Because I was curious,' he said. 'Because I had already come all the way from Mumbai to Kumarakom. Because I had already arranged for a boat to ferry me. Because Kishan was threatening to kill Ruhi.'

'Why would you believe anything Danuj said? You knew him to be a liar.'

Sahil let out a long breath.

'Well… when Ruhi's life was at stake, I couldn't just ignore what Danuj said—even if there was a high chance that was lying. This was too serious a matter to ignore.'

'Okay. Go on.'

'In any case, I had come here all the way from Mumbai to meet him, and I was not going to back out at the last moment.'

'Were you not afraid that he might try something funny?'

'What if he did? I could handle it.'

'Did you go armed?'

'Armed!' Sahil seemed to find the suggestion amusing. 'Of course not. Danuj was not a particularly strong guy. And he was terrified of pain. When we were growing up, I could always get the better of him.'

'Okay. What did you do after you received his call?'

'I called the boat owner and told him to come to the pier a little short of 11 p.m. I then alternated between walking around the lawn and sitting in my room. I was understandably nervous. Just before 11, I got into the boat and, like a fool, got my shoes soaking wet. Then, I went to the houseboat.'

'What happened there?'

'Danuj was in a very good mood. He welcomed me heartily, opened the gate for me to board, gave me a hand and pulled me up, and even offered me a drink. It was as if we were the best of friends like before.'

'And your boat? Did it stay there?'

'Yes. I told the boatman who ferried me to wait till I was ready to return.'

'What then?'

Sahil turned back to face the lake and leaned on his elbows, which he placed on the railing.

'It was a bizarre meeting, Mr Athreya,' he said softly. 'Danuj seemed to be in a world of his own and quite removed from reality. He seemed absolutely convinced that Ruhi and I had an affair going. He believed that we were desperate to get together and it was only he—Danuj—who was standing in the way. Where he got this notion, I have no idea. But he seemed certain that such was the case.'

'Was it?'

'No. Not at all. I've said that to you before, Mr Athreya.' Sahil paused with a hint of annoyance and a trace of resignation on his face. He let a moment or two pass before resuming. 'By the way, he tried to bring Ruhi into the conversation.'

'But I thought she was in the bedroom?'

'She was, but Danuj talked to her through the closed door and said that I had come to meet them. It was time, he added, that the three of us sat down and sorted things out. He had

178

no objection to the divorce if certain conditions were met. The three of us meeting face to face on the boat was supposed to be the culmination of this elaborate drama Danuj had enacted.'

'What did she say to that?'

'Nothing. Absolutely nothing. She merely clicked the latch and locked the door from inside. She neither uttered a word nor made any other sound. She might as well have not been there, except for the clicking of the latch.'

'But Danuj went on with his plan?'

'He was sure that she was listening to every word and continued with the little speech he had prepared. He made it appear that he was doing us a favour. Given that I was his childhood bosom friend and that Ruhi was no longer interested in him, he was willing to step aside, he said. Step aside so that the two people closest to him could get together and be happy. All he wanted in return were a few small things.'

'Like 35 crores?' Athreya asked.

'Correct. But he had told me earlier—just as I boarded the houseboat—that the 35-crore payment was only between the two of us—between two men of the world. Being a woman, he said, Ruhi would find it insulting that money was involved. It was best to leave her out of it. She was not to know of the monetary angle. She would, of course, have to sign up to the other conditions like waiving alimony and sharing her Gauria inheritance with him. Minor paperwork, Danuj called it.'

'Didn't Ruhi react to that?'

'No. She maintained absolute silence. I admire her.'

'Tell me, Sahil. Were you willing to pay the 35 crores?'

'Honestly, sir, I was willing to *consider* it as a last resort if it freed Ruhi from her nightmare and lifted Kishan's threat from her head. But it's a heck of a lot of money. In any case, I didn't think Ruhi would want me to do it. Danuj might stoop to putting his wife up for sale, but she was not a commodity to be bought and sold.'

'Then why did Danuj propose such a thing?'

'He thought it would work because he was convinced that Ruhi and I were having an affair and were dying to get together. You see, Danuj had taken to measuring everything in monetary terms—just as Kanika does. He believed that everything had a price. It was only a matter of discovering it. Towards the end of the meeting, he began negotiating and dropping his ask from 35 crores to 30 and then to 25.'

'And Ruhi was listening all the while?'

'I don't know. He conducted the negotiation in an undertone. But it was a small boat.'

A houseboat went past them at a distance. Both men gazed at it as it passed, thinking about their own entanglement with another houseboat.

'What then?' Athreya prompted.

'After talking past each other for fifteen minutes, it was clear that it was going nowhere. Meanwhile, seeing his ill-conceived plan fall through, he was turning nasty and abusive. I decided it was time to go even though I feared for Ruhi's safety. I did feel a little guilty, but I really couldn't interfere between husband and wife.'

'Wasn't Danuj getting sleepy?'

Sahil looked up in surprise. 'How did you guess? He kept stifling yawns and seemed low on energy. He went through with the meeting mostly on willpower, which he had a lot of.'

'Did he have a dagger with him?'

'Yes, a brown-and-gold one. He was fiddling with it all the time.'

'Did you notice anything else in the sitting area?'

'It was dark. So I couldn't see much. But I did see that he had two phones, probably his and Ruhi's. I thought I also saw a file on the chair, under the phones.'

'Colour?'

'Blue.'

So, if Sahil was speaking the truth, someone had boarded the houseboat *after* he left and had taken the papers from the file. That would have caused the houseboat to rock twice more. Athreya filed that thought away.

'And then?' he asked.

'I left the houseboat. He was getting into a foul mood by then and was sulking on the sofa. I opened the gate and got down into the boat I had come in.'

'Time?'

'Maybe 11:15 to 11:20 p.m. Can't be absolutely sure, but I don't think I was on the houseboat for more than fifteen to twenty minutes.'

'Were the phones and the file there when you left?' Athreya asked.

Sahil nodded.

'Was the file open or closed?'

'Closed. There were papers in it—I could make that out by the thickness of the file. I assumed that they were the papers Danuj hoped Ruhi and I would sign.'

'Why did you assume that?'

'When Danuj had talked about our signing an agreement earlier, he had gestured towards the file. That's why I thought that the papers to be signed were in it.'

'But you don't know that for sure?'

'There was no way to be sure short of actually reading the papers.'

'Fair enough. Tell me, did the houseboat rock when you got off it?'

'Oh, yes. It had rocked when I had boarded it as well. Why?'

'Just wondering. Then you returned to the resort?'

'That's right. The boatman who ferried me will bear witness, I'm sure. I paid him and gave him a tip once I got off at the resort pier. I can give you the boat owner's number.'

'Was Danuj alive when you left?'

'Of course! The boatman saw him too. Danuj latched the boarding gate after I disembarked.'

'Now, think carefully and answer me, Sahil. Was anyone other than the boatman and Danuj watching?'

'Well,' Sahil frowned as he tried to recall. 'There was the other houseboat, you know—the one hired by Kanika and Jeet. I saw them walking about in their sitting area. Theirs was a larger and a fancier boat, unlike Danuj's. I heard their drunken voices too, especially Kanika's high-pitched laughter. They seemed to be having a good time. They sounded sloshed.'

'Was anyone watching from the resort or elsewhere on the shore?'

'I can't say, Mr Athreya. It was dark. All I can say is that I didn't see anyone.'

'One last thing—I will have to speak to Ruhi about our conversation. I need her corroboration.'

'Certainly! Knowing her, she's probably not told you about my being on the houseboat that night.'

'Why do you think that?' Athreya was curious. Sahil, of course, was right. 'After all, her husband was murdered that night. In all likelihood by someone who boarded their boat.'

'Loyalty to an old friend, perhaps? Or because she hasn't had the time to think things through. It's complex, Mr Athreya. We are very good friends, but I don't think she has feelings towards me as I have towards her. But she wishes me well.'

·   ·   ·

After his chat with Sahil, Athreya went to find Ruhi. On discovering that her dagger had not caused the fatal wound, Inspector Anto had relaxed the restrictions on her. Like the other members of the family, she too could move about the resort freely, but not leave it. As Athreya had expected, he found her in Mahesh's suite in Veni's company. Mahesh and Manjari were there as well. Ruhi was looking much better than the previous day.

'Feeling better?' Athreya asked her.

Ruhi nodded. 'I managed to get some sleep. The inspector allowed Pari *Bhabi* to be with me last night. It was such a relief, Uncle!'

'Hari,' Veni said softly. Her face was uncharacteristically worried. 'There is something I need to tell you: I was followed by a stranger on my way here from Kurup's house today.'

'Man or woman?' Athreya asked, his head snapping to her. He was acutely aware that she and Kurup's family were soft targets for anyone wishing to disrupt the investigation.

'Man. He looked like the one we saw last night, watching the house. But I can't be sure that it was the same man. He was tall and well-built and didn't look like a local.'

'I'll inform Anto about him. I'll also ask for an escort when we move between here and Kurup's house.'

'Would you like to stay here for a couple of days?' Mahesh asked. 'That would make things easier for you both, and it's probably safer too. Don't worry about the expense. With the room rates being so low, one more room won't make much difference. I'll ask them to give you the room next to this suite.'

Athreya glanced at Veni, who nodded.

'Okay,' Athreya said, turning to Mahesh. 'We'll accept your offer. Thanks very much. We'll go shortly and bring enough of our stuff to last a few days.'

'Excellent. That's settled, then. However, please do be careful. We don't want any harm coming to you.'

Silence descended on the group. After a few long moments, Ruhi spoke in a small voice.

'Uncle,' she said hesitatingly. 'I saw you with Sahil just now. Did he…'

She left the sentence unfinished, but Athreya knew what she was referring to.

'Yes, Ruhi, he did. Would you like to talk in private?'

She shook her head. 'No. I'd rather say it in front of Papa and Mummy. He told you that he came to the houseboat that night?'

Athreya nodded and waited for her to tell it in her own way, without his prompting. Mahesh and Manjari turned to her as well.

'What a mess,' she said, staring unseeingly at the large Tanjore painting on the wall that depicted deities and Kamdhenu, the divine cow from Hindu mythology. 'I held back talking about it yesterday because I wanted to sort out my thoughts first. I decided last night that I should tell you about Sahil's visit. There is nothing to hide, but I just wanted to be sure.'

'Understandable, Ruhi,' Athreya said and sat back.

'It was just as I had told you earlier,' she began. 'I went into the bedroom at about 9 p.m. and cried. I took the Restyl at 10-ish and tried to go to bed. It was a nightmarish night despite the Restyl, and I kept drifting in and out of sleep.

'At about 11 p.m., I felt the boat rock, but paid no attention to it. My brain was sluggish due to the drug, and I didn't realize the implication of the rocking. In fact, it was only the next day that I grasped its significance—that too, only when you pointed it out. Looking back, I wish I had paid more attention to it, especially to the rockings that happened after Sahil left. But I'm getting ahead of myself.

'So, I heard a thump and some creaking at about 11 p.m., and felt the houseboat rock. The next moment, I heard Danuj's voice, welcoming someone who had boarded. It was only after a minute and some overheard conversation that I realized the visitor was Sahil.

'With my mind being slow, I was confused. But I was curious too. I got up silently, switched off the air conditioner so that I could hear better and went to the door to listen. Imagine my surprise when Danuj called my name as if he knew that I was standing inside the door! He said that Sahil had come to talk to us and insisted it was high time the three of us sat down and sorted things out. He said that we were all adults who understood the realities of life, whatever that meant.'

'He spoke from outside the room?' Athreya asked. 'Did he try to open the door?'

'He spoke from outside. The door was hardly soundproof. He knew very well that I could hear every word. As he continued talking, it dawned on me that he really was convinced that Sahil and I were having an affair. That's why I wanted the divorce, he thought. He said that he knew that the two us wanted to get married.

'To facilitate that, Danuj explained, he would stand aside—he wanted his best two friends to be happy again. However, he had a few conditions that needed to be met, and that's what we needed to discuss and sort out. That's why Sahil had come.'

'What was your reaction to that?'

'I was confused and afraid. I didn't know if Danuj was playing some trick. As a precaution I engaged the latch on the door and locked it.'

'What did you say to Danuj?'

'Nothing. I thought it best to remain silent. Danuj was completely off the mark about Sahil and me having an affair. There wasn't even an iota of truth in it. But why Danuj decided to believe it, I don't know. And as far as my marrying Sahil, I have never had such thoughts. He is a very dear friend, but I had—and have—no such feelings towards him.'

'Does he have feelings towards you?' Athreya asked gently.

'I don't think so, although Kanika likes to believe that he does,' she replied. 'We are close friends and professional colleagues. He is the producer of several of my films and keeps his distance. He is a thorough gentleman.'

Athreya thought it best not to say anything. Out of the corner of his eye, he saw Veni watching him. He didn't respond in any way and let Ruhi continue her narrative.

'It was a bizarre and humiliating twenty minutes during which Danuj seemed to be living in his own alternate reality. How Sahil put up with all that nonsense Danuj was spouting is beyond me. I presume he did it for me. At the end of it, I was left more confused than ever.'

'But you remained silent? You didn't want to set right Danuj's misconceptions?'

'What was the use, Uncle?' Ruhi asked. 'He wouldn't listen. And as Sahil was there outside the door, I decided not to go out. My lawyer has said, very clearly, I should not meet Sahil at all. So I was also wondering if this was some ploy of Danuj to make me meet Sahil face to face. That would strengthen his case. Anyway, Sahil left at 11:20 p.m.—'

'You looked at the clock?' Athreya cut in.

'Yes, I looked at my watch when I heard the boarding gate creak. An instant later, I felt the boat rock again. Danuj then said something nasty and shut the gate.'

'And then?'

'Danuj came to the bedroom door and called me names through the door. He then lit a cigarette and went away. A few minutes later, I heard him talk on the phone.'

'To whom?'

186

'I don't know. I couldn't make out what he was saying. By then, I had got back into bed and had switched on the air conditioner. Its noise made it difficult for me to hear him. I just ignored him and tried to go to sleep.'

'Did you go to sleep?'

'Not right away, but I must have drifted off into troubled sleep in a little while—perhaps fifteen minutes to half an hour.'

'Did you hear or feel anything after that?'

'Yes… like I said earlier, I felt the boat rock a few times. Unfortunately, I don't know when or how many times, even though my sleep was shallow and disturbed.'

'Okay, Ruhi,' Athreya said. 'It's good that you told me this of your own accord. Anything else?'

Ruhi shook her head. 'Can't think of anything.'

'Do you know what Danuj's proposal was?'

She nodded and repeated the proposal except the part about Sahil paying 35 crores. Mahesh, who had been listening silently so far, let out an inarticulate rumble that Ruhi seemed to understand.

'Yes, Papa,' she said. 'He wanted me to sign a paper to that effect. Now that I think of it, the blue file might have contained the papers he wanted Sahil and me to sign.'

'Good lord!' Mahesh exclaimed, clearly alarmed. 'And now, somebody else has those papers. I hope it doesn't leak to the press.'

'Ruhi,' Athreya asked slowly, watching the young actress's face. 'Are you aware that Danuj had asked Sahil to pay him 35 crores as a part of the deal? For him to sign the divorce papers?'

'What!' Ruhi's head snapped to him even as he heard Mahesh suck in his breath. 'Is that true, Uncle? That is abominable even by his standards.'

'Yes, it's true. He didn't want you to know, as you would have stopped it.'

'Of course I would have stopped it!' Ruhi's eyes blazed. 'What am I? Some cow to be bought and sold?'

'Sometimes I wonder,' Mahesh whispered in puzzlement, 'if Danuj was in his right senses.'

13

When Athreya walked out of the suite, he discreetly gestured to Veni to follow him. Once outside, they went to the railing at the lawn's edge.

'I need to consult the Bollywood encyclopaedia in your head,' he said with a smile. 'What can you tell me about the Gauria family and the others here from Bollywood?'

'I thought you'd never ask!' she shot back at him. 'What took you so long?'

'Veni, my dear, you have strong views on most matters. I didn't want to be influenced by them right at the start. I wanted to talk to everyone first.'

'Hmpf!' she snorted. '"Strong views," eh? Don't you—'

'Don't get upset, Veni. You know how much I value your opinion. Now tell me. Please.'

'Okay.' She calmed down as quickly as she had got her back up. 'The Gauria family... they are one of the top Bollywood families. Third generation now, I think. Mahesh's father was a producer-director too but not as successful as Mahesh has been. All of them live in the same house—a large one, by Mumbai standards—as a joint family. Three generations—including Hiran's and Kanika's children—live together under the same roof and eat at the same dining table.

'There is huge respect for Maheshji, as he is called in the film industry. He is a doyen of Bollywood. He is tough but fair, and he drives a hard bargain. He has a nose for talent and has been instrumental in bringing up several new stars. Because of that, he enjoys tremendous goodwill all around. Of course, he is very rich, thanks to many of his films becoming box office hits.'

'Does he continue to make films at this age?' Athreya asked.

'Not actively. But he does fund a few and co-invests in projects that he believes are worthy. As a result, he still makes money.

'The same cannot be said of his sons. Hiran has made some successful films but hasn't had a blockbuster, a runaway box-office success. He is considered a cautious producer who doesn't waste money. He avoids high-budget films and stays away from expensive stars. He prefers to make films with a good story and a message. While he too has lost money, it's nothing compared to what Danuj has lost. None of Danuj's projects has succeeded. Not one!'

'Then, Danuj must be losing a lot of money.'

'Oh, yes! Heaps of Gauria money, which, I'm sure, has irked Kanika and Hiran. Each time Danuj made a dud, the family lost dozens of crores.'

'According to Bhagya,' Athreya said, 'he ran a casting couch and didn't pick his actresses based on their acting abilities. Is that true?'

'Probably. His films often featured new actresses who didn't do a good job. Most of them weren't seen again on-screen.'

'Does that go for Bhagya too?'

'Bhagya can act, you know. She may not be brilliant, but she clearly passes the bar. She did a decent job in some support roles she was given. I read somewhere that she went to a film school or acting academy.'

'Really?'

'Yes. Her parents wanted her to do nursing. After training for six months, she quit and went to learn acting. She was one of those thousands of starry-eyed hopefuls who come to Mumbai every year, attracted by Bollywood's glitz and glamour. She got a break in TV, where she did well and caught the eye of a Bollywood producer. Although I haven't watched her first film, I believe she gave a good account of herself.'

'Then, she has talent?'

'I'd say so. She could have done better but for her misfortune.'

'What happened?'

'For one, she got into a public spat with Danuj, just as Hiran said. It showed both of them in a bad light. She made accusations about the casting couch and said things that were probably true. But many in the industry don't like such things to be made public, especially by an insider, which Bhagya is. They don't like their dirty linen washed in public.

'In retaliation, Danuj said that he wouldn't work with anyone who gave Bhagya a role. Being from the Gauria family, his threat carried weight, at least then. Because of a combination of these two reasons, Bhagya stopped getting any substantial roles.'

'No wonder she is wild!' Athreya said.

'Yes, but something else happened that actually broke her—her younger sister committed suicide. The sister was known to be troubled, but it was nevertheless a huge shock. Her death broke Bhagya completely and she ended up needing psychiatric help.'

'She still is pretty volatile,' Athreya observed. 'Probably a tad unstable too. She flies off the handle at the slightest provocation. Anyway, go on. What happened then?'

'That's when Maheshji stepped in and helped her,' Veni continued. 'He requested people in the industry to support her during her crisis, and he gave her a role in one of the projects he had co-invested in. He also got Hiran to give her a role in one of his more successful films—a horror movie in which Bhagya played a vengeful ghost. She did a pretty good job. That reopened the doors for her, and she started getting small roles. Given her figure and dancing ability, several of them turned out to be item numbers.'

'I'm sure she is not satisfied with that.'

'Correct. Her career never really recovered, and it's all thanks to Danuj.'

'That's useful, Veni, thanks,' Athreya said. 'What do you know about Kishan?'

'Nothing,' she replied, shaking her head. 'I'd never heard of him until we came here. But that's not surprising as he is in the background—fixing and arranging matters. The media doesn't cover such people.'

'There is something between Kishan and Bhagya... some deeper relationship. We need to find out what it is.'

'Why do you say so?'

'Gut feel, I guess. What can you tell me about Sahil?'

'Very successful producer. One of the best we have now. He cut his teeth working with Maheshji. He is considered top-notch.'

'Then, he should be able to afford the 35 crores Danuj demanded, right?'

'I guess so. But would he really pay up and become a part of the abominable scheme?' She turned her head at a movement from a resort building. 'Hello? What's up?'

A door had suddenly flown open and Anto was hurrying out of the temporary office. Seeing Athreya and Veni, the inspector hastened to them across the lawn, taking long strides. When he came close, he stopped to bow theatrically to Veni.

'Ah, good morning, madam!' he said. 'Good morning, good morning. Trust you are well?'

'Very well, thank you, Inspector,' she replied with her Malayali accent in evidence. 'You seem to be in a hurry?'

'Yes, yes! I have a piece of good news for Mr Aadhreiah.' He turned to the investigator and went on as if he had won the lottery. 'You were right, sir—bang on! We found a small coracle floating on the lake south-west of here. The wind and waves had taken it quite some distance away. Unless we were looking for it, we wouldn't have connected it to the case.'

'Excellent, Anto!' Athreya praised. 'You are working wonders!'

'The most interesting thing is this: a rope was attached to the coracle! The rope is exactly like the piece we found tied to the railing of the houseboat.'

'And the end of the rope?' Athreya asked. 'Was it cleanly cut?'

'Yes! With a sharp blade. There is also a corresponding blood-stain. There is no doubt that it is the other half of the rope that was tied to the houseboat's railing.'

It took a little over an hour for Veni and Athreya to take a police vehicle to Kurup's house and bring their personal belongings to the resort and check in. After moving into their room, they went over to Mahesh's suite a little short of lunchtime, where they were in for a surprise. In the suite was Bhagya, dressed conservatively in a *salwar* set and commiserating with Mahesh, Hiran and Pari. It was clear that they knew each other well. Bhagya rose as they entered and did a *namaste* to Veni and Athreya.

Veni, who was meeting Bhagya for the first time, was a little taken aback by the demure impression the younger woman conveyed. There wasn't the slightest suggestion of an item girl or a jilted lover. Nor was there any hint that she could be unstable and volatile. She seemed entirely in control of herself, and was a completely different person from the one Athreya had described. It appeared that she had now come to pay her respects to the bereaved family.

Which was the real Bhagya, Veni wondered. This modest, self-possessed woman in the suite, or the volatile woman who had repeatedly flown off the handle while talking to Athreya? Bhagya showed no signs of the illness that required her to see a psychiatrist. But come to think of it, Veni mused, why would a

193

mental condition always be more visible than a physical illness like, say, diabetes or hypertension? At the same time, she also knew that the mood of some psychiatric patients could swing considerably—sometimes from one extreme to another. It was best not to make any judgements.

Wondering what was going through her husband's mind, Veni glanced at him. Athreya was smiling amiably at Bhagya after returning her *namaste* and he showed no sign of resentment from the earlier meeting. Bhagya, in turn, seemed to appreciate it. Trust Hari to win her over!

Veni remained content watching the interactions as Mahesh and Pari enquired about Bhagya's well-being with concern that seemed genuine. From her replies, it appeared that her career hadn't really recovered from the setbacks despite the help from Mahesh and Hiran, for which she was visibly grateful. To Veni, it seemed that Bhagya was suppressing bitterness as she spoke.

Presently, Mahesh changed the topic and asked, 'Would you like to join us for lunch, Bhagya? You've come at the right time.'

'No, Maheshji, thank you,' Bhagya replied. 'I'll be meeting Sahil Sir now. I told him that I'll hop over after seeing you all.'

'You can meet him after lunch,' Pari suggested with genuine warmth.

'I'll join you tomorrow or something, *Didi*,' Bhagya said. 'Sahil will be waiting for me. I don't want to delay him.'

'As you wish,' Pari replied, smiling sweetly at Bhagya. 'It's never a good idea to keep your producer waiting!'

A round of restrained smiles greeted Pari's words, making Veni think about how little grief had followed Danuj's death. Manjari seemed to be the only one to have shed copious tears. Veni recalled Bhagya's words to Athreya: *'Nobody other than his mother will grieve for Danuj. You don't have to look far to find his killer.'*

Veni's thoughts were interrupted by Bhagya, Pari and Hiran rising. Bhagya touched Mahesh's and Manjari's feet, did a round of *namastes* and left the room with enviable grace. Veni looked around the room silently. Yes, there was a disturbing lack of grief among the Gaurias, except for Manjari, and possibly Mahesh.

Veni turned quietly and left the room.

Five minutes later, they were the only people in the dining room. Ruhi and Manjari had joined them and were sitting together. Veni noticed that the family had dropped the habit of sitting in a fixed order at the dining table with Mahesh at the head. She also noted the absence of Kanika and Jeet but didn't comment on it.

'What's the relationship between Bhagya and Kishan?' she heard Athreya asking Hiran after a waiter had served soup.

'None that I know of,' Hiran replied. 'I was rather surprised to see her here with him. Any idea, Pari?'

'No.' Pari shook her head. 'I was surprised too. Kishan is an eminently avoidable character.'

'Surely, it's not hard to guess, *Beta*,' Mahesh interposed. 'She came here to turn the screws on Danuj. She and Kishan must have joined forces solely for that purpose—Kishan to recover his money and Bhagya to teach Danuj a lesson.'

Pari shook her head sadly. 'Not good, Papa. It's not right for a girl like her to associate with a gangster. I wish she hadn't done that.'

'Too late for that, Pari,' Mahesh replied. 'That's water under the bridge. You do know that Bhagya had resolved to make Danuj's life hell, don't you? She was following through on that promise.'

Something stirred in Veni on hearing that.

'In that case,' she asked, 'why were all of you even talking to her? After all, she was coming after one of the Gaurias.'

'It's a complex situation, Veni,' Mahesh answered wearily. 'As I said earlier, Danuj wronged her. Wronged her badly. We are trying to restore some balance by being kind to her. She is impulsive, perhaps, but not a bad sort. And she's been through a very difficult time because of Danuj. We are trying to compensate for what he did to her.'

'Then as far as you know,' Athreya asked, 'there is no real relationship between her and Kishan? They are just being opportunistic?'

'I would be surprised if there is an amorous or romantic relationship,' Hiran said slowly, as he paused drinking his soup. 'She isn't that kind of a woman.'

'I agree,' Pari added empathically. 'I feel sorry for her that she had found it necessary to associate with someone like Kishan. I hope that's over now. Nothing good can come out of it. I'd like to see her return to Mumbai and pick up the threads of her life. She is still young. I'm willing to help her.'

'I'm told that Bhagya can be erratic and, frankly, quite explosive,' Veni said. 'Especially after her nervous breakdown. She was pretty volatile when she met Hari yesterday—flew off the handle a couple of times and eventually walked out of the conversation. However, she seemed perfectly normal today.'

'Hers is a manic disorder,' Hiran explained. 'It makes her swing from one extreme to another. She can be very agreeable and sweet one day, and completely frenzied and a bit irrational the next day. Poor girl, she wasn't like this earlier.'

They fell silent and turned their attention to the food that had just arrived at their table. The only sounds were that of spoons and forks.

'Isn't Kanika joining us for lunch?' Athreya asked, looking up suddenly as if he had just realized her absence.

'She sent word that she isn't feeling very well,' Mahesh replied. 'They'll have lunch in their room.'

'Nothing serious, I hope. She was fine this morning.'

'I hope not. We'll know shortly. I've requested the resort doctor take a look at her.'

Watching the conversation, Veni saw Athreya become thoughtful and distracted. His right index finger twitched as if it wanted to be released to start tracing its indecipherable words. But Athreya firmly picked up his spoon and began doing justice to the lunch.

A few minutes later, when Veni was enjoying her coconut rice and *mor kozhambu*, the resort doctor appeared with news about Kanika.

'Nothing to worry about,' he told Mahesh. 'She's just a little tired.'

'Nothing serious, I hope?' Mahesh asked.

'No, no. She's actually quite fine—no temperature, body pain, phlegm or cough. I wouldn't have known that she was under the weather had you not told me. Both of them were quite active, as far as I could see.'

'Good.' Mahesh nodded. 'Thank you, Doctor. Have you pre-scribed anything?'

'Nothing other than rest. I suspect that her brother's death is affecting her. She is visibly anxious and high-strung. She just needs to rest and calm down. Good afternoon.'

Veni could see that the doctor was not convinced about what he had said. Kanika had been all chirpy and energetic just that morning. Her brother's death didn't seem to have bothered her then. Why did it suddenly begin affecting her? Veni decided to keep her thoughts to herself.

'Thank you, Doctor,' Hiran and Pari said in unison, as the doctor turned to go.

When Veni brought her gaze back to her husband, she was surprised to see an intent look on his face. It was as if something had occurred to him. Simultaneously, his right index finger, which had been busy with his spoon a few seconds ago, was furiously tracing something on the table. Even as she watched, Athreya snapped out of the trance and picked up the cutlery with a hint of a smile.

Her gaze lingered on him as she wondered what had struck him. The conversation with the doctor seemed quite unremarkable to her. The rest of the lunch proceeded normally, and at the end of it, all of them returned to their respective rooms. Within a minute, a knock sounded on the door, and Veni went to answer it. Anto and Saju stood outside, wanting to meet Athreya. Veni ushered them in.

'Ah! Thanks for coming, Doctor,' Athreya greeted them. 'I believe Kanika is under the weather and the resort doctor has seen her. I just wanted a second opinion. Would you mind checking her out?'

'Sure,' Saju replied. 'Anything specific you need me to look out for?'

'I don't want to bias you. Just give me your impressions. The inspector can go with you and give his opinion too.'

The two men turned to leave the room.

'Oh, Doctor,' Athreya called after them. 'Just check Jeet too.'

Athreya sat down on the easy chair and waited patiently, deep in thought. Fifteen minutes later, a knock sounded again. Saju and Anto had returned. Veni ushered them to chairs and sat down on the bed.

'I met the resort doctor first,' Saju began. 'His opinion is that there is nothing wrong with Kanika. She was just overly anxious and rather tense.'

'High-strung was how he put it,' Athreya said.

'Yes. That's my opinion too. Everything is normal except her pulse rate.'

'And Jeet?'

'His pulse rate is high too.'

'So nothing is really wrong with either of them. Could they be faking illness, Doctor?'

Saju thought for a moment, blinked, removed his glasses to polish them and nodded.

'Could be,' he said. 'They could be faking it. But why is the pulse rate high?'

Athreya turned to the inspector. 'What's your reading, Anto?'

'They are frightened, Mr Aadhreiah,' the policeman replied at once. 'Spooked. That's why their hearts are beating fast.'

'You are a gem, Anto!' Athreya enthused. 'That's what I think too. Consider this: they were perfectly fine at 9 a.m. this morning—a mere four hours ago. She came to pump you for information. If I remember right, she was very pleased with herself; looked like a satiated cat, in fact. Yet they are spooked now.'

'Yes, Mr Aadhreiah. Something happened after that discussion. Something that has frightened them enough to make them lock themselves up in their room. I wonder what.'

'You remember the conversation you and I had yesterday, Anto? On the houseboat? I had talked about how little physical evidence we have in the case. I had feared that if the murderer remained content with killing Danuj, we might never crack this case.'

'I remember!' Anto sat up. 'You had said that murderers sometimes get overconfident after a successful murder.'

'Correct! I wonder if the murderer in this case is starting to overreach.'

'What's that got to do with Kanika and Jeet being frightened?' Veni asked.

'We'll find out soon enough. Eh, Anto?'

'I hope so, sir. I have the same question in my mind... the one madam asked now. I don't have the answer.'

Athreya rose and stretched. His face seemed clear and there was no sign of uncertainty.

'I think I'll go and have a chat with Kanika and Jeet.'

14

Kanika and Jeet's room was the last one at the end of the wing and was closest to the lake. Having windows in three of the four walls, it was bright and airy. But the mood inside was not as sunny when Jeet guardedly opened the door at Athreya's knock. Kanika's face, which was visible over Jeet's shoulder, was a picture of anxiety.

'Can I come in?' Athreya asked gently. 'I'd like to help you if I can.'

Having no alternative, Jeet stepped back and let him enter. Kanika's eyes followed him warily as he went to the chair Jeet indicated. She seemed to have stopped pacing the room when Athreya knocked. Looking at her, Athreya agreed with the doctors that she was tense but not tired. In fact, she seemed to be full of restless energy.

'I've just spoken to the doctors,' he said, as he took his seat. 'The good news is that there is absolutely no sign of any infection. In fact, they say that both of you are quite well, except for an elevated pulse rate. You father is quite relieved.'

Kanika nodded absently and continued watching him as if she was waiting for him to get to the point. Athreya obliged.

'Both of you were fit and cheerful when we met last about four hours ago,' he said in a measured fashion. 'Something has happened since then that has made you feel unwell. Would you like to talk to about it?'

Kanika averted her gaze even as Jeet looked to her for guidance. She probably hadn't expected such a direct approach by Athreya. Silence dragged for a few seconds as she was unable to come up with a response.

At length, she mumbled, 'There's nothing to talk about.'

She sat on the bed and stared at the wall, saying nothing further. The silence lengthened uncomfortably.

'I realize that you are in a difficult position,' Athreya said, breaking it. 'Sometimes, talking to someone about your predicament can help in finding a way out of it. I'm happy to listen if you wish to talk. Alternatively, you could talk to your father or brother.'

She threw him a quick glance. There was no animosity in it or resentment. Just curiosity and much wariness. The arrogance that had earlier characterized her was absent as well. She quickly averted her eyes and shook her head. Meanwhile, Jeet had chosen to remain on his feet, watching her with concern from the other side of the double bed.

'There is nothing to talk about,' she mumbled again. 'You are mistaken.'

'Fair enough,' Athreya conceded. 'I won't press you. But my offer stands. If you change your mind and want to talk to me, you would be most welcome. I'll be staying here at the resort for a few days at your father's request. I'm just four doors away, next to your father's suite.'

This time, she looked at him for longer with a searching gaze. Athreya could tell that she was confused and uncertain. And afraid. He didn't want to confront her with his suspicions yet. Time, he knew, would soften her stance. Unless she had killed her brother, she would eventually decide to confide in someone.

'How does it look now, Mr Athreya?' she asked softly. Athreya noticed that, unlike before, she had used the title now. 'It's been a day and a half since Danuj died. Is there anything you can tell me?'

'Yes, there is. But in return, you and Jeet must be completely honest with me.'

202

She nodded. His implied suggestion that she hadn't been fully honest with him went uncontested.

'We found the coracle that was used to board Danuj's houseboat that night,' he said.

She stared at him with wide eyes. 'A coracle?' she asked. 'What's that?'

'A kind of a small, circular basket boat made of bamboo. It seats one person who uses a paddle to propel it.'

'I see… I think I've seen a picture of it somewhere.'

'Did you see a coracle the night Danuj was killed?' he asked.

She shook her head.

'We didn't,' she said. 'You must believe us.'

'You did have your binoculars, didn't you?'

She nodded.

'Did you watch Danuj's boat through it?'

'On and off. Looking through binoculars when you are inebriated is unsettling. Especially when you are on a boat that wobbles. Images float around in your vision, and you feel nauseated. So, we didn't use it very much.'

'You didn't see a coracle?'

'No. Or any other boat.'

'What did you see? Anything that you haven't told me?'

'Well, I watched Ruhi and Danuj fight. I then saw her go into the bedroom and close the door. Danuj cursed and kicked the furniture. He smoked a couple of cigarettes, spoke on the phone and lay down on the sofa where he was later found.'

'Thank you. What else?'

'Nothing else on their boat, but we did see people in the resort—Hiran, Pari, Sahil and Mummy. I saw them several times. They all seemed tense and were walking in and out of the suite and their rooms. Pari took a dip in the pool—trying to relax, I guess. We were all pretty high-strung that night.'

'Did you watch the adjacent resort too? Sunset Bay?'

'Where Kishan and Bhagya are staying? Yes, I did look in that direction occasionally, but I didn't see anyone I recognized. Did you, Jeet?'

'No,' he answered. 'But then, I would recognize only Bhagya. Nobody else. Everybody else would be a stranger to me.'

'Okay,' Athreya nodded. 'Is there anything you haven't told me, Kanika? Jeet?'

The couple looked at each other and shook their heads.

'Nothing,' Jeet added. 'Nobody approached Danuj's house-boat while we watched. No boat did, at least.'

'Would you have seen the coracle? It would have been low in the water.'

'Probably not, especially if the person boarded on the port side. Unless one was looking for it, which we weren't.'

'Fair enough. Were you both on your houseboat all night?'

'Yes, of course!' Jeet was quick to assert.

'Never got off it?' Athreya asked.

'No,' Jeet insisted.

'Not even to take a dip in the lake?' Athreya went on casually.

Silence. Athreya let it drag for a couple of seconds.

'The police know that you both swam in the lake that night,' he said slowly. 'It would have been better for you if you had told us proactively.'

Kanika's hands flew to her face, and she began trembling. Jeet hurried to her and held her shoulders. Athreya stayed silent. His suspicions were based on the wet swimwear the housekeeping staff had found in their room the next morning. That now stood confirmed.

Athreya sat there, looking down at his fingernails, giving them what little privacy he could. Suppressed sobs and soft groans reached his ears, but he didn't look up.

A couple of minutes passed.

'Since when have you known this, Mr Athreya?' Kanika asked pitiably.

'For about twenty-four hours.'

'Yet you didn't confront us?'

Athreya remained silent.

'Does Papa know?' she asked.

'I haven't told him. There was no need to. Can you tell me about your swim? When was it?'

'I don't know the precise time, but it must have been pretty late. The fight on the other houseboat had long finished, and both Jeet and I were pretty tipsy. We had this silly idea to take a dip in the lake at night. Looking back, it was a stupid idea, but it seemed fun then. We swam around for ten to fifteen minutes and returned.'

'Why didn't you tell us earlier, Kanika?'

'It's obvious, isn't it, Mr Athreya? Danuj had been killed by someone who probably boarded his boat at night. It wouldn't do us much good if people knew that we had left our boat for a short while. We thought that nobody had seen us. We decided to keep quiet about it.'

'One more question: did you see anyone on Danuj's house-boat at about 11 p.m.?'

Kanika and Jeet looked at each other. Slowly, she nodded.

'Sahil. He and Danuj talked for a while, and he left.'

'Did Ruhi come out of the bedroom?'

'No,' Kanika said with a decisive shake of the head. 'Danuj was talking to her through the door.'

'And then, Sahil left?'

'Yes.'

'You did see his boat, didn't you?' Athreya asked.

Kanika bit her lip. 'I didn't want to get a friend into trouble,' she said.

'By not telling me earlier, you have damaged your own credibility. Well, so be it. Is there anything else you haven't told me?'

'No… nothing.'

Athreya let out a long breath and shifted in his chair.

'Coming back to what I was saying earlier, something happened in the last four hours or so that has frightened you. Did anyone threaten you?'

Kanika and Jeet shook their heads in unison. Athreya stood up. Suddenly, his head spun. He had risen too quickly. He took support from the wall and got back his bearings.

'One last piece of advice from someone who has seen a lot of crime in his career,' he said softly, still leaning on the wall. 'Please don't take offence. I mean it for your own good.'

Kanika nodded silently, her curious eyes on Athreya's face as he steadied himself.

'The *only* way to deal with blackmail,' he said quietly, 'is to nip it in the bud. Once you engage with a blackmailer, you're done for.'

Her face froze into inscrutability. He had taken her by surprise, but she had been quick to recover. Before either of them could say anything more, a knock sounded on the door. Jeet opened it. Outside were Mahesh and Manjari. Presumably, they had come to enquire after their daughter.

'Goodbye,' Athreya said and went out unsteadily, feeling a little disoriented from the brain fog that had suddenly come on.

When he stepped into the corridor outside the door, he saw Hiran, Pari, Sahil and Bhagya strolling on the lawn a dozen yards away. Bhagya's head was thrown back as she laughed wildly, and perhaps a little hysterically. Sahil looked on with a wide smile. Even Hiran and Pari seemed to be smiling, though not as much as Sahil. Athreya steadied himself by leaning on a decorative wooden pillar and stood still for a moment or two. Bhagya's recent words passed through his befogged mind again: '*Nobody other than his mother will grieve for Danuj…*'

She had been right—none of the four on the lawn showed signs of much grief. Noticing him, Sahil, Hiran and Pari stopped smiling. But not Bhagya. She called out merrily as if she were tipsy.

'Good afternoon, Mr Athreya,' she said with a manic giggle. 'How is the case coming along? Do let me know if you need help. Maybe I can help.'

Athreya didn't reply. His clouded mind was busy recalling what Hiran had said about her manic disorder—that she could swing from one extreme to another. She had been measured and stable a mere hour ago. Yet, here she was, showing signs of hysteria now.

Athreya had hardly stepped into his room when an overpowering wave of exhaustion swept over him. Once again, his head swam, making him sway drunkenly. If Veni hadn't caught him, he would surely have fallen, and probably hurt himself badly. The next few moments were a daze during which he was vaguely aware of Veni steering him to the bed. She removed his leather sandals and made him lie on his back with a pillow under his head.

When he regained his bearings a short while later, Veni's reassuring face was smiling at him from above as she bent over him, stroking his forehead.

'You'll be fine,' she said comfortingly. 'That was just the aftereffects of dengue. You've pushed yourself too hard over the past day or two.'

He reached out and held her hand as she sat beside him on the bed. He closed his eyes and breathed deeply, trying to regain his strength. He knew that he was in the best possible hands.

'Take a break today, Hari.' Her soothing voice went on gently, 'We are not as young as we once were, and your recent illness hasn't helped.' Her free hand rested on his forehead. 'You have a slight temperature. How are you feeling?'

'Bushed,' he muttered. 'I suddenly feel dog-tired.'

'Post-dengue fatigue. It'll pass. Just relax. Shall I get you some *mousambi* juice? It'll help.' Sweet lime was called *mousambi* in Hindi.

Athreya nodded.

'Just lie down. I won't be a minute.'

He sensed her rise and leave the room. He exhaled and let his body relax. Veni always knew what exactly to do when he was ill. He smiled gratefully to himself. He then emptied his mind and focused on his slow, deep breathing. Impromptu *pranayama* always helped.

Before he knew it, the door opened, and two pairs of feet entered. Whom had Veni brought? He opened his eyes and saw Dr Saju.

'Good afternoon, sir,' Saju said cheerily. 'Do you mind if I check you out?'

'Not at all, Doctor,' Athreya mumbled. 'I didn't think you'd still be here. Thanks for coming.'

Saju quickly checked Athreya's vitals and pronounced his verdict.

'You're fine,' he said. 'Just tired... dengue's parting gift. Post-illness fatigue is well-documented, you know, and is known to be debilitating. You probably pushed your body a bit too hard. Just rest and eat well. Lots of fluids. Take a break today, sir. The world can wait. You'll be as good as new tomorrow.'

'Good to hear that, Doctor,' Veni said with relief. 'I brought him here to Kumarakom for him to rest and recuperate after his illness. The next thing I know is that he's gone and found himself a murder case here too!' She smiled fondly at her husband. 'You heard, Hari? This is what the doctor has ordered—rest. I'll ensure that Anto and Maheshji don't bother you today. You just take it easy, okay?'

Athreya smiled and nodded.

'There's no way they can get past you, my dear,' he chuckled. 'Not when you are in this mood.'

'They better not try, then!' She wrapped up, 'You're quarantined for today. Eh, Doctor?'

'Precisely, Mrs Athreya. I see that he is in excellent hands. I'll see you tomorrow. Do call if you need me. Goodbye.'

Saju left the room accompanied by a round of grateful noises from Veni. She shut the door and returned. She ruffled Athreya's long, fine mane and pulled up a chair.

'Good man, Dr Saju,' she pronounced. 'Competent and a no-nonsense type.'

Athreya nodded silently. Speaking seemed to require more effort than he was ready to expend.

'Try and take a nap, Hari,' she said as she picked up her book to read. 'I'll be right here. You can have your *mousambi* juice after you wake up.'

When Athreya finally awoke, it was dark outside.

'Well done, Hari!' Veni said, inserting a bookmark into the novel she was reading and closing it. 'You slept for five hours on the trot.'

'Really?' he asked. 'What time is it? Wow! 7:30? I must have dropped off a little after 2 p.m.'

'How are you feeling?'

'Better. Much better. I think I needed that.'

'Hungry?' she asked.

'I do feel a little empty inside,' he confessed.

'Good! Have the *mousambi* juice. There are some cut fruits as well. They'll be easy on the stomach and give you the fluids you need.'

She rose and arranged a small table next to his bed, which he gratefully accepted. With Veni allowing only small talk while he ate, he didn't get to mention the case until she had cleared away the table and the cutlery.

'Ah!' he exclaimed. 'That was good! So, what's been happening in the world while I was asleep?'

'Not much,' she replied. 'A few assaults on our door by the Gaurias and Anto. I shooed them away.'

'Trust you!' he grinned. 'Did they call in the army?'

'Wouldn't have done much good! Now, stay awake until dinner, Hari. Otherwise, you won't sleep at night.'

'Am I allowed to talk about the case now, your Highness?' he asked, bowing and folding his arms as if he were seeking permission.

She responded with her own playacting as if she were a queen who was looking down her nose at her subject.

'You may,' she said, waving a royal arm.

'Did Anto or anyone else bring any news, Veni?' he asked.

'No.' She shook her head. 'But to be fair to them, I didn't let Anto or the Gaurias talk when you were sleeping. I didn't want them waking you up prematurely.'

'I guess they can wait till tomorrow. What are your views, Veni? You know as much about the case as I do. Any thoughts?'

'Let's see now,' she began, getting comfortable in her chair and putting her feet up on the bed. 'Like you said, we have very little physical evidence. Lots of motives and opportunities, but not much by way of tangible evidence. Even if you do figure out who killed Danuj, you're going to have a heck of a time proving it.'

'True. It is one of those cases. We need a lucky break.'

'All you have is a dagger—which, incidentally, is not even the murder weapon—and a coracle. And we don't know how the alprazolam got into Danuj's body. The issue we have here is that, if the murderer stays content with that one crime, and doesn't get greedy, the case might remain unsolved. If his or her objective was only to get rid of Danuj, we may get nothing new. So, our hope is that the murderer—as you said—overreaches and does something more.'

'Or something outside their control makes them do things. Go on.'

'You have told me several times in the past that the very act of killing, even if it was the sole aim to begin with, could spawn additional objectives that spring from that act.'

'Example?' Athreya asked.

'If someone has witnessed the murder or saw something connected to it, the murderer will have a new objective of silencing that witness.'

'Is that a possibility here, you think?'

'Reading between the lines of what you've said so far, Kanika might be involved in some such thing. You probably feel that she is concealing something significant that connects her to the murder or some other, yet undiscovered, act or crime.'

'Go on. What could that act be?'

'I don't know. This thread unfortunately ends here. We can pick it up once you discover the act that incriminates her of something, or just embarrasses her socially.'

'Agree. I'm hoping that this attempted blackmail will lead us somewhere. But for that to play out, Veni, we must wait.'

'So, let me switch tracks and consider motives. Wealth and inheritance are very strong ones for Danuj's two siblings and their spouses. That's true for all four of the younger Gaurias, but particularly for Kanika and Jeet.'

'Why so?'

'Because money is the most important consideration—even probably the sole consideration—for Kanika. Jeet, of course, does as his wife says. Considering that Mahesh was contemplating paying Kishan off with 25 crores, the urgency of that motive became stronger.'

'And in the larger scheme of things,' Athreya added, 'Danuj was blowing up dozens of crores on every failed project. That could add up significantly over the rest of Danuj's lifetime—hundreds of crores.'

'Correct! And a third of the money he might blow up would otherwise go to Kanika. You know, Hari, I've heard Kanika tell her father that *he* has no right to squander away *her* inheritance?'

'What?' Athreya exclaimed. 'But that money is Mahesh's. He can do as he pleases. How can his daughter lay claim to "her inheritance"? Amazing!'

'That shows how she thinks, doesn't it, Hari? That's why I feel that money is the strongest motive for Kanika and Jeet. They could do almost anything to bolster their gains.'

'Now with Danuj gone, Kanika should have no other objectives, right?'

'Yes… unless she has been seen in a compromising situation that is connected to the murder.'

'Something that makes her vulnerable to blackmail? Perfect! Go on, Veni. What about the other Gauria couple: Hiran and Pari.'

'The motive is the same as it is for Kanika and Jeet. In addition, as Hiran and Danuj were partners, he has had to pick up half the losses Danuj incurred. Surely, that couldn't continue as far as Hiran was concerned. When these films bomb, he loses not just his future inheritance, but he also loses some of his personal money. Not to speak of any reputation loss he might suffer. In some ways, his motive is stronger than Kanika's.'

'He could just refuse to co-invest with Danuj,' Athreya countered.

'He could, I guess. But we don't know what other equations existed between the two brothers, what pies they had their fingers in. There could be shady deals they have jointly floated. There is a lot there that we don't know.'

'True, that's a black box for us. And Pari?'

'You may think me silly and sentimental, but I don't believe Pari is capable of participating, even passively, in Danuj's murder.'

'Just as we've heard people say that Ruhi is incapable of murder?'

'Yes. I agree with that too. Ruhi is a sweet girl. But remember what Bhagya told you when she was upset.'

Athreya nodded, recalling Bhagya's words clearly: *Nobody other than his mother will grieve for Danuj. You don't have to look far to find his killer.* Athreya continued to feel that there was a ring of truth to her statement.

'Let's go to the non-Gaurias and start with Kishan,' Veni went on. 'I don't know whether he came to Kumarakom to kill Danuj or to get his money back. Either way, his motive is strong. Especially given his reputation. If it's true that he has killed before, getting rid of Danuj would be just another murder. Unlike our other suspects, he's unlikely to lose sleep over it.

'But the interesting part about Kishan is that his two motives—killing Danuj and recovering his money—are at odds with each other. If he kills Danuj, he can't recover his money. It is particularly so after Mahesh entered the picture.'

'Bang on, Veni! Now that Danuj is no more, his potential deal with Mahesh will probably fall through.'

'And that,' Veni went on intensely, 'creates a new objective for Kishan. He will now try to recover a part of the 25 crores in any way he can.'

'Including by blackmail? Brilliant, Veni!'

Veni blushed at her husband's praise.

213

'Let's move on to the two young women,' she continued. 'Ruhi and Bhagya. Both had motives, albeit different ones. Ruhi's motive was to free herself from abuse and a failed marriage, while Bhagya's was to get back at Danuj.'

'How do you rate these motives?' Athreya asked.

'Not very strong,' Veni replied. 'Ruhi was filing for divorce anyway. The papers were ready, and the family also knew about it. She would get her freedom *very* soon. It was a matter of weeks. Why should she go and commit a murder at this stage? For a future Gauria inheritance? Unlikely. She doesn't covet that.'

'Well, she had the best opportunity.'

'Yes, but it has been established that someone other than Sahil boarded the houseboat. Did Ruhi manufacture that evidence? The very few pieces of physical evidence we have?'

'You believe that's not possible?' queried Athreya.

'It's possible, Hari, but not likely. It's too much risk for little additional gain. It would be foolish of Ruhi, and she isn't a stupid girl.'

'And Bhagya? What about her?'

'People move on from relationships, Hari. Particularly in showbiz. It's been a while since their affair took place. The fires would have died down.'

'Yet she came to Kumarakom with someone like Kishan.'

'An alliance of convenience. As Mahesh said, she came to turn the screws on him. From what I overheard on the cruise boat, her mere presence here unnerved him. I would say that she succeeded in giving Danuj a virtual punch in the gut.'

'That leaves Sahil. What's your take?'

'His motive is straightforward—if Danuj is removed, he can free Ruhi from her living nightmare, and in due course lay claim to his secret sweetheart. Now with Danuj dead, he needs to do nothing more. If he is the murderer, he will remain quiet.'

'I agree, Veni. That's pretty straightforward. That completes our list of suspects. Anything else?'

Veni considered for a moment and shook her head. 'I guess not. What's going through your mind, Hari? You seem preoccupied.'

Athreya let out a long breath and lay back on the bed.

'I can't get rid of the feeling that this attempted blackmailing hasn't fully played out yet,' he said.

'Wouldn't that be good? It might produce evidence that could help you crack the case.'

'Yes, it could be good. But it could also be bad if it leads to another crime. Let's see what tomorrow brings.' He turned to look at her. 'Any overall remarks?'

'Only one.' Veni smiled affectionately at him. 'I don't have a clue who killed Danuj. I hope you do!'

15

Athreya was jolted awake the next morning by loud knocking on his door. His eyes snapped open to see a cross-looking Veni hurry to the door and swiftly open it before it could be knocked on again. Outside was Anto, grinning sheepishly.

'Did you have to knock so loudly, Inspector?' Veni berated him in Malayalam. She threw a backward glance at the bed and continued irately, 'See, you've woken him up. What's the hurry? It's just past seven o'clock.'

'Twelve dozen apologies, madam,' Anto lamented, professing regret despite having deliberately created the ruckus to wake up Athreya. 'There have been developments overnight that Mr Aadhreiah needs to know about.' He added as an afterthought, 'I hope he slept well?'

Before Veni could think of a suitably cutting reply, Athreya spoke from the bed.

'Come in, Anto,' he called as he sat up. 'What's all this excitement about?'

Veni, however, didn't budge from her spot where she barred Anto's way. She wasn't done with him yet.

'I will have you understand, Inspector,' she said sharply, reverting to English, 'that I don't approve of your actions. Hari is recovering from a serious illness. He needs rest. Couldn't you have waited for a more decent hour?'

Anto shuffled his feet like a schoolboy facing his headmistress and apologized again. Veni refused to move for another moment or two, glowering at the embarrassed man and making her displeasure amply clear. Then, she stepped aside and let him enter.

As he did, Anto stooped and picked up an envelope from the floor. Neither Athreya nor Veni had noticed it. He grinned and held it out to Athreya, saying, 'Joseph slipped this under the door last night. It looks like you haven't seen it yet.'

Athreya accepted the envelope and waved Anto to a chair.

'Would you like some tea?' Veni asked Anto, as she picked up the electric kettle. She had already cooled down after ticking the inspector off. 'I'm going to make some for Hari and me.'

'Yes, madam,' Anto answered as he took his seat, visibly relieved at the change in her. 'Thank you.'

Athreya opened the envelope and read the typewritten sheet that was folded inside it:

> Good morning, Mr Athreya.
>
> I trust you had a good rest and are feeling energetic enough to indulge me. I will come to the resort at 7 a.m. with the fond hope of meeting you. As your wife was very clear that she would allow no visitors yesterday, I couldn't meet you.
>
> There have been developments that we need to discuss.
>
> Thanks & regards.
> Anto

'Shoot,' Athreya said, folding the sheet and putting it back into the envelope. 'What's happened?'

'Bhagya was attacked last night,' Anto replied.

'What!' Concern erupted on Athreya's and Veni's faces.

'Yes. Fortunately, she is alive even if injured.'

'How badly is she hurt?' Athreya asked.

'She has a few wounds, and her ankle has been hurt badly. She's using crutches. No life-threatening injuries, thankfully.'

'Where was she attacked? In her room or elsewhere in the resort?'

'Not at the resort. On the road to Kochi.'

'Kochi!' Athreya exclaimed. 'Why was she going there? Where is she now?'

'In her room at the resort. Under police guard. Would you like to talk to her?'

'Right away! This might well be the break we were waiting for.'

Athreya hurriedly swung his legs out of bed, almost kicking Anto in his haste. He apologized and rose swiftly to his feet, only to sway and clutch Anto's shoulder for support. Holding onto the inspector, he steadied himself.

'I'm okay,' he assured a sceptical Veni, as he let go a moment later. 'Just stood up too quickly. That's all.'

'Sure,' Veni replied drily. 'I'm not letting you go out alone. I'm coming to Sunset Bay too.'

Athreya thought for a second and nodded.

'Good idea,' he said and turned to Anto. 'Let Veni and me meet Bhagya alone. I'll report back to you on the meeting. She may say more if you aren't there.'

'No problem,' the inspector smiled. 'I've already talked to her. Let me know if you need any assistance. A constable will accompany you as an escort.'

A short while later, after a hurried cup of tea and a lightning-quick shower, Athreya entered Sunset Bay with Veni, and made his way to Bhagya's room. There, they were met by a constable who was watching the corridor outside. On knocking on the door, it was opened by a female nurse. She conveyed their names to Bhagya inside the room and got her approval before admitting them.

Wearing a pair of shorts and a T-shirt, Bhagya was propped up in a single-seater sofa, with her injured right leg stretched out and resting on a padded stool. A thick pressure bandage was wound around her right ankle. Her left arm was bandaged at the elbow and a pair of crutches stood against the wall to her right. Her arms and face showed colourful bruises and healing scratches.

'It's very kind of you to look me up, Mr Athreya,' she said with a weak smile when they entered. 'Thank you for coming, Mrs Athreya. Forgive me for not rising.'

Unlike on a couple of earlier occasions, Bhagya showed no signs of volatility or hysteria. She seemed fully grounded today.

'Nothing to forgive, Bhagya,' Veni responded, stepping forward and going close to the young woman. 'How are you feeling?'

Her maternal instinct had come to the fore on seeing the bandaged woman who was the same age as her own daughter. She gently stroked Bhagya's head as the latter smiled gratefully.

'Not too bad, Aunty,' she replied, slipping comfortably into a friendly relationship with the older woman with whom she was speaking for the first time. 'It's only my ankle that hurts real bad. Especially when I put weight on it.'

'You'll be fine in no time, my dear. No bones broken, I'm told. Are they looking after you well at the resort? Do you need anything? Can I help in any way?'

'Thank you, Aunty. The resort people have been very kind, and Susan—' She gestured to the nurse '—is very efficient. The doctor has already come twice. I'm being looked after very well.'

'Do you want something to read?' Veni asked. 'I have tons of books, both fiction and non-fiction.'

'No, Aunty,' Bhagya laughed. 'Thanks. I don't read very much.'

'Music, then?' Veni persisted. 'I'll lend you my Bluetooth speaker. I have lots of Malayalam songs too.'

'Thanks, I have this.' Bhagya indicated her mobile phone and a pair of earphones. 'I carry my music with me.'

'You youngsters are so self-sufficient! It's the same with my kids too. They are forever using their earphones. Not good for the ears, you know. I keep telling them, but they don't listen.' She lifted her hands in a mild apology. 'Okay, I won't pester you any more, but please do let me know if you need anything. I don't want to leave you alone when your family isn't around you. I'll come and look you up a couple of times a day.' Veni smiled broadly. 'We can chat about all manner of things.'

'Of course!' Bhagya agreed. 'Why don't both of you sit? Mr Athreya?'

Bringing Veni had been a good idea, Athreya thought. Within a minute, she had established a rapport with Bhagya. As a result, the atmosphere in the room had become markedly relaxed and Bhagya didn't seem to be on her guard.

'I'm sorry to see you hurt, Bhagya,' Athreya said gently, as he remained standing. 'But I'm happy to see that you are largely okay except for your ankle. Is it all right if I stand?'

'Of course! As you please.'

'Thanks. Would you like to tell me what happened?'

'Sure, sir.' She nodded. 'I'll start from the beginning. After meeting Maheshji and then Sahil yesterday afternoon, I took the boat shuttle from Crystal Waters to the boat terminal. When I came out on the road, a couple of tough-looking characters followed me.'

'On the road from the terminal to this resort?'

'Yes. They seemed to have been waiting for me there. As soon as I came out, one followed me on foot while the other started his bike. Fortunately, there were other pedestrians around and some vehicles too. So, they didn't come close to me. I walked as fast as I could and entered this resort. They didn't follow me in.'

'Did they seem familiar? Had you seen them before?'

'I'm not sure... one man seemed a bit familiar. But I can't place him.' She paused for a moment, frowning as she tried to identify the men she had seen. Then, shaking her head, she went on, 'When I went out a couple of hours later to buy something from the shop across the road, I saw them again. They were waiting outside the resort gate. I hurried back inside, and I guess I started to panic. The more I thought more about it, the more I grew scared. I kept thinking about what happened to Danuj.

'But I had nobody to talk to as Mr Kishan had gone to Kottayam. I called a close friend in Mumbai and told her about the situation. She suggested that I take the next flight out. She thought that I should get out of here as soon as possible. She'd come and pick me up at Mumbai airport, she said. I decided to take her advice.

'As I packed, she looked up the flights and found an 8:10 p.m. flight to Mumbai. While I called for a resort car to drop me in Kochi, she booked me on the flight and sent me my ticket.' She held up her mobile to show Athreya the ticket. He peered at it. It seemed genuine. 'I decided to leave behind my suitcase in the room and go with only hand baggage. I didn't want anything to delay me or bog me down. I thought I'd ask Mr Kishan to bring my suitcase or send it across.'

'Didn't you try calling Kishan?' Athreya asked.

'I did,' Bhagya answered. 'More than once. But he didn't answer. By the time he called back, I was already in hospital after the attack.'

Athreya ambled pensively to her French windows that opened out onto her veranda. He made a mental note to check the location history of Kishan's mobile. That would show if he had really been in Kottayam when the attack took place, or elsewhere.

'Nice view,' he said appreciatively, gazing out of the French windows at the swimming pool just outside and the resort garden beyond. 'The pool looks like a sheet of glass from here, and you have an excellent view of the lake. Not a single boat or barge mars the blue waters of the lake. Lovely!'

'Yes,' Bhagya agreed. 'This *is* a nice resort and the view from here is outstanding.'

'Go on,' Athreya urged, turning away from the French windows. 'What happened after you left the resort for the airport?'

'About ten minutes later,' Bhagya went on, 'a bike with the two men suddenly intercepted my car, forcing my driver to stop. The men came to my door, yanked it open and hauled me out. I fell onto the road and my foot got caught between the car door and its body. It got twisted as I fell. Then, one of the men pulled out a long knife.

'Fortunately, I am in the habit of carrying pepper spray in my handbag, which had fallen with me on the road. As soon as I fell, the driver of my car shouted and got out. That gave me a couple of seconds to pull out the pepper spray.'

Athreya understood why she carried the pepper spray. Some men would take liberties with an item girl who performed raunchy dances on-screen. She needed some way to defend herself.

'I jumped up and sprayed the man with the knife in the face,' Bhagya went on. 'But I didn't realize that my foot was injured. It gave way and I fell onto the road once more. A couple of passers-by came running and the goons decided to flee. The man whom I had sprayed was clutching his face as the other goon started the bike. The first man clambered onto the bike and they sped away.'

'Thank goodness for the driver and passers-by,' Athreya said softly. 'I wonder what you would have done had they not intervened. The men who attacked you... what can you tell me about them?'

'They didn't look like locals, and they spoke in Hindi. As I said, one looked vaguely familiar, but I still can't place him. I've given their descriptions to the police.'

'Okay. What happened after the men fled?'

'Seeing that my foot was badly hurt, the driver took me to a hospital. While the doctors were treating me, he called the resort, which informed Inspector Anto. By the time the doctors had bandaged me up, the inspector reached the hospital.'

'And the flight?' Veni asked.

'I missed it, Aunty. And now that I have twisted my ankle and am on crutches, I would be a sitting duck for the goons at the airport. The inspector recommended—strongly—that I return to the resort with a police nurse. As you saw, he has also posted a constable outside my door.'

'Any idea why the men attacked you?' Athreya asked.

'None,' Bhagya replied. 'No idea whatsoever. I can't think of anyone who would wish me harm. I wonder if they mistook me for someone else. Ruhi is the closest to my age.'

'Well, I'm happy that you are safe now,' Veni pronounced. 'You are young, and your ankle will heal soon. But be careful, my dear, and take a lot of rest. Don't go out of the resort for anything. Call me if you need something. Don't feel awkward. I'll come and see you two or three times a day till you are back on your feet.'

'Thanks, Aunty. You are really very kind.' She turned to Athreya. 'If we are done, Mr Athreya, I think I'll take a nap now. The medicines they gave me make me drowsy. I had my morning dose a short while back.'

'Of course, my dear,' Veni said, not letting her husband answer. 'Let me help you up.'

Athreya watched Veni and the nurse help Bhagya get up from the sofa. Grimaces contorted the young woman's face as her right foot moved. Very gingerly and visibly in pain, she put her left foot on the floor and stood up. She reached for her crutches and tucked them under her armpits. She then hobbled to the bed using them, where she turned around and sat down with a groan. The nurse helped her lift her legs and put them on the bed.

'This is how ankle twists are, Bhagya,' Veni commiserated. 'Very painful at the beginning, but they quickly improve. You need to be careful not to put weight on it too soon.'

'Yes, Aunty. I'll be careful. Thanks for everything. Do drop by later in the day if you have the time. Thank you, Mr Athreya.'

On returning to their room, the preoccupied couple didn't notice an envelope lying on the floor until Veni stepped on it. Out of long-bred habit, she picked it up with her right hand and touched her eyes with it. Kicking a book, which was considered a manifestation of Goddess Saraswati, was taboo in her family. The status accorded to books was often extended to other forms of paper like envelopes and letters. Touching the inadvertently kicked paper to the eyes or heart was the prescribed apology.

'Looks like it's the season for slipping envelopes under doors,' Athreya chuckled, as he took if from Veni. 'Two in two hours!'

Inscribed on the front in a flowing, feminine hand was the name: 'Mr Harith Athreya'. He opened it and read the notepaper folded inside it:

Dear Mr Athreya

Good morning. I hope you are feeling better today.

Jeet and I thought it over last night and decided to take your advice. We will take the bull by the horns. We would like to meet you as soon as possible.

Please call me when you are free.

Take care.

Kanika

He read it twice, noting a politeness that was uncharacteristic of Kanika. He then handed it over to Veni to read. Her response was a snort.

'She spews bullshit each time you meet her, and now wants to take the bull by the horns?' she bristled. 'Don't trust her, Hari. Whatever she says will be half-truths or outright lies. Bull by the horns, indeed!'

'Relax, my dear,' he laughed. 'As you yourself said yesterday, we are no longer as young as we were. We are mature enough to handle deceptions. We'll take it as it comes.'

Athreya glanced at the clock. It was about 8:30 a.m. He texted Kanika, saying that he would come over to her room in fifteen minutes and received an acknowledgement. Precisely fifteen minutes later, he knocked on the door and was admitted by Jeet.

'Good morning, Mr Athreya,' Kanika greeted him. 'We have work to do.' As an afterthought, she added, 'I hope you are feeling better today?'

'Yes, thank you,' he replied and took a seat.

The Kanika of today was markedly different from the one he had encountered the previous afternoon. Gone were the hesitation, trepidation and tension. Today, she was a fiery, take-no-prisoners Amazon. He could almost imagine a sword in her hand and a helmet on her head. Jeet, on the other hand, was distinctly timid, perhaps in response to his wife's bellicose avatar.

She wasted no time in getting to the point.

'I take it that you have read my note,' she began, speaking rapidly. 'Now that we all are on the same side, I'll tell you everything. Yes, you were right—we are being blackmailed. Blackmailed because Jeet and I took a dip in the lake that night and didn't tell anyone about it. Someone saw us and decided to chisel money from me. But that won't happen, will it, Jeet?'

'Not if you can help it, Kani,' was the dutiful response.

'Let me make it abundantly clear, Mr Athreya, in case it isn't already so. Our taking a dip in the lake had *nothing* to do with Danuj's murder. Nothing! Zilch! And now that you and the police know about our little nocturnal escapade, the blackmailer has no hold on us. Let's go after him hammer and tongs. He'll regret that he even thought he could blackmail me. I'll show him that I'm no gullible weakling.'

'Him?' Athreya asked. 'Is it a man?'

'It was a male voice. Didn't I tell you?'

'Perhaps, you should start at the beginning. I don't know anything about the blackmail attempt.'

'There's nothing much to it,' she went on irritably. 'I got a call from an unknown number at about 10:30 a.m. yesterday. It was a man speaking in a muffled voice, asking if I was Kanika. When I answered in the affirmative, he spoke very briefly and hung up.'

'Was it a regular call or a WhatsApp one?'

'WhatsApp.'

'Smart,' Athreya conceded. 'That makes it hard to track him.'

'Why?' she asked. 'The phone number and WhatsApp number are the same.'

'In your case, yes. But it needn't be. For instance, I can transfer my WhatsApp number to your phone.'

'Really?' Her eyebrows rose. 'I didn't know that.'

'Yes, Kani,' Jeet interposed. 'I can put your WhatsApp number on my phone if I wish. I can instal WhatsApp even on a device that doesn't have a SIM card—like your tablet.'

'Let's keep that aside for now,' Athreya interrupted. 'What exactly did the blackmailer say?'

'I don't remember the words verbatim, but it was something to the effect: "*I know what you did that night. I know why you entered the water. You'll hear from me again soon.*" That was all he said. Now that I look back, I think I overreacted and ended up panicking.

I should have gone to Papa right away or come to you. But you know what it's like—once you start imagining the worst, there is no end to it. You get sucked into the vicious cycle.'

'I hope you haven't deleted the call from your phone log?' Athreya asked.

'No,' she answered. 'It's there—the number, time and duration.'

'Did you recognize the voice?'

'I am not a hundred per cent certain. It sounded like the man was speaking through a cloth to muffle his voice. But I think I know who it is.'

'Who?'

'Kishan.'

'Have you spoken to him before?'

'Oh, yes! So have Papa and Hiran.'

'Business dealings?'

'Correct.'

'I see. Has he called back yet?'

'No. Not yet. That's why I was in a hurry. I wanted to know what to do when he calls again.'

'Good thinking.' Athreya nodded. 'Let's meet the inspector right away. Is there anything else about the call or the caller that I need to know?'

'I don't think so.'

'Was there only one call?'

She nodded. 'Only one.'

'No message? SMS, WhatsApp, and things like that?'

'Nothing.' Kanika shook her head. 'Only one call yesterday morning.'

Athreya stood up.

'Come,' he said. 'Let's go. Be prepared for the police to examine your phone.'

227

Fifteen minutes later, Anto and Joseph were fully abreast with the blackmailing attempt. After taking down the blackmailer's number and call details, Anto returned the phone to Kanika with the suggestion that she answered when the blackmailer called again.

'Buy time and keep him talking,' he advised, as Athreya watched appreciatively. This was a sure and competent Anto. 'The longer he is on the air, the better are our chances of catching him. Prolong the call but don't commit to anything one way or another. Say you need to think it over. Ask questions. Ask him what he wants. He'll, of course, want money. Ask how much, where it must be sent and in what form. Cry, if you can. He might feel that you are at his mercy. He will then underestimate you.'

As soon as Kanika left the room, Anto and Joseph swung into action. While the former called Inspector Holkar in Mumbai, the sub-inspector spoke to the local mobile phone operators. Anto hit pay dirt within a minute of reading out the blackmailer's WhatsApp number to Holkar.

'A lucky break!' Holkar's excited voice came over the speaker-phone. 'At last! We've been waiting for this. You know, Anto, this is one of the ten numbers Kishan's sidekick bought last week with fake papers. The shopkeeper who sold them confessed and gave us the list of the ten numbers.'

'Excellent!' Anto replied in glee. 'Then, the SIM card Kishan is using could be one of the other nine SIMs.'

'Exactly!' Holkar went on. 'I'm sure that the SIM number and the WhatsApp number will be different, but both will be from the same lot of ten.

'What's more, Anto, is that we have set up alerts for all ten numbers. When any of them connects to the network, its location will be recorded, and it will be automatically tracked for as long as it remains on the network. Hang on a minute. My man is checking the records.'

Athreya waited impatiently, thinking how much things had evolved since he had been a young police officer. Technology had changed everything and had put so many tools in the police's hands. Even ten years ago, it would have taken days to do what Holkar was now doing within a minute or two. Two minutes later, they had the latest location of one of the other nine SIM cards.

'Right next to you!' Holkar enthused. 'At a resort called Sunset Bay.'

'Bingo!' Anto responded in the same vein and rose. 'That's where Kishan is staying. We'll go get him.'

'Just a minute, Anto,' Holkar cautioned. 'What we have so far is circumstantial evidence. We can't convict him on this.'

'Really?'

'Yes. We've been here before. A good lawyer will get him out of it, and Kishan has some very good lawyers. What you need to do is to catch Kishan red-handed with the SIM cards in his possession. You will need a search warrant for that. Can you get one right away?'

'Er…' Anto hesitated, his face losing the eagerness it had just been suffused with. 'I am not sure. My boss hasn't even heard of Kishan—'

'Don't worry, Anto. I'll send you one. We have a long record on Kishan and his three associates.'

16

Athreya returned to his room once Anto and Joseph had hurried away to raid Kishan's cottage with the help of a bunch of constables. Considering that he was working for Mahesh as a private citizen, it was best to not get involved in an official police raid. He would go over later if Anto found something concrete. Moreover, he didn't feel energetic enough to handle a raid, which was, as a rule, unpleasant. Fatigue was still dogging him despite a good night's rest and the adrenalin surging in his veins. Besides, the exertions of the morning, minor as they were, had sapped some of his stamina.

Back in his room, he updated Veni, after which they went together for a late breakfast. A hungry Athreya attacked the food, much to Veni's amusement.

'Good,' she remarked. 'Your appetite is returning. Nothing like a thorny case to get you back to normalcy, eh?'

Athreya grunted something unintelligible through a full mouth, making Veni shake her head indulgently and turn her attention back to her plate. They spent a few minutes in agreeable silence.

When they were midway through their meal, Athreya's phone buzzed—it was Anto calling. The raid had begun, he said, and they had met with success in the first ten minutes. They had found several of the illegally procured SIM cards that Holkar had mentioned. They had also found the phone from which Kanika had received the WhatsApp call. Uncharacteristically careless of Kishan, a delighted Holkar had thought. However, the raid was not complete yet as they had more searching to do.

'Proceed cautiously, Anto,' Athreya said, as he continued with his breakfast. 'Technically speaking, Kishan did not blackmail

Kanika because he did not actually threaten her or demand money. All he said was that he knew that she had entered water. Blackmail is our inference.

'Holkar can proceed against him for being in possession of illegally obtained SIM cards, but you and I are not on firm ground as far as our case is concerned. We need Kishan to talk.'

'I see that, Mr Aadhreiah,' Anto replied. 'Kishan too realizes that. He actually said so—said that he has threatened nobody. Nor is there proof that it was he who called Kanika from that phone. After all, we only found the phone in his possession a full twenty-four hours after the call was made.'

'Would you mind if I had a chat with Kishan alone? Whatever he may say to me he would not have said to the police.'

'I see what you mean. No objection as long as you fill me in afterwards.'

Twenty minutes later, Athreya and Kishan sat alone in the latter's bedroom.

'As I told you the last time,' Athreya began, 'I am trying to help Maheshji by investigating his son's murder. That is the sum total of my interest in this affair. Whether you have illegal burner SIM cards or not isn't my concern. Nor am I going to ask if you threatened Kanika.'

Surprise flashed across Kishan's habitually inscrutable face and his eyebrows rose a fraction of an inch.

Athreya went on, 'I, therefore, have only one question in my mind: how did you know that Kanika and Jeet swam in the lake that night? Let's look at the possibilities: either you saw them swimming, or someone else witnessed it and told you. If you saw them, that shatters your alibi that you were in Kottayam at the time of the murder. If it was someone else who witnessed them swim, I would like to know who that was.'

Kishan's face had become unreadable after the brief involuntary surprise. But Athreya could make out that his mind was racing. Given Kishan's reputation, a false alibi could get him into considerable trouble. Especially if his alibi-provider was seen as a professional witness. Coupled with his very visible motive to kill Danuj, the circumstantial evidence of his having watched Crystal Waters from a boat and of possessing illegal SIM cards, his freedom in the near future was in jeopardy. Kishan was undoubtedly on a sticky wicket.

Athreya gave him time for that to filter through the thug's mind. When a few moments had elapsed, he spoke again.

'You know Kanika, and you have done business with her,' he said. 'You probably know the kind of person she is. I don't. But I'm told that she is unforgiving and doesn't necessarily play by the rules, especially if she could get away with bending or breaking them.'

Kishan continued to watch Athreya intently.

'I'm saying this,' Athreya went on, 'because your stance that you didn't *threaten* her rests solely upon her word. What you say won't really matter. If she were to claim that you did blackmail her and did demand money, you will have no way to disprove that. It would be your word against hers, and both of us know what will happen. Your goose would be cooked.'

Kishan's face darkened in anger. Athreya paused again to let it all sink in.

'But on the other hand,' he went on, 'if she knew that you helped us catch her brother's murderer, she might just stick to telling the truth. That would make a *huge* difference to what happens to you.'

Athreya sat back. He had said his piece and had to now wait for Kishan to respond. The gangster took less than a minute.

'What do you want?' he asked.

'I want to know who told you that Kanika and Jeet took a swim in the lake that night.'

'If I told you, will you stick to your side of the bargain?'

'What is my side of the bargain?' Athreya asked. 'That I do nothing, say nothing? I have no interest in your SIM cards or how you obtained them. Nor am I convinced that any blackmailing was done. So, my side of the bargain is silence, other than to tell Kanika that you helped me.'

'Okay.' Kishan nodded. 'Maheshji is a respectable man, and you are representing him. I therefore assume that you will keep your word.'

Athreya nodded silently. Kishan took a long pause before he spoke again.

'Bhagya,' he said. He let out a long sigh and closed his eyes as if he had done something he hadn't wanted to. 'Bhagya saw them from her French windows that night.'

'When did she tell you?' Athreya asked.

'The next morning... as soon as we heard about Danuj's death.'

'Does she know that you called Kanika?'

Kishan shook his head firmly.

'No,' he said. 'You must believe me. Don't involve her in my affairs. She is a good girl whose only mistake was to trust Danuj.'

'What is your relationship with her?'

'It's not what you think—'

'I think nothing. That's why I am asking you.'

'I am just someone who has occasionally helped and pro-tected her. She is an unfortunate young woman who has been shafted by the rich and powerful of Bollywood. She has suffered a lot, and I don't want to add to her woes.'

Athreya considered it for a moment. It didn't add up. Why would Kishan be a protector of Bhagya, a young woman who seemed to have no connection with him at all? He was missing something here, some connection, perhaps. Unfortunately, he hadn't had the time to enquire into the backgrounds of Kishan and Bhagya. He made a mental note to correct that right away through a combination of Anto and Holkar.

He brought his attention back to the conversation.

'You are aware that Bhagya is pleased that Danuj is dead,' he said.

'Undoubtedly,' Kishan shot back. 'Who isn't? Everybody except Manjariji is happy. You would be pleased too, had you been deceived by Danuj as Bhagya was. That man was a leech and a downright cheat. He got what he deserved.'

'Perhaps he did,' Athreya agreed. 'But his death put you in a fix. The 25 crore you lent him might never come back. You, therefore, had to recover whatever you could from the Gaurias. Kanika was an easy target once Bhagya told you about their swim.'

Kishan merely shrugged.

'Do you know who attacked Bhagya?' Athreya asked, changing track abruptly.

Kishan's face darkened again in anger. But he said nothing.

'You recognized the men from Bhagya's descriptions,' Athreya persisted. 'They are thugs from Mumbai.'

A quick, almost imperceptible nod from Kishan.

'But you don't know who sent them,' Athreya finished. 'Or do you?'

'Not yet.'

Athreya walked briskly back to the boat terminal from Sunset Bay, trying not to appear to be hurrying. Last night's developments and the morning's discussions had flipped a switch and made him optimistic. Suddenly, his fatigue seemed a thing of the past. The 'Case of the Rocking Boat', as Veni had playfully called it last night, which he had feared might peter out for lack of evidence, had roared back to life. There was much to do now and little time to do it in.

On getting off the boat at Crystal Waters, he made for Anto's temporary office, where he found the inspector on a video call with Holkar in Mumbai.

'Just the men I wanted to see,' Athreya began, as he shut the office's door behind himself. 'I'm afraid I have been lax, gentlemen. I should have asked you to initiate information collection as soon as the murder took place. By not doing it, we have lost two days. My profound apologies, Anto.'

'What information, Mr Aadhreiah?' Anto asked, his Malayali accent nowhere in evidence, now that Holkar was listening over the video call, except in how he pronounced Athreya's name.

'The usual stuff. We should have built dossiers on all the people in this case by now—the Gaurias as well as the others. Specifically, we must compile a list of all the people Danuj cheated—both the business associates he duped and the young women he wronged. It's possible that the motive for his murder lies somewhere in his past that is littered with people who wished him ill.'

'We have opened files on each of the Gaurias and the other people in this case—Kishan, Bhagya, Sahil. Did you have anyone else in mind?' asked Anto.

'That will do for now,' Athreya replied. 'Do we have their backgrounds, families, friends, business and financial interests, past and current relationships, gossip, rumours, press coverage, et cetera?'

'Well…' Anto hesitated. 'We have some of it. We were going slow because we were focusing on the investigation here.'

Athreya turned to Inspector Holkar's image on the laptop screen.

'You must have a dossier on Kishan, I suppose, Inspector?' he asked. 'You've been pursuing him for a while now.'

'Yes, sir, we do,' Holkar answered. 'Quite a thick one, I must say. We also have one on the man in Kottayam who supplied Kishan's alibi. We can share digital copies of both dossiers if that helps.'

'Yes, please do so right away. In that case, you must have the answer to this question: is Kishan originally from Kerala?'

'Yes, sir,' Holkar replied, much to Anto's astonishment. 'He is a Keralite or Malayali, whatever you wish to call him.'

'Where in Kerala is he from?'

'Kollam. His hometown is on the banks of the Ashtamudi Lake. He spent much of his childhood there and goes back there occasionally. His associate in Kottayam—whom Kishan had visited on the night of the murder—is a childhood friend.'

'Is Kishan his original name?'

'No. It was Gopal Krishnan. He changed it to Kishan after coming to Mumbai.'

'You see, Anto?' Athreya turned to the local inspector. 'A boy who grew up on the banks of Ashtamudi Lake is likely to have learnt to use a coracle. And he would have all the local connections necessary to walk away with murder. By neglecting our suspects' backgrounds, we have missed this important piece of circumstantial evidence.'

'Yes, sir,' Anto agreed sheepishly. 'I should have thought of that. I am a Keralite too, but I didn't recognize Kishan as one. How did you guess?'

'Remember, when we went to meet him the first time at the swimming pool at Sunset Bay? He said something in Malayalam. How likely is a Mumbai-wala to know Malayalam unless he was from Kerala?'

'Good guess, sir!'

'We need to stop guessing, Anto. That's why we need information on all the people in this case. Without them, we won't know what we are missing.' Athreya turned to Holkar and continued, 'You have dossiers on Kishan and his friend. What about the Gaurias? Anything on them?'

'Yes, but not much. We do keep tabs on Bollywood personalities, as you probably know. But we haven't done in-depth information gathering.'

'Yes, I'm aware that you have a team that monitors Bollywood personalities. Can that team help us? I can speak to Mr Sardana if that helps.'

Sardana was a very senior police officer in Mumbai Police, with whom Athreya had worked in the past.

'Not required, sir. I need to keep Mr Sardana informed anyway. I will reach out to the Bollywood team right away and get whatever I can on the Gaurias, Sahil and Bhagya. Is there anything specific you want?'

'As I said, let's gather as much information as we can on the people Danuj has duped and wronged. Create a full list of all such people and add whatever details you have on them, including their photos and videos. Include everything, even if it is gossip and rumours. Make sure that you cover tabloids, cine magazines and Page-3s of newspapers. Please assemble the dossiers as electronic files that we can read on laptops and tablets.'

'Not a problem, sir. We'll get to it right away.'

Holkar's image turned to someone who was off-screen and spoke in Marathi. A moment later, the figure of a khaki-clad woman hurried out of the door behind Holkar, presumably to carry out his instructions.

'You see our oversight, gentlemen?' Athreya asked. 'We have so many motives here in Kumarakom that we did not bother to look elsewhere for more. How do we know that the real motive doesn't lie in the past or in Mumbai? We have been remiss, don't you think?'

'Yes, sir,' Anto acknowledged.

'By the way,' Athreya went on, 'we need to find out what the relationship between Kishan and Bhagya is. Any idea, Holkar?'

'No, sir,' the inspector answered from Mumbai. 'I don't think she figures in his dossier. Why do you ask?'

'Because Kishan claims that his intent is to help and protect her. How did that come about? Why did he become her protector? Out of the blue? I don't think so, Holkar. We are missing something there.'

Anto hesitated for a moment and spoke tentatively, 'If you don't mind my asking, Mr Aadhreiah…'

'Go on, my friend. Ask.'

'You seem to be suddenly charged up, sir,' Anto said hesitatingly. 'Did you find out something new in your discussion with Kishan?'

'You remember, I was telling you that if the killer remained content with just Danuj's death, we might never catch him?'

'Yes, sir. With little evidence so far, we might get stuck if the killer went into his shell and did nothing more. However, if the killer became ambitious or overconfident, he might make an error. Then, new evidence might emerge that could be used to identify him or her.'

'Precisely, Anto! That's what has happened. It seems to me that the killer is *not* content with just killing Danuj. Either he wants to do more, or his hand has been forced.'

'What are you referring to, sir?' Holkar asked. 'The blackmailing of Kanika or the assault on Bhagya?'

'Both, I suspect,' Athreya replied. 'Why do you think Bhagya was attacked? There is no doubt that her attacker was trying to kill her.'

'No doubt, sir,' Holkar agreed. 'As to why he tried to kill her, I can only guess.'

'Go ahead, guess.'

'She probably knows something that makes the killer nervous,' Holkar said.

'But she says that she has no idea why the men tried to kill her!' Anto protested. 'I asked her several times.'

'Either she is lying,' Holkar responded, 'or she doesn't know that she possesses incriminating information.'

'Obvious, isn't it?' Athreya agreed. 'So, the question now is: what does she know? Consciously or unknowingly. The killer thought it important enough to send thugs from Mumbai to silence her. Which, in turn, lends weight to the suspicion that the killer is from Mumbai.'

'But, Mr Aadhreiah,' Anto objected again, 'all our suspects are from Mumbai. That doesn't make us any wiser.'

'Which is why we need dossiers on all of them,' Athreya said. 'The answer lies in one of them. I kick myself for not having initiated the information creation as soon as we discovered the murder.'

'Don't worry, sir,' Holkar interposed from Mumbai, 'I've already put a team on it. You'll get the first dossiers in a few hours. They will be updated several times a day, as and when we gather more information. I'll send you a PDF version of Kishan's dossier right away.'

'Good,' Athreya approved. 'We need to move fast. I fear the killer is already preparing to make the next move.'

If the first half of the day had Athreya darting from room to room, the second half saw him closeted in his own room, poring over Kishan's dossier on his iPad. Beside him, Veni was on *her* iPad, scanning all the Bollywood news, rumours, photos and videos Holkar was sending her way. Four hours of staring at their screens was making their eyes water and necks stiff. They longed for a break but were also acutely aware that they had already lost time. They had to catch up.

Meanwhile, having spotted an inconsistency in what different people had said, Athreya had developed a tentative theory, which he had shared with nobody. Except to ask Veni to look out for something specific as she sifted through the vast amounts of Bollywood-related material Holkar was sending. Knowing him well, Veni had not pressed him to share his theory with her. She was content in keeping an eye out for the requested information as she sifted through what she called 'Holkar's Dump'.

The welcome break from their tasks came in the form of a knock on the door. Eager to put down their iPads, both husband and wife vied to open the door. Outside was Mahesh Gauria, leaning on his walking-stick.

'I was wondering if I might trouble you, Mr Athreya,' he said in his gravelly voice. 'My apologies, Veni, if I have interrupted something.'

'Not at all, Maheshji,' Veni beamed, ushering him in. 'You have no idea how happy we are to take our eyes off electronic screens and talk to a human. Please come in! Tea? I have some nice Roasted Darjeeling Tea.'

'What are you two up to?' Mahesh asked, glancing around as he hobbled into the room and took the chair Veni offered. 'Chained to your iPads, are you? Yes, tea please. I do like Roasted Darjeeling. Thank you.'

'We should have done it earlier,' Athreya replied. 'We are trying to catch up on lost time. I'm burrowing into Kishan's past and Veni is boiling the Bollywood Ocean to see if she can find any new piece of insight.'

'Can I help?' the elderly man asked. 'I do know a lot about Bollywood and Indian filmdom.'

'We are compiling a list of people Danuj has cheated or otherwise wronged. I'm looking for motives beyond the ones we have in the group here. Once I have the list, I'll come to you with it. Your insights would be invaluable.'

Mahesh looked up sharply at Athreya.

'You think someone outside Kumarakom is involved in Danuj's murder?' he asked.

'I can't be certain. But I do know that I am missing something.'

'What, for instance?'

'For instance... who sent the men who tried to kill Bhagya? Indications are that they came from Mumbai. Why does someone want to kill her? What does she know—knowingly or otherwise—that makes someone want to silence her? What is the connection with Danuj's death?'

'Hmm. Someone here could have sent the men too. All of us are from Mumbai. All it takes is a phone call. I dare say that all of us here have the necessary connections.'

'I agree.' Athreya nodded. 'However, the questions remain.'

'I see what you mean. As long as we had only Danuj's murder to explain, it was probably simpler. But with Bhagya's attempted murder, it has become complicated. What is the connection between the two events?'

'Exactly. Once we find the missing pieces, it'll all fall into place. Hence the search.'

'Any theories as yet, Mr Athreya?' Mahesh asked.

Athreya smiled and said nothing.

'He always has theories, Maheshji,' Veni chipped in, stirring the tea leaves in the steaming water. 'At every stage of the case. Hari believes that imagination is often the key to solving difficult mysteries. Because you seldom have all the pieces of the puzzle, you need to use imagination to fill in the gaps. So, he usually has multiple theories in his mind at any time, each one based on a different set of imagined components. But he doesn't talk about them, even to me.'

'Really?' Mahesh offered a smile. 'You are an intriguing man, Mr Athreya. Any theory on how alprazolam entered Danuj's body?'

'Some suspicions but nothing firm that I can tell you.'

'Fair enough. Is there anything you *can* tell me? Especially about my late son?'

'Well, yes. It is now clear what Danuj was planning in Kumarakom and why he enacted all this drama. You probably know all the bits and pieces already.'

'I might. But do indulge me. What was he trying to do?'

'I think it began when Kishan threatened Danuj with dire consequences,' Athreya began. 'By all accounts, Danuj was truly unsettled and fearful, for he genuinely believed that he would come to grief unless the 25 crores were repaid to Kishan along with the interest. But unfortunately, he had no way of raising such a large sum.'

'Until I entered the picture,' Mahesh said, accepting a mug of tea from Veni. 'Until I told Danuj in confidence that I would talk to Kishan.'

'Precisely. Once you stepped in, Danuj must have begun seeing things differently. He would have been quite certain that you would get Kishan off his back and pay him off. Once the fear receded, Danuj began seeing Kishan's threats as an opportunity to make a profit. You would eventually repay Kishan quietly and without anyone else knowing about it. Isn't that right?'

Mahesh nodded. 'One doesn't advertise the fact that one has paid a blackmailer.'

'Which meant that, if Danuj could raise an *additional* 25 to 35 crores from another source, he could pocket the money raised.'

'Ostensibly for the purpose of paying off Kishan?'

'Correct. The person who was going to provide the additional money would not know that you had paid off the debt. Danuj could then pocket the second tranche of money he raised. With that in mind, he began planning his artifice.

'The first thing he did was to contact Sahil, whom he thought he could deceive into providing him the money. He believed that his childhood friend was deeply infatuated with Ruhi and would do anything to get her. By then, he had also begun to believe his own lie that Ruhi was having an affair with Sahil and wanted to marry him. And, as luck would have it, Sahil already knew of Kishan's threats. Whether Kishan really threated to kill Ruhi, I don't know, but there was nobody to contradict Danuj's claims.

'And so, he told Sahil that Ruhi's life was in danger and if Sahil could provide the money to pay Kishan off, she would be safe from the thug. And in return, Danuj would agree to a divorce, and Sahil could claim his sweetheart. That way, Sahil and Ruhi would get each other, and Danuj would get his money—a win-win outcome for all concerned.

'The venue for sealing this deal was a place far from Mumbai's and Bollywood's prying eyes; a place where strangers and visitors were the norm—Kumarakom.'

'Are you suggesting that Danuj planned all this before we came here?' Mahesh asked.

'Judging by the fact that he had his first conversation with Sahil before you arrived here, I would think so. I suspect that he also had all the necessary agreements drawn up in Mumbai before he came to Kumarakom.'

Mahesh's eyes bored into Athreya's. 'The infamous blue file?' he asked.

'I believe so, but we can't be sure,' Athreya agreed. 'Neither Danuj nor the file is available to us, but I believe Danuj made all his preparations in Mumbai. After coming here, he secretly called Sahil and told him to come to Crystal Waters. And when Sahil arrived, Danuj acted as if he was surprised. He enacted a drama and threw a fake fit to take Ruhi away to the houseboat for the night, where he had secretly asked Sahil to come at 11 p.m.'

Mahesh groaned and rubbed his leathery face.

'I fear you are right, Mr Athreya,' he said. 'So, Danuj could act very well when he wanted to… well enough to fool his own family.'

'Indeed.'

'My heart bleeds, Mr Athreya. He so cunningly used his father, wife and childhood friend towards his own selfish ends.'

'And brother too,' Athreya added. 'Remember, he used Hiran's name to convince Sahil to come to Kumarakom. He said that Hiran and he had decided not to involve you in this "settlement" with Kishan.'

Mahesh nodded slowly.

'It all seems to add up, Mr Athreya,' he said. 'He expected to get away with this dupery by ensuring that Sahil and I didn't talk to each other. That's how he would raise 25 to 35 crores *twice*.'

'And pocket the money he raised from Sahil.'

'But matters didn't go as he expected, obviously.'

'They didn't,' Athreya nodded. 'For one, Sahil was not as gullible as Danuj had supposed—'

'Sahil? Gullible?' Mahesh cut in. 'One can't be a successful film producer if one is gullible! Danuj should have known that. He should have also known,' Mahesh went on fiercely, 'that Sahil would never covet another man's wife, especially a close friend's. Danuj's expectation that he could make money from his divorce was utterly misplaced.'

'Further,' Athreya added, 'Danuj expected Ruhi to give him half her inheritance from you.'

'Honestly, Mr Athreya, I wouldn't be surprised if she gave him all of it. That's the kind of woman she is... she doesn't hanker for money. That's why I added certain clauses in my will... to prevent Danuj taking away what I give to Ruhi.' Mahesh paused and let out a long sigh. 'Sometimes,' he muttered, as if he were talking to himself, 'I wonder if Danuj was in his right mind. He even tried to extort money from his own sister.'

'From Kanika?' Athreya asked softly. 'How?'

'I don't know if it was in jest or if something more serious was at play. He got hold of some document that could potentially prove embarrassing to her socially. Very embarrassing. When she asked for it, he refused to return it. He made her cry and run around, just as he used to do when they were kids.'

'When was this, Mr Gauria?'

'Oh, a couple of weeks back, I think. It's got nothing to do with Danuj's murder.'

Mahesh paused. When Athreya remained silent, he put down his empty tea mug, looked up at the investigator and went on, 'It was some silly thing, Mr Athreya. Some indiscretion that Kani is very touchy about now and rather embarrassed. She had social and commercial links with someone who has since turned toxic. That's what that document shows. If word of those links reaches her social circles, she would be very embarrassed. Believe me, it can't be a motive for murdering one's brother.'

'Fair enough,' Athreya responded. 'We'll set it aside. What is the feeling in the family now, Maheshji? Who do they think killed Danuj?'

Mahesh rose and leaned on his walking-stick.

'We are at a loss, Mr Athreya,' he replied. 'But we don't think it is anyone from the family. Hiran and Pari are convinced that it is Kishan. There seems to be no doubt in their minds.'

'What makes them so sure?'

'Elimination, presumably. Once you exclude the family, there aren't many left. Of the remaining, Kishan stands out.'

'But his alibi holds strong. And as far as Kishan is concerned, Danuj's death has reduced his chances of recovering the 25 crores he lent.'

'True. You probably need to ask Hiran about why he is so certain that it's Kishan. I'll see you later. Thanks for the tea, Veni.'

Mahesh hobbled to the door and left the room. Silence hung in the air as Veni shut the door.

'So, the Gaurias want it to be Kishan,' she said softly. 'Or, at least, so they say.'

'We can't expect them to name one of their own, can we?' Athreya asked. 'Or Sahil.'

'Probably not. But there is one thing about Hiran that is bothering me.'

'His claim two days ago that Kishan had specifically threatened to kill Danuj?'

'Yes,' Veni nodded. 'He deliberately misstated his conversation with Danuj, which I overheard.'

'I've asked you before, Veni... are sure that you remember the conversation correctly?'

'*Absolutely* sure, Hari. Danuj said very clearly that Kishan had threatened to track down and kill Ruhi. "Cut her up" were the words Kishan had reputedly used.'

'Hmm.' Athreya's index finger began tracing words on his chair armrest.

'Right from the beginning, Hiran has been trying to pin it on Kishan,' Veni added. 'You've noticed that, haven't you?'

'Yes, I have. I wonder what it is that he hasn't told me. While he hasn't been avoiding me, he hasn't been particularly forthcoming either.'

'True,' Veni agreed. 'Even Kanika has spoken more to you than he has.'

'One more thing, Veni,' Athreya asked. 'Are you sure that Hiran can't swim?'

'Oh, yes. Both Mahesh and Manjari told me that. So did Pari.'

'When did they tell you?'

'Before Danuj was killed—they were pulling Hiran's leg. There was no reason for them to lie.'

They were interrupted by a knock on the door. Veni went to the door and opened it. Outside was Anto.

'I think we have found the murder weapon, Mr Aadhreiah,' he said softly, entering the room and closing the door behind him. 'A large kitchen knife that is also called Chef's Knife. It is available online for anyone to buy. The blade is eight inches long and two inches wide at the handle.'

'The same dimensions as the fatal wound. Where did you find it? On the lake bottom?'

'Yes, we've been searching the lake since Saturday. We began under Danuj's houseboat and looked for it in expanding circles.'

'Where exactly was it relative to the houseboat?'

'If you drew an imaginary line from the houseboat to the Crystal Waters pier, the knife was found near the midpoint of that line.'

'That would make it about a hundred feet from the boat and an equal distance from the resort,' Athreya mused. 'I wonder if the killer could have thrown it that far.'

His right index finger had suddenly sprung to life and was furiously tracing invisible letters on the armrest again.

'The knife is heavy,' Anto volunteered. 'I don't think any of the women in this case could have thrown it that far. Even Bhagya, who is probably the strongest of them. Someone like Kishan or

Sahil might have managed it but a hundred feet is a long way for them to throw such a heavy knife.'

'I agree… it's more likely that the killer dropped it on the way back from the houseboat… after killing Danuj.'

17

Just as it had happened the previous morning, Athreya's slumber was once again disturbed by the sound of knocking at his door. But unlike on the earlier occasion, the rapping was not loud. Instead, it was soft and persistent, as if the person knocking was trying to be discreet while being intent on waking him up. At first, Athreya, who was fast asleep, thought he was dreaming. But as the insistent tapping continued, he began surfacing and heard Veni's mumbled protest. Abruptly, the subdued sound was joined by a shriller one, jolting Athreya awake. It was the landline extension in his room clamouring for attention.

Snapping to consciousness, Athreya was temporarily disoriented. It was still dark, and it took him a moment or two to get his bearings right. Guided by the blinking red light of the strident telephone instrument, he reached out and groped for the receiver.

'Hello?' he croaked.

The response was a confused utterance in a combination of English and Malayalam.

'What?' Athreya asked. 'Who is this?'

'One second, sir,' the caller replied and handed over the phone to another person.

'I'm calling from the reception, sir,' a new male voice said with a pronounced Malayali accent. 'We are sorry to disturb you, but something has happened. Inspector Anto suggested that we wake you up. We need your advice. The resort manager is knocking at your door.'

'Okay, I'll open the door.'

Athreya hung up, swung out of bed and hurried to open the

door. A contrite resort manager was outside. He apologized profusely and repeated what the caller had said.

'Inspector Anto is on his way, sir,' he added. 'He wants you to take charge till he comes.'

'What time is it?'

'Four o'clock, sir.'

'Give me a minute,' Athreya said. 'I'll dress and come.'

He shut the door and changed out of his night clothes as he briefed a now-awake Veni. As a policeman's wife, she had seen numerous late-night and early-morning calls. He was usually woken up when there was some sort of an emergency. She wondered aloud what it could be this time.

'Don't want to speculate,' Athreya responded. 'There are so many possibilities. I'll know soon enough.'

'You have been expecting something to happen, haven't you? I could see that you were tense yesterday.'

'Well, yes.'

'Be careful, Hari. It's still dark outside.'

When Athreya came out of his room and shut the door, the resort manager handed him a large flashlight and hurried away past Mahesh's presidential suite and towards the resort office. Athreya followed silently. The manager then turned right and went towards the opposite wing that housed Sahil's and Pari and Hiran's rooms in addition to some vacant ones.

'This way, sir.'

The manager turned into the gap between the two buildings that formed that wing and went towards the cottage on the lake shore. He then went around the corner behind the wing and gestured towards the water. Three men—presumably the resort staff—stood at the shore, gazing out into the lake. On hearing footsteps, they made way for the resort manager, who had now switched on his flashlight.

Wordlessly, the manager halted at the water's edge and shone his torch at a spot in the lake a dozen feet from the shore. The other men switched on their flashlights and added illumination to that spot.

Floating in the lake, still and face down, was a body. It was bobbing gently with the waves that lapped the shore, and seemed to be a man who was wearing a light-coloured shirt. Athreya couldn't make out the legs very well as they were a few inches under the surface. With his face in the water, there seemed no doubt that the man was dead.

'Shall we pull him out, sir?' a security guard asked. 'Or should we wait for the police? They'll be here any moment.'

Athreya considered for a second. There was no question that they were looking at a corpse. Nothing would be achieved by pulling it out now. It was best to leave the scene as untouched as possible for the police.

'Let's wait,' Athreya replied. 'Do you know who it is?'

'I… we are not sure, sir. It looks like a man.'

'One of your guests, or a stranger?'

'Can't say, sir.' The security guard shook his head. 'We can't see the face.'

There was no way to tell who the dead man was. He could be a stranger, or someone connected with the case. The body could have floated in from the lake too. Until the police took him out and identified him, there was no point in speculating. Yet Athreya's mind churned with possibilities and his index finger traced words on the side of his leg.

Athreya turned away and looked down at the soft ground at his feet. He grimaced in disapproval at what his torchlight showed. The ground between the cottage and the water—which was about ten feet wide—was full of footmarks. Several pairs of slippers, shoes and naked feet had trod there recently. The slushy

251

mud at the water's edge was all churned up. Whatever evidence might have been there was now lost.

'Let's move away from here,' he said, backing towards the cottage. 'Is the resort boat available?'

'Yes, sir,' the manager assured him, pointing towards the pier. 'Should I get it ready?'

'Yes. The police might want to go by boat to inspect the body and to retrieve it.'

The manager nodded to one of the men who hurried away to fetch the keys to the boat. Athreya pulled out his mobile phone, turned on its light and captured a video of the trampled ground as the others shone their torches for additional illumination.

'The inspector should be here any moment,' the manager repeated when Athreya finished. 'Meanwhile, is there anything you want us to do?'

'Yes. Post your staff in the corridors of all the buildings. Let them stay there until they are recalled. We want to ensure that nobody enters or leaves any room or cottage. If the guests wake up, tell them to stay in their rooms until further notice.'

'Nobody is staying at the cottage, sir, and the clubhouse is shut at night.' He jerked his thumb at the cottage they were standing beside.

'All the more reason to keep an eye on them... in case someone is hiding there. I will stay here and keep watch till the police arrive.'

As the manager hurried away to mobilize enough people to keep watch over all the buildings, a light came on in one of the rooms of the wing behind the cottage. Athreya went to see which room it was. The window opened, and Sahil peered out through the bars.

'What's going on here?' he asked in English. He then caught sight of the investigator and continued in surprise. 'Oh, Mr

Athreya? What are you doing here at this unearthly hour?' His voice sharpened as realization struck. 'Wait! Has something happened?'

'Well, yes. Please stay inside your room. Don't come out.'

'What's happened?' Sahil's voice dropped. 'Nothing bad, I hope?'

'We don't know yet. It could be nothing to do with us.' Realizing that Sahil's window was close to where the body was found, he asked, 'Did you hear anything during the night? Any noises or voices?'

'No.' Sahil shook his head. 'I didn't hear anything. My window was closed, and the air conditioning was running. Noisy appliance, I must say. Makes a racket.'

'When did you go to sleep?'

'A little after midnight.'

'Deep sleep?' Athreya asked.

Sahil nodded. 'Yes. Your voices just woke me up.'

'Okay. I'll talk to you later. Please close your window and draw the curtain. Go back to sleep if you can.'

Athreya walked along the wing towards the pier. The last room, he knew, was Hiran and Pari's, while the other rooms were vacant. However, Pari was spending nights in Ruhi's room to keep her company after the trauma the younger woman had just endured. Hiran would therefore be alone at night. Athreya stopped outside his window and gazed at it. The room was dark and the outdoor unit of the split air conditioner was running noisily in the still night. He could see or hear nothing else.

He went past the wing to the pier, where he halted and swept the resort with his gaze. Everything seemed normal except that a handful of men and women were spreading out to watch all the walkways. At the pier behind him, the resort's motorboat floated lazily in the water.

Noticing nothing out of the ordinary at Crystal Waters, he turned his gaze to Sunset Bay. Everything seemed peaceful there too. He wondered if the body could have drifted in from Sunset Bay or elsewhere. Corpses tended to get washed ashore. And in the short time Athreya had been watching it, the body had drifted a few feet in different directions.

Turning to the lake itself, he saw that the two houseboats— Ruhi's and Kanika's—lay anchored and dark where they had been when Danuj's murder had been discovered. Anto had followed Athreya's instructions and seen to it that they hadn't been moved. He hoped that the inspector had recorded their positions scientifically enough for it to stand up in court. This could turn out to be an important piece of evidence.

His thoughts were interrupted by voices that he recognized—Anto, Joseph and the resort manager, and others. He hurried back to near where the body was floating.

'Anto,' he called. 'Before you and your men add to the footmarks on the ground here, I suggest you capture a high-resolution video of this strip.'

Once the police photographer had complied, Athreya went to the waterline. Seeing that the corpse had drifted closer to the shore, he shone his light on it, hoping to find some clue to the dead man's identity. But the face was still submerged.

'Any idea who it is?' Anto asked.

Anto's and a couple more torch beams joined Athreya's on the body. He heard cameras clicking to record the scene.

'I hope it isn't someone we know,' Athreya answered, peering at the island of illumination surrounded by predawn darkness. 'But I am fearful, Anto.'

'So am I, sir. What you said yesterday is stuck in my mind: *I fear the killer is already preparing to make the next move.*'

'We don't need a boat, sir,' Athreya heard Joseph say. 'We can wade in and retrieve the body. We have hooked bamboos that can reach it.'

'Go in as soon as the camera work is finished. Let the cameras record your retrieving the body.'

'Yes, sir.'

A few minutes later, the corpse was lying in the mud at the waterline. It was still face down but the clothes were clear. Athreya noted with dismay that the dead man was wearing a light pink half-sleeve shirt and dark trousers. Suede shoes on his feet. Athreya's heart thudded as one of theories he had grew stronger. He had the inescapable feeling that he knew the dead man. But he waited for Joseph to turn over the corpse. When he did, Athreya's suspicion proved right.

Lying lifeless before him, with his shirt and trousers deeply soiled and stained, was someone he knew well.

Hiran Gauria.

Anto and Athreya were in the temporary office, discussing the case as they waited for Dr Saju to return. The police doctor was conducting a preliminary examination of the body, which had been moved to the cottage after it was pulled out of the water.

'Did you have the security cameras activated in the two resorts?' Athreya asked.

'Yes, sir,' Anto replied. 'Did it yesterday morning. But they record footages in the buildings and the entrance. The rest of the resort—the lawn, pier, pool, walkways, et cetera—is not covered.'

'That might still prove useful. Hopefully the footage will show Hiran coming out of his room. And the additional camera... did you have that installed too?'

Anto nodded. 'I did, but I am not sure why you wanted it. I can't see a connection between the pool and anything else in this case.'

'Maybe you are right. But no harm playing safe. I hope the resort staff have been instructed not to gossip or speak to anyone?'

'Yes, Mr Aadhreiah.'

Athreya had suggested that they wait for the Gaurias to wake up before informing them. Pari, of course, would be absolutely devastated at the news of her husband's death. As would Mahesh and Manjari. Out of kindness, Athreya had suggested that they be left undisturbed until the resort was secured. Anto had agreed.

'The two people who were to receive the lion's share of the Gauria inheritance are now dead,' Anto mused softly, as they waited for Saju. 'The surviving daughter stands to benefit the most.'

'True,' Athreya agreed. 'She and the grandchildren.'

Kanika's two children and Pari's two were in Mumbai under their respective nannies' care.

'Yes, of course,' the inspector agreed. 'The grandchildren too. But of the three women, Mahesh will probably leave more to his daughter than to his daughters-in-law. That's what would happen in most families. Blood is thicker than water, after all.'

'Are you suggesting something, Anto?'

'Well… step back from all the details and look at it, Mr Aadhreiah. Two of the three Gauria scions are dead… only one is left.'

'Is that suggestive?'

'Isn't it? Come on, sir. Don't tell me you haven't thought about it.'

'Oh, yes, I did,' Athreya replied. 'As soon as I knew that the dead man was Hiran. But it is far from conclusive.'

'Of course. It's one possibility, though. Don't you get the feeling that Kanika and Jeet are not telling everything there is to tell?'

Athreya nodded. 'I do. They are hiding something. I'll get it out of them soon.'

They were interrupted by a knock on the door. A moment later, Dr Saju and Joseph walked in. Anto and Athreya looked at him enquiringly.

'I have, obviously, not done the autopsy yet,' Saju began. He sat on a chair and continued in his usual measured fashion. 'What I'm going to tell you are the results of my preliminary examination of what I could do here.

'Death occurred between 1 a.m. and 3 a.m., and the highest probability is around 2 a.m. The body was fished out at 4:30 a.m., and I don't think it has been in the water for more than three and a half hours. That places the first boundary at 1 a.m. The body temperature suggests that life ceased at least two hours before I examined it, but not more than four hours. Considering that I took the temperature at 5 a.m., the other boundary falls at 3 a.m.'

'Quick work, doctor,' Athreya complimented him. 'Thank you.'

Saju blinked and went on, 'There is some question about the cause of death—'

'You know that Hiran could not swim, right?' Anto asked. 'Didn't he drown?'

'There is a complication, Anto. On the one hand, his lungs and stomach are full of water. So, drowning is clearly indicated. But there are also two deep stab wounds in the heart, which were inflicted by a long, narrow blade. Either wound could have been the cause of death, as could the drowning.'

'I see your point,' Anto nodded. 'Did he fall into water imme-diately after he was stabbed?'

'I believe so. He was alive when he went into water—that's how he swallowed and inhaled water during his dying moments. He died very soon afterwards. He would have died of the wounds very quickly even if he had not fallen into the water.'

'Stabbed from the front?' Athreya asked.

'Yes,' Saju replied.

'Direction of the wounds?'

'Slightly upwards. Both times, he seems to have been stabbed with an underarm jab. The killer stabbed forward and upwards. The blade entered the chest slightly below the heart and cut upwards into the heart. The blade was kept horizontal so that it could slip in between the ribs.'

'Underarm stabs, eh?'

'Yes.'

'Any views on the blade used to stab him?' Athreya asked. 'You saw the wounds on Danuj too. How do you compare the three weapons?'

'The short, blunt dagger that was left in Danuj's chest was not much of a weapon to kill someone with. So, I'll leave that out. Of the murder weapons in the two cases, the first one was a heavy kitchen knife, while the second one seems to be a more professional weapon.'

'Professional weapon?' Athreya asked.

'Anto will agree, I think,' Saju replied, adjusting his glasses. 'In many cases where gangs or professional criminals are involved, we see stab wounds like the ones on Hiran. Many thugs carry long, narrow blades that are very sharp—ideal for quick underarm stabs. They do that for the simple reasons that they are easy to conceal and very efficient to kill with. They penetrate deeply and cause death quickly. The hilt is often made of wood or leather.'

'I concur,' Anto added. 'We do see such wounds and knives in professional killings.'

'That's interesting, isn't it?' Athreya asked with a smile. 'The first murder was with a kitchen knife while the second is with a professional knife.'

His eyes shone brightly, and he looked pleased. Something had just fallen into place in his mind.

'We must search for it, Anto,' he went on. 'Right away. Before the people in this case get to know that Hiran is dead. Have you brought metal detectors?'

'Yes, we have four. You want every room in this resort searched? I have the warrant to do it.'

Athreya nodded. 'And some in Sunset Bay too. Apart from the knife, wet clothes and muddied footwear, I need you to look for something else too.'

Athreya rose.

'Get your people ready for the search,' he said. 'Let's start with Mahesh and Manjari. They should be told first. I'll get Veni to join us. She will be a support to the unfortunate mother who has just lost another son.'

Athreya sat beside a thunderstruck Mahesh in the latter's suite. On an adjacent sofa, Veni held a devastated Manjari's hand as the resort doctor checked her vitals and a nurse looked on. While her octogenarian husband sat stunned, Manjari's tears ran down her face as sobs racked her bony shoulders. Neither of them could believe that they had lost both their sons within a span of four days. The couple who had taken their younger son's death so stoically, was shattered by the older one's. The profound grief in the room had moved Veni to tears as well.

'Why Hiran?' Mahesh asked for the umpteenth time of nobody in particular. 'I can't understand.'

He could think of no reason for anyone to kill his elder son. Danuj's death had not been a total surprise as he had been a wayward man. But not Hiran. He was known to be a gentleman who was often courteous to a fault. Who would want to kill him?

There was little Athreya could say or do to console the broken father. He stayed silent, his hand resting on the old man's forearm. Behind him, a group of four police personnel were approaching the end of their search. They had already searched the sitting room of the suite and were now about to finish the bedroom.

Mahesh had not objected. In fact, he had encouraged Anto to go through all rooms with a toothcomb. By examining Mahesh's suite first, Anto would set a precedent for someone like Kanika, who was sure to object and even bodily resist.

Presently, Joseph came to Mahesh.

'Thank you, sir,' he said almost reverentially. 'We have completed our search.'

'Found anything?' Mahesh asked haltingly.

Joseph shook his head. 'No, sir. We didn't expect to find anything in your rooms, but we have to search all rooms. I'm sorry.'

Mahesh nodded.

'If anyone from my family objects,' he said slowly and clearly, 'tell them that I *want* you to search *all* rooms. The same goes for Sahil, Kishan and Bhagya. If they resist, they will have to answer to me personally—tell them that.'

'Yes, sir. I'm very sorry for the inconvenience. Thank you, sir.'

Joseph bowed and left the suite. The other searchers had preceded him. Athreya steeled himself for what was to come next: Pari and Ruhi.

He turned to Veni and nodded. Veni understood the unspoken message. She summoned the nurse and made her sit next to Manjari, holding her hand. She then left the room quietly and hurried towards Ruhi's room, where a policewoman was already knocking at the door. The unenviable task of telling Pari had fallen to her.

Two minutes after Veni left the suite, the sound of a broken wail reached Athreya's ears. It caught Mahesh's and Manjari's attention too.

'Pari!' Mahesh gasped. 'Oh, how will I face her? I was the one who insisted that we come to Kumarakom.'

'You weren't to know,' Athreya whispered gently to him. 'Nobody knew. Don't blame yourself. Be strong, Maheshji. Pari needs your support.'

Mahesh blinked and said nothing. He seemed to steel himself for what the running footsteps in the corridor outside augured.

'Papa!' Pari's cry preceded her. 'Mummy! *Yeh kya ho gaya?*' What is it that has happened?

Clad in a pink nightie, her hair flying and tears streaming, she flew into the suite with Ruhi close behind her. An older and roly-poly Veni came in a distant third. Pari went straight to Mahesh and hugged the old man, bringing rare sobs to his lips. He hugged her and squeezed his eyes shut, sending teardrops down his face. The two sobbing people held each other, unable to utter a word.

Meanwhile, Ruhi went to Manjari, displaced the nurse and flung her arms around Manjari. Seeing her younger daughter-in-law, tears poured anew down the old woman's face as she broke into a fresh bout of weeping.

So intense was the tragedy in the room that not an eye remained dry, including Athreya's and the resort doctor's.

Athreya, who had given his place to Pari, stood a few feet away and turned his mind to the investigation. Searching Ruhi's and Pari's rooms had never been seen to be a problem. They would have raised no objection even if Mahesh hadn't weighed in. One team had already searched Pari's room when the other team was examining the suite. The second team had gone to Ruhi's room while the first was now on the way to Kanika's.

That's where Athreya expected fireworks—Kanika was not going to give in without a fight. However, there was no question of not searching her room. Searching all the rooms, in some ways, was a cover to gain access to hers. Anto was tenacious enough to not let go, however unpleasant be her tantrums. He was not called a bulldog for nothing.

Sure enough, Kanika's shrill voice reached their ears a minute or two later, from her room at the end of the wing. Jeet's voice barked at Anto. Athreya had no doubts about the outcome. Unable to browbeat Anto into submission, Kanika's fallback would be to unleash hysterics at her father and get him to intervene. But she was in for a surprise.

Five minutes after Kanika stormed into the suite, she was a spent force. The police had a warrant and Mahesh had been categorical in telling her to cooperate. There was no way out for her.

'But at least let me change into something decent!' she protested gracelessly. 'I'm in a nightie, for God's sake.'

'So are the others,' Mahesh countered. 'You needn't go out of this suite. Stay in the bedroom if you wish. Now, Kani,' he admonished gently, 'don't be difficult. Do as I say.'

That took the wind out of her protests. She sat down heavily on a chair.

Athreya, who had been watching her closely, wasn't surprised to see that her face was several shades paler than usual. She was scared. There was something in her room that she didn't want found. Glancing at Jeet, he saw fear in his eyes too.

Noticing that Athreya was studying her, Kanika retreated into the bedroom with her husband following her. Athreya strode out of the suite and made his way to their room.

18

Athreya halted just inside Kanika and Jeet's room and surveyed the scene. The large room, which could comfortably house a family of four, was being searched by several police constables. Two had removed the mattress, pillows and all sheets from the bed, and were thoroughly examining the bed and every piece of bedding.

Another policeman had climbed onto an aluminium ladder and had removed several panels of the false ceiling. He had stuck his head into one of the square openings and was studying the space above in the light of a powerful torch. A fourth constable was examining a cupboard while the fifth was standing over four pieces of luggage and contemplating them.

'Any luck?' Athreya asked Anto, who was standing outside the bathroom and watching a policeman search inside. In his hand was a metal detector like the ones used by security staff at airports.

'Not yet,' the inspector replied. 'We are checking the obvious and easy-to-hide places first. 'Next, we'll search the concealed spaces with the help of a resort maintenance staff member. Last, we'll open the luggage.'

'Concealed spaces?'

'Like the toilet cistern. It's behind a removable panel in the bathroom wall. You'd be surprised how often we find weapons and drugs there. There is space behind the water heater too. We also have a couple of cubbyholes used by the resort's electricians and plumbers, including a closet in the corridor outside.'

'What about the other rooms?'

'Mahesh's rooms are clean… not that we expected to find anything there.'

'Unless one of his family hid something there,' Athreya corrected.

'Yes, of course.' Anto seemed a tad abashed for a moment or two. 'That's possible, isn't it?'

'Yes. But thankfully, nobody did that. I'm interested in Hiran and Pari's room. Pari, of course, slept in Ruhi's room. Anything interesting in Hiran's room?'

'Nothing suspicious. While his bedspread had been disturbed, he hadn't actually gone under the sheets and slept. He probably just lay on the bed and waited for his rendezvous time.'

'Rendezvous? With whom?'

'The killer, I suppose. Don't you think Hiran had a clandestine meeting with someone behind the cottage? Someone who killed him?'

'Possibly. Wonder what time the meeting was for.'

'We will know what time he left the room when we review the footage of the security camera in the corridor outside his room.'

'No security camera behind the cottage, I suppose?' Athreya asked.

'Unfortunately not.' Anto shook his head. 'It's possible that the spot was picked for that very reason.'

'Anything else in Hiran's room?'

'Well… everything was in order. He seems to have locked his door when he came out for the meeting. The room key was in his trouser pocket. Funny thing is that he left his mobile behind in his room.'

'Ah! I wonder why?' Athreya's index finger began scribbling furiously on his leg. 'Interesting, isn't it, Anto? One would think that he would carry his mobile to the meeting. What if the person he was meeting got delayed? What if he needed to contact that person for any reason?'

They were interrupted by a series of beeps from a metal detector. They turned to see that the constable searching the cupboards had grown visibly excited.

'What's this?' she called. 'A dagger!'

She reached behind a pile of clothes and triumphantly pulled out a brown-and-gold dagger. It looked exactly like the one that had been left in Danuj's chest.

'It's probably Kanika's,' Anto guessed, utterly unmoved by the find. 'See if the blade has her name.'

The policewoman drew the blade and nodded, looking crest-fallen. 'Yes, sir.'

'That's okay, then. We found Pari's dagger in her room too.'

For the next fifteen minutes, Athreya watched the police go about their work systematically. These people were well trained. Using their hands, eyes and metal detectors expertly, they covered every square inch of the room. They found no knife or anything remotely suspicious. From a corner of the room, a camera recorded everything they did and found.

They then brought in the resort's maintenance man and asked him to point out every crevice and cubbyhole he knew of. Within another ten minutes, they had searched every nook and cranny. What was left were the four pieces of luggage.

One by one, they placed them on the bed and opened them. They took out the contents in small piles so that they could replace them as they had been. The biggest suitcase was a standard one that was very popular. It was mostly empty as the clothes it had probably held now hung in the cupboards or sat folded there. A laptop was there too, enclosed in its sleeve. Its charger lay beside it.

The next two suitcases were half empty and of little interest. All they held were personal effects such as clothes, toiletries, chargers and a couple of electronic gadgets. Kanika's binoculars were in one. All that was left now was a capacious leather bag that was clearly full.

'Interesting that the other pieces of luggage are mostly empty,' Athreya mused aloud, 'but this bag is full. I wonder if it has been filled recently.'

The searchers hauled it onto the bed and opened it to find several pairs of shoes at the top, kept in plastic bags. Under them were shopping bags bearing the names of shops in Kochi and Kottayam. These were the results of Kanika's shopping expeditions. Right at the bottom were two sweaters and two plastic boxes with medicines.

'Show these boxes to Dr Saju and ask him what each of these medicines is for,' Anto instructed.

'Yes, sir.' One of the constables took the boxes and went away.

'That's it,' called the policeman searching the bag. 'Nothing more.'

Anto stepped forward and waved his metal detector over and around the bag. It beeped at multiple spots, but it was for the rivets used to bind the leather. Some beeps were for other attachments such as buckles and hooks.

He lifted the bag and waved the metal detector under it. A few more beeps sounded. On inspection, the culprits turned out to be metal-mounted castors that made the bag wheelable. When Anto inserted the metal detector into the empty bag, the beeps were fewer and fainter.

'Leather is heavy,' Anto remarked, as he switched off the detector and dropped the bag back on the bed. He turned to Athreya. 'I'm disappointed, Mr Aadhreiah,' he said morosely. 'We've found nothing.'

Athreya didn't respond. He was contemplating the leather bag with a frown.

'What is it, sir?' Anto asked.

'Do you have a metal tape measure or a long ruler?' Athreya asked. 'Or a stick?'

'Yes, sir.' One of the constables came forward with a yellow plastic tool that had a metal tape measure rolled up inside it.

Athreya picked up the leather bag and placed it on the wooden floor. He then took the tape measure and pulled out about three feet of the metal tape and locked it. He inserted it into the mouth of the empty bag till the end of the tape touched the bottom. He peered at the number on the tape at the top of the bag. It read: 21.

'The depth from the top to the bottom of the bag is 21 inches,' he said aloud. 'That is the *inner* depth. Now, let us measure the *outer* depth.'

Keeping the metal tape vertical and beside the bag, he measured the height of the top of the bag from the floor and peered at the tape.

'The top of the bag is 26 inches from the floor,' he said. 'That's a difference of five inches. The castors are about two inches high. That leaves three inches as the difference between the inner and outer depth. Even if the base of the bag is an inch thick—which is probably too much—we still have two inches to account for. Eh, Anto?'

'False bottom, sir!' the inspector growled softly. He moved forward and shone his torch into the bag. 'Let's see now... how do we access the hidden compartment?'

He pulled on a pair of latex gloves and dipped his right hand into the bag. Systematically, his fingers explored the base and all around it. He paid particular attention to the edge where the horizontal base met the vertical leather sides. Intense concentration showed on his face. His eyes were closed as he focused on what his fingertips were sensing.

Abruptly, he stopped. His eyes snapped open.

'There's a hole or a depression here,' he said softly. 'I need a hook to insert into it.'

The man who had supplied the tape measure stepped forward again and offered a stiff bent wire.

'Careful, Anto,' Athreya cautioned, as the inspector took the wire. 'We need to test whatever is in there for prints. And please ensure that the wire doesn't tear anything.'

He pulled out his mobile phone and began capturing a video of what Anto was doing. A police cameraman did likewise—they would have an official record of whatever they found there.

Five seconds later, a soft click sounded from inside the bag. Simultaneously, Anto's face lit up. Flushed and smiling widely, he pulled out a flat slab of dark plastic from the bag. It was exactly the same shape and size as the base. He showed it to the police camera and put it aside on the bed. It would shortly be tested for prints, especially its underside.

He then opened the bag's mouth wide and shone his torch into it. He and Athreya peered into it. At the very bottom, in a shallow, newly revealed compartment was a black plastic pouch that was rectangular and flat.

'Gently, Anto,' Athreya warned again. 'Don't smudge finger-prints. Take it out slowly. Hold only one corner.'

Thirty seconds later, the flat pouch lay on the floor.

'Test it for fingerprints before opening it,' Athreya said. 'Make sure that you record a video of the fingerprinting.'

'The fingerprinting man will be here soon,' Anto said as he stood up.

'Excellent, Anto. Call me before you open the pouch. I'll be in my room.'

Athreya already knew what they would find in it.

.   .   .

268

Meanwhile, Veni was busy in her room. Once Athreya had left Mahesh's suite to go to Kanika's room, she too had decided to return to her room. She felt that she should leave the grief-stricken family to themselves. They would want privacy at this time.

Back in her room, she found that Holkar had sent more photos, clips and written matter overnight. Among the latest lot were some that had been 'scraped' from websites and social media. She began flipping through them.

Within five minutes, she began to feel awkward—she was viewing private material. While they were not stolen, they were never intended for her eyes. She felt that she was prying into strangers' lives. She shifted queasily in her chair and looked away from her iPad screen.

No sooner had she done it than another thought passed through her mind. The people who had posted these photos and clips might not have intended them for someone like her, but they had nevertheless posted them in the public domain. Facebook, Instagram, Twitter and TikTok posts were visible unless the owner made them private. The fact that they had not done so meant that she could view them, especially if she was doing it for a legitimate and virtuous purpose.

She went back to her iPad.

She began flipping through the assorted material Holkar had sent. It was not indexed or sequenced in any particular order. She guessed that they just hadn't had the time to do that. This was a raw dump of what they found.

Suddenly, she came across a face she had not seen before in Holkar's Bollywood dump—Kishan. She hadn't seen a single photo or clip of him, or an article. He was not even a minor celebrity, and he didn't attend parties either. As a result, the media had no cause to cover him. They probably seldom came across him. Curious at where this photo might have come from, she delved into the details.

It turned out to be scraped from the Facebook page of Kishan's teenage daughter. It seemed to be a family photo, showing ten people including Kishan, his wife and his daughter. It seemed to have been taken on the banks of a water body fringed with coconut trees. It looked very much like the Ashtamudi Lake. That fitted well with what little she knew of Kishan—he hailed from that part of Kerala.

Her curiosity piqued, Veni zoomed in and ran her eye over the rest of the group. The next moment, her eyes popped wide open and she stared at the photo, stunned. Among the remaining seven was another face that she recognized—that of a very pretty young woman.

Bhagya!

She quickly scanned the accompanying material and digested what she discovered. Holkar had sent extensive information from the Facebook page of Kishan's teenage daughter and other sources. Slowly, the relationships that had been murky so far were beginning to get clearer.

The impression she carried of Kishan also began changing. Earlier, based on what she had heard about him and his alleged notoriety, she had formed an impression of a tough, cruel man. A man who killed for money had to have a heart of stone.

But now, seeing the family photo, especially his gentle-looking wife and his shy daughter, she began seeing him as a caring husband and loving father. The humanness in him grew apparent to Veni. What had made this family man acquire the image of a ruthless killer?

Her reverie was broken by a knock on the door. Hoping that it was her husband, she hurried to open the door. It was Athreya, giving some instructions to Anto.

'Hari, Anto!' she called softly. 'Come in! I have something to show you.'

Closing the door after the two men, she hurried to pick up her iPad.

'See,' she said, thrusting it at Athreya. 'This is a photo of Kishan and his family. Look at the third woman from the right.'

Athreya stared and froze for a moment. Anto peered over his shoulder.

'Bhagya,' Athreya murmured. 'She and Kishan are related?'

Veni nodded furiously.

'Bhagya is Kishan's cousin's daughter.'

'That makes his motive stronger,' Anto said. 'In fact, he has a double motive—money and revenge.'

'See if you can break his alibi, Anto. We haven't given it the attention it deserves.'

'No, sir, we haven't,' Anto agreed. 'And I am responsible for that.' A determined look came onto his face. 'Kollam and Kottayam are my backyards. I will find all there is to find.'

'Send the photo to Kollam and Ashtamudi. Find out whatever you can about the others in the photo.'

'Yes, sir!'

The inspector strode out purposefully.

'Come, Veni,' Athreya said when Anto was out of earshot. 'Let's go look up Bhagya.'

'And Kishan,' Veni replied. 'I'm interested in meeting him.'

Fifteen minutes later, Athreya knocked at the door of Kishan's cottage. Kishan was fully dressed when he opened it despite it being 8 a.m. He stared enquiringly from Athreya to Veni as he stood in the doorway.

'Can I have a word with you?' Athreya asked softly.

In response, Kishan's gaze shifted to Veni.

'I saw a family photo of yours,' she said in Malayalam. 'It seems to have been taken in Ashtamudi. I wanted to meet you after seeing it. Mr Athreya let me come along with him. Can we come in, please?'

Veni's gentleness seemed to have an effect on Kishan. He nodded and stepped back, letting them enter the cottage. They silently took chairs. Kishan had still not said a word. He gazed expectantly at Athreya.

'This my wife, Veni,' Athreya said.

As courtesy suggested, Veni joined her palms in a *namaste*. Kishan responded in kind, as most men would have.

'I'll come straight to the point,' Athreya went on quietly. 'Veni came across a family photo of yours on social media and showed it to me. There were ten people in the photo. One of them was Bhagya. On further research, she discovered that Bhagya is your cousin's daughter.'

Kishan continued to stare without uttering a word. But his features had softened.

'As you can see,' Athreya went on, 'I have not come with the police. Instead, I've come with my wife. She sees you as a family man, a husband and a father. She has trouble accepting the image Bollywood paints of you.'

Kishan's eyes moved to Veni. He slowly dipped his head in acknowledgement.

'May I smoke?' he asked her.

'If you want to,' Veni replied.

Kishan picked up a cigarette packet from the nearby table and lit a stick. He drew two deep puffs and cleared his throat.

'Thank you,' he said to Veni. 'It's not often that folks outside my family see me as a normal person. My reputation usually precedes me. May I ask where you came across the photo?'

'Inspector Holkar of Mumbai sent it,' Veni answered. 'I'm helping my husband in the investigation. I do know more about Bollywood than he does.'

'Where did Holkar get it?'

'He didn't tell me,' Veni replied, sticking to the literal truth. She had never spoken to Holkar and she had no intention of getting Kishan's daughter into trouble. 'His team is scouring the Internet and social media posts for information. They have thousands and thousands of photos. This one caught my eye.'

Abruptly, Kishan stubbed out his cigarette and stood up.

'Come,' he said. 'Let's go see Bhagya.'

A few minutes later, they entered a very surprised Bhagya's room. The young woman was on the same sofa as she had been the last time Veni had visited her. Her foot was in a pressure bandage but her other bandage had been replaced by a Band-Aid.

'We need to have a private conversation,' Kishan told Susan, the nurse, in Malayalam. 'Would you mind giving us privacy for fifteen minutes?'

The way he had spoken, Veni noticed, was how any decent man would have. He didn't seem a bit like what his reputation suggested. The nurse nodded and left the room. The visitors took their seats.

'Bhagya,' Kishan began without preamble. His voice was gentle and caring. 'They have discovered a family photo that was taken in Ashtamudi. Mrs Athreya realized that you and I are related.'

Bhagya closed her eyes, took a deep breath and exhaled slowly.

'That was bound to happen, Kishan Mama,' she replied when she opened her eyes, referring to Kishan as her maternal uncle. 'I am happy that it was Aunty who discovered it, and not that police inspector.' She turned to Veni and asked, 'Do the police know, Aunty?'

Veni nodded. 'They do.'

Bhagya turned back to Kishan. 'I guess Mr Athreya will want to know why we concealed it. Shall I tell it, or will you?'

'Let me do it. It's easier that way.' He pulled out his cigarette packet. 'Forgive me for smoking, Mrs Athreya. This is a difficult moment for me. A cigarette makes it manageable.'

Veni nodded and he lit a cigarette.

'There isn't much to tell,' he began after blowing a cloud of smoke out of the open French windows. 'You know my reputation—I'm a moneylender, a killer, a crook, a mafia man, a pimp... take your pick. I've had this image for years.

'When Bhagya initially came to Mumbai and got a break in Bollywood, I told her not to mention me at all. If people came to know that she was related to me, whatever chance she might have had would have evaporated. So, we agreed that we would never talk about each other in public. We spoke mostly on the phone, and when we did meet, we made sure that we were not seen.'

'Bollywood is a dangerous place for a young woman,' Bhagya added. 'Especially when you are a newcomer from the south. Wolves are always prowling around you. You could do with a friend or a relative who knows the territory. I had many close shaves, but Krishnan Mama protected me from the worst. He was the only person I could trust.'

'I did the best I could without being seen,' Kishan went on. 'I failed sometimes, but thankfully, things didn't take a bad turn. Eventually, Bhagya learnt the ropes, after which she didn't need my help. She would reach out to me once in a while.' He paused and took another two puffs. 'But my biggest failure was that I was unable to protect her from Danuj.'

'That was my fault, Kishan Mama. I didn't tell you. Don't blame yourself for it. Please.'

'Yes, but had I known of it earlier, I would have told you what to expect. Danuj was well known for the wrong reasons. Anyway, it's over now. We can go back to Mumbai in peace.' He turned his gaze to Athreya. 'So, you see, sir? This is why we have kept our relationship secret—to protect Bhagya's reputation and career.'

'I do see that, Kishan,' Athreya replied. 'Thank you for confiding in us. We will not speak of it. I'll ask Anto and Holkar to keep it confidential as well.'

'Thank you, sir.'

Athreya went to the French windows and stood there, hands in pockets, gazing out at the swimming pool and the lake beyond. Like the last time, the still water in the pool looked like a sheet of glass. Where it ended, the lake began. Today too, the expanse of water was clear of boats or barges.

'What a lovely view,' he remarked to nobody in particular.

'If you don't mind my asking you, Mr Kishan,' Veni said, changing the topic. 'How did you acquire such a notorious image? I couldn't reconcile it with the photo I saw.'

'Krishnan Mama is a good man, Aunty,' Bhagya said. 'But once you start acquiring a bad reputation, it just keeps growing even if you do nothing wrong.'

'Since you ask, madam, I'll tell you,' Kishan said, pulling out another cigarette. 'When I came to Bombay as a young man, I didn't get any good breaks. The chances I got were all shady ones. I had no option but to take them. The alternative was to return to Kerala, which my ego didn't permit.

'The first name I earned was that of a moneylender—a "financer" who charged usurious rates and preyed upon the vulnerable. But the truth is that I have never had the money to lend! I was the front for a big name with big bucks and a virtuous image. Even now, I lend in my name, but the money is his. When my "client" repays, I pass it on to him. He gives me a cut of the interest.

'When a client defaults, he sends his men to deal with the client, and my reputation as a thug gets reinforced. On the rare occasion when a client refuses to pay despite several "reminders", his men kill the client. Guess who gets tagged as the killer?'

'In Danuj's case…?' Veni left it hanging.

A bitter laugh escaped Kishan.

'Where would I go for 25 crores, madam?' he asked. 'I live in a small flat in a dirty chawl. If I had 25 crores of my own, why would I live there? Why would I do all these nefarious things on someone else's behalf? I would invest the 25 crores and live off the interest of two crores I'd get every year. That would be more than enough to live comfortably in Kerala. I would be happy!'

'So, you see, Aunty,' Bhagya concluded, 'Krishnan Mama is as much a victim as I am. He has never killed anyone.'

19

Athreya had requested Mahesh call the Gauria family to the suite at 10 a.m. They had had the time to bathe, change into fresh clothes and have a sparse breakfast. A pall of gloom hung over them when Athreya, Veni and Anto entered on time. It had been just a few hours since they had lost a second member of the family. For all that, both Mahesh and Manjari looked stoic as they faced the changed reality.

Pari and Ruhi, both newly widowed women, sat together, taking comfort in each other's presence. Athreya wondered if the news had reached Pari's children. Probably not. Elsewhere, Kanika and Jeet sat close together, looking subdued and apprehensive. Athreya had not said anything about the pouch found in the hidden compartment in their luggage. Whether Kanika had checked and found it empty, Athreya had no idea.

He hadn't wanted anyone else here and had kept the participation to the minimum. Joseph and his team were in Kottayam, trying to break Kishan's alibi.

'This is an absolutely rotten time to have this conversation,' Athreya began, as soon as Anto and Veni took their seats. 'It's been but a few hours since you heard about Hiran. However, we are now in a position to clear up one part of the mystery, and that's why I requested Maheshji to call you all here. I hope it's okay if I get straight to the point.'

'There's no better way,' Mahesh rumbled. 'Let's have it, whatever that may be.'

'Thank you. As you know, we searched all the rooms this morning. It turned out to be a useful exercise because we did find something.'

That caused a stir. Several Gaurias glanced at each other and sat up. Kanika and Jeet seemed to shrink into their sofa. They didn't utter a sound.

'Where?' Mahesh asked, his voice a whiplash. Kanika shut her eyes and clutched her husband's arm.

'In Kanika's room,' Athreya replied. 'We found a secret compartment in her large leather bag.'

All eyes, some angry, others incredulous, snapped to her. Jeet and Kanika paled. Their faces became white as sheets.

'What did you find?' Mahesh demanded, keeping his eyes on his daughter.

'This!' Athreya held up the flat pouch. 'As you can see, this is a pouch that holds A4 size documents. Do you recognize it, Kanika, Jeet?'

The couple stayed silent.

'Any idea what it contains?' Athreya asked the others.

'I'm not sure,' Ruhi answered hesitantly. 'Papers from Danuj's blue file, perhaps?'

'Correct. We have seen the papers inside. They include the agreement Danuj had wanted you and Sahil to sign the day he died. There is also the document that Danuj had taken away from Kanika—an agreement that would cause her considerable embarrassment if it went public. There are two other documents that I will let Maheshji decide what to do with. They relate to some dealings between Danuj and Hiran.'

'Kanika, how did these papers come into your possession?' Mahesh demanded, his voice hard as granite.

Kanika didn't answer. Instead, she buried her face in her hands.

'The contents of Danuj's blue file being in your possession can mean only one thing,' Athreya said slowly. 'You boarded Danuj's houseboat that night.'

278

Two gasps sounded but Athreya didn't know where they had come from. Kanika began shaking, her face still buried in her hands. Jeet was staring mutely at the coir mat on the floor.

'Is that right, Kanika?' Mahesh thundered.

Thoroughly intimidated, Kanika swivelled where she sat and took refuge in her husband's shoulder.

'Jeet?' Mahesh demanded. 'Speak, man!'

Jeet nodded. 'Yes… yes, we boarded Danuj's boat.'

'From the starboard side?' Athreya asked.

Jeet nodded. A pregnant silence enveloped the room. Horror showed on several faces as they wondered what more the confession meant. Did Kanika and Jeet kill Danuj?

'We boarded the houseboat,' Jeet repeated, his thin voice wavering. 'But… but we didn't kill Danuj.'

Pin-drop silence greeted the words. Even Kanika had stopped sobbing. Athreya sat down.

'Honest!' Jeet pleaded earnestly. 'We took the papers from the blue file. But we didn't kill Danuj. He was already dead when we boarded.'

This drew more gasps and groans.

'Jeet!' Mahesh snapped again. 'Speak the truth.'

'I swear! It is the truth. Danuj was dead when we boarded the boat.'

'Kanika!'

Mahesh's voice was like the crack of a whip. Most people in the room were startled. Kanika almost jumped. Her hands flew from her face.

'Yes, Papa,' she whispered. 'Danuj was dead.'

'Then, why didn't you call for help?' Mahesh asked. 'For God's sake, he was your brother!'

'Because it was too late… he was already dead. And… and if

I said that we had boarded the boat, we would be arrested for the murder. That's why we remained silent.'

Mahesh groaned and rubbed his leathery face.

'Mr Athreya,' he appealed to the investigator. 'Tell us what happened. Please. I think you know.'

'There are still some holes in what I know,' Athreya replied. 'But this is what I think happened.'

Athreya's imagination flared, and the happenings of that night flashed past his mind's eye as if he were watching the events unfold.

It was forty-five minutes past midnight. The two houseboats bobbed lazily on the lake, anchored to their spots. The only sounds were from the generators on the boats and the air conditioners. And the gentle breeze of course—always the breeze. The two nearby resorts lay still and silent in the moonlight. Only the night lights in the corridors and public areas were glowing. All the windows were dark.

The boat had already rocked twice that night. Sahil had come and gone more than an hour back. He and Ruhi had heard a bizarre proposal from Danuj and had rejected it. The boat hadn't rocked again after Sahil had left.

The world was asleep. Or so it would seem.

Danuj lay on the sofa in the sitting area of his boat, knocked out by the massive dose of alprazolam that had somehow entered his body. Figuratively, if not literally, he was dead to the world. A single light glowed above him, powered by the boat's generator. A blue cardboard file lay on a nearby table with two mobile phones on it, acting as paperweights against the breeze. Ruhi's ornamental dagger, which he had been playing with, had fallen from his hand to the coir mat on the deck. Danuj's chest heaved gently as he breathed deeply in his sleep despite the cramped sofa.

On the other side of a thin wooden door lay Ruhi. Unlike her husband, she lay on a bed behind the locked door. After a terrible evening, she had finally drifted off to sleep, thanks to a small dose of alprazolam she had taken. The drug had helped her overcome the discomfort brought about by the constant movement of the boat due to the waves.

All was still on this boat.

The other houseboat, however, was witnessing activity, albeit silently. Kanika and Jeet whispered to each other as they took turns to peer through binoculars at Danuj's boat. The blue file was visible in the light of the overhead lamp. Also visible was the fact that Danuj was fast asleep. They had been watching him for fifteen minutes, and he hadn't stirred even a little bit. Nor had there been any sign of movement from the bedroom where Ruhi slept.

The time was ripe. Kanika made her decision.

'Let's go,' she whispered to Jeet. 'Swimsuits.'

The couple entered their bedroom and began changing into their swimwear—Jeet into a pair of trunks topped by a swim shirt, and Kanika into a one-piece swimsuit. Both pulled on disposable gloves.

Finally, she picked up a plastic pouch to hold the papers from the blue file. The stiff cardboard file, she knew, couldn't be rolled up and inserted into her swimsuit. But the flat pouch could be. It could easily be tucked in. The adhesive seal would keep the papers dry. Hopefully.

From inside their bedroom, they couldn't see Danuj's boat, where something unforeseen was happening—a coracle had arrived on the port side. Had they seen it, they might have changed their plans.

The coracle rider, with hands enclosed in latex gloves, took a length of rope and tied the small craft to the railing. The boat rocked for the third time that night... rocked gently as the visitor climbed cautiously onto the boat and glided in over the railing. Once on board, the figure crouched and listened.

No sounds came, other than from the generator and the air conditioner.

The first thing the nocturnal visitor did was to locate the lamp switch and turn it off. Once the sitting area was dark, the intruder moved to study Danuj's sleeping form. The person knew what to expect, it seemed.

The act took less than five seconds. Up rose the hand holding a large knife. It paused for a moment and flashed down, sliding the blade cleanly into Danuj's chest and severing his heart almost in two. A gurgle sounded from the stricken man's throat and a few muscles jerked.

A minute later, he lay still. Breathing ceased.

Something lying on the deck caught the killer's eye—Ruhi's brown-and-gold dagger. The interloper contemplated it for a few moments. A smile slowly blossomed on the intent face.

The killer picked up the dagger and clicked it open. The hand rose and fell three more times, stabbing the dagger into Danuj's chest each time. After the fourth stab, the hand let go, leaving the dagger lodged in Danuj.

That would incriminate Ruhi! At the minimum, it would confuse the police. Good!

Suddenly, the sound of two splashes came across the water. Jeet and Kanika had entered the water from their houseboat. The killer crouched close to the deck and listened. Rhythmic sounds of freestyle swimming strokes reached the killer's ears… they were coming closer. Two people. Swimming towards Danuj's boat.

Damn! Not a second to lose! Panic flared.

Staying low, the killer darted towards the gate in the railing and tried to untie the rope that moored the coracle to the boat. But trembling fingers wouldn't cooperate. The darkness made it even more difficult.

Precious seconds ticked away. The sound of swimming was much closer now. The killer looked around desperately. The eyes fell on the murder weapon.

Cut it!

The next moment, the rope lay in two pieces and the severed ends were stained with blood from the knife.

The killer went over the railing and dropped gently into the water, knowing full well that the approaching swimmers wouldn't hear the splash over their own swimming sounds. The boat rocked again, for the fourth time that night.

The killer began swimming, pushing the coracle in front. Now, the killer couldn't hear sounds! Panic surged again. Kick harder! The killer made a snap decision—it was best to swim back, rather than get in the coracle.

A rider in the coracle might be seen in the moonlight, but a swimmer was hard to spot if they used breaststroke or swam underwater. The coracle just needed to be pushed a short distance from the boat for the night to shroud it. Overnight, it would float away, taken by the waves and the breeze.

A minute later, when they were far enough from the boat, the swimmer let the coracle go and began swimming towards the pier. Halfway there, the killer let go of the knife and continued to swim away.

Meanwhile, Danuj's boat rocked for the fifth time that night as Kanika and Jeet boarded it together. Danuj seemed to be fast asleep. Sparing nary a glance at her brother, Kanika went straight to the blue file. She didn't know that he was now literally dead to the world.

She opened the file and removed the clasp that held the papers in place. Holding the entire sheaf of papers in the file, she pulled them out from the two springs. A rasping sound came from the file as the papers slid over the springs. She glanced at her brother in alarm. He was not moving, but Jeet's bearing seemed odd. He was peering at Danuj strangely. Ignoring it, she brought her attention back to the file. Stay focused!

Once the papers were out of the file, she threw the empty file overboard. The waves would take it away. She pulled out the pouch, opened its adhesive seal and slid the papers into it. She glanced again at Danuj to see if the sound of the seal had awakened him. It didn't matter now if it did—she had already taken possession of the embarrassing document in the file. By now, Jeet was gaping like a goldfish, unable to say a word.

Concentrating on what was important, Kanika rolled up the pouch tightly and pushed it in from the top of her swimsuit, between her breasts, to her belly. Once it was safely tucked away, she glanced at her water-resistant watch. It was 12:59 a.m. Well done, she congratulated herself. This had been her last resort, and it had worked out well. Pleased, she turned to Jeet and the still unmoving Danuj. That's when it finally struck her that something was very amiss.

'Dead!' Jeet whispered when Kanika came and stopped a few feet from her brother, well short of the pool of blood. 'He's dead! Killed, Kani!'

Kanika stared for a long moment, her eyes taking in her dead brother, the pool of blood on the coir mat and the dagger in his chest.

'Ruhi killed him!' she hissed. 'That's her dagger!'

Her gaze dropped to the deck where the dark pool was spreading towards them.

'You fool!' she hissed at her husband. 'You have stepped in the blood.'

She was right—the blood had reached Jeet's right foot and was less than an inch from his left foot. Instinctively, he sprang backwards. His right foot made a fresh red mark on the coir mat, a couple of feet from the maroon pool. The ball of the foot and four toes showed clearly.

'Stay still!' Kanika hissed again. 'Now, raise your right foot and don't put it down. Hop away on your left leg. Don't let your right foot down!'

Kanika bent and picked up one of Danuj's slippers. She dipped the front half of it into the blood and smeared it over the mark Jeet's foot had made. She did that twice, making the stain irregular in shape. In her haste the blood got on the strap as well. She dropped the slipper into the blood and backed away as it came to rest on its side.

Seconds later, they slid off the boat together, which rocked for the sixth time and final time that night. They began swimming back to their boat.

A stunned silence reigned after Athreya stopped narrating. Shock and horror etched most faces. Manjari was staring at her daughter with incredulity. Mahesh might have been carved of stone with his jaw drooping in astonishment. The Gauria daughters-in-law were appalled; they gaped fearfully at Kanika as if she were a demon. Ruhi looked as if she might throw up any moment. Jeet sat frozen while Kanika had bent double in shame to place her face almost between her knees.

The suite was a picture of abject misery. A family in utter despair.

Athreya rose. So did Veni and Anto.

'I will say this in Kanika's defence,' he said softly. 'She boarded Danuj's boat as the last resort. She had probably pleaded with her brother several times to return the papers he had taken. But he didn't budge. Petrified by the spectre of its contents going public, she was left with no option but to steal it back. When the opportunity presented itself that night, she took it with both hands.'

He went to Mahesh and spoke gently to him, 'We still have work to do, Maheshji. I will take my leave if you don't mind. Please call me if you need me.' He dropped his voice into Mahesh's ear. 'I'm sorry to have been the bearer of bad news. Please forgive me. I hope to name the killer this evening.'

Athreya, Anto and Veni left the suite in silence and walked out to the lawn.

'How did you know?' Anto asked, as soon as they were out of earshot of the suite.

'It's quite straightforward, Anto,' Athreya replied. 'We already knew that the murderer came in the coracle. The cleanly cut rope had Danuj's blood at its ends.'

'Yes, but how did you know that Kanika and Jeet came immediately after the murderer?'

'Why would the murderer cut the rope if he or she could have untied it? Why leave a piece of evidence on the houseboat? The only reason I could think of was that the murderer was in a tearing hurry. Why? Because he or she was surprised by someone and had to leave the boat within seconds.

'If so, who surprised the murderer? There were two possibilities. One, Ruhi might have come out of the bedroom. Two, someone came to the boat. All indications are that Ruhi was sleeping under the influence of alprazolam. Besides, had she stepped out of the bedroom, she would have come face to face with the murderer *immediately*. The murderer might have killed her too. I therefore picked the second possibility—that someone came to the boat unexpectedly.'

'Okay, that makes sense. But why did it have to be Kanika?'

'The coracle was tied to the *port* side of the boat. The fact that the murderer was able to cut it loose meant that the surprise visitor did not come from that side. So, the visitor came via the *starboard* side. That was also consistent with the damp patch we saw on the deck on the starboard side.

'Who could it have been? What was there to the starboard side? Only Kanika's houseboat. Kanika and Jeet were the only people on that side. All the others were in one of the two resorts, which were on the port side. So, chances were that Kanika and Jeet boarded the boat. Besides, we already knew that they had entered the water.'

'And the discovery of the papers under the false bottom confirmed your suspicion,' Veni concluded. 'A clear chain of logic. Well done, Hari. Such a simple explanation for the irregular patch of blood!'

'Yes, Mr Aadhreiah,' Anto agreed. 'Clear and simple.'

'So that's why Kanika and Jeet took time the next morning before coming to Mahesh's suite,' Veni exclaimed, as something else clicked into place. 'When they returned to their room, they had to empty the leather bag, open the secret compartment, hide the pouch and replace the contents in the bag.'

'Exactly.'

'What will happen to Kanika now?' Veni asked.

'That's up to Mahesh,' Athreya answered. 'Technically, Kanika only took back what Danuj had stolen from her. So, no crime was committed there. Although I suspect that Danuj stealing it was not playful fooling around between brother and sister. I suspect he was trying to extort money from his sister.'

'I agree,' Veni said. 'That was in keeping with Danuj's personality.'

'She did tamper with evidence,' Anto bristled. 'I mean the patch of blood.'

'A minor matter, Anto,' Athreya said. 'Not very material.'

'What were the embarrassing documents that Danuj had taken from Kanika?' Anto asked. 'The ones with which he was trying to extort money from her?'

'You remember the Bollywood con man named Mandal?' Athreya asked.

Anto nodded. 'The man who was arrested after he duped several Bollywood personalities two years ago? He fled the country while on bail, and is reputed to be hiding under a different name.'

'That's the one. Kanika had some dealings with him and had also entered into contracts with him. The papers Danuj stole from her are agreements that show that she had financed him and had invested in his businesses. She probably has since lost that money, but she retained the documents in case she wants to claim it back sometime in the future.'

'Ah!' Veni exclaimed. 'So, that's it! Not only has Kanika been chummy with a con man, but she has also financed him! She wouldn't want that to come out—Mandal is hugely toxic.'

'That's not all,' Athreya added. 'Her carefully cultivated image of being a hard-nosed businesswoman would take a beating. She prides herself on being like her father. If it emerges that she fell for Mandal hook, line and sinker, that image will crumble.

'So, Anto, when the case is over, you can decide whether or not to charge Kanika for tampering with evidence. The only thing you can charge her with is smearing blood over a footprint.'

'Are you close to cracking it, Hari?' Veni asked in a hushed voice.

'I think I know what happened. I just need evidence that will stand up in court.'

'Video footage from the security cameras, sir?' Anto asked.

'Yes. And one more piece of evidence.'

'What are we waiting for, sir?' Anto grinned. 'Let's go. The footages are waiting for us.'

20

Athreya and Anto sat in the temporary office with a young woman whom Joseph introduced as 'Marisa, our technology person'. She and Joseph had collated all the camera footages onto an external hard drive, which Marisa had connected to the computer. Also attached to the computer were a large TV and a specialized control pad that Marisa used expertly to manipulate the videos.

'We have all the raw footages from last night,' Marisa began. 'You can view them whenever you like. But that would take hours, even if you watched them at high speed. To make it easier for you, we have watched them and extracted the key parts into another video file.'

'Brilliant!' Athreya applauded. 'By key parts, I presume you mean the portions where people appear in the video? You have removed footage that shows an empty corridor?'

'Yes, sir. That's what we did in the first iteration. Then, we reviewed the extracted video and cut out the portions that are of no importance—a steward walking down a corridor, for instance. Joseph guided me in that. Wherever we had the slightest doubt, we let it remain. The most important parts of the footage from this resort are from the wee hours. However, nobody came out of their room or entered it until 1:47 a.m. Shall I show you?'

'Before we do that, Marisa, give me a verbal summary of what your footages show after, say, 8 p.m. last night,' said Athreya.

'Several people were walking around till almost 11 p.m.,' she replied unhesitatingly. 'That's what the footages show. Joseph, would you like to add anything?'

'The Gaurias and Sahil were up and about till 11 p.m., as Marisa said,' Joseph offered. 'Ruhi and Pari were in Mahesh's suite most of the time, except when they went for dinner. Sahil, Hiran, Kanika and Jeet spent several hours together in the evening.'

'Where?' Anto asked.

'In Sahil's room. Judging by the ice, soda, coke and snacks that went in, we think that they were having drinks.'

'All of them?' Athreya asked.

'Yes, sir. All four. I spoke to the stewards too. They did not get drunk or anything like that. It was a sober and low-key affair. They were mostly reflecting on Danuj's death and what it meant for the Gaurias and for Ruhi in particular. They also speculated on what the rumour mills might be saying.'

'Okay. What happened after 11 p.m. last night?'

'The four of them went for a late dinner, after which they returned to their own rooms.'

'Did they stay in their rooms?'

'Kanika and Jeet did. Sahil and Hiran strolled on the lawn, smoking and talking. At about 11:30 p.m., they separated, and Hiran returned to his room.'

'Sahil?' Athreya asked.

'He was outside till about midnight. He then went to his room and didn't come out again.'

'Hiran came out, I suppose?' Athreya asked. He glanced at Marisa. 'Is that what you were going to show us?'

'Yes, sir,' she replied. 'Shall I?'

'Please.'

Marisa's fingers flew over the control pad. A moment later, a video sprang to life on the TV. It showed a covered corridor that had rooms on one side and was open on the other. Most of the picture was dark, except where night lights illuminated the corridor. The top right corner showed the time: 01:47.

'That's Hiran's room,' Marisa pointed to a door with a pencil. 'It will open in… twenty seconds.'

They waited. Exactly twenty seconds later, the door opened, and a thin man stepped out. He was dressed in dark trousers and a light shirt. It was Hiran. He was wearing the clothes he was found dead in.

'Stop!' Athreya cried suddenly.

Marisa responded swiftly, and the image on the TV froze.

'What's in his hand?' Athreya asked.

'A mobile phone, sir.'

Marisa was nonplussed by the intensity of the interruption. It was quite apparent from the image that Hiran was carrying a mobile phone.

'Can you zoom in?' Athreya asked. 'I want to see the mobile.'

Marisa's fingers flew over the control pad again. The image on the TV expanded outwards slowly and stopped when the mobile filled the screen.

'It's a mobile, sir,' Marisa repeated. 'No doubt.'

'Anto?' Athreya asked. 'What do you think?'

'It's not his usual phone, sir,' Anto replied. 'His regular phone is the latest iPhone, while this—' He pointed to the TV '—is a cheaper instrument.'

'I agree. He left his regular phone in his room.' He glanced at Marisa. 'Continue playing the video, please.'

After shutting the door and locking it, Hiran disappeared into the darkness. The time the TV showed was 1:48:13.

'That's all, sir,' Marisa said. 'He didn't come back.'

'And nobody left their rooms around this time?'

'No, sir. Everyone was in their rooms—Mahesh and Manjari in the suite, Ruhi and Pari in Ruhi's room, Kanika and Jeet in their room and Sahil in his.'

'What about Kishan and Bhagya?'

'The footage from Sunset Bay shows that Bhagya didn't come out of her door from when the security cameras were switched on. Her nurse and several visitors walked in and out, but not her. I'm told she is injured and can't walk without crutches?'

'That's right,' Athreya concurred.

'Her nurse left at 7:07 p.m. Joseph says that her duty schedule is from 7 a.m. to 7 p.m.'

'And Kishan?'

'We have a problem there, sir. The footage shows that he entered his cottage at 10:13 p.m. through the front door. And didn't come out until the next morning. But—'

'But he could have come out through either of the veranda doors in the hall or the bedroom,' Athreya interrupted. 'Is that what you were going to say?'

'Yes, sir. Unfortunately, none of the cameras covers his verandas.'

'Anything on his alibi during Danuj's murder, Joseph?' Athreya asked.

'It still holds, sir,' Joseph replied dejectedly. 'The man in Kottayam stands by his earlier statement, and we have not yet found anybody who can contradict him.'

'Kishan and he must have gone out, I guess?'

'Yes, they did… first to buy liquor and later for dinner. But they insist that they were together all the time.'

'Until 1:30 a.m. or thereabouts? Kishan entered Sunset Bay at about 2 a.m.'

'Yes, sir.'

'Danuj was long dead by then.'

'Yes, sir.'

'Okay,' Athreya stood up and stretched. 'From what you have said about Kishan and Bhagya, I don't need to view the rest of the footage. We have already seen enough Crystal Waters footage. What remains to be viewed are the footage of the swimming pool and the video of the attack on Bhagya. Let's view them.'

'I'll show you the footage of the swimming pool,' Marisa responded. 'It's interesting for sure. But the video of the assault on Bhagya is not very clear. It was dark when she was assaulted and the surveillance camera on the road wasn't close to where it happened.'

'Aren't the figures clear?' Athreya asked. 'The assailants, the driver and Bhagya herself?'

'Well... yes and no. Since we know there are four figures, we can make them out. But the video is currently not clear enough to stand up in court.'

'I thought you were going to enhance it?'

'Yes, sir, but that takes time. That's currently being done at our lab.'

'You know what I am looking for, right? All I need from you is confirmation that my suspicion is correct.'

'Yes, sir,' Marisa nodded. 'Joseph told me what you are expecting to see in the footage. Once we enhance the video, we'll apply different filters and see what comes up.'

'How long will that take?' Athreya asked.

Marisa glanced at her watch. 'Another two hours is my guess.'

'Good! Can you have it ready by 5 p.m.? Enhancement, filters and all? I need it here at Crystal Waters at that time.'

'Will do, sir,' Marisa replied crisply. 'Leave it to me.'

'Thanks, Marisa. I intend to close this case today and your work will be crucial.'

'Understood, sir.'

'Okay. Let's have a look at the swimming pool footage.'

Once again, Marisa's fingers did their dance. The TV sprang to life again, showing a swimming pool from a distance. The time displayed at the top right corner was 01:26:27—very early in the morning of the night Hiran was killed.

All was quiet in the image. The camera registered no movement. There was no sign of life, and the world was asleep. If the gentle night breeze created small ripples in the pool, the hidden camera—which Anto had installed at a distance from the pool out of necessity—didn't register them.

'Five seconds,' Marisa announced.

Athreya tensed. This could be the make or break point. Without this, the case might not stand up in court.

A figure appeared at the near edge of the large swimming pool. The light was not enough to show where the figure had materialized from. But it was clear that it was carrying something. Something that Athreya recognized despite the distance between the camera and the figure.

'Enhancement will show it clearly, sir,' Marisa assured him.

'Will we be able to recognize the person?' Athreya asked.

'I think so. But I can't be sure until I enhance and apply filters.'

The figure entered the swimming pool and swam, carrying the burden it had brought. On reaching the other end, it came out of water. The things it carried became more visible and discernible.

'Excellent!' Athreya exclaimed. 'This will do.' He rose and shook hands with Marisa. 'Well done!' he said. 'You have helped us no end!'

The young woman reddened at the praise.

'It was my pleasure to work with you, sir. I've heard a lot about you. I'm grateful for the opportunity.'

Athreya turned to Joseph.

'Breaking Kishan's alibi may no longer be important,' he said. 'I think we have everything we need.'

Anto, who had been silent all along, came and shook Athreya's hand.

'You were right, sir,' he gushed. 'It has been a delight to watch you crack the case. What next, sir?'

'Get everyone to gather at Mahesh's suite at 5 p.m.,' Athreya replied.

'Everyone?'

'Yes. The Gaurias, Sahil, Kishan and Bhagya.'

When Athreya returned to his room, he found Veni in a state of high excitement. He knew at once that she had something to tell him but had refrained from calling or messaging him because he was viewing crucial footages with the police. She had waited impatiently for him to return.

'You were right, Hari,' she enthused as soon as he closed the door. 'The motive for Danuj's murder lies not in Kumarakom, but in Mumbai; in Danuj's past.'

A surge of excitement ran through Athreya. This was what he was waiting for—the final piece in the puzzle.

'Wonderful, Veni!' he said. 'Show me.'

She opened her iPad and showed him Kishan's family photo.

'Look at the second person from the right. Study her face.'

Athreya stared at the indicated person for a few seconds. He then nodded.

Veni swiped furiously on her iPad for a few seconds and brought up another photo. She thrust the screen in her husband's face.

'See?' she hissed. 'See what I mean?'

The second photo showed the person whose face he had just memorized. She was at a restaurant with a man. With her fingers, Veni zoomed in to show the man's face clearly. It was a familiar face.

Danuj.

21

The usually gregarious Veni was uncharacteristically nervous and quiet when 5 p.m. came. They had all gathered in Mahesh's suite and were waiting for Athreya to begin proceedings. Veni sat alone and watchful in her corner, away from the Gaurias and the police. Marisa was in another corner, having connected her laptop to the large wall-mounted TV. Bhagya was on a sofa beside Kishan, with her crutches leaning on the wall behind her.

Mahesh and Manjari, having prepared themselves for hearing the truth about their sons' deaths, tried to keep their faces impassive. The prayer beads were still absent from the mother's hand. The younger Gaurias and Sahil sat quietly but Veni could see the tension in their faces.

From the few terse sentences Athreya had uttered earlier in the privacy of their room, Veni guessed that the family was not going to like what he was about to reveal. She felt sorry for them—hadn't they endured enough?

Presently, Athreya stood up. Veni closed her eyes for a moment and took a deep breath. Here it comes!

'I will start with Danuj's murder and resume from where I left off this morning,' Athreya began without any preliminaries. 'I will conclude this sordid affair here and now. We had established this morning that Kanika and Jeet had boarded Danuj's boat and had inadvertently surprised the killer just after Danuj had been killed. That had made the killer flee by cutting the coracle's rope with the murder weapon. We had, however, not established the identity of the murderer.

'Danuj's killer had come in a coracle but, due to the sudden paucity of time, had cut it adrift and swam back to the shore.

Halfway to the pier, the murder weapon had been dropped and fell to the lake bottom, where it was later found.

'Now, a small coracle tends to be unstable and difficult to handle unless one knows how to do it. This peculiar little water-craft is used widely in Kerala, and many youngsters there learn to use it rather early in life, especially those who grow up near lakes and other water bodies. Veni herself has used them in her younger days. Then, did it mean that the killer, who was adept at manoeuvring a coracle, was from one of the lake regions of Kerala?'

All eyes, except Bhagya's, turned to Kishan, who was a Keralite from Ashtamudi. He sat there impassively with his face and body language giving nothing away. His eyes were fixed stonily on Athreya.

'But that theory ran into a problem. Everything about Danuj's murder suggested that the killer knew what was going on at and around Crystal Waters—Danuj's fake tantrum, his sudden decision to hire a houseboat for the night, Sahil visit-ing the houseboat and Kanika and Jeet spending the night in their houseboat. Kishan couldn't have known any of this in advance.

'The murder, as you all saw, was executed almost perfectly. That could not have happened without knowledge of the minute-to-minute happenings at Crystal Waters. How then did Kishan manage it when he was not at this resort? He was at Kottayam by all accounts, which is half an hour's drive from here. To com-pound the problem, none of the guests at Crystal Waters seemed to be able to handle a coracle.'

Veni scanned the faces in the room as Athreya paused for breath. Every pair of eyes was riveted on him. Expressions gave nothing away other than deep interest. They were hanging on to his every word.

'That's how matters stood until Sunday evening,' Athreya went on. 'As I said, the murder had been executed so well that we were left with almost nothing to go on—no fingerprints or any other physical evidence. Just a severed rope and an empty blue file. I began fearing that if the murderer remained content with one crime and made no further moves, we might never solve this case. Nothing more might happen that could give us new leads.

'But I have seen in other cases that murderers sometimes grow overconfident after a successful crime and make a slip up. Or something happens outside the murderer's control that sets a new chain of events into motion.'

'That's what happened,' Mahesh rumbled. 'Bhagya was attacked.'

'Correct,' Athreya agreed. 'Two men from Mumbai assaulted her with an intent to kill. The street camera shows it clearly. As you yourself told me, Maheshji, all of you here have the contacts necessary to put out a contract to kill her.'

Mahesh nodded. 'We call it "offering *supari*" in the Mumbai language.'

'*Supari*, indeed. But why? Why did someone want Bhagya out of the way? Did she know something that was incriminating to the killer? Or was there some other reason? We were not sure and had no option but to wait for things to play out.'

'With events in motion again,' Anto interrupted, 'there was a good chance that more things might happen. That's why you asked me to switch on the security cameras in both resorts.'

'Correct, Anto. And that gave us a vital lead: Hiran was carrying an old mobile last night when he left his room after 1:45 a.m. He had left his regular iPhone in his room.'

A couple of soft moans sounded at the mention of Hiran's name. After all, it was a mere ten hours since they had learnt of his death. Athreya paused for a few moments before continuing.

'Pari,' he asked gently. 'Did Hiran bring a second mobile to Kumarakom?'

'Yes,' a perplexed Pari replied. 'But it was an old spare one.'

'Do you know why he brought it here?'

'There were some phone numbers in it. He brought it along just in case they were needed. But it had no SIM card.'

'That was, in all probability, true. However, if a new SIM card was inserted, he would have had a different number for making and receiving calls.'

'Yes. So what?' Pari was puzzled.

'We'll come back to that soon, Pari,' Athreya said. 'Right now, the questions we need to answer are: why did Hiran leave his room at the dead of night, and where did he go? Was he going to meet someone at that unearthly hour? If so, was the rendezvous near where his body was found? To answer these questions, we need to go to the video footages from last night—the night Hiran was killed.'

Marisa hit a key on her laptop. The TV screen sprang to life.

'When Inspector Anto got both the resorts to turn on their security cameras after Danuj's death,' Athreya went on, 'he did one more thing. He installed a night camera some distance from the swimming pool. We are about to see the footage that this new camera captured.'

He nodded to Marisa, who hit the play button. An image of a large, aesthetically shaped swimming pool came on the TV. Behind it were the rooms of a resort. The time at the top right corner showed 01:26:27.

It was the same clip Athreya and Anto had watched earlier in the day. Only now, the picture was considerably clearer. Marisa had enhanced the video and applied filters.

'That is not our swimming pool,' Mahesh objected. 'Ours is a rectangular one.'

'That's right,' Athreya concurred. 'This is the swimming pool at Sunset Bay. We are watching something that happened there last night.'

Brief murmurings sounded. Once again, eyes stole glances at the impassive Kishan.

'Watch,' Marisa said in a low voice. 'Five seconds.'

A figure appeared at the far edge of the pool. But unlike on the earlier occasion, the video enhancement showed the figure emerging from French doors behind it, carrying some things.

'A French window,' Athreya explained. 'Stop! Zoom!'

The image froze with the figure centred on the TV screen. Marisa zoomed in. The top half of the figure filled the screen.

Bhagya.

She was carrying a single crutch and a small bag.

Veni was stunned. She gawked at Bhagya in disbelief. The image of a wounded Bhagya sitting bandaged and forlorn on her sofa was fresh in her mind. She remembered, very vividly, the sympathy she had felt for the young woman. How well Bhagya had faked her injury! An accomplished actress if ever there was one. With a jolt, Veni realized that she had developed affection for a murderer!

'Zoom out slightly,' Athreya's voice said, bringing Veni back to the present.

The figure on the TV shrank until its feet were also visible.

'See… no bandages. She is walking normally on both feet, but she is carrying a crutch and a waterproof bag.'

Bhagya had become white as a sheet. Kishan was gaping at her in horror, stunned speechless. All the others were dumbfounded too.

'This, by itself, is not conclusive,' Athreya went on relentlessly. 'All it proves is that Bhagya faked her foot injury and that she went out of her room a little before 1:30 a.m. this morning with her crutch and a waterproof bag strapped to her back. Remember, she is an expert swimmer—she swam with the crutch on her back. This video also shows her returning at about 2:15 a.m., which I will not show you. But do note the swimsuit—it has a distinctive red and blue diagonal pattern.

'After her nocturnal adventure, Bhagya couldn't afford to have a telltale wet swimsuit in her room. It would be a dead giveaway. Nor could she throw it away into the lake or elsewhere, as it would be discovered soon. She therefore needed to hide it somewhere. The one place that came to mind was the swimming pool itself.'

In a corner of the room, Joseph picked up a large plastic bag. Veni's heart thudded. She knew what was in it.

'Sunset Bay is an old resort whose pool has been modified several times,' Athreya continued. 'At the bottom of the pool, near the deep end, are some old notches in the wall that used to house pipes that circulated and cleaned the water. With a new purification plant now in place, those pipes have been removed. But the notches remain and are excellent hiding places. Joseph searched the pool this afternoon. What he found is interesting.'

Joseph opened the evidence bag and pulled out a colourful garment—a woman's wet one-piece swimsuit with a red and blue diagonal pattern. Bhagya's. He put it on the floor and dipped his hand into the bag again. This time, it came out holding something long and slender, metallic and sharp. A knife that Dr Saju would have characterized as a professional weapon.

Veni shuddered as she felt her blood run cold.

'What an evil-looking blade!' Mahesh exclaimed. 'Where did she get it?'

'From the Mumbai thugs who attacked her on the road to Kochi,' Athreya replied. 'One of them had it and was going to kill her with it. But she got him first with the pepper spray. In his agony, he dropped the knife. We have examined the enhanced footage from the street camera. It shows her picking it up from the road.'

'Does the blade match the stab wounds on Hiran?'

'Yes, Maheshji, it does. I also expect the DNA collected from the knife to match with Hiran's.'

Silence prevailed after Athreya stopped talking. Everyone was still, including Bhagya. She studied the carpet with contemplative eyes. Veni looked around. The Gaurias had taken it well, but Kishan was gutted. Sahil looked thoughtful. Presently, Bhagya looked up at Athreya.

'How did you know?' she asked. 'When did you catch on?'

'When you told Kishan that you saw Kanika and Jeet enter the water. You said you saw them from your French windows.'

'I could have,' Bhagya countered. 'I had my binoculars.'

'No, you can't see the two houseboats from your room. I checked. They are just not visible from there—Kishan's cottage stands in the way. After your first success, you grew overconfident and told Kishan a half-truth without verifying its possibility.'

He glanced at Veni.

'Remember, Veni? Not a single boat or barge was visible to me when I stood at her French windows. Even though both the houseboats were still anchored to their spots. I verified that again when we visited Bhagya today.'

Veni nodded. A penny had dropped in her mind. Clever Hari! That's why he had strolled to the French windows and admired the view from Bhagya's room. Twice! He had even said, '... *you have an excellent view... Not a single boat or barge mars the blue waters of the lake.*'

'Besides,' Athreya went on, 'Kishan is not the only Keralite here from a lake region. As his cousin's daughter, you are one

302

too. You would know how to handle a coracle. By the way, the family photo was useful in another way as well. We also know the motive now—Bina.'

'Bina?' Mahesh asked. 'Who is that?'

'Bhagya's younger sister... the one who died by suicide. Do you know why, Maheshji? She was one of the many women Danuj cheated. After he used Bina and dumped her, the young woman couldn't take the heartbreak. She killed herself. Bina was all of nineteen years old.'

A cold finger ran down Veni's spine.

'Oh, God!' an agonized Mahesh whispered and squeezed his eyes shut. 'Why, Danuj? Why?'

Sahil's face was a picture of revulsion. Tears filled the eyes of Ruhi and Pari. Manjari had shut hers tightly.

'That was not all, Mr Athreya,' Bhagya said in a wavering voice. 'My mother couldn't take little Binu's suicide. Our beautiful, innocent Binu! Unable to bear the sorrow, my mother's heart failed. She passed away three weeks after Binu.'

Silence descended on the room. Each person was contemplating the tragedies they had just heard about.

'Mr Athreya.' Kanika broke the silence. 'If Bhagya couldn't see the boats from her French windows, how did she know that Jeet and I entered the water?'

'She was probably watching you through her binoculars from the veranda of Kishan's cottage, where she was waiting for an opportunity to board Danuj's boat,' Athreya replied. 'Remember, Kishan was away in Kottayam. Subsequently, when she was on Danuj's boat, she heard splashes from the starboard side and sounds of swimming. Only your boat was in that direction. She figured that you and Jeet had entered water.'

'You seem to have all the answers, sir,' Bhagya said, steely-eyed. 'But please note that I have not accepted what you have said about my killing Danuj. I have not confessed. You still don't have evidence to show that I killed him.'

'Perhaps not!' Anto bristled. 'But we have enough on Hiran's murder. How do you respond to that? You cannot deny it.'

'I don't. That was in self-defence.'

'Self-defence?' Anto let out a snort. 'You'll have to try harder than that!'

'Hear me out, Inspector. You can then decide.' She turned to Athreya. 'Do you know why I killed Hiran, sir?' she asked.

'Because Hiran had tried to kill you,' Athreya answered. 'He was the one who hired those thugs to silence you.'

Bhagya nodded as gasps and protests sounded all around. Pari was half out of her chair in agitation.

'He put out a contract on me, Maheshji,' she said, glancing at him. 'Those two men who attacked me are not unfamiliar to Mr Kishan. He is already gathering proof for you, Inspector. You will have confessions to the effect that Hiran hired them to kill me.'

The Gaurias had not recovered from the earlier jolt when this one exploded in the room. They were stunned speechless. All except Mahesh.

'Is that true, Mr Athreya?' he asked in a hard voice. 'Was it Hiran who offered *supari*?'

'I'm afraid so, Maheshji,' Athreya replied. 'Hiran was also the one who kept Bhagya informed on the happenings in Crystal Waters. That was how she managed to kill Danuj without being seen.

'Earlier, knowing of Bhagya's thirst for revenge, he quietly fanned the flames and encouraged her to kill Danuj. That's why she came to Kumarakom. Hiran then supplied her with minute-to-minute information so that she could carry out her plan when the opportunity arose.'

'Wait!' Pari exclaimed. 'That other phone... the spare one that Hiran brought here... was that... did he...'

Her question ended in a shudder as she realized the truth behind the second phone.

'Yes, Pari. That's how he kept in touch with Bhagya. I suspect she too had a second phone. That way, there would be no call records or messages on their regular phones. I suspect both phones are under several feet of water by now.'

'Are you saying that Hiran *Bhaiya* and Bhagya planned and executed Danuj's murder?' Ruhi asked.

Athreya nodded.

'It was all planned in advance, then?' She sounded incredulous.

'Well in advance, Ruhi. Well before you all came to Kumarakom. I suspect that the Chef's Knife that killed Danuj was brought from Mumbai.'

'But they couldn't have known that Danuj would hire a houseboat that night.'

'Correct. That's why they had to be in constant touch through their other phones. They were waiting for an opportunity to arise. As soon as it did, they acted.'

Ruhi shuddered and wrapped her arms around herself.

'You see, Ruhi,' Athreya continued, 'Danuj had planned to make 25 crores from his divorce by misleading Sahil. But independently, Hiran and Bhagya had made other plans for him. Kanika, of course, was opportunistic. When she saw a chance to take back the blue file, she grabbed it with both hands.'

'But why?' Ruhi asked in an anguished voice. 'Why did Hiran *Bhaiya* want to kill Danuj?'

'Financial matters, Ruhi. And the family inheritance too. I suspect Hiran had already lost a lot of money due to Danuj's poor business sense and he probably expected that to continue. In addition, if Danuj went on chipping away at the family's wealth, it would be seriously eroded in a few years.'

'Being equal partners,' Mahesh interrupted, 'Hiran and Danuj shared profits as well as losses. Hiran lost dozens of crores over the past few years due to Danuj's recklessness.'

'But they could have terminated that partnership and gone their separate ways, Papa,' Ruhi protested.

'I suggested that, *Beti*, but Hiran said that he couldn't do it. I didn't understand why.'

'Maybe, I can throw some light on that too,' Bhagya interrupted. 'There should be a couple of agreements from that file that Danuj had tricked Hiran into signing. They barred Hiran from going away and setting up his own production house. I know that these agreements were a part of his motive.'

'Yes, there are two such agreements,' Athreya confirmed, glancing at Mahesh. 'It is for Maheshji to decide what to do with them. My recommendation is to shred and burn them. In fact, you should destroy the entire blue file.' He turned back to Bhagya. 'Go on. You were telling us that Hiran put out a contract on you.'

'Yes.' Bhagya nodded. 'But I don't know why Hiran turned against me. Why did he want to kill me?'

'I can only guess,' Athreya said. 'I don't know whether you do it deliberately or it is your nature, but you do come across as being volatile and unstable—'

'Well, I have had my share of problems, thanks to Danuj,' Bhagya interrupted with palpable bitterness. 'You probably know that I had to undergo psychiatric treatment. I was not like this before Bina's and my mother's deaths. I was sane and stable, and I was fully focused on my career. But Danuj changed that forever by killing Bina. I've not been the same since.'

'Yes, I am aware. Coming back to Hiran, he perceived you as being volatile and unstable. His exact words to me were this: *Hers is a manic disorder. It makes her swing from one extreme to another. She can be very agreeable and sweet one day, and completely frenzied and a bit irrational the next day. Poor girl, she wasn't like this earlier.*

'He took advantage of it and fanned the flames of revenge in you. But once Danuj had been killed, Hiran was probably afraid... afraid that you might let the cat out of the bag in one of your irrational moods. That would land him in big trouble.'

Bhagya gazed at Athreya mutely.

'I remember one thing you said in public on Sunday,' he went on. 'You, Hiran, Pari and Sahil were together on the lawn. You seemed tipsy. I had just come out of Kanika's room. You said to me: *How is the case coming along? Do let me know if you need help. Maybe I can help.* You sounded hysterical.

'Already worried about your instability, your words might have spooked Hiran into precipitating matters. You had killed Danuj with his help. If you "helped" me, as you put it, it would be curtains for him.'

'That's why he actioned his last resort of putting out a contract on her?' Mahesh asked.

Athreya nodded.

'I wish he had talked to me instead,' Bhagya rued. 'He would have been here today. But you do see why I had to get him first, don't you, sir? It was him or me. He made the first move. I *had* to defend myself. If I didn't, it was only a matter of time before he killed me. The men might have failed in their first attempt, but they were sure to succeed sooner or later. There was only one way out for me—to eliminate the person who put out the contract.' She glanced at Anto. 'That's what I mean by self-defence, Inspector.'

Anto remained silent. There was nothing more to be said. The case would play out in the courts.

'Tell us about last night, Bhagya,' Athreya suggested.

'There's not much to tell. It was as you said—I came out through the swimming pool, which was very convenient. In under two seconds, I could go from my room to the pool. I could then swim to the other end of it, which touches the lake. Only a low partition separates the pool water from the lake. It's very easy to slip over it. I could therefore go from my room to the lake more or less unseen. The crutch posed no problem—it is very light and fits snugly on my back. The waterproof bag was small too as it had only a knife and a tee.

'After crossing the pool, I swam from Sunset Bay to Crystal Waters and reached the rendezvous point behind the cottage. Once most of the water had dripped from my swimsuit, I put on the tee, which was long enough to conceal my swimsuit. I tucked my crutch under my arm and waited for Hiran to show up. I had told him that I had papers from Danuj's blue file that he might find interesting. He agreed to come and asked how I could swim when I was injured. I replied that I had a boat, and he was not to worry about it. He didn't know the full extent of my "injuries".

'When he turned up, he smiled at seeing me on a crutch. My apparent helplessness put him off his guard. He became completely relaxed. When I asked him why he was trying to kill me, he smiled again but didn't answer me. In the next minute or two, I got confirmation that it was he who had put out the contract on me.

'Meanwhile, he had become complacent on seeing me defenceless and using a crutch. He didn't view me as a threat at all. He came close and demanded the papers from the file. It came as a shock to him when I suddenly let go of my crutch and lunged at him with the knife. It was surprisingly easy to drive the blade into him. It just took a couple of seconds for each stab. Having a smattering of medical knowledge, I knew where to hit. As he staggered backwards, I pushed him into the water.

'Two minutes later I was swimming back to Sunset Bay in my swimsuit. I hid it, the bloody clothes and the knife in the pool and came out naked. The next moment, I was inside my room. Using my nursing experience, I retied my foot bandage and applied sticking plaster.'

Anto rose and nodded to Joseph. It was time to take Bhagya away.

'You will have to come with me, madam,' Anto told her formally.

Bhagya sighed and rose without the support of anyone or her crutches. She stood with both feet planted on the ground. Kishan stood up slowly and like an old man. He suddenly seemed ten years older. He took her elbow and prepared to pilot her towards the door.

'Inspector,' Bhagya said, glancing at her crutches. 'Can you do me a favour please? Kindly give these crutches to a poor person who needs them. They are of excellent quality. Thank you.'

She lifted her arms did a *namaste* to the Gaurias and Sahil before turning and walking out of the door unaided.

EPILOGUE

Two days later, Mahesh and Athreya sat beside the swimming pool in wicker chairs, watching Akuti conduct her yoga class on the lawn. She had resumed the class that morning after a hiatus due to the murders at the resort. Unsurprisingly, none of the Gaurias was participating today. Veni too had refrained from taking part, respecting the tragedies that had befallen the Gauria family.

'The last time I was watching Aku's class,' Mahesh lamented softly, 'both my sons were alive. Today neither of them is. Eight Gaurias came to vacation at Kumarakom. Two of us are going back in coffins and two more are returning as widows. We never know what fate has in store for us.'

'No, we don't,' Athreya agreed gently. 'But I must say that you all have taken it very well.'

'I don't know, Mr Athreya... as Kishan said, we all are actors. Danuj's death was not as much of a shock as Hiran's was. What do you think will happen to Bhagya? Will she be convicted?'

'For Hiran's murder, yes. Her lawyer could make a strong case for self-defence, but that will only mitigate the punishment. She *will* go to jail.'

'And for Danuj's death?' Mahesh asked.

'I am not sure. There is very little evidence.'

'But what is the alternative? Who else could have killed him?'

'That is not the defence's concern. They just need to establish reasonable doubt or show that the evidence isn't conclusive.'

'But the two are linked,' Mahesh protested. 'The motive for Hiran's death lies in Danuj's. Hiran wanted to silence Bhagya because of his involvement in Danuj's death.'

'How does one prove that in court?' Athreya asked gently. 'Hiran is no longer with us. Bhagya will say that she had no idea why Hiran tried to kill her. Or her lawyer will concoct some story that paints Hiran in darker hues than was really the case.'

Athreya turned to Mahesh and spoke softly.

'Maheshji,' he asked, 'is there anything you can now tell me about how the alprazolam ended up in Danuj's blood? The case is now closed.'

'Yes, there is something I learnt the night before last,' the old man replied, his watery eyes on the waters of the lake that had claimed both his sons. 'Although I suspect you already know.'

Athreya remained silent.

'At dinner that fatal night,' Mahesh began quietly, 'the family ate together as usual, except for Kanika and Jeet, who had already boarded their houseboat. It was a tense dinner and we tried hard to maintain a normal façade in the dining room.

'Manjari usually serves coffee to the family after dinner, and she has carried on this routine here too. It's her little ritual that keeps the family together. So, for whoever wants it, she pours coffee into a cup and gives it to them. Hiran and Danuj always have coffee after dinner. The others do so sometimes.'

Athreya's eyes opened a trifle wider. He had an inkling about what Mahesh was going to say.

'That night, all of us were tense, and everyone opted for coffee. Manjari poured out the cups. And when she did, she dropped a pill of Restyl into Danuj's and Ruhi's cups. Her hope was that the drug would calm them down and prevent Danuj from precipitating something irreversible.'

'That's how alprazolam entered Danuj's blood,' Athreya said softly. 'Restyl in his coffee.'

'Not only that, Mr Athreya. Ruhi changed her mind after the

coffee was poured and decided to not have hers. Danuj then drank hers too.'

'Ah! Two pills of 0.5 mg each! He ended up taking 1 mg of alprazolam. It must have knocked him out!'

'Now you see why Manjari blames herself?' Mahesh concluded. 'She did it thinking that it would help. Instead, it put him to sleep. And when his murderer came to kill him, he couldn't fight her off or call for help. Had Manjari not put the Restyl in the coffee, Danuj might be alive today.'

The two men fell silent. Beyond the lawn and the railing, two houseboats and a barge were passing at a distance. A couple sat in the sitting area of one of the houseboats. Athreya contemplated them silently. Mahesh let out a sigh.

'Life goes on,' he said, 'as it should. The lives of one family might have been broken irreparably, but nothing much has happened to the rest of the world. You know, Mr Athreya, I find that the last few days has changed my attitude towards money.'

'In what way?'

'My mother used to say that having some money is a boon but having lots of it is a curse. After a certain point, it robs you of your happiness. I think I see what she meant. I have tons of it, making what I have evil. If I were to distribute bits of it to many people, I would be creating small parcels of goodness, while chipping away at the evil I possess.'

Athreya remained silent. Mahesh went on.

'We return to Mumbai today and will probably never come back to this place. But I will remember you and Veni for the rest of my life; remember you both with gratitude. You were the messenger of bad news, but you gave me the truth. For that, Manjari and I will be eternally grateful to you.'

At the sound of voices, they turned. Veni, Manjari and the two daughters-in-law were coming towards them. The prayer-bead

312

necklace was back in Manjari's hand. Athreya rose to his feet and did a *namaste* to her. It occurred to him again that he had still not heard her voice.

'*Namaskar*,' he said to her, as she came close, and went on in Hindi, 'Maheshji tells me that you have ended your *maun vrat*.'

'I have,' Manjari replied in Hindi. Her voice was thin and feeble. 'Thanks to you, we know who killed Danuj and Hiran.' She paused for a moment, struggling with emotion. 'I don't know how to thank you and Veni. May God's blessing be upon you both and your family.'

She did a *namaste* to them. Veni and Athreya accepted it with folded hands and bent heads.

'I have one last thing to say to you,' she said, holding Ruhi's shoulder for support. 'It's about why I took *maun vrat*. I think you already suspect it... I was the one who put Restyl in Danuj's and Ruhi's coffee. My intent was to prevent something bad from happening, but God willed it otherwise.'

She looked at him shrewdly. 'You knew, Mr Athreya, didn't you?' she asked.

'I suspected that your taking *maun vrat* had something to do with the alprazolam in Danuj's blood,' Athreya replied. 'But I can't say that I *knew*. Maheshji just told me the details.'

Manjari closed her eyes and did another *namaste* to him.

'You spared me the pain and embarrassment of the authorities and my family knowing. For that, I am deeply grateful. You have a good heart, Mr Athreya. God bless you!'

She nodded and went towards her husband. Pari came forward and held Athreya's hands.

'I hope I will have the pleasure of meeting you again, sir,' she said. 'But not in your professional capacity. You will always be welcome at our home. Always. Do come by sometime.'

Ruhi came last with her eyes brimming. She gazed at him for a moment or two. She then darted forward and hugged him.

'Thank you,' she whispered in his ear. 'For everything. I don't know what would have happened to me had you not been here.'

Athreya and Veni were walking back to Kurup's house. The thugs who had been watching them were no longer in evidence. The Gaurias had just left for the airport, and the couple had seen them off at the boat terminal.

'How I misjudge people!' Veni exclaimed softly, indulging in the self-criticism that she often fell into. 'I took a liking to not one murderer, but two! Bhagya and Hiran. How could I have been so wrong?'

'That's because you always like to see the good in people, Veni. That's why so many people are fond of you and so few take to me.'

'I still feel sorry for Bhagya—she never asked for any of this, and Danuj ruined her life. He was the real fiend in this affair. In some ways, Bhagya was a victim too.'

'Well, so much for our restful retreat in God's Own Country!'

'I hope the rest of our stay here goes without incident, Hari,' Veni said earnestly. 'You still have much ground to cover in your recovery. Don't go nosing around for another case.'

'Don't worry, I won't,' Athreya chuckled. 'I've had my fill for now. By the way, did you return Ruhi's will to her?'

'Yes. This morning.'

A ping sounded from Athreya's phone. He pulled it out and saw that he had received a message from his bank. He tapped the message and read it.

'This can't be right,' he said, frowning. 'My eyes are playing tricks on me. I'm counting one zero too many.'

'What is it?'

'Mahesh has just transferred my fee to the bank. I don't think I am reading the amount correctly. Have a look. What's the amount?'

Veni took the phone and looked at it. She stopped in her tracks.

'Good lord!' she whispered. 'He said he would be generous, but *this*?'

'Am I not seeing a zero too many?' he asked.

'No, Hari.' She handed back the phone. 'Maheshji has just expressed his gratitude in his characteristically grand fashion.'

'And, he is living up to his promise of creating small parcels of goodness and handing them over to others.'

'Yes... except that this isn't small!'

MIST

Ageing millionaire Bhaskar Fernandez has invited
his relatives to the remote, and possibly haunted,
Greybrooke Manor, high up in the misty Nilgiris.

MOUNTAINS

He knows his guests expect to gain from his death,
so he writes two conflicting wills. Which one of them
comes into force will depend on how he dies.

MURDER

Fernandez also invites Harith Athreya, a seasoned
investigator, to watch what unfolds.

When a landslide leaves the estate temporarily isolated,
and a body is discovered, Athreya finds that death
is not the only thing that the mist conceals…

RV RAMAN

A HARITH ATHREYA MYSTERY

'A rollercoaster... perfect for fans of Agatha Christie' Harini Nagendra, author of *The Bangalore Detectives Club*

GRAVE INTENTIONS

On the banks of the Betwa, an excavation goes fatally wrong

PUSHKIN VERTIGO

SECRETS

Seasoned detective Harith Athreya is back, this time to investigate suspicious thefts on a riverside dig in the heart of remote Bundelkhand, steeped in myth and history.

SUPERSTITION

Here the legend goes that anyone who sets foot on nearby island Naaz Tapu will be cursed forever.

SLAUGHTER

When an archeologist defies local folklore, the fallout is swift and deadly. Is the death a result of the ancient curse, or is it a more down-to-earth case of murder? Athreya needs to unravel the truth from legend before the curse strikes again...

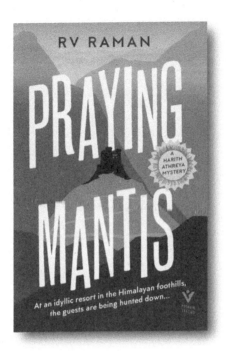

RV RAMAN

PRAYING MANTIS

A HARITH ATHREYA MYSTERY

At an idyllic resort in the Himalayan foothills, the guests are being hunted down...

ISOLATION

Detective Harith Athreya is taking a well-earned break at a boutique hotel in the Himalayan foothills. But his holiday is cut short when mysterious bloody handprints appear on the walls around the resort.

INCRIMINATION

When a guest falls to her death, the hotelier casts suspicion on five young people who checked in at the same time as the victim but who all claim not to know her – or each other.

INTRIGUE

Does one of these guests have something to do with the tragedy? Harith Athreya must get to the bottom of the case before the murderer strikes again...